the Syracuse Codex

ALSO BY JIM NISBET

—NOVELS—

THE GOURMET (1981) (REPRINTED AS THE DAMNED
DON'T DIE; 1986)
LETHAL INJECTION (1987)
DEATH PUPPET (1989)
ULYSSES' DOG (PUBLISHED IN FRENCH ONLY; 1993)
PRELUDE TO A SCREAM (1997)
THE PRICE OF THE TICKET (2003)
DARK COMPANION (FORTHCOMING; FRENCH
EDITION, 2005)

—POETRY—

POEMS FOR A LADY (1979)
GNACHOS FOR BISHOP BERKELEY (1980)
MORPHO (W/ ALASTAIR JOHNSTON) (1982)
SMALL APT (W/ PHOTOS BY SHELLY VOGEL) (1992)
ACROSS THE TASMAN SEA (1997)

—NONFICTION—

LAMINATING THE CONIC FRUSTUM (1991)

—RECORDINGS—

THE VISITOR (1984)

the Syracuse Codex

JIM NISBET

20 05

FIRST EDITION
Published September 2005
(A French edition appeared in 2004)
Second printing January 2006

Dustjacket and interior artwork
by Carol Collier.

ISBN 0-939767-52-X

DENNIS MCMILLAN PUBLICATIONS
4460 N. HACIENDA DEL SOL (GUEST HOUSE)
TUCSON, ARIZONA 85718
TEL. (520)-529-6636
EMAIL: DENNISMCMILLAN@AOL.COM
WEBSITE: HTTP://DENNISMCMILLAN.COM

In memory of Michel Lebrun

"But what an agonising truth was now contained in those lines of Alfred de Vigny's *Journal d'un Poète* which he had previously read without emotion: 'When one feels oneself smitten by love for a woman, one should say to oneself, *Who are the people around her? What kind of life has she led?* All one's future happiness lies in the answer.'"

— Marcel Proust, *Swann's Way.*

"One is shy asking men under sentence what they have been sentenced for; and in the same way it is awkward to ask very rich people what they want so much worry for, why they make such a poor use of their wealth, why they don't give it up, even when they see in it their unhappiness; and if they begin a conversation about it themselves, it is usually embarrassing, awkward, and long."

— Anton Chekhov, *A Doctor's Visit*

"I got some place I gotta be, but I don't know where it is."

— John Borland (1946-1994)

Heartiest thanks to Jean-Pierre Deloux,
whose hospitality and intelligence nurtured the
fortitude by which this book was begun;

to Emmanuelle Lavoix: *formidable*;
to David Koepcke, for being himself;
to Tom Goldwasser, Sydna Jones and Bruce Richman
for timely expertise;
to the editors of *Pangolin Papers, Gat,,* and *Polar,*
wherein excerpts of the present work first appeared;
and to Carol, for a thousand felicities.

• • •

For much of the historicity battered within the
present work, its author plundered a number of books.
He hastens to assure these respective authors,
as well as their readers, that nothing contained
in the present tale intends disrespect of
the quality or integrity of diverse scholarly endeavors.

Anthony Bridge, *Theodora, Portrait in a Byzantine Landscape*
Robert Browning, *Justinian and Theodora*
Charles Diehl, *Theodora, Empress of Byzantium*
Edward Gibbon, *The Decline and Fall of the Roman Empire*
Robert Graves, *Count Belisarius*
Harold Lamb, *Theodora and the Emperor*
Procopius, *Secret History*, translated by Richard Atwater
Procopius, *The Secret History*, translated by G.A. Williamson

In addition, acknowledgement is here made to Mr. Bernard Knox's
extremely informative introduction to Robert Fagles'
translation of Homer's *Odyssey*, pp. 3-67.

the Syracuse Codex

AN ENCOUNTER

ONE

The first time I saw Renée Knowles she was falling out of her dress. A yard of black fabric, its spaghettini—though it would be more *Zeitgeist*-accurate to say yuppie squid-ink linguine—straps kept slipping off one or another of her shoulders. She would then run the edge of a self-conscious fingernail under the strap to realign it, up and over her bare shoulder, much as one would deal with a thrown fanbelt. The shoulders were tanned and articulated, as were the upper arms, and along the forearms a fine brunette down swept, like cloud-shadowed windrows of rain-laid grain, if I do say so. Like such grain, her skin had taken the sun well. Still it would have remained tawny and soft—she'd rarely burn or desiccate, there was some genetic protection there; so that her belly, lanuginous also, as one might speculate, would tan to a burnt chocolate, and the sun would evolve the belly, if closely watched, like a darkening Mandlebrot landscape.

Her falling out of the dress had nothing to do with the will-fulness of the straps. It had to do with the woman's advanced drunkenness. Lipstick smeared and knees wobbling, she yet remained attractive. Pretty like a woman who's taken care of herself—or over whom care has been taken, judging by the rock on her wedding finger—but a kind of pretty not often granted. One could discern, for example, none of the care that children can bring to a complexion, nor little of the hardness that lack of them can. Children had not shown her,

1

as is said, more about herself than she had ever wanted to know. She had learned it some other way. There was a sadness in her eyes that made for a temporal suspension, a disjunction, a gulf to be broached when traveling to the world beyond that unlined face.

Informed or not, it was troublesome for her to stay in the dress, though the dress wasn't much to start with. She'd been modestly shaping its contents at the gym. The dress displayed the results as intended. A lot of men at the party were watching her, or trying not to watch her, or shying away from her, or failing to shy away from her, much as filings waver uncertainly at the approach of the magnet.

There was another obvious reason for this frank interest. Two of the dozen or so paintings displayed on the walls around us were sumptuous portraits of her, quite naked. By sumptuous I mean to say that not only were they approximately 40 by 60 inches—good-sized paintings—exquisitely rendered, but every stroke was such that one could positively feel the sable as it drew the pigment over her limbs. And they were beautifully framed, not strictly because I myself had framed them, but because the purchaser had not stinted the quality of this final touch. That's what I did in those days; I framed pictures. Some of them were expensive pictures. These two portraits, for example, had gone for seventy-five thousand dollars apiece. Each frame had cost five thousand. Hand-carved, slightly distressed, patinaed by a secret gilding process, altogether *quattrocento* . . . that's quite enough of that bullshit. In framing them I'd become curious as to their lush subject. And here she was.

I'd been paying my compliments to John Plenty, the artist whose vernissage this was, when she asserted herself. There were quite a few people around John of course. Patrons, owners of work lent to the show, friends, a dealer or two.

"John," was all she said, as she burst into the circle of people around him, interrupting various inane remarks. Himself drunk in his lordly way, he stared at her. If one might have guessed that his eyes had once twinkled, now they only gleamed; two storm lanterns aloft over the raft of his intelligence, adrift in a sea of alcohol.

I'd known Plenty for some years. Despite the strata of society he'd become accustomed to inhabiting and the large prices his work now commanded, along with the tuxedos and the box at the opera he'd come by necessity to affect, he was a tough customer. When this woman in her little black dress called his name, he turned automatically toward her, warming, it was obvious, at the sound of her voice. But their eyes met and something went wrong. Draping an ursine forearm over her slight shoulders, he drew her awkwardly aside. They exchanged a few words before she broke away. John watched her go, his expression a curious mix of desire and resignation.

Girly Renquist, who owned the gallery, sailed in, deploying her considerable girth between her artist and his distraction. A professional moment. With a backward glance Plenty allowed himself to be carried off to meet a Mr. Kahane from Beverly Hills, who was "in the market."

The knot of people dispersed. The woman in the black dress defaulted to me.

I was curious.

"Come," she said abruptly. She put her arm through mine and drew us to a floor-to-ceiling window. "Look at this view," she declared. "Wouldn't you like to jump right into it?" The edge to her voice turned the question into a dare, and suffused it with an element of truth.

Undeniably it was a buena vista. If the twin towers of the Golden Gate Bridge had a length of inner tube to go with them, you might have slingshot the sun right back to New York. As it was the sun depended in the tremulous atmosphere beyond them, a five ball dipped in glycerine and visibly descending, the light thickening as its tangent to the global caustic angled magisterially through what cinematographers call the magic hour. Its penultimate rays, spangling around us, caused the stemware to gleam on the sterling salvers like clusters of vertical minerals. The scene both beckoned and repelled, like some Platonic vestibule gone Mertzbau. The blended mechanics of social drinking and its chatty accompaniment sounded not unlike a glass carillon randomly abraded by vellum mallets, muted and incoherent. Perhaps I exaggerate; but certainly, looking back, it was the moment between one world and, not merely another, but the next.

One knew this vernissage as a tony affair because the decanters were glass instead of plastic, and there was little yelling. In the event, all one could discern was the subdued prattle that precisely defines a given moment at almost any such party, an abrupt calm that arises like a swell between the second cocktail and the third, and passes on. The woman in the black dress looked and acted as if she'd been drinking all day. And now that she had a good heat on, she manifested only two desires: to be out of that black dress and into the sunset.

Where her skin touched mine, it was warmer than room temperature, exuding a scent of night-blooming flowers. I asked her name.

"Renée." She tightened her grip on my arm and repeated the name as if thoughtfully, failing to ask my own. Even in heels she was shorter than I by two or three inches, so I inadvertently achieved the smell of her hair. There were hints of lavender, tobacco, lime-scented gin; of new upholstery; of fused electronics. It was a breeze from another world.

What man doesn't like a woman to take his arm, even when she doesn't care who he is? It allows him to make a second mistake without even thinking about it, which is, he begins

4

to trust her. She can do collateral damage with her eyes, if she wants. But the thing with the arm is pretty effective.

"If the fall weren't fatal, one might swim to Japan and commit *seppuku.*" And she added, as if to herself, *"Ku,* abdomen; *seppu,* cut. I looked it up." In a louder voice she continued, "That's if you don't get dragged under by a giant squid, of course. Before you get to where you're—"

"Speaking of sushi," I interjected, watching the window, "there's a restaurant in Japantown. Perhaps you've been there? The chefs prepare the food within the circumference of the bar, encircled by a moat." She made no reply. "They place the dishes on little barges?" I made a circle with the forefinger of my free hand. "Within the periphery of the bar?" She squeezed my arm. "The diners pluck up what dishes they fancy. And, since I'm a charter member of the club called Isn't Sushi at the Bottom of the Food Chain Where Heavy Metals Rising Meet Fecal Dust Descending?—" I shrugged "— what I genuinely enjoy about the place is its black Sapporo beer. Served by the foaming draft, it's completely vegetarian. I can sit with barm on my upper lip and watch plates of urchin gonads go purpling round and round without paying for them to colonize my cecum." She grimaced, then smiled in spite of herself. "The liver," I finished, "is a different story. A necessary organ. It's always good to have an extra liver between oneself and the food chain. Two livers is better than one is the best objection to vegetarianism. Therefore, may I buy you a steak someplace else?"

She turned her eyes on mine as I turned mine on hers. There was no trace in hers of the notion that I might be mad. Not only were they the grayish-blue of the nacre you see in guitar purfling, a striking color to find embedded in any deeply tanned face, but they were about to weep. The barely-elicited smile appeared to have left her a heartbeat from hysteria.

"You look as though you could use one," I added quietly.

"I hate sushi," she said huskily, the tears just barely contained.

"Sushi is not the end of the world," I hastened to assure her, my voice nearly robbed of its levity by the precipitous vertigo broadcast by her eyes. "Television is. But for the end-of-the-world meal, there's nothing like a slab of elk venison, with hot marrow on fresh crackers and a swarthy Cabernet. Although," I indicated the view, "let's leave by the door instead of the window."

Her grip on my arm plainly declared that she was depending entirely on momentum to get her through the next few moments of consciousness; from, as it were, one lamppost to the next.

"Maybe if you practiced wearing that dress at home before you went to parties in it," I suggested, taking the liberty of delicately pinching one of the fallen straps into place on its shoulder, "strange men might leave you alone."

The skin afforded a lambency in which to bask. I don't offer that concept lightly—no more so than her skin beamed it consciously. It's amazing what a little money and time and a beach and the sun and a good coconut oil can do, not to mention a complexion of considerable natural pulchritude. Which train of thought led me right back to one of the very first I'd entertained upon spotting her, laughing too loudly at something a stiff in a suit had said; laughing, clearly, by way of dismissing him: a crescendoing trialectic of thought which was, She's beautiful; No, she's very beautiful; and, Yes, I can't afford her.

"All it takes is one," she said.

As I was failing to shake the truth of this quip, the son of the gallery owner passed close to us and Renée abruptly suggested that, even though she wasn't "in love" with sushi, she had however been to that particular restaurant many times, usually in conjunction with the film festival. She was sorry to add that there was a much better sushi place in St. John's. St. John's, I queried, puzzled. Isn't that a little river community near Benicia? And giving me a look whose gratitude nearly dried her eyes all by itself, she said, as frostily as you please, St. John's is the capital of Antiguan, island of Antigua, population 72,000, and added that, unlike Japantown, they serve excellent conch fritters there.

The son had moved on. "Not a bad repartee by way of class putdown for a girl with tears in her eyes," I said brusquely. "What was that about? Are you able to brunch in your sleep, too? Or do you rake more feebly with your nails than your tongue?"

She touched two fingers to my lips, a move that utterly startled me. Sincerely and with not a little fire she said, "If I rake you with my nails, you stay raked," and she said it with such tenderness it shut me up. She'd caught me judging her by the company we were both keeping. But at least John Plenty didn't affect to daub crap bridging the horrible loneliness between his morning Irish coffee and his noon *apéritif* in which he suffered to think up titles like "Sepsis Huit" and "Plage de Tristesse." And at least that's not what I was framing—not lately, anyway. I caught the hand in my own.

She pulled away. I thought, she's wasted enough time on a conquest meant only to reassure her. And by now I'd nearly convinced myself I could do with less of her company than more. It always helps to second-guess your leaps of faith, even as you fall.

On the far side of the room Mrs. Renquist rapped the edge of a knife against a champagne glass to attract the attention of the assembled, providing a fateful interruption. As if startled, Renée shook off her opprobrium. She stood away from me, adjusted the thin straps, and coolly thanked me as

7

if it were I who had disarranged them—that is to say, thanked me for less than nothing, and muttered something else. I didn't hear it. But drunk as she was, in order to stay vertical she had to place her feet somewhat far apart, causing the narrow little black skirt, short enough to begin with, to ride up her tanned thighs, which presumed to catch the last golden rays available to the West Coast that evening.

Lanuginous, I was thinking, and embarrassing. The down of a baby's face, yet not on no baby. What Jason was after in Colchis? Maybe I got the story wrong. But before I could get it straight, Renée sat down on the floor.

This too was something to see, and I won't describe it, having plenty of faith in the reader's imagination, and finding nothing to relish in this woman's humiliation. She was drunk. We've all been there. But she was pretty, too, and the two are mostly irreconcilable. What we might forgive in a close friend or never forgive at all in a relative lacks meaning to witness in certain others, of whom she was one. But there she was. She had a whole life behind her, which at that moment conspired to bring her to the floor, lipstick askew, a delicate trace of eyeliner drawn over one cheek by a single tear.

The crowd affected not to notice. But the son of Mrs. Renquist, Gerald by name, an attentive homosexual in a lovely suit, reappeared to whisper fussily about how Renée shouldn't have to show so much to accomplish so little. He gently chided her, solicitous about helping her to her feet; but neither of them achieved a grip on the situation before she failed to restrain a sob that seemed unpretentiously dramatic. It conveyed to me, all at once, that Renée was frightened.

Gerald embraced her kindly, and his eye caught mine. We knew each other slightly. I saw no reproach. I could guess that he sympathized, or perhaps had been through this before with her; not often enough to have tired thoroughly of it, but sufficiently to evince no untoward concern while attempting

8

to minimize her embarrassment. Whatever the facts, he was willing to help. Gerald didn't need a scene at the gallery but on the other hand he'd have only a little moxie to spare, being present to manage the infrastructure, catering and parking and whatnot, chores that probably only peripherally included unruly drunks, while his mother sold paintings. He began to coo—words of comfort, I imagined, some of which reached my ears. "There there, darling. Just give me the keys. The rest will take care of itself. The keys, darling. That's a good girl. Everything's going to be all right. . . ."

I looked around. Mostly it was backs turned, people ostensibly paying attention to what the hostess had to say about what the artist had to say about what his art had to say about what the world refused to admit; thank God for artists like John Plenty who are ready and talented enough to take the risks sufficient to map the dilemma; and so forth. Until now the rest of us had thought of him as merely talented.

Gerald took Renée into the kitchen and I followed. It was a bright sheet-metal affair with a tile floor whose purpose was industrial-scale alimentation. There were people in white jackets reloading batteries of champagne glasses, readying the next application by way of furthering Mrs. Renquist's hope to loosen grips on checkbooks. Seventy-five grand is a lot of cake, and John Plenty liked to live high. But at that price a painting might glower from a gallery wall, aloof, for a long time.

There was a chair just inside the door. Gerald sat Renée down on it, out of the way of the door's busy swing as the help bustled to and fro. He asked me to hold her erect while he sought water, coffee, aspirin. As soon as he had turned his back, Renée adroitly swiped a brimming glass off a passing tray and downed it. White wine in anger. It's a sobering sight.

Gerald returned just as I accepted the empty glass from her hand, and for the first time he showed his exasperation by daintily stamping his foot, as if he'd felt a ladybug crawling on the calf under his pant leg and wanted to shake it out.

I told him not to worry, that I had a busy day tomorrow. I was ready to leave. I would be perfectly happy to see the lady home.

TWO

Gerald didn't even ask me if I knew her but allowed his features to flood with relief. It was like watching a chameleon waft from chartreuse to cobalt. Only his gills pulsed. With the end to this shabby episode in sight, he could foresee getting back to selling paintings to drunks, his mother's priority.

Once again a little black strap draped the triceps, a Möbius of fashion and flesh, but now there was a gibbous aureole visible at the upper seam of the bodice, and tawny, too. Gerald had the adroit delicacy to straighten the social contract without apparently touching her, nor revealing his distaste for the suavity of her skin, as he deftly realigned the strap: but the gesture was tender, too.

A member of the caterer's staff appeared with Renée's wrap and Gerald helped her into it, a sleeveless jacket that wouldn't have warmed a chihuahua. Then Gerald retrieved her purse from me and rummaged it for car keys, allowing one eyebrow to rise in a little fit of delicacy as he fingered aside a half-pint bottle.

By now, Renée's eyelids were at half-mast. "Last month," Gerald confided as he showed me her keys, "we called a cab to take Mrs. Knowles home from a shambles of a dinner at Postrio. But we neglected," he added, in a singsong voice, "to collect car keys." He bent perfunctorily toward Renée and dangled them in her face. "Didn't we forget to take our nasty old car keys?" He straightened up, affecting mock severity. "Once home, did our little vixen go straight to bed? *Nooo.*

11

She gave the cabbie a twenty and told him to wait. Inside the house, she downed a couple of stiff belts of–what–vodka? Schnapps?" He leaned toward her again. "*Grappa?*"

"Heroin," Renée muttered, though her eyes were nearly closed.

"I don't doubt it." Gerald sniffed and straightened up. "The idiot taxidriver took her straight back to Postrio. The idiot valet-person retrieved her car–with every sign of respect, I'm sure, due the proffered tip: it cost him his job. She got about ten blocks before she *destroyed* her car, absolutely piled it up against the back of some Deadhead's school bus parked on Grove Street." He shook a finger under her nose. "Right beside Louise Davies Symphony Hall, *just* as intermission had deposited two or three hundred socially prominent cigarette smokers onto the sidewalk, right across the street, not forty feet away. How she got that far, nobody could fathom." Renée snapped audibly at the finger, like a dog at a pesky housefly. But Gerald had already withdrawn it, to touch my forearm for emphasis. "The police were already there, of course, so they and fully half Renée's friends–the smoking half–could watch her stagger from the wreckage, as drunk and out of place as Truman Capote at Bobby Kennedy's funeral. Can you imagine?" He detached a rubberized key and alarm switch from the ring and showed them to her. "No matter what the question, driving drunk is not the answer."

Now Renée swiped at the key, much as she had swiped at the passing drink tray. Gerald easily snatched it away, smiling grimly. "Heroin. Not a bad idea. It might make us less *active.*" He pocketed the car key and dropped the others back into the purse, which he handed to me. "When you get her home," he said, "tell her husband I'll messenger the car keys to her tomorrow morning.

Ah, I thought. The husband.

12

"I'd let you have them," Gerald added darkly, "but without them you'll be less exposed to the *tentacles* of her *wiles.*"

"That squid has surfaced twice tonight," I said.

Gerald didn't miss a beat. "Usually they stay very deep," he observed darkly, "where they belong."

Steadied between us, we steered Renée among stainless steel tables paved with trays of prosciutto-wrapped cantaloupe and escargot-shaped pâté–capers for eyes and parsley for eyebrows–past the silently rolling screen of a portable television, to the service entrance at the back of the kitchen. Gerald named an address at the far end of Broadway, just east of the Presidio. He politely emphasized that it would be a good idea to escort Renée through the front door and directly into the arms of her husband or at least the butler, and no sooner had we cleared the threshold than he closed the service door behind us. Clearly, he was glad to be seeing the last of Renée Knowles.

As I dropped the purse into the passenger footwell, I thought she probably attended three or four of these party-like things a week. Such drinking would mean a lot of reciprocity at the gym in order to maintain her terrific shape. Not an ounce out of place, I noted, helping her into the passenger seat; warm, too. A diminutive bundle of energy, perhaps energetic to a fault, verily convulsant to channel her nerves and perhaps her intelligence into something useful or even meaningful or at least consuming. Drunk and disorderly, even on the verge of a long nap, she burned.

The truck started. Blessings come as they may. Halfway across the lot she tapped a fingernail on the passenger window, indicating a black BMW, one of those frowning-panther jobs with tinted windows, turbofan wheels, fat adhesive tires, and an antenna that facilitates demands upon, among other things, the Global Positioning System. It looked brand new. "It's just like mine," Renée Knowles said, almost desperately. "Except," she turned to me, "mine has a little bumper sticker on it. You know what it says? 'Look at me when I'm hitting you'." She laughed. I was trying to drive but I looked at her anyway. "Little blue sign." She made a rectangle with the thumb and forefinger of each hand. "Like this."

"Sure," I said.

She turned so she could see out the back window. "You like my car?" She watched it recede into the darkness. "Drive it?"

"I thought you said it wasn't yours."

She turned and placed a hand on my arm. "Please?"

I steered around the end of a file of parked vehicles and shrugged politely. "Gerald has the key. You saw him take it. You'll get your car back in the morning, when you're in shape to drive it."

She ignored this. "Not tomorrow. Now. And not around the block. I mean to Tahoe—or Reno. How about Malibu? Palm Springs?"

"Sure," I humored her. "But let's wait till all the headlights are pointing in the same direction. Tonight we take the pickup. Try to look on it as a unique experience."

She blinked. Then she leaned back against the passenger door and watched me. "Oh really? Do you think so?"

"Maybe it reminds you of high school."

"High school!" She laughed much too loudly. "High school. . . ."

"Didn't your boyfriend drive a truck? Did you always drive BMWs?"

"I was fourteen," she shouted. "Four-fucking-teen—!"

She stopped.

"High school." She pulled together the lapels of her little jacket. "What the hell were you doing at a party like that?"

We bounced over the gutter between the parking lot and the street. The radio, which had a short in it, abruptly began

14

a recitation of John Coltrane's cover of "Don't Take Your Love Away," right at the beginning.

"John Plenty's a friend and a client," I said, turning down the volume. "So I showed up."

She said nothing.

"The artist? The guy who painted all those pictures back there?"

Silence.

"The walls." I glanced at her. "They had paintings on them?"

She watched me.

"Two were portraits of you?"

No response.

"Anyway," I shrugged, "I framed them."

She said, "So you were the guy."

I didn't know what to make of that, but I was willing to accept it as derogatory, and shut up. After a couple of minutes of silence she touched a hole torn into the dashboard vinyl and asked, "How many miles on this thing?"

"Ninety-two thousand," I said proudly, glancing at the odometer, "eight hundred and two. I paid $600 for it eight years ago. Showed sixty thousand, then. Haven't put a wrench on it. High-octane gas, change the oil and filters regularly, blow out the carbon on the freeway once in a while." I patted the dash. "A solid ride."

"Six hundred dollars." She would not have been more awed if I'd told her the light from Orion's head had begun its journey toward her head the year Christ was born.

"Come to think about it," I reflected, pausing at a cross street, "that's probably one monthly payment on that black BMW."

"Payment?" She angled the rearview mirror for a look at herself. "I paid cash." She touched her hair once and sat back in the seat.

15

"One of these days," I said, readjusting the mirror, "a giant squid's going to rise up out of the pavement and–"

"–Make sushi out of the upper classes," she laughed.

"Did you pay cash for the one you wrecked, too?"

"Tattle-tale faggot," she snapped. "Of course I did." She regarded me. "Off the cuff, I'd think that a man who could hang on to the same ratty truck for eight years could hang on to a woman, too."

"What makes you think I haven't?"

"You're looking for trouble."

"Since when does lending a hand mean trouble?"

"Since it means you're only doing it to impress people."

I hadn't meant to turn onto Lombard, but now I found I had done so. "You did a pretty thorough job of that yourself."

"Meaning?"

"I'm impressed. Everybody was impressed."

"Hah. Those people don't give a rat's ass what happens to me–or anybody else, for that matter. They're just glad I'm gone. Out of it. Finished."

I looked at her. She was as far away from me as she could get, angled into the corner between the seat and the door, watching me. Lights slid over her face, but her eyes remained in shadow.

"I thought you were drunk."

"Maybe I am. But you're not. You could have stayed. Who knows? You might have bought a painting."

I laughed and looked away, only to find I'd missed the turn at Divisadero. "I don't have the wall space."

"All taken up with pictures of your mother, no doubt."

"Don't forget my sister."

"Those are my paintings, you know."

"I noticed they were sold."

"They were never for sale. They're *of* me, and I *own* them."

"Those paintings are portraits of you?" I asked, slightly

16

disappointed. It hadn't been five minutes since I told her I'd framed them. "You sat for them?"

"Yes."

"I don't believe it. Plenty could have done a better job using telepathy."

She giggled. *"Au contraire,* it was a very hands-on experience. And what do you mean?" she said archly. "Those are *very fine* portraits."

"Now we're talking about the John Plenty I thought I knew."

"You don't know a damned thing about him," she said, even more sharply.

I looked at her. She glowered back.

The light at Broderick went green and I bore left. "Broadway at Baker?" I asked, my patience waning.

She said nothing. At the Presidio Gate I turned up Lyon, and we found ourselves behind a 41 bus. But it turned east on Union, and I turned east a block further, at Green. We climbed up out of Cow Hollow, past the old Russian Consulate, where a single light now burned in a third-floor window. We took a right at Divisadero and ground up the steep hill to Broadway, where I turned right. A block and a half later she pointed at the driveway of a place not quite so big as a dirigible hangar, but much nicer.

"Listen," she said abruptly, not moving, watching the house. "Come in for a nightcap?"

This surprised me.

"My husband will be very grateful to you for driving me home," she added.

"Husband," I said.

"Grateful," she repeated.

"Maybe some other–"

"Please." She put the hand on my forearm. "I've been very rude."

I looked from the big house to her.

"You got a sister?"

She smiled. "Park under the cypress."

It was a big cypress, about halfway along a row of them lining the drive. The needles they dropped weren't allowed to languish. Someone with a leafblower appeared once a week to whisk them elsewhere, and afterwards devoted a great deal of time to the rest of the landscaping. At thirty yards I could smell the night-blooming jasmine that cloaked the entire eastern corner of the three-story mansion. A towering explosion of bougainvillea draped the western corner.

I should have been yawning at this point, or combing the yellow pages for a new hairdresser, or redistributing the earth in my coffin in preparation for a long day's sleep—anything but parking in the shadows of a rich man's villa with his wife. But the truck parked itself, as it can do; what could be more natural? I switched off the engine. Then it became quiet enough to hear the fog as it moved through the cypress boughs, seeking the desert heat a hundred miles inland, whose upward convection had drawn the layer of cool marine air through the arroyos of the coast range. What could be more natural? I suddenly became conscious of the odor of mildew that rose from the floormats. And there was the musk of motor oil cooking off the exhaust manifold below a leak in the valve cover gasket. I was nervous and annoyed by that intrinsic, tricky foreboding that runs like a thread right through the predication of such a moment, the breathless anticipation at the edge of the unknown. I might have wished myself some-where else altogether. But you know how it is when you're a loner. You get lonely.

I pulled at the door handle.

"Wait."

I looked at her.

She pulled me toward her. The next thing I knew my head was in her lap and she was kissing me.

I couldn't easily sit up again. I admit I'd considered hesitating; but I didn't even have time to admit to myself that I was going to hesitate for just that moment I thought necessary, to plumb perhaps this beauty's intentions, her instincts, her emotions, her ability to talk, her willingness to share for just another moment the odoriferous cab of an eleven-year-old pickup truck that may or may not have reminded her of a guy she dated in high school–who am I kidding?

She jumped me as my mind hesitated in the thicket of impulses between turning off the engine and saying good night. I need not have wondered–I never had the chance, and I never would have guessed. She'd drawn blood from my lower lip with her teeth before I knew what bit me, before I even realized that one arm had escaped its little strap completely, before I realized that in my mouth was no longer her tongue but a nipple. Only the roof of the cab arrested her ascendancy, sideways and upwards like a lateral moraine of flesh and silk, a geology of woman, clothing reduced to mere detritus caught between us. In the darkness her breast moved over my face, its aureole now streaked by the blood of my lip, and she moaned. Too soon, as I thought, for even such stored potential as my own to go kinetic with. Though I was welcome to let it try. As brashly and out of focus as she had risen, she descended, and before I could arrest the acceleration she had three of the five buttons below my belt disgrommeted, an imperious ripping aside of the flap of her concubine's tent, making a noise as she did so of triumph, frustration, urgency, demand. So that when I grabbed both her wrists, even as one of her hands was grabbing me–already it was very easy to grab me; I admit it; put your hands on a loner and get a loner's response; who isn't precisely aware of this? Who doesn't depend on it? Who isn't alert for it when it's needed? But there're so few things in this world one can depend on, this being one of them, that she was very surprised when I took one of her wrists in each hand, arresting their motions mid-deliberateness, and I folded her arms behind her own back, crushing her to me so I could say no. Stop. Please.

Urgency gave her strength. What you get when you drink every night and work out every day and infuse it all with prolonged desperation is strength. Mine, on the other hand, was eroding. She felt and smelled wonderful, like beauty, like sin, like corners of hell I don't usually get to visit, like cigarettes and perfume and talcum powder and perspiration and chardonnay and tanned leather. The impulse was to cover her mouth with my own. But instead I whispered, "I don't do this anymore."

"Do what?" she rasped, breathless. "You aren't doing anything. You don't have to do anything. I'm the one who's doing. Just lie there and enjoy it." And she moved her hands again. They were strong. I was weak. Gripping her wrists I forced her hands to my thighs. She spread them flat and dug in her nails. She looked me in the eye. "Don't you want me?"

Her eyes gleamed, ever so slightly almond, which I hadn't noticed before. The hair at her temples tapered to nothing along the back of each cheek, anterior to each ear, and if my mouth was saying one thing, the rest of me was saying something else.

"Oh, my," she whispered, her eyes holding mine. She was a woman, after all. I was a man. That much we knew. She took the tip of my nose into her mouth and touched the tip of her tongue to it.

"No," I whispered, trying not to laugh or sneeze. "I'm trying to behave. It's later on in life."

"Behaving," she said, "is for much, much later in life."

"I couldn't have agreed more—earlier. Now it's later."

"Now is now," she said, fiercely, and she forced me to force her to move her hands. "Do you like my breasts?"

"It's not a question of liking," I said, looking at them, as it were, with my hands as guided by her hands. The dress was gone. "It's not. . . ."

Abruptly she tore one hand from my grasp and presented a breast to my inspection, somewhere between my upper lip and the tip of my nose and my eyes. "You don't think they're too small?"

"Jesus, Renée–" I should have kept my mouth shut. If you say her name aloud, you'll understand why. She presented me with the nipple as if I were a nursing child.

"That's it," she whispered.

Suddenly I felt as peaceful, as comfortable, as purposeful, as reposed, as self-contained, as driven, as necessary, as. . . . What? A force of nature? A cataract? A falling safe? I suppose one could say anything to avoid the subject. Which was that I now had her breast in my mouth and my fly was open and she, petite and agile as she was, had somehow parked herself between me and the steering wheel, astride my lap. And if before her desperation had made her repellent, now it made her gravity itself. She now allowed her breath to hiss as her hips figured themselves around mine. She took a handful of my hair in one hand and the rim of the steering wheel, behind her, in the other. I dropped my left hand along her calf to the seat lever, and the seat sprang away from the wheel as far back as it would go.

Since it was war, we took a long time. Many died. At some point I became disturbed. It was curious. But to put a name to it, what began to disturb me, as the experience progressed, was the way we fit together. Neither of us said a word. A gesture, a touch, a look, even in semi-darkness, sufficed to compile, through an anthology of vignettes, an album of desire. With a thrust of her hips she met me in a way that I'd

21

always wanted to be met, but hadn't until that moment realized. The way she guided me with her hand, the way my hand cupped the base of her spine, the way her thumb left a bruise just above my hip, dot dot dot . . . this was not common. The little dress became a thin cumulus ineffectually scarving a lunar presence. Every gesture, touch, sign, whisper accumulated to the pitch of our conspiracy. So that, in the end, having the intimacy of saying *Renée* into her ear, the only thing I really missed was the reciprocal pleasure of hearing my own name in my own ear, called by her. How could she? She never learned it.

THREE

Y ou should come in and meet my husband."

"What, so we can get tested together?"

"That's not nice."

I grunted, annoyed. "My nerves aren't wired like that. Why would I want to meet him? Put another way, other than to get his face rubbed in your indiscretion, why would he want to meet me?"

She touched the tip of her tongue to a trickle of sweat at the base of my ear. "How do you know he has a face?"

I touched her nose. "Can't we keep it just between the two of us?" I looked at the house. "I imagine the guy who owns that building has a face."

"Suppose you're wrong?"

"Me? Wrong?"

Her eyes were bright in the gloom. A certain puffiness accented her lips. "No," she said softly. "So far, so good."

"I surrender," I said.

She covered my lips with her fingers. I touched her hair and somewhat incredulously watched my hand doing it. She watched me back. "No no," she said, very quietly. "I surrender."

As go men and women, this might have been a moment for pillow talk–the floorplan for the new addition, a niece's odd remark at a family dinner, one or two atomic secrets–as

23

natural, as unconsidered, as the flow of an undammed stream carried along by the lay of the land. But we were strangers. The only knowledge we shared was our mutual carnality, and the fact that she had a husband to go home to.

"And you don't?"

"I haven't noticed a particular need for a husband."

"So scrupulous."

"Oh," I said, looking around the truck, "I wouldn't go that far."

She moved against me and I responded without hesitation. "If we keep this up. . . ."

"Yes?"

"One of us is going to lean on the horn."

"This thing has a horn?"

We were like two children hidden in a thicket, watching the amusing world of adult behavior beyond the scrim of leaves and pretending not to notice we were holding hands. A delicious, tenuous intimacy. A rather too-grown-up game caught in a rather too-simplistic reflection, I could have been home, "safe in front of the television"–if I had a television. And I recalled at that moment a cartoon of the same title, drawn by the English poet Tom Raworth, depicting a squat combination safe, its dial prominent on its locked door, angled toward a television. Exactly. One's emotions are locked up in the safe, see, and one has lost the combination. . . . To tell the truth, I didn't need a television to keep it that way. In 1950 Jacques Ellul wrote, "The radio, and the television more than radio, shut up the individual in an echoing mechanical universe in which he is alone." To think it was so obvious, even then. I lived otherwise. Think of it as penance–two or three years without television, you get a night like this.

She took one of my hands and flattened it over the center of the steering wheel behind her, and covered my hand with one of her own. A little pressure would honk the horn. She

24

locked her eyes with mine. She moved against me. A sudden exhale escaped the damp embouchure of her lips.

"Don't," I suggested. "Don't interrupt this."

"Oh darling," she said, "you always say the right thing."

"Yes," I agreed, "all three times you've heard me speak."

We kissed.

Longing enveloped us. At the moment of penetration she closed her eyes and bit her lip, a portrait of concentration, as if no amount of untoward detail could distract her from the timeless delicacy of this instant, as if, certainly, nothing else mattered. A classic stolen moment. Little psychiatric chipmunks in my attic presumed her to be a woman in a loveless marriage who had much to give, much pent up, no one to take it—quite used to doing whatever needed to be done about it. It took no such chipmunks to conclude that my own longing came of a man too much alone, who, having expressed a token compunction, ceased to hesitate to take what he needed, too. Whatever drove it, the fusion made for a soaring hour, and the better part of another. By the time we thought about talk or breathing or stopping or anything else at all, it was well past three in the morning.

We'd moved to the passenger seat, and wrapped ourselves in a quilted furniture blanket: two kids lacking, for the moment, a single care.

"They throw people out of the army for this kind of stuff."

"Better they should deploy every government vehicle with padded blankets."

"It would save the taxpayers a lot of legal fees."

"It would give those in uniform something to fight for."

"But what would the politicians do?"

The lanthorn remained illuminated, along with a couple of windows on the second floor. I say lanthorn, but you could call it a porch light. Except it looked like a lantern, slung from two perpendicular catenaries of chain; it was as big as an upended motorcycle. Tapered ochre bulbs flickered like gas flames within it. And I say porch because I don't know what else to call that, either, unless portico connotes greatness of size as well. Would a husband affecting such ostentation, seeing his wife desired by another, not be capable of suddenly rediscovering her beauty, and wanting her back? What might implement this claim? An elephant gun? A hit man? Air let out of the suitor's truck tires?

Renée had closed her eyes and may even have been dozing. Stray wisps of damp hair clung to her temples. I touched them gently. She opened her eyes, saw me, smiled, and closed them again. It was hard to square such a lovely, confident repose with the drunkenness I'd so recently witnessed. But what's to square? Alcohol can make a monkey out of anybody. It was beside the point anyway. I liked being wrapped in a quilted moving blanket in the front seat of my pickup truck at three in the morning with this particular woman asleep on my shoulder, a woman who affected absolutely not a care for where her clothes might be at that particular moment. What's a few drinks earlier or a hangover later to that?

"Are we through fighting?" she murmured, not opening her eyes.

What a question. What if I said yes? Would she dress, walk up the drive, disappear forever? And wouldn't that be best? It's one thing to pass a few hours in a moving blanket with another man's wife. But to continue past that? Into ring-twice-and-hang-up, anonymous hotel rooms, the don't call me here, the I'll call you when I need you—I mean, when I get a chance—in short, the claustrophobic clandestinities of adultery? Were we both so bereft? What we'd already proven ourselves so wonderful at might drive six months' or even a year's worth of philandering, but anything more serious would quickly prove impossible. I, for starters, wouldn't be able to afford a third or even a second dinner in the manner to which she would be accustomed–let alone the electric bill for all those bulbs in the lanthorn. And at first she'd say no problem and produce her husband's credit card to cover the bill. And I'd forestall the gesture, refusing to cuckold a man and see him pay for it, too. I'd pull out the sum total of my meager pelf, and it would come just short of the bill, forget the tip, and I'd be forced to allow her to go ahead with the credit transaction. I'd awkwardly insist she accept all my cash anyway, which she would grudgingly, without intending to be spiteful or insulting, throw into her purse uncounted. And then, when we were snuggling at adjacent stools elsewhere over a nightcap, she'd have to provide the cash for the drinks. This would suit a cad down to the ground. But for most people within a month or two the whole thing would have become a confusion of embarrassment and desire, of cashlessness and strained understanding, of pride and adultery and lust and the nifty excuses like, oh, the battery was dead on the cell phone, on the pickup, in my pacemaker. . . .

So I said, "We've both won." Then I added, "You want to be finished with fighting?"

Eyes closed, she smiled, and snuggled against me. "No," she said simply. "I like fighting with you. What was your name?"

As I opened my mouth to tell her, she added, "Or how about a phone number? Do you have a phone in here? To go with your blanket, I mean?"

"If I had a phone in here, I'd have to move in with it so I could hear it not ring all the time."

"Oh, Mr. Lonelyhearts." She opened her eyes. "You have women crawling all over you."

"Is that supposed to be a compliment? Or is that why women always never call me on my non-carphone? Truckphone. Because they're too busy crawling all over me?"

She shook her head. "The girls are good to you."

I stifled the impulse to declare the obvious, that she didn't know a thing about me. "Sure," I said mildly. "They call from the Cousteau Society, Greenpeace, The Sierra Club, Democratic Party Headquarters. . . . They're dying to talk to me, and they'll only charge me thirty or forty dollars a year for the privilege."

She watched me. I looked away.

"That's pathetic," she said.

I shrugged. "Hey, I talk to them. Invariably, they're nice girls. Women, too. Liberal true believers. And, I might add, they're safely far away, in Washington, D.C., mostly, where I can't crawl down the phone line to violate them."

"They don't know what they're missing."

"Is this sadism? Or masochism?"

"What do you discuss with them?"

"The environment, speaking of sadism, the current House bill mandating exploratory oil wells in Golden Gate Park. The subject doesn't make any difference. The trick is to turn the whole thing into a sexual metaphor."

"You're not serious."

"Not often. But yes. They're between the Scylla of duty and the Charybdis of curiosity. They're navigating a fog of wrong numbers, answering machines, angry hangups— boredom, in short—and emboldened by anonymity."

"You're telling me this so I'll think you're a creep."

"No, I'm telling you this so you'll realize how desperate I am."

"Ohhh, poor baby," she said, and kissed me on the forehead.

"Do you think a normal, well-adjusted, moral creature, who merely hangs up on well-meaning female volunteer telephone solicitors instead of trying to seduce them, would have allowed you to jump him like he just did?"

"That's a good point," she said thoughtfully. "But you left out heterosexual."

28

I grunted contentedly. "The radio should break into *Let's Get Lost* about now. But who said anything about heterosexual?"

She snuggled. "Nobody."

"Ou-tiz."

She abruptly pushed away, to get a good look at me. "What did you say?"

"Pardon?"

"Why did you say that?"

Her eyes were serious. "It's Greek," I said simply. "It means *nobody.*"

"I know that," she snapped.

I frowned, amazed. "Really? Dare I hope that you've read Homer? Or Ezra Pound?"

Now she frowned, but uncertainly. "Homer? No. Is that where you learned it?"

"Yeah. I mean, no. The only place I've ever seen it is in Ezra Pound's *Cantos,* but it's Homer he's quoting, whom of course I read in translation. But you. . . ? Surely. . . ? I mean, no offense, but. . . ."

"You're right," she nodded. "I'm mostly illiterate."

I dismissed this. "There's literacy and there's literacy. So where did you learn *outiz?*"

"Skip it," she said curtly. "Otis is a lousy name anyway. It doesn't fit you. It sounds more suitable for a nineteen-year-old bagging groceries."

"Hey," I said sourly. "What's in a name?"

"Glasses, maybe. Creased chinos and a thin belt. Sensible gunboat shoes. A name tag."

"Don't forget sleeve garters."

"Sleeve garters!"

"And vertical hair."

"A squeaky, unbroken voice."

"You'd take the squeak out of any man's voice."

29

"Oh, what a nice thing to say to a girl." She did her trick to the tip of my nose, adding teeth.

"Yum," I said, rubbing it vigorously, "rhinophagy."

She recoiled with affected horror. "Is that more Homer?"

"No, it's nose-eating."

"That's a relief." She came back. "Mmmm. . . ."

"Let's switch to Latin."

She snuggled dreamily. "You can do anything you want."

"Sort-of-modern Latin. In Calô, which is what certain tribes of gypsies and low-riders speak, when they're not speaking Spanglish, there's a *mordisuerbe,* which is your loud, wet soul kiss." I kissed her nose. "Onomatopoeic—no? Then there's the *mordibeso,* which is your soul kiss with bite."

"Ouch!" She squirmed away and rubbed her nipped nose with the back of her wrist, like a cat might.

"Fair's fair," I suggested.

She sneezed daintily. I attempted to *mordibeso* her nose again, and she hid her face against my shoulder. After a long moment she sighed. "Thank you."

"For what?"

"For making me feel at home."

"Really?"

"Really."

"In that case. . . ." I held her at arm's length and looked very serious. "Would you iron my sleeve garters?"

She chose a fold of skin over my third rib and pinched it, hard.

"Ouch!"

"Got a Latin name for that?"

"Yes! Pain!"

"That's better."

"Domestic pain," I added, when she'd turned me loose.

"You're welcome. Notice I didn't dump a pan of hot grits over your head."

"Thank you." I gestured toward the house. "Has it occurred to you that you really are home?"

She looked toward the illuminated portico. "No, it hasn't."

The lanthorn gently swayed in the fog, a dark, cold breeze that made us reluctant to unfurl the moving blanket, as if it were time to get up and go to work of a winter's Monday morning.

"This is your home—right?"

"Oh," she replied, "I live here—there." She turned towards me. "But it's not my home." Again she covered my mouth with the tips of her fingers. "Enough." Her eyes had that mildly surprised look of someone who's been drinking, but by now she was pretty sobered up. And along with this sobriety and its exhaustion came a frank clarity, compounded by intimacy. Whether or not I might find myself trusting this situation, I wanted to trust her. But with what? With my decrepitude, I suppose. With those non-optional salients of my humility, my truck, my little apartment, my job. Later, I'd trust her with my bad back and long silences and the nightmares and the one or two other weaknesses that might gradually differentiate me from a thousand other men. Maybe I could rely on her to watch that back while I faced the predators in my dreams. And in a flash I intuited that she'd stay until she got bored. As she was leaving, rather than tell me the truth, she'd think up some excuse. "Oh," she might say, "you need somebody who can really look after you."

I didn't like this intuition. I wanted to like her. All I had to go on, of course, was sex and a little banter. If not sempiternal, it wasn't trivial either. Far from it. And who reading this wouldn't settle for equidistant? And, again: How stupid can a man get?

Pay attention, says the little voice, and you might find out. Besides, what else do you have going tonight or this week—or this month or this year?

"Otis, will you take me home?"

I knew what she meant and I almost said yes. She meant the little apartment. She knew I knew. Whatever was going on beyond the lanthorn, she was ready to push it over the edge. Yet my instinct was to dissemble. And not because I wasn't stupid enough to say yes, I'll take you home: I was that stupid. It's just that I wasn't so stupid I didn't know better. That's different from action. Okay, sure, I'd been through it before. Women I couldn't afford, women who lived in worlds quite distinct from mine, women who. . . . I'd played out the scenarios with their *Zeitgeist* subroutines of credit cards and worldly accession. It could not but come to a grisly end, with a lot of sex along the way—sex and an inevitable intimacy that would delude me, by the time the grisly end arrived, into denying its arrival. Silly boy. Adios. Take a couple months off, get over it. Maybe six months. But darling, I have to work anyway, whether I'm having sex or not; whether you're bored or not; whether or not, in fact, it was your husband's money that bought dinner last night. Can't you just hole up with me here in desperate but witty poverty and *live with it?*

"Hah!"

"Are you laughing at me?"

"No. I'm laughing at what I would imagine to be the look on your face as you stepped through the front door of my *portico.*"

"That's presumptive," she declared, "and singularly unromantic."

She was taking this entirely too seriously. "Yes. I *presume* your unromantic reaction would be analogous to that of a bare-footed woman who's just stepped on a snake in the dark."

She wasn't laughing. "There're things worse than snakes."

"You should hiss when you say that. But it's true. And life with me might be one of them."

32

"What about life with me?"

"All things being equal, it might be hell."

"Hell?" Her upper lip quivered.

"I . . . I suddenly don't understand."

"I was thinking about getting out of hell, Otis. Not into it."

"Excuse me, Renée, but hell, short of Sartre or war, is usually tailored by the individual to suit the individual's needs."

She was crying.

"Hey," I added hastily, "I have no idea what I'm talking about." I shut up and held her. She cried pretty hard.

Two lonely people with their own reasons to cling to each other, and just enough humanity between us to momentarily cope. Which is as much as to say that I continued to hold her, to stroke her hair, and to silently wonder whether I might have even a remote hope of helping her. She continued to sob. We exchanged not a word. After a while her tears subsided. We made love for the last time.

Much later we were pretty cute, handing back and forth mismatched bits of clothing in the dark, and the half-pint of cognac, extracted from her purse. She had a nip while I pulled on a sock. I took a sip while she rummaged for a shoe.

All this took time. There was no talk of our seeing each other again. But we would. It went without saying. We scrawled telephone numbers on the back of a gas station invoice and tore it in half. She told me hers was for the cell phone in her purse. She labeled mine "Otis." And before we knew it, I was watching Renée in what was left of the black dress walk barefoot up her driveway, shoes and purse in hand, hair all undone. And already I was scarcely able to credit my memory of the evening.

We have an interesting phenomenon in San Francisco. Sufficient numbers of parrots, cockatiels, and parakeets have escaped or been freed that the birds have found one another, each its own kind, some even cross-breeding, and the resultant flocks have taken up residence in various locations around the city. It is quite common to see them in the palms along Dolores Street, for example, or up and down the Filbert Steps below Coit Tower, or perched along limbs of the Monterey pines lining the Stockton Street block of Washington Square Park. These flocks gather noisily in the crowns of certain trees at dusk, preparatory to roosting, and sally raucously over the city just before dawn. They generate a surprising amount of noise. It's a foreign clamor, too, consisting of sharp, piercing shrieks and braying cackles, endemic to the jungle habitats of equatorial and South America, and quite distinct from, say, the single whistle of the solitary red-tail hawk, native to the arid bluffs of coastal California.

It was a large dawn flock of boisterous parrots, loudly wheeling out of the easternmost eucalyptuses of the Presidio, less than a block away, that distracted me, as, its brake released, the truck rolled silently backwards down the driveway. Once into the street I started the engine. Then I paused to watch the flock circle to accrue members before inaugurating its vector over the city toward some stand of foliage, where the birds would find nourishment peculiar to their adapted ecosystem. These particular parrots were a brilliant chartreuse, the males showing a fuchsia blaze at their throats, all of them with bright orange beaks, black legs, and yellow claws, their coloration as loud against the gray fog as their strident nagging against the silence of dawn. It was this sensory racket, compounded by the worrisome tapping of a seized lifter in the truck engine, that prevented my hearing the shot that killed Renée Knowles.

34

THE BEREAVED

FOUR

I've reproduced as much of the scene as I can remember. How long have I been here? Anybody with a brain should be able to understand that Renée and I came honestly to our amusement, and parted on good terms. To say the least."

"Fat chance, peanut."

The big tired cop smelled like a health problem. He had listened to the whole story, chainsmoking silently. Having interrupted my coda, he lit a fresh cigarette and sat astride a chair for a while, forearms over the back of it, directly in front of me. Though the cigarette was a filtered one, he occasionally plucked an imaginary flake of tobacco off the tip of his tongue, examined and dismissed it as if it were equivalent to an implausibility in my story.

At length he stood up. Setting the chair thoughtfully aside he took a turn about the room, looking into the faces of three or four associates, glancing over the shoulder of the stenographer.

Finally he barked and hissed, half dog and half adder, an expectoration of slander by turns excoriating and coarse, insidious and intelligent, and directed with an uncanny hazard, as if I were a corner spittoon.

"Likely *fucking* story, Kestrel. You think a guy doesn't have a blemish on his complexion never ate peanuts out of his Coca-Cola?"

Before I could respond to this absurdity, he shouted: "Shut up! I know better. You ain't never visited a peanut farm, is

35

you, buddy? Let alone turned them up? You never dug peanuts! But me? In my time? I dug me some peanuts. Until further notice, consider yourself one of the species. One among thousands. The work of a harvest moment. It's enough to give you ambition, forking peanuts."

He abruptly wheeled and asked, "You know that story about Ulysses and his last task?"

Otis, I suddenly remembered, and sat up straight. "As a matter of fact I–"

"Don't panic," Bowditch shouted. "I didn't know either. Not until Sergeant Maysle, sitting over there, put me onto it. Ulysses had to walk inland with an oar over his shoulder, see, and he had to keep walking until he found somebody who didn't know what the oar was for. That's a long way from the beach, peanut. Still a little shook up? Caught so soon and all? Relax. You can re-read *The Odyssey* on Death Row. Refresh your memory, so soon to be erased. Good project. Maybe read it in Greek. The state-sanctioned snuff takes a long time. Wheels within wheels. Our liberals grind your agony into very fine particles, but the State is inexorable. After ten or twelve years all them wheels cook down to just the four on the gurney."

"*Otis*," I began again.

"Shut up. But the peanut is New World. And thus," he opened one hand, "we get the peanut fork. Same deal as the oar. Some guy—me—walks inland with the peanut fork over his shoulder till he meets some guy—you—who don't know what it's good for. Good question, I say, you're just the mother-forker for me to turn up with it. You drive the tines into the dirt just in front of the plant, deep into its roots. Crickets and grasshoppers and maybe even a firefly snap out of the leaves, into the musty twilight. You lever the whole plant up and over, roots and all. There they are: dirty little nodules of truth. Dirty, but nutritious. Truth is good for us."

36

"Is it my turn yet?" I asked.

"No," said Bowditch. He blew on the coal of his cigarette and showed it to me. "See that? You hold a lit cigarette to a tick's ass, he'll back right out. It's the same with the truth. That's the point."

I looked around the room, then back at him. "I don't believe this."

"Oh, well, it's metaphorical *insalata mista,* that's all. A new interrogational technique. Torture, you might say. Leaves marks only on the psyche. Keep mixing the metaphors until the subject loses his bearings and pukes–that's my job. *Metaphor* means to carry, and what's carried is meaning. I ain't going to hold no actual match to your ass, but that's what you're going to think I'm doing." He sucked loudly on the cigarette. "Don't let me confuse you. You got anything to say, just blurt it out. When it comes to the truth, we got all the time in the world."

Before I could speak, he said, "Shut up. We were discussing peanuts. Common coin for small, minuscule, diminutive, no-count: and that's what you are, Peanut: Nobody."

"Otis," I tried again.

"We been checking up on you. You do nobody so good you must like it. We-all around here are surprised such a nobody as yourself can afford even to live in this town anymore. Rents being what they are. Gentrification being the rule. Nobodies being the exception. Times is changed, Peanut. Tsk. But then, somebody so peanut as yourself gives an old peanut harvester like me something to turn up out of the infra-structure once in a while. Here's where I put my face right into yours and say," he put his face right into mine, 'Here's a dirty nodule to turn up and *eat whole and green* if I'm a mind to.' And I am thereof. I think you're pretty green, Peanut: green as a treefrog's dick."

He paced away, came back.

"You get far enough back in the woods, boy, it's a delicacy."
He paced away, turned. "You pretty far out in the woods."

Then he said, "Cigarette? Don't mind if I do," and lit himself one.

"These officers are laughing at you, Peanut. Not me. You. You ever see that movie, *Wild at Heart?* Peanut's a term of affection, that picture. The novel, too, they say, though only Sergeant Maysle here's read it. Sergeant's the Cultural Liaison, down here, liaison between headquarters and all that bullshit out there. That ninety-percent of the human brain nobody can explain? It's a bullshit filter. Take it from me. Except it's no longer sufficient. Since more than ninety percent of what goes on *is* bullshit, it stands to reason that the brain can't cope. Shut up. Far as I'm concerned—if they made a filter you could wear on your head? Auxiliary, like? I'd be all for it. Even so, we have to be at least marginally informed. So while her resumé says the Sergeant's a stenographer and a forensic anthropologist with a minor in philology, what she really is is our Auxiliary Bullshit Filter. If it's a movie, she's seen it. If it's a book, she's read it. If it's music, she's heard it. If Camille Paglia said it, the Sergeant can quote it. And that's all right, for the culture. Here, 'culture' means something else. Here, 'culture' is something to prop the car up with while we rotate the tires. See?" He came very close to me. "Pardon my cigarette-and-salami breath, but I'm about to rotate your tires."

"More like diapers," I said, "diaper breath."

Bowditch let the titters in shadows around him die out before he leaned in, his face six inches from mine, and continued quietly, "I'm just gonna love you to death, fuckface. Gonna love you right onto the gurney. I can smell the alcohol swab right now. Can you? It's cool on your inner elbow. Ain't it? Man, oh man, there ain't no injection like a lethal injection. It cuts through liberal smog like an F-103 on afterburn."

When Bowditch stood up, a vertebrae at the top of his spine cracked audibly, like a pine knot in a hot fire. "Shit!" he ejaculated, and grabbed his neck. "All things considered?" he almost shouted. "That's a likely fuckin' story, Peanut. Taking the woman home. She's drunk. You're a total stranger. It's a favor to several other strangers. Even so, the bitch deals you a piece. That's hard to swallow." He massaged his neck. "Let's see. They invite you to their fancy soirée? So what? You make picture frames for them? And so what? No way that means they're going to give you one of their women. It's a class thing, Peanut. They got it and we don't. Your going with her is about as likely as me going with her, which is about as likely as Roland Kirk playing three saxophones on the *Love Boat*—if I may be allowed a couple of cultural referents that may go right straight over your head. Yes, Peanut, Sergeant Maysle, there, she just loves jazz. She leads us in seminars. Cultural *insalata mista* throws the suspect off his feed, get it? Trips him up on his story. Him being you. We got us two-three techniques, down here to Headquarters, one of which is, we get your cultural metaphors all screwed up through the course of the interrogation and you eventually go nuts and hurl dirty little nuggets of truth all over the room. So why not cough up, Peanut? Otherwise we'll just love on you all night long. And Peanut? Before you see daylight again, I promise you will be squealing like a hinge on a bathroom door in a cheap hotel. That's because, in this precinct, we equate love with the fucking truth. And hey, Peanut? Just like the quotidian, the normal, the everyday, these concepts are *incontrovertible*. Not to mention how they're horrible and bright. Now, if you will condescend or crumble or cave in or merely flip out and cop to murdering Mrs. Renée Knowles, it'll save everybody a lot of secondary smoke inhalation. We found her phone number in your pocket and your come in her snatch, if you'll forgive my frank forensics. It'll be six

39

weeks before the DNA test comes back, but so what? We make you for the killer, dude. Your phone number had *Otis* written next to it, but it was still yours. You can explain that shit after you confess."

Otis, I thought. *Otis.*

Bowditch gestured toward the stenographer. "Look at the Sergeant get nervous. How those lacquered fingernails dance over the keys! She's nervous because she knows if I thought for a minute she was a suspect in this crime I'd hold her down and draw the blood myself. She respects me because I got this motto engraved on the barrel of my gun, right before the bullet comes out: *Justice Served, Medium Crispy.*" He smiled. "It's a long gun."

He took two steps away, hitched his pants, turned and said, "Two bucks says the DNA is yours." He pulled several bills from his pocket and showed them to the room. "Any takers?" I didn't rise to the bet. "Not against you, Chief," someone said. "Chief's always right," somebody else said. "Confess, peanut," Bowditch said, "and do life." I confessed nothing. Bowditch shrugged and put the money away. "That's almost as good as dodging the special circumstances, huh Peanut? That's okay." He smirked. "They'll rectify that oversight in the showers at Q."

He pointed at me. "Which reminds me. I'd like to thank you for keeping your philosophical resistance to DNA sampling at a minimum, so it took only four men to hold you down and a fifth to draw the two syringes of blood. Elephantine syringes, it's true." He smiled. "Your arm will heal in time for the trial." The smile went away. "Speaking of contusions, there's a bruise above your left hip that precisely matches Mrs. Knowles' right thumbprint."

This was true.

Bowditch sighed. "We'd all be better off, Peanut, if you'd just give it up. Now, I'm tired, but I'm not so tired that meta-

40

phorical *insalta mista* won't sicken you before it does me. I'm a professional. My mind is sharp and my stomach is sour. My synapses spit like a backyard fly-zapper. My tongue tastes like a welcome mat at a massage parlor. But the truth's slicker than a porn-booth doorknob, Peanut. Once you get your hand on it," he rubbed three fingers with their thumb, "it sticks." He sniffed the fingers, then held them under my nose. They smelled like he said. "Even the mildest aroma leaves my hound-neurons surging, like balls on a sea-going pool table. But truth? Nothing clears the mind like truth—except the feel of a vein as it sheathes a needle: itself a form of truth." He rubbed the inside of his elbow thoughtfully. "It's enough to make you puke just thinking about it." He raised his voice. "You *ambushed* the Knowles broad, Peanut. She coulda took a cab. But you weaseled your way in on a favor. You got the lush off their turf and onto your little half-acre of naugahyde. The gallery was distracted and grateful and relieved. In fact, as far as I can tell, they don't give a shit she's dead. But that's another story, Peanut. Your story is, a half-hour later, in her own driveway, she said yes. My story is she said no, so you raped her. It's simple. In the daze of your post-coital *tristesse,* the broad makes a break for it. You catch up with her just as she gets the front door open. You slap her around. Rape her again. Then you shoot her for some reason. The autopsy will tell us you raped her after you killed her."

I tried to stand up. "You don't know what you're taking about, peckerhead."

Bowditch smiled broadly. "Peckerhead? Oh, my. Are we pissed?" And he laughed most genuinely. "Peckerhead. . . ."

Hands came out of the darkness and forced me to sit again.

"Necrophilia! You sick fuck. We're running your profile in similar unsolved cases."

He paused to light himself a new cigarette. "I'm into you for the *truth*, Peanut. Understand? You will never escape my

41

affection for the truth. You're dead meat and I'm a bluebottle fly. I *breed* in decaying matter. It's like a magnet for me. I'm gonna lay *eggs* in your *eyes*. And just as sure as there's cherries in a chocolate sampler, the truth's somewhere inside you." He exhaled smoke into my face. "And I'm goin' to get at it if I have to eat the whole fucking box."

He paced away. "The D.A.'s psychological profile says if we dig deep enough, there'll be others. You've done this before. It's a pattern. This is our lucky break. That college girl in Berkeley last year? In you we think we see a guy we can *love to death*."

He cleared his throat, hawked something up, and almost gagged. "A cigarette." He hooked a wastebasket out from under a desk with the toe of his shoe. "Christ." He spit into the basket and kicked it away. "The old lady tried to make me give them up. Wanted me to quit the force, too. Got the idea from watchin *Columbo*, this show on TV." You watch TV, Kestrel?"

I ignored him.

He ignored me. "That guy, I forget his name. Gives good *Columbo*. His personal identity's totally wrapped up in the character. Took it on the chin, professionally speaking. Even in that Vim Venders film, completely in character. Even though he's some kinda angel."

Bowditch wiped his lips with a dirty white handkerchief. "But you know, this is a good example of why these cultural metaphors solve so much crime. Take *Columbo*. You look at enough movies—you with me, Peanut? Pay attention. You see enough films? Eventually, sooner or later, you get around to *Diabolique*. Am I wrong?" he asked the room. The room murmured assent. "Huh? Sooner or later? *Diabolique?* Am I right? Sooner or later, you get sick of World Music, masturbation, Paul Auster novels, whatever, and you take a look at a real classic. It's called reversion therapy. If it's not, it should

42

be. And there he is! Our Columbo–in *Diabolique!* The guy stole everything! The raincoat, the lugubrious disarming demeanor, even the cigar! So he could play this paragon of integrity! Is the world twisted?" He turned a full circle until he faced me again, one hand on his cheek. "Or is it just me? That guy in *Diabolique?* That French actor?"

"Charles Vanel," somebody said.

"Oh, wow," another cop piped up. *"Wages of Fear."*

"No way," Bowditch continued, "no way Vanel saw residuals from that movie–forget the TV show! Is that fair? He probably died broke in a fog of absinthe and heroin, tortured by his imprisoned talent; singing weepy duets with L'Hirondelle. *Où sont tous mes rezids. . . ?* Boulevards of Montmartre. *Sirop de la rue."* He crushed his cigarette underfoot.

"Artists suffer. What's your excuse? That's not the point. The point is–culturally speaking? You dig deep enough? The guy who stole the role is busted. *No problem.* If you love hard enough, Peanut, you give birth to truth. That's the point. That's the real deal. That's what sex is all about, down here at headquarters. It's not about promiscuity. It's about truth." He leaned in again. The red folds of his jowls brimmed with sweat. "D.A. says, you plead guilty to rape and second degree murder, we'll drop the premeditated with the deadly weapon, call it a crime of opportunity. I'm against it myself." He shrugged philosophically. "You should be for it. No premeditated and no weapon means no special circumstances: *ergo,* no lethal injection. Settle for twenty-five to life. By the time you get out, your hardons won't be anybody's problem." His lower jaw undershot his grin. It looked like the bucket on a steam shovel.

I just watched him. How could this be happening to nobody, anyway?

"No?" said Bowditch. "Not giving nothing away? You shouldn'ta said no to a lawyer." He fed a cigarette from the

43

pack directly to his mouth. "Somebody give me a match." Somebody gave him a match. Bowditch inhaled smoke. "No? Nothing?" He exhaled the smoke loudly and said to nobody in particular, "Call whatever M.E.'s on duty. Tell him to meet us downstairs."

FIVE

Her tawny skin had assumed the gray blush of a winter sunset. The upper lip curled asymmetrically, revealing a canine and marbled gum the grayish brown of gone bacon. A tiny garnet stone set in a circle of tinier gold beads, pinned dead center to a delicate earlobe, was all that twinkled in the room. The other earring, Bowditch told me, was in evidence.

"We found it crushed into a rug in the entry hall." He stood with his hands in his pockets, the panels of his jacket crumpled over his forearms. A lapel crooked outward, revealing the brown strap of a shoulder harness. "Whoever killed her stepped on it."

That's why they'd taken my boots. Bowditch pointed the tip of his ballpoint pen and sucked a tooth. "Some of those little beads are missing from the setting." Then he looked at me, but instead of menace he projected only exhaustion. He'd been up all night. He had drunk only coffee, and now the lining of his stomach would be tighter than a can of botulized soup. He needed a shave. What remained of his hair had been allowed to grow grotesquely long, and he combed it laterally across the arctic waste of his balding skull, like so many paths to be followed by migrating caribou. He smoothed these strands habitually. When he smiled his seldom-seen smile, as now, his teeth matched the varied ochres of a used cigarette filter. "One little gold bead, embedded in the sole of a boot," he exhaled loudly, "your ass is mine." He measured an iota off the tip of his pen with a thumbnail. "No bigger than the dick on a circumcised louse."

So I was standing in my socks on a freezing tile floor in the city morgue. It was four-thirty in the morning and Bowditch remained hyperbolically abrasive, but I wasn't paying much attention to him. He didn't have a case against me, and so what if he thought he did. Before us, beneath a coarse sheet, with just her head exposed, lay the corpse of the only woman who had taken the trouble to touch me in a long time.

"And suppose you find no little beads," I asked absently, "what then?"

He dismissed this. "You'll still be number one."

Rooms away, a door slammed. An occasional shout penetrated from an even greater distance, probably from the drunk tank in the new city jail, two stories above us.

"Nothing to say, Kestrel?"

Say? I looked at Renée's face, twisted in death. Overhead, a fluorescent tube buzzed like a tattoo machine. Behind a fabric partition on the far side of the room a piece of cutlery fell to the tile floor. The room was cold. On its filtered air drifted an improbable odor of rock cocaine fired by a butane lighter. A distant toilet flushed with a muffled roar. A pale green sheet the color of a malignant sea flowed over the puny salients of her unbreathing body. A hinge whined. A voice squawked over a radio. One of my socks had a hole in it.

Hers was a negative presence, its face under light no complexion would court willingly. I had seen corpses before. Fate throws a switch and what was once a repository of sensation and meaning becomes something else entirely. It's a fact.

"And a waste," I said aloud.

"You should have thought about that before you wasted her," Bowditch suggested.

"You know," I said tiredly, "you're pushing this bullshit pretty far."

46

He cocked an interested ear. "You gonna crack?"

She wasn't beautiful in death, but you could see that she might have been in life. Of all her features it was the hair that remained alive. Brunette, ringletted, well-cut, it remained lustrous and amazingly tactile.

"Did I mention that word?"

"What word? Confession?"

"Beautiful."

"Oh, Christ, Kestrel, she's dead! That's what happens when you kill somebody. They get dead. And in case you've forgotten—" Without another word Bowditch drew back the green cloth, exposing the naked corpse from the hips up.

Disemboweled.

"That incision usually comes with the autopsy," Bowditch said brutally, watching my reaction, "not before it."

He covered her again.

I couldn't get a fix on my feelings. I admit that. I knew better than to try, at a time like that, but I wanted to control myself. I needed to understand. Waves of sensation swept through me. I'd been in battle. I'd even been in a morgue before. My parents—well, parents get dead. I'd pulled a woman from a wrecked car who hadn't been dead more than five minutes. I'd found three corpses in a burned-out tank, dead for a week in the tropics. In both cases, years apart, a radio still played. In both cases the sun shone. Upside down and smoldering, with gas leaking on the grass beneath it, the car still had a turn signal going. The woman's family's laundry was strewn all over the deserted highway. The safety was off on the tank commander's sidearm, but it was still holstered. There was a joint in his package of cigarettes.

This wasn't any different. Renée was dead. She was a body, no longer a person. After that would come a lot of silly details, flash-frozen at the moment of death, extraneous to the woman I'd briefly known. Even without her, such details

47

would persist in sharing our continuum for a while, like sparks falling from a star shell. And finally they, too, would expire.

But this was different, too. Most of those other people I had never known, or known too well. I had never touched them, they had never touched me, or we had touched each other plenty, thank you. It wasn't like what Renée and I had experienced, or might have experienced. There'd been a former girlfriend, suicided years after we'd parted, who'd left behind the usual lingering questions. Friends and acquaintances got killed racing cars or shooting drugs or fighting the war or crossing against a light. Men and women I'd known well or hardly at all had dropped dead or wasted away or simply disappeared. Different. I hadn't known Renée. In an evening we'd made love and a little talk. She had never known my proper name. Perhaps—

"Hey," said Bowditch, "Peanut." He snapped his fingers in front of my face. "You're fixing too much nitrogen."

I tore my eyes away from the table and looked at him.

"You better get a HIV test."

I began to shake. This hadn't happened in a long time. I had to muster some self-control in order to leave Bowditch alone—physically, that is. I still had my mouth, however. "It's two hundred and fifty pounds of chickenshit," I observed, "that hides behind a badge."

Bowditch didn't even flinch. "Long before you come along," he smiled thinly, "I been called everything from pig to plerocercoid. I don't care about names, see? All I care about is getting to you. You Peanuts are all alike," he added dispassionately. "You gun a woman in the back, even carve her up a little; but the law that comes after you is chickenshit. Don't make me laugh. I could take a nightstick to your face like it was a slab of abalone. Usually all it takes is one lick—" he slapped one hand into the other "—and a punk drops like a two-inch turd down a four-inch pipe. Hollers for mercy, hollers for lawyers, hollers for mama. I'm not allowed to do it, of course, though there's always hot pursuit. But sooner or later it's down that pipe for you, Peanut. A finger-print inside the front door of her house, a piece of her earring in the sole of your boot, that special pistol you can't bear to part with, the knife you carried all the way through Boy Scouts. . . ." He snapped his fingers. "You're on the gurney to Shangri-la. When you get there, be sure to tell everybody what chickenshits we are."

A door opened behind us and one of Bowditch's detectives appeared, the uppers of my boots pinched delicately between thumb and forefinger.

"Well, Evans?" said Bowditch, watching me.

"Nawp," Evans shook his head. "Cleaner'n momma's sexual persona."

Bowditch made a face. "You tell Clarence—"

"Clarence went over the kicks with a fine-toothed comb," said a voice behind Evans. "There was white wine soaked into where one of the toes is worn—there." Clarence pointed with an unlit cigarette. "Carpet fibers on both insteps from a mid-eighties Toyota, don't have the exact year and model yet. . . ."

"Eighty-four extended cab," I said.

"Thanks. There's antifreeze, aluminum sawdust, a blade of grass, and beach sand embedded in the seams and soles of one or both boots. But no trace of the earring."

"Sounds like a singles ad," Bowditch said.

"The heater in the truck leaks," I offered.

Bowditch ignored this. "No fibers from the hall carpet?"

Clarence shook his head. He was a worn, bespectacled, aging chainsmoker, gaunt in a white lab coat and baggy slacks.

Bowditch said, "You sure you dug deep enough?"

Clarence shot his cuff wearily. There was no watch on the wrist. "What the fuck time is it?"

49

Bowditch scowled. "What, the ex-wife get your watch, too?"

Clarence's face tightened. "Formaldehyde leaches dyed leather." He tapped the cigarette on the inside of the wrist. "Kind of like you leach the spirit." He parked the cigarette on his lower lip. "I want outta here."

Bowditch produced a Vantage for himself. "Give the guy back his footwear." He lit Clarence's cigarette, then his own.

"Smell like cat piss." Evans held out the boots.

I took them. "Yours don't?"

"That's not cat piss," said Clarence, "it's adrenaline pumped to his extremities by abject fear." He cocked his head and sucked his cigarette alive.

"Shit," said Evans.

"No, really," said Clarence, exhaling. "Look at him." He squinted at me through the smoke. "Terrified." After a moment he added, as if casually, "Did you bother to find his records, yet?"

Evans looked at me with renewed interest. "This guy has a record?"

Clarence nodded. "If you look in the right place."

I dropped the boots in front of a folding chair and sat down. The chair's metal legs generated echoes in the vast, tiled room. "That's enough, Clarence." I crossed one ankle over the opposite knee and brushed off the heel of the sock. "How's it going?"

Evans looked from me to Clarence and back. Bowditch just watched Clarence.

"I don't know," Clarence said. "Where do they keep that stuff, Danny?"

I pulled on a boot. "Beats me."

"What stuff?" said Evans, looking from Clarence to Bowditch. "What stuff they talking about?"

"A box of doughnuts says they're talking about fly-casting," Bowditch said, glowering.

50

Evans frowned. "Fly-casting?"

"The yuppie pussies," Bowditch spat.

Clarence smiled. "You're popping your P's, Charlie."

Bowditch looked at me. "Flycasting's the only goddamn thing Clarence does outside this building."

Evans moved his forearm back and forth. "At the casting pools? In the park?"

"It's a club," Bowditch said. "They see who can land a tied fly in an inner tube. Then they have cocktails and talk about Montana. It's a tranquil endeavor in a hectic world. Not to mention, it's a surrogate for sex."

Evans frowned. "Somebody should tell my daughter about it."

"Haven't seen you out there much," Clarence observed mildly.

"I got bored," I said simply.

Bowditch nodded my way. "Murder One's more compelling?"

"Not like drinking," I said.

"Stay away from my son," Evans said.

I had both boots on. "Any reason to keep me?"

Bowditch looked at the corpse.

"You should check on him before you waste any more time," Clarence persisted, clearly enjoying this hitch in Bowditch's program. He tapped an ash into the palm of one hand and spread it on the apron of his lab jacket. "Danny's a vet with a war record. Two tours, a commendation, one Purple Heart. Besides that, he's twenty years self-employed; he's got a business license; he even pays taxes."

This information annoyed Bowditch considerably. "You didn't tell me you're a vet."

"It was bad enough I had to go through it then. Now I should go through it with you?" I pulled a cuff over a boot and stood up. "No thanks."

51

"You mighta saved us a lot of time, asshole."

"What—you mean since I was stupid enough to go to Vietnam, I'm not smart enough to kill somebody and get away with it?"

"Marines?" Evans asked hopefully.

"Oh, Christ," I said, "let me out of here."

Clarence chuckled. "You should see Danny float those moth larvas, Charlie. They're really light, see, and eiderdown fletches make them particularly unaerodynamic. Only the hook weighs anything at all and—"

Bowditch shot Evans a look that stopped him mid-guffaw. "Listen," he said. "We got a broad here, cut down in the prime of life. We got this guy having sex with her until five minutes before she died. If he didn't kill her himself, he almost certainly saw who did, and if he didn't see who it was, he must have smelled them. He must have something we can use: a make of car, a head of hair, a shirttail, a radio, the smell of after-shave, of garlic. . . ."

"I didn't," I said. "I was busy. Now what? Are you finished?"

Bowditch held himself very still. His eyes looked like tired fuses. "As a matter of fact, I'm very close to finished. But not with you."

I massaged my neck. "Bowditch, I didn't kill this woman. I hardly knew her. We parked a few hours in her driveway, right? Sure, we had our moment. Sure, I enjoyed it. So did she, maybe. Somebody could have been dropping mortar rounds on the hood for all I might have noticed—get it? But in fact it was very quiet out there. Nobody took a picture through the windshield. No vehicles came or went. I saw nobody, not even a cat. You found my phone number in her pocket. She gave me a pet name to go with it. How does that conflict with what I'm telling you? It makes sense. You can't find anybody who can tell you I knew Renée Knowles at all, and only one or two people who ever saw us together."

I looked at the corpse. "I wish she were still alive."

Clarence moved over to the table and, holding his cigarette as far away from her as possible, he drew the green sheet over Renée's face.

"Why the hell would I kill her?" I said quietly. "I hardly knew her. I liked what little I did know. I never even saw her in daylight, for Chrissakes. . . ."

Bowditch nodded, his eyes closed as if against a distraction. "I know," he said suddenly, wearily. "I knew the minute I showed you the belly wound."

I blinked.

Bowditch sighed. "It was a complete surprise."

"He's got lots of points, Charlie," Clarence surmised.

"Yeah," said Evans. "And we got none."

"Shut up," Bowditch said to him. He opened his eyes. "Get the fuck out of here."

SIX

Colma is south of San Francisco, and a lot of people are buried there. Wyatt Earp for one example, Joe Dimaggio for another. Currently there's talk of moving a few acres of graves to make room for a casino. Gambling interests have convinced the burghers that, after 150 years of farming the dead, the municipality might want to get something else going. Survivors of the interred are upset. As there's a lot of money involved, relatives of the interred are likely to remain upset.

The mourners barely made a crowd. Some were dressed appropriately, a number of them expensively; but this is the West, where dress is virtually unproscribed under almost any circumstances. John Plenty, for example, was there. Grief-stricken, he wore paint-streaked jeans and a seersucker jacket that would have looked more appropriate at a lawn party. He was also drunk. Gerald Renquist was there too, in a beautifully cut suit of somber charcoal with a subtle mauve pinstripe. On his arm he wore his mother, or vice versa, in very large dark glasses and a conservative jacket and skirt of dark navy blue. She and her son seemed reserved; in shock, perhaps. We all had a nodding acquaintance, but in respect, no doubt, of the pall of suspicion that hovered over the affair, no one approached me.

Man, that is born of woman, hath but a short time to live, and is full of misery. . . .

54

The Episcopal priest read from his scarlet *Book of Common Prayer* while a light breeze tugged at his achromatic alb. The evergreen leaves of a nearby oak rustled audibly, and I suddenly noticed an Alaskan tang to the air, the taste of fall that a Californian learns to anticipate, bringing with it the hope that, after the four or five months of summer drought, some rain may come at last. And with the rain all the imperatives of drought must wash away: the odors of micturition in the streets and alleys, the flat beiges and umbers of the dessicated grasses, the tourists that throng the coast highway, and the land that remains stable only so long as it remains dry. With the invasion of the southerly latitudes by this tundral cool come also the salmon catch, art openings, the opera, elections. The sun continues nevertheless to glare down from its brilliant blue firmament which, once freshened by so much as a single storm, renews all at once the hope that finds itself daily and meticulously betrayed by the teeming nefariousness below.

He cometh up, and is cut down, like a flower; he fleeth as it were a shadow, and never continueth in one stay. . . .

No doubt, many of those graveside were aggrieved; whether they wore their sunglasses against the grief or the sun was impossible to discern. Certainly, the sun was bright. But, uncertainly, there were few of the outward manifestations of grief one had come, over many years of burying the cut down, to expect.

In the midst of life we are in death. Of whom may we seek for succour, but of thee, O Lord, who for our sins art justly displeased?

The Lord wasn't the only one displeased with this particular sinner. Two or three among the crowd plainly watched to make sure Renée Knowles didn't fly up out of her coffin to perpetrate some last-minute peccancy. They stood not shyly, either, but staunchly graveside with sharp eyes on the proceedings.

Yet, O Lord God most holy, O Lord most mighty, O holy and most merciful Saviour, deliver us not into the bitter pains of eternal death.

"Au contraire," a voice whispered behind me, not so loudly as to disturb anyone, but theatrically *sotto voce* sufficient to be heard within ten feet, "Let it be eternal." It was a woman's voice, and I was curious if not rude enough to turn and see whose it might be. There were a certain desperation, a certain despair, a certain irresolution and a certain hopelessness, all resonant in its quaver.

"Now Ruthie," another woman, also behind me, said firmly, "God's will be done."

"A-fucking-men," the first voice declared, *"but she never treated me right."*

I took a look. She had short-cropped gray hair, stood not five-foot-three, and appeared to be a very trim if weathered sixty-five to seventy years old. A red kerchief was tied at her throat. She wore sneakers on small feet, denim shirt and jeans, a fleece vest. An enameled button pinned to her lapel declared: US GOV'T OUT OF MY WOMB.

A strong resemblance haunted her face. This would be Renée's mother.

"Ruthie," her companion said. "The girl is dead."

Thou knowest, Lord, the secrets of our hearts. . . .

56

"Ain't no heart," Ruthie hissed, *"buried here."*

The friend clasped Ruthie's shoulder. "Get a grip!"

Unlike Ruthie the friend was dressed like an urban matron, in a long cloth coat, sensible but stylish heels, a leather purse. The two were approximately the same age. Ruthie wore no makeup, wedding ring, or jewelry at all. Her friend wore plenty of cosmetics, along with diamond clasp earrings, a thin gold necklace, and a gold ring on the wedding finger of the hand she was keeping on Ruthie's shoulder. "Ruthie's upset," she said, to no one in particular.

. . .suffer us not, at our last hour, for any pains of death. . . .

Someone in the crowd snickered and abruptly fell silent.

People are unpredictable when faced with death. Laugh or cry, it doesn't make much difference. But there is a moment in the ceremony that's more or less guaranteed to get the genuine sentiment out of the crowd, just in case their brains were to stray from the business at hand, and this moment came now. The priest closed his book on his forefinger and, shortening the length of his chasuble with a fastidiousness worthy of a princess confronted by a gutter, he took a step backwards, carefully redistributed his skirts, and gestured toward the spectators.

The casket had been lowered prior to the service. Uncertainly, at first, then determinedly people began to file past the heap of dirt piled on a bright green tarp at the foot of the open grave. Each took a quantity of earth to cast over the deceased. One took a pinch between her fingers and sprinkled it timidly, back and forth, as if adding seasoning to a broth. Another cut a hand decisively sideways into the mound, like a Hunan chef angling a spatula into a bowl of diced peppers; but no matter the amount, these handfuls of dirt and stones made a loud impression upon the coffin lid, startling some of

57

the onlookers, imparting to others an apparent satisfaction. Eight or ten people, including a fascinated young boy and an even younger girl, participated in the ritual.

When each had taken his turn, the priest stepped forward, pried open his scarlet book, and adjusted his own pair of tinted spectacles.

Unto Almighty God we commend the soul of our sister departed, and we commit her body to the ground. . . .

And even I, who despite or because of a certain familiarity retained a modicum of respect for death, now committed my own small sacrilege, commencing a reverie upon that very body now enshrined in malodorous disinfectants and wasted brass, quick-rotting velvet, and slow-leaking teak. I saw shadows different than the ones Renée may well have encountered by then, shadows that moved because we were moving, or because the tree protecting us had stirred in the westerly, or because a seagull drifted between the grave and the sun; shadows that lived.

. . .earth to earth, ashes to ashes, dust to dust; in sure and certain hope of the Resurrection unto eternal life, through our Lord Jesus Christ; at whose coming in glorious majesty to judge the world, the earth and sea shall give up their dead; and the corruptible bodies of those who sleep in him shall be changed, and made like unto his own glorious body; according to the mighty working whereby he is able to subdue all things unto himself.

The old anti-entropy con, whereby love squandered comes back for more; whereby ice cubes impart cold to whiskey, rather than the calories of whiskey winning their ceaseless war against ice; whereby a body stung into shredded meat by fifty-caliber insects rearranges itself into the blinding sublimity of a Caravaggio; whereby time goes backward, as if in a dream, and takes the dreamer's heart with it. The old perseverance of blind hope in the face of a rank stench. The old ploy for *pesetas* to further gild the ornaments of the church. What must this priest think, mouthing these words, emitting them like so many mild and randomly elected phonemes against the cruelties of this world? What must these people think, if they were listening to the priest at all, of the vague pusillanimity of these syllables, ticking against their shirtfronts like so many motes of sterile pollen at dusk?

I remembered the nipples raking my face; erasing weeks, months, perhaps years of desuetude, like a pair of beautiful pedagogues buffing the coarse orthography of errant slang, blanking a scarred *tabula* with each energetic pass of their weightless felts. Or some such impious reflection. . . .

I heard a voice from heaven, saying unto me, Write, From henceforth blessed are the dead who die in the Lord; even so saith the Spirit; for they rest from their labors.

At these words a collective sigh emanated from the crowd, from such a crowd of urbanites who might readily admit to their singularly urbane fatigue, but never, indeed, admit to boredom. For when the priest invited them to participate, even so fractionally, in his liturgy,

The Lord be with you

only two or three knew to respond,

And with thy spirit

although when the priest raised his hands and said

Let us pray

many of those present actually bowed their heads; not omitting to touch their forefingers first to the bridge of their sunglasses, in order to inhibit them launching off their noses to follow the dear departed into the grave. And they listened as the priest recited,

Lord, have mercy upon us

and then surprised themselves and all the rest of us by responding, as if out of some common ethno-genetic reflex,

Christ, have mercy upon us

allowing the priest and the rest of us our first real, as heartfelt as if retaliatory, antiphon,

Lord, have mercy upon us,

which, however, faded audibly through the next phase, called the Lord's Prayer, in a halting, jerking, miserable, badly conducted performance, not unlike a buggy with two mismatched horses and an incompetent teamster, everybody uncertain of the whip, one horse pulling as the other loafs, while at times neither pulls at all, as they allow the momentum of the vehicle to push them downhill.

A cellphone trilled. Girly Renquist threaded her way among the gravestones, away from the crowd, holding a phone to her ear. A man standing at the head of the grave glowered. I thought he might be the husband.

O Lord Jesus Christ, who by thy death didst take away the sting of death. . . .

Isolated among the crowd the man looked somewhat quizzical, distracted, not particularly aggrieved, but by turns thoughtful and exasperated. Nobody seemed to be with him, yet most among the attendees had spoken to him at the beginning of the service.

. . .Grant unto us thy servants so to follow in faith where thou hast led the way, that we may at length fall asleep peacefully in thee. . . .

I looked into the open grave. I hadn't noticed before, but now saw the six-inch striation of compacted refuse that snaked along one face of the excavation, about two feet below the grass. This recalled to me that, in the background, there was a steady din of heavy equipment–lurching motorgraders and caterpillar tractors–moving and leveling truckloads of garbage over the upper quarter or fifth of what had once been a thousand-foot-deep arroyo. Less than a quarter-mile from where we stood a perpetual raft of seagulls undulated over the dump site, just above the eastern boundary of the cemetery, demarcated by a tall windbreak of shimmering eucalyptus trees.

At the corner of the grave the striation cornered too, and angled across the earthen face at the head of the coffin; and I realized that, if I were to stand on the opposite side of the grave, with the priest and the husband, I'd see this same striation passing beneath the ground on which I presently stood. This site, along with most of the graves around us, if not the whole of the cemetery, maintained its altitude above sea level primarily because it was atop the graded surface of a vast landfill.

. . .and wake up after thy likeness. . . .

The woman with the anti-abortion button on her fleece vest began to weep. She made no effort to conceal her emotion, nor to be quiet about it, and this immodest outburst seemed to unsettle something in the man I presumed to be Renée's husband, who now allowed a single tear to escape his eye and slide over his cheek unimpeded. Renée's mother, as I'd come to think of the woman in the fleece-lined vest, displayed an uncommon complexity in her emotion, exposed there for any who cared to study it. Anger and yearning, love and frustration, relief and despair and much more conflicted there. A desire to call her daughter back warred with a, perhaps, life-long need to be rid of Renée for good. Certainly something more than the mere fact that they'd not been able to say goodbye remained unresolved between mother and daughter, and now their narrative would hang in stasis, insoluble, forever.

. . .through thy mercy, who livest with the Father and the Holy Ghost, one God, world without end. Amen.

Various voices among the crowd raggedly repeated the particle of assent, all of them faintly. When the priest turned sideways to encompass us within his benediction, his profile exposed Bowditch, whom I'd not noticed before, behind him. The inspector stood with his hands clasped before him, like the good choirboy he once might have been, and stared back at me as he mouthed the word, *Amen.*

Immediately the crowd began to disperse among the gravestones. Just inside the gate of the cemetery two men in coveralls sat side by side in the bucket of a front-end loader, one watching the crowd, the other contorting his mouth around one end of a large burrito. They might wait a decent interval for us to disperse, depending on the celerity of their lunch, before pushing the final measure of earth over Renée Knowles; they might not.

Bowditch leaned forward and said something to the husband. Startled, the husband glanced over his shoulder. Bowditch was watching me, and after a moment the husband turned to look at me, too.

The man blinked, then shook his head.

Bowditch straightened up, nodding grimly.

The husband excused himself–curtly, it seemed to me– and walked my way.

This took a few minutes. He had to circle the open grave. I waited. Almost everybody he encountered stopped to shake his hand or buss his cheek or give him a hug. He courteously dispensed a word or two to each of them.

Bowditch watched this scene with interest, and I quickly worked up a certain amount of dread for what he might have said to the husband. Nothing, certainly, would be beneath his incitement. But even if Bowditch had said very little, it had to be an unfortunate certainty that the husband already knew the story of the last hours of the last evening of his wife's life, of what she'd been doing, of where, and with whom.

Now, with a little nudge from Bowditch, he had a face to put to the story.

"Kestrel?"

He was a dumpy little man. Older than Renée, too, he was dressed in a Western leisure suit, of a yellowish tan fabric with brown cordage woven into a yoke on the back of the jacket, outlining the breast pocket as well, complete with a bolo tie. The gold clasp holding the strings of the tie looked like a cattle brand, a pair of capital K's surmounting a curved bar. The black kerchief tapering out of the breast pocket represented the sartorial nod to the occasion.

63

I acquiesced to my name, not at all sure whether I should be preparing to accept a blow, but certain that, if such a blow were to arrive, I had no right to do anything about it.

He stuck out his hand. "I'm Kramer Knowles."

I was surprised enough by his courtesy to be slow in returning the proffered handshake, so that he modestly added, with a gesture of his head toward the open grave behind him, "I am—I was—Renée's husband."

We shook hands. He was at least twenty years older than Renée. "Mr. Knowles. . . ." I began.

"Kramer," he said, not relinquishing my hand.

"Kramer," I began again, "I'm . . . very sorry for you and for your wife, sir."

"Thank you," he said sincerely. He glanced toward the grave, turned back and said, "I'm going to miss her."

What could I say to this? "Had you been married long?"

"Yes, we had." At this point he realized he was still holding my hand and, slightly flustered, relinquished it. "Tell me something."

"Yes, sir?" I answered, not without trepidation.

"Will you come to see me?"

"Will I—what?"

"Come visit. Tomorrow, if you have the time. Yes, tomorrow. At two o'clock, shall we say?" He checked a little smile. "I think you know the address."

Though I wasn't amused, I had no idea how to respond to this invitation.

"I'd like to . . . to talk," he added. "Maybe have a drink."

"Talk?"

"Talk. You've heard of it?"

"I've heard of it."

"You'll come, then? Tomorrow at two?"

I looked past him. Bowditch was watching us with a slightly puzzled expression on his face, as if someone had just

64

informed him the remains of the eel he'd wolfed for lunch had tested positive for selenium. I must have looked a little strange myself. Bowditch obviously had no more idea about what Knowles was up to than I did: and I could hear what the man was saying. I shifted my eyes back to Knowles and said, "Sure I'll come see you."

He took my hand again and shook it. "Thanks," he said; sincerely, as I thought. "Thanks very much."

He turned away quickly. But not before I'd seen that a tear had formed in his eye.

Knowles walked toward the cemetery gate between Renée's mother and her companion, who each took one of his arms. None of them looked back.

SEVEN

A mottled afternoon. The sky was white on cerulean and moving rapidly over towers of fog that rose above the eastern edge of the Presidio. Along Divisadero between Broderick and Baker a phaser of sunlight traced the gold leaf along the upper heights of the columns of the portico of what, they tell us, is a scaled-down copy of the *Petit Trianon,* a modest palace Louis XIV caused to be built on the back forty at Versailles, a triumph of secular absolutism. Which partially explains why, when the atheists finally achieve demolition of the huge cement cross atop Mt. Davidson, certain other elements of society may succeed in replacing it with an equally stark guillotine.

Two doors west stood the burghers' den Kramer Knowles called home. Characteristic of any neighborhood sprung entirely from the fruits of ambition, this edifice imposed itself over the street like a cliff-face of the Channeled Scablands, and kept only the scale of its opulence in common with its neighbors. A cursory nod toward civic politeness, unmistakably aloof, took form in the studied neglect of the cypresses lining the drive. Even so, brown windrows of cypress needles clustered in the granite corners formed by the stairs' leeward risers and treads. The lanthorn remained lit even in daylight. Two or three of its bulbs had burned out. Only a week had passed since Renée Knowles' death, but already signs of neglect were settling in.

The smells of juniper and jasmine released a flood of memory, of course. But I stepped aside to let it cascade down the steps and sluice over that fatal parking place beneath the tallest cypress. Only an affectedly casual glance over my shoulder hinted that I might have been there before. That, and my blank stare at the large front door. Would any sign linger of the tragedy that had taken place beyond it?

Kramer Knowles, the *Chronicle* reported, had made his money with a single idea. He patented the process whereby a thickness of cardboard is embedded in almost every cake of motel soap sold in the United States. In his tenure as a motel supplies salesman canvassing a vast territory, extending from the Humboldt River north to the Snake, from the versants of the East Cascades and the Sierra Madre to the Green River in eastern Utah, Knowles realized that no guest ever used up an entire cake of motel soap. Motel soap gets used once; then it's replaced. Even if a guest has not moved on, management daily replaces the soap, if only because each fresh cake is wrapped in the handsome logo of the host motel. If a cake were used up entirely, it was because the guest was cheap enough to take it with him, or the motel was too cheap to replace it in a timely fashion.

The customer who takes the slim bar with him? Forget that guy. The establishment whose maids are instructed not to replace the soap during a continuous tenure? Beneath consideration. But in the multi-storied hotel towers of Reno, and in the isolated high desert tee-intersection six-room gas-station/cafe/motel/casino/bars for which the Great Basin is justly famed, in businesses that made a point of treating their customers honorably, Knowles perceived his market.

He converted a shed behind his Carson City rental ranchette into a laboratory. Carson City anchored the southwest corner of his sales territory without forcing him to actually live within its perimeter, cloaking the two days a month he actually spent

67

there in a kind of mercantile purity, from which he could serenely contemplate his betterment. Prostitutes were readily available there, and reasonably priced; as was Basque food. Knowles loved hookers and mutton. The whole setup–the hookers, his 28-day absences, the other two or three days in the lab–had cost him his first marriage. But also, it had made him his fortune.

"Good riddance and worth every minute of it," Knowles suddenly told me, "ten-fold." It hadn't taken him ten-fold minutes to launch into the story of his life. Clearly, he was telling it to me because he didn't have anybody else to tell it to. This was, after all, the first Wednesday of his widowerhood.

We were sitting on opposite couches, facing each other over a glass coffee table. To hand, on a leather coaster branded with the Rocking Double-K logo, stood a crystal decanter containing three ounces of single-malt whiskey and two ice cubes. Not that I have a predilection for after-lunch whisky; but it was offered and I accepted. Knowles didn't seem to mind when I asked it to be sullied with plenty of ice, but his butler winced fastidiously.

"Soon as I get myself organized," Knowles said, watching the door close behind the departing servant, "is as soon as that pretentious bastard gets replaced by a nice babe." He swirled a glass containing his own ice, floating in a Seven and Seven. "Little uniform and everything." He loudly inhaled an ounce of his cocktail. "Black mesh stockings. Seams up the back." He chewed some ice and lifted his glass. "Straighter than a military runway."

A copy of *Design Unlimited,* a fat, slick magazine aimed at interior decorators and their customers, lay on my side of the table. Its cover featured the front façade of the Knowles house. Beyond the magazine, dead center on the table's rectangle, a little sterling silver cowboy boot offered a fistful of filtered cigarettes. Next to that was a stand-alone cigarette lighter shaped like a flintlock pistol, its wooden base surmounted by an engraved brass plaque. Then came a telephone with LCD display and many buttons, its console angled toward Knowles. Between these and his edge of the table ranged a disarray of financial magazines, a stack of what looked like annual reports or balance sheets, a note pad with the rocking double-K brand centered atop its pages, pens, pencils and paperclips, a half-bowl of cashews, and a 3-1/2" floppy disk, which Knowles was using as a coaster.

He contemplated Alcatraz, the lighthouse of which was visible out the north wall of the room. This wall rose ten feet, up from an upholstered settee to a box-beamed ceiling, and was mostly glass. Through it could also be seen the tops of the cypresses in the driveway and a wall of eucalyptus beyond, demarking the eastern boundary of the Presidio, beyond which could be seen the upper third of the north tower of the Golden Gate Bridge, and the hills of the Marin Headlands perhaps three miles away. The trees surged silently in the afternoon westerly.

"Dropsy was a good girl," Knowles continued. "But she didn't believe in science. And she didn't have any . . . what you call. . . ." he moved his drink vaguely, indicating our immediate environment, ". . .class."

An ice cube popped in my glass, spitting expensive whiskey onto my cheek.

"Not like Renée," Knowles added. "Renée was a natural."

Somewhere in the depths of the house a door chime sounded.

A silence passed with neither of us looking at the other, both of us staring at the glass wall. I wondered if this were what a nice view was for, to help people through those awkward moments of social intercourse that, otherwise constricted by the cracked plaster of a small apartment, could only culminate in mayhem or hilarity.

69

"This cardboard you put in your soap," I ventured into the silence, "is it recycled, by any chance?"

"Our first Federal subsidy," Knowles nodded, not taking his eyes off the view, "mandated recyclables. That grant was Renée's idea, in fact. . . ." His voice faltered.

"I'm sorry," I said.

He shook his head. "She —"

The butler opened the hall door. "Mr. Knowles?"

Knowles didn't respond.

"Sir?"

Knowles interrupted his thoughts to look at him.

"Your two o'clock, sir?"

The expression on Knowles' face changed so abruptly, as he stared past me toward the door, that I turned to see why. The butler stood aside, one hand on the doorknob, and into the room walked a very pretty woman.

I say woman, but she was no more than college age, twenty-one or twenty-two. She was tastefully dressed, well-groomed, and knew how to walk in heels. The new maid?

A few paces into the room she stopped to look from me to Knowles and back.

"Hell," said Knowles, shooting a cuff and angling the face of his watch toward the light. "I completely lost track of the time." He narrowed his eyes toward the girl and nodded just perceptibly. "This won't take long," he said to me. "Care to hang around?"

I shrugged.

"Freshen his drink, Alfred." Knowles stood up and drained his own. "And for you, Miss. . . ?"

"Anne," the young woman said. "Cognac."

Knowles set his glass on the coffee table, empty, and pointed at Alfred.

"I'm afraid we've only brandy," Alfred said, inclining his head slightly. His face might have been the glacial escarpment

70

of an Alp, placidly aloof despite centuries of crampons up and down it. "Mrs. Knowles consumed the last of the cognac that–" He stopped.

Knowles stared at him. His face, too, betrayed nothing. "Brandy, then," he said softly. "Order more cognac. Brandy's better than cognac anyway," he said to Anne with a smile. "You can put it on ice without people wincing. Will that do, Miss. . . ?"

"Anne," the woman repeated firmly, her eyes shifting momentarily toward me. She looked back at Knowles. "Brandy on ice will do nicely."

"I'll have another as well. We'll be in the study." As Alfred the butler backed through the door, Knowles added, "We'll continue in half an hour, Danny. Make yourself at home. Alfred will see to your drink."

I nodded.

"Fine. Half an hour then." Knowles ushered Anne out of the room and closed the door behind them.

I was alone in Renée's living room.

I regarded the copy of *Design Unlimited*. As an artifact, in juxtaposition with those across the table, as a clue to Renée, it already made sense. Knowles wouldn't have the taste to own this house, let alone decorate it or even to hire someone to do it, let alone whip it into a showplace. Certainly Knowles would not care, one way or another, about seeing his home on the cover of a magazine. But a woman of a certain ambition, using his money, would be just the ticket. He would take pleasure in her pleasure, and pride in the result. But in the end as in the beginning, other than finding and encouraging her, he would have no idea how to bring it about by himself. True, along with his pride, he would also bring, certainly, a degree of possessiveness. And there, within his possessive pride, might not she find her own? Or would she, out of his accomplishments and money, mine only contempt? What sort of marriage had the Knowleses' been?

I took up the flintlock pistol and read the brass plaque screwed to its base.

AWARDED TO

KRAMER KNOWLES

TOP SALESMAN

BY HIS GRATEFUL EMPLOYER

INLAND FURNISHINGS & SUPPLY CO., INC.

"WE'LL MISS YOU BUDDY!"

I pulled the trigger a couple of times. Metal parts feebly scratched, but no flame was forthcoming.

I bet he doesn't miss them, I thought.

I replaced the lighter on the table. Presuming Inland Furnishings and Supply Co., Inc., to be the outfit for whom he had repped supplies to motels throughout the Great Basin, this cheesy souvenir represented to Knowles, no doubt, something not cheesy at all; on the contrary, it was emblematic of his permanent release from servitude. It was a milestone.

Another moment of speculation, and I wondered that Mrs. Knowles had allowed Mr. Knowles to retain this knickknack in public view. Had it been out of consideration for his achievement, or over her objection? Perhaps it had reappeared since her death? Over, say . . . her dead body?

Maybe the butler was in on it, too.

Wouldn't that bring the drawing room mystery neatly to a close?

I picked up the copy of *Design Unlimited* and leafed through it. To be found therein were golden spigots in bathrooms with pristine views of the Mediterranean; replacement windows two-and-a-half stories high and nearly as wide; clapboard gables over-looking twilit, multilevel redwood decks; gardens with topiary motifs, one being the stock market crash of 1977; a five-Ferrari garage floored entirely in Carrara marble; another garage, which provided a view of Lake Tahoe for its meticulously restored Stanley Steamer; a private exercise terrace with a commanding view of the Hudson River; until finally, there it was: a variation of the cover shot of the front of the Knowles mansion. On the facing page appeared a photograph of the exact coffee table at which I currently browsed. In the picture was a tall vase of hand-blown glass containing three colors of long-stemmed tulips, a large book the spine of whose dust jacket read *Louis Le Vau;* an ornate dagger with bejeweled scabbard and handle, shaped like a scimitar, perhaps a letter-opener, if not too precious to function at all. On the wall beyond the couch hung one of the nude portraits of Renée, a wall currently bare, as I looked up to check: the painting remained on loan to the Renquist Gallery. The photo caption identified the artist as John Plenty, and the glass vase as Lalique. No cigarette-lighting flintlock pistol, nor miniature sterling silver cowboy boot, stood in evidence.

Whose taste had dictated the lighter's absence from the photo session? Renée's? The decorator's? The art director's? Perhaps mutual affinity had spirited it away with not so much as a word spoken aloud?

The next page showed Mrs. Knowles' bedroom, her "getaway," her "home away from home," in which there was not a trace of Knowles himself—or anybody else for that matter. There were a big four-poster bed with crocheted drapery from Arles, lots of pillows, a two-hundred-year-old counterpane. Two armoires "from Province" flanked a floor-to-ceiling bookshelf, before which squatted a Regency chair that could not be comfortable for prolonged sitting; an ornate vanity table; shelves full of collections of things, the contents of which were highlighted in inset photos. There were wooden crucifixes from southern Mexico; many *lagrimas,* also from Mexico; dozens of votive candles, their wicks unburned; there was a plate of sand dollars, symmetrically arrayed. The books were old, leather-bound, in many languages and not particularly valuable, in her possession "'. . .just because I like them,'" Mrs. Knowles was quoted as saying, "with a modest shrug. 'They're so old, so hand-made. It's a textural thing,' she laughs, punning on textual, tactile, and textile. 'Aren't they beautiful?' She takes one up and runs her hand over its tattered vellum. 'I simply treasure them as objects!'" In this breathless tone, perhaps the result of editing, perhaps the result of her acting, I failed to detect Renée's voice.

Atop each shelving unit, out of normal reach, stood a collection of wire-frame mannequins, each two to three feet high, ". . .peculiar to the nineteenth-century dollmaker's trade in France. Talented seamstresses used them to tailor exquisitely detailed clothing for 1/4-scale dolls. Each has its featureless head inclined slightly forward, as if to cast down its glance, demure in its modesty...." Did Mrs. Knowles own any of the actual dolls, highly prized for their compulsive detail, or any of the clothing, equally prized for scrupulous workmanship and period exactitude? "'Oh, no,' she says, gazing fondly up at her diminutive mannequins. 'I just treasure them as female forms, so minimal yet so idealized, so reserved yet so empty, devoid of the distinguishing characteristics of personality, yet so obviously feminine. . . . They're fascinating!'"

Her little collections, her objectification of books, the hollow, wire-frame female mannequins, all in the context of a room that had no real personal touches—they fascinated me, too. Despite the obvious fact that the place had been cleaned up for the photographer and journalist, under the stern eye of the fussing interior decorator for whom this article was an important advertisement, and despite the fact that it was an inference I was reluctant to make about a woman I wanted to like, the conclusion, that her decor could all too easily be interpreted as an outer formulation of an inner desolation, seemed almost inescapable.

So absorbed was I by these thoughts that I didn't hear Knowles reappear, even though he was carrying two large decanters tinkling with ice.

"Nothing like a piece of ass to clear a man's head," he declared heartily, handing me a fresh drink. "Especially when he's mourning."

EIGHT

K nowles propped his feet on the edge of the coffee table with a satisfied air. "Ever read that motto below the clock on the south gable of St. Mary's?"

"As a matter of fact I have. *Son, mark the time and fly from evil.* Old Testament? *Ezekiel?*"

"Beats the fuck out of me," Knowles shrugged. "But if that was my church, it would read *Son, mark the time and go get yourself a good piece of ass.*" He laughed heartily and showed me his glass. "Cheers, Danny."

"Cheers," I said. "But it's not your church."

"Ah." He removed his hand from the pocket to take a swipe at the landscape beyond the window. "You can't own it all." It sounded as if he didn't quite believe it.

"I've often thought," I mused aloud, "that when Dana returned to San Francisco. . . ."

"Who?"

"Richard Henry Dana. Author of *Two Years Before the Mast?*"

"Oh," he said vaguely, "a book."

"A book," I agreed. "When Dana first visited San Francisco, in 1835, there was only one man living on this side of the bay, a white trader called William Richardson. That silted-up inlet between Sausalito and Mill Valley is named for him. All the other natives, mostly Ohlone so-called Indians, lived on the eastern side of the bay, where it's always a lot warmer."

"The guy was probably Irish," Knowles grunted.

"Then our climate suited him," I laughed. "Twenty-four years after his first visit, Dana returned to San Francisco, only to discover a metropolis of 100,000 people. There'd been a gold rush in the interim."

"1849," Knowles confirmed wistfully.

"The change shocked Dana's mind, but not his wit. One of the ways in which he studied this instant city was by visiting all manner of churches, two or three a Sunday. One Catholic service, he marveled, was conducted entirely in French. He also attended services at St. Mary's—the very parish of which we now speak."

Knowles' expression, reflected in the window glass, was sad.

"The service, Dana noted, was stifling. In this and other respects he found it surprisingly similar to what he'd experienced in churches in Boston and Cambridge, replete with, and I quote, 'intelligence in so small a proportion to the number of faces.'"

Knowles turned around, smiling. "Did he now? Did he say that?"

"He wrote it, yes."

"I don't wonder. . . ." He turned back to the window. "Would we find it so different today after—how long?"

"A hundred and forty years, more or less. And no, I don't think we'd find it so different. Between the two of us, however, there would be no standard to compare it to. This is to presume that you don't venture over the threshold of St. Mary's any more than I do? That you just read the south gable as you go by on the cable car, on your way to lunch at Taddich Grill?"

He nodded. "By god I like this man. What was his name?"

I told him. Knowles recorded Dana's name and the name of his book on the memo pad. "Hot damn." Knowles dropped the pen. "I forgot all about the game." He retrieved a remote control from a drawer on his side of the table and aimed it toward the wall opposite the window. A tambour door rolled away to reveal a large television, just beginning to glow. Soon enough, football players ran around on the screen. Crowd noise and the voices of commentators flooded the room, loud.

"Knowles," I shouted, "turn it down!"

He looked at me in surprise. "It's an exhibition game."

I pointed my fingers at my ears. "You want to talk or what?"

He raised an eyebrow as he muted the sound. "Sure."

"I don't mean to lose my cool, but one of the things I hate worse than football is television."

"Really?" Knowles affected surprise. "How can you live with yourself?" He smiled. "What about an empty glass? Hate that, too?" He held up his glass.

I held up mine. "You got me."

"Goddamn intellectual." He pressed a button on the phone.

"Sir?" came Alfred's voice.

"Two more," Knowles said, as he drained his drink.

"At once, sir."

On the big screen, lizards sold beer. After thirty seconds of it, Knowles broke the silence.

"She was a spectacular little brunette, wasn't she? Just about on fire with ambition, too. Her looks she got from her momma, I guess. In any case, she didn't know her father. The ambition she got from her early years, passed mostly in a trailer park in Steamboat Springs. Her mother still lives in the sticks, in northwestern Nevada. She was at the funeral."

"Is her name Ruthie?"

He nodded. "She was there with my ex-wife."

I blinked. "There's a package."

"You got that right." He pointed toward the upper left hand corner of the television. "Way up in the northwestern corner. Cotter Pin, Nevada. Ever been there?" He chuckled. "Nobody's been there. After that Japanese guy bought the

78

ski hill–I believe it's called Mount Warner; guy who sold it made a killing on that deal–Steamboat got too civilized for Ruthie. Cotter Pin, on the other hand, will never have a ski hill, and that suits Ruthie fine. There's not even a motel up there to sell soap to. Come fall, all the elk hunters sleep in their trucks behind the bar. In the five years Renée and I were married, she never took me there. I talked to Ruthie once or twice a year if I happened to pick up the phone when she called. But she didn't call to talk to me; she called to argue with her daughter. If the call lasted more than ten minutes, it was because neither of them would stop yelling long enough to hang up."

He opened the drawer on his side of the table. "Ruthie wanted some attention Renée couldn't give her. Care for a cee-gar?"

"Well, I. . . ."

"It's a good one." He pitched me the cigar and produced a second one for himself. "Don't smoke, don't like football, don't watch TV. The fuck you do all day, Danny?"

"Work."

"Oh." He licked his cigar. "Some folks don't like cigars, and they're wrong about that." He retrieved a tool from the drawer and clipped one end off his stogie. The tip fell into his lap. "But you're mostly right about television. I can't stand the way those guys talk about the game." He slid the tool over the table. "Bunch of idiots."

"They're a poor substitute for silence."

He dragged a wooden match along the table top until the head exploded, then let the fumes dissipate before holding the flame under one end of the stogie. "I used to sit in them motel rooms in places like Winnemucca and Pahrump and Jackpot and Eureka and Wendover and Tonopah and Denio and Austin, just to name a few. . . ." He looked past the cigar toward me. "At least once, in every one of those motel rooms, I'd come face to face with silence."

Part of the wrapper tore away as I clipped the cigar.

"Lick it first," Knowles said, waving out his match.

"Garlingus is undignified," I muttered.

Knowles looked at me, surprised. "You ever watch a broad do it?"

The door opened and Alfred appeared with a tray and set new drinks before us.

"Every half hour, Alfred." Knowles blew a smoke ring. "Keep 'em coming."

"Very good, sir." Alfred took the empties away.

I took up the flintlock pistol and scratched it under the cigar.

"Hey," said Knowles, "you don't want no kerosene fumes in no Havana."

I looked at the cigar. "Really? This is a Havana?"

He slid a box of kitchen matches over the table top. "We were speaking of silence."

"Yes, we were."

He loudly inhaled from his drink. "I'd do it deliberately. Just sit on the bed, listening. There'd be trucks on the highway, of course."

"I'd imagine."

"And a little casino noise, maybe, depending on how cheap the room was."

I nodded, puffing.

"Maybe a drip from the sink or the showerhead. . . ."

I blew smoke without inhaling.

"About then I'd notice the air conditioner was on."

"Turn it off?"

"Yeah. For science. It gets hot as hell out there. Cold too. Anyway, then I'd hear the mice or the termites, or maybe a rattlesnake shedding its skin against a footing in the crawl-space. So I'd turn the air conditioner back on."

We both chuckled.

"Well," he said, "the noise of an air conditioner always helped me sleep in a strange bed."

I nodded, my head leaking smoke.

"But the strange bed ain't the problem. Without the air conditioner, if I shifted, there'd be creaks from the bedsprings. There'd be doors slamming down the hall and muffled voices. The snaps on suitcases? They flutter when they open. TVs. People fucking. The plumbing. Somebody visiting the ice machine. A car moving slowly over gravel."

"Doesn't sound so quiet to me."

"That's just it. That's the point. There's no such thing as silence anymore. I doubt there ever was."

"How can you say that? You were smack in the middle of a desert. All you had to do was go outside."

"I'm way ahead of you. I did go outside."

"And so?"

He shrugged. "The freeway was loud. The lights were so bright you could call them loud, too. If I was in town, a car would go by with them big speakers in it. You know. *Boom, ba-boom. Boom, ba-boom. . . .*"

"That's in a town."

"In town, out. Point is, there was no longer any such thing as silence. Not in the world I lived in then."

"Did you try the desert?"

"Sure I tried the desert. You can't tell me about the god-damn desert. I lived out there seventeen years. It's never si-lent out there. Not like it is here, in this place," he tapped his head with the remote, "or in here," he waved, indicating the rest of the room, "or in there." He pointed the wand back at the television. "It's pretty damn quiet, though." He puffed thoughtfully. "I was an ex-salesman who made a killing with

81

a single, dumb idea. The only difference between me and a thousand other guys is, I was bullheaded enough to see it through. If I'd wanted, I'd never have had to work again. All I had to do was establish diverse portfolios with a couple reputable brokerage houses and never hit a lick. Spend it all on hookers and booze and maybe even gamble, within limits. Get a houseboat up the Delta and spend all day fishing."

"Sounds like a life," I lied.

He snorted. "I don't know how people do it, and you don't either."

"That's true," I said. "I'd rather live in a one-room apart-ment with guys throwing skillets and tureens around the restaurant kitchen next door and be safe from the sound of a fish hitting a lure. I am a bedlamite."

He looked at me. "One room, eh?"

I looked at him.

He pointed the cigar at me. "If you was twenty years younger and didn't have a dick, I'd help you do something about that one-room apartment." He grinned salaciously.

"Cool," I said dryly. "I might even let you, too."

"It's too late though, ain't it."

I said nothing.

"So," he said, "thrill me. What allows you to enjoy things just as they are?"

I looked at him. We were just two guys with a television, drinking and shooting the breeze. Right? I took a sip of whis-key and wondered what Knowles was after. "I frame art and I read a lot. It's a quiet life, and I can just about stand it."

He made his face ugly. "You're not some kinda artist, are you?"

I shook my head. "No. I'm addicted to privacy. I can't get enough of it."

"Privacy." He looked around him. "Gives me the creeps."

"As for the rest of so-called culture," I pointed my cigar

toward his television, "I had my belly full of culture a long time ago."

"In the war?"

I didn't answer.

"You're a misfit, then."

"I could accept that."

"I was—am—one, too. I saw the light in Korea. But I tell you, I'd rather pass the time with them rich idiots," he indicated the men moving their mouths on the TV screen, "than be alone entirely. Being alone is just too freaky. I spent lots of time alone. I had my belly full of alone. I may be a misfit. We're all misfits one way or another. I figured that one out. But—"

"—you just love people," I finished for him, somewhat dryly.

"That's right, soldier." He cocked his head at me. "You were a soldier—right?"

I nodded.

"Well, soldier," he said. "I just love people."

Alfred returned with a fresh round.

"Excuse me," I said, "could I get a soda back?"

"Certainly, sir." Alfred took the empties and went away and came right back with a liter of mineral water, a saucer each of lemon and lime slices, two tall glasses, a silver bowl full of ice cubes, a pair of silver tongs, a cut-glass salad bowl full of salted cashews, three dishes with three kinds of olives, two finger bowls, a couple of cloth napkins, and a small ormolu cup for the pits.

"I could get used to this," I said, watching Alfred arrange things.

"I'm sure you could," Knowles said, watching me. After a pause he took up a fistful of nuts and tossed three or four into his mouth. I chose a wrinkled black olive and poured myself a glass of soda water with a squeeze of lime. "So, into all that silence came Renée."

83

He kept his eyes on the muted ballgame. "She was hanging around a casino in Elko, hooking a little." He looked at me. I looked at him. He looked back at the television. "Cute little thing. This was after I'd spent about two and a half years doing nothing but advancing the soap idea, which by then was pretty established. There was a trademark. I parlayed that into a license with a big manufacturing operation, and opened an office in Reno. After being my own sales force, R&D department, procurement officer, shipping clerk, and so forth, I figured ways to sub out all the grunt work. Finally I had enough dough to sign up the best damn patent attorney in D.C., and so that aspect was nailed down. This global enterprise was set to take over the entire operation, and eventually they did. Advertising, marketing, sales, manufacturing, packaging, distribution—the whole shooting match. I was weeks from closing the deal. After years of nothing but work I was going to sit back and clip coupons. Everything was beautiful, and I was high as a kite.

"Renée had broken up with a cowboy who owned a ranch about seventy miles outside of Elko. She took me out there once, and it was beautiful. You went up this little draw off a dirt road far, far off the main paved road, and that little draw opened out into the prettiest damn place you ever saw. The guy had three, four hundred acres up there, a year-round creek with willows and cottonwoods and aspens all up and down it, a deep well, an orchard, fifty or sixty head of quality Charolais or some such beeves, a herd of sheep, and maybe ten head of the most spirited cow ponies you ever saw. Those horses would come up and eat an apple right out of your hand, but they were wilder than shit, too. They were an important part of his dream, see, because what he really wanted to do was breed cutting horses. He'd built a little house, with a barn and a milk cow and chickens and everything. Just the prettiest place you'd ever seen.

"And crazy about Renée? He couldn't do enough for her. That was one problem. She was nothing but independent. Plus, the scene reminded her of where she was from, of her mother, you know. Her mother's a sheep rancher, and they never got along. Whatever the reasons, Renée was restless and bored up there. That cowboy would have cut his wrists for her, and that's a fact. But she would drag him forty miles to town every Saturday to hear music or to pretend-gamble, just to be around people and noise and cars and bright lights, just to shop or look at godforsaken galleries full of cowboy art or whatever, just to see other people walking around wearing clothes and talking and stuff.

"That beautiful little ranch, that dedicated, good-looking guy, it just wasn't enough for Renée. He wanted kids and peace and quiet, he wanted the sun rising and setting on all that loveliness for fifty years, and he wanted to share every minute of it with her. Maybe by the time he died, he might have gotten enough of it, but I doubt it. He was a happy man.

"Renée? All along, she'd had ambition. She wanted to be somebody on her own. It had to be quasi-artsy, but it had to make a buck, too. That was another thing. The cowboy could carve a cradle out of stumps of apple wood, but he never had any money. He sprung that apple wood cradle on her one day, by the way, built it on the sly, see, life-sized, and just scared the daylights out of Renée. She told me it even smelled like a baby. Turned out the last thing she ever wanted was kids of her own. What Renée really wanted was money. And people. It developed she had a talent for putting what decorators and architects call 'elements' together. Like this place." He waved his hand at the room and added softly, "I offered to help set her up in the big city. Simple as that."

He took a long draw against his drink. "She never lost her taste for that long-legged kind of dude, though." A couple of cashews tumbled out of his fist, onto the couch. "When she left that cowboy, I thought it would kill him. I know how she felt, anyway. I done the same to Dropsy. Left her for Renée after seventeen years. Seventeen hard, hard years. But me leaving Dropsy for Renée, that was understandable. Even Dropsy could understand it. And to be perfectly frank, if Dropsy got it, anybody could get it. All I did was leave a completely understood old something for a completely unknown and fresh new something. The whole world understands that. But Renée. . . ."

I took a long sip myself. I'd been staring out the window at the eucalyptuses. The westerly was giving them hell. Wraiths of fog blistered past the window at twenty knots in complete silence.

"Renée left a handsome, hardworking, clean-living young man with a family in his future and a place to raise them— and for what? For a guy twenty-two years older than her, that's what, with a paunch to show for it, the hair going, bad teeth, not much education—all he had that anybody could see was a pile of money. I'll tell you, everybody in her life, everybody she knew out there, her mother, the cowboy, well. . . . They were just disgusted with her." He discovered one of the cashews among the buttons on his shirtfront, inspected it for a moment, and popped it into his mouth. "Me, I wasn't completely stupid. I only asked her about Wesley a year or two later. That was the cowboy's name. I asked if she'd been in touch with him at all. And she said no, except indirectly. She said her mother had heard from somebody in Elko that Wes had sold up the ranch and moved to Hawaii—Hawaii, for god's sake. And I professed amazement at this development, though I wasn't surprised the guy had to take some radical steps, you know, to get this girl out of his system. She was something, Renée was. A real beauty. And a devil in the. . . ."

He let his voice trail off. I watched the trees. I know a little bit about silence, too, but it was pretty damn quiet in that living room at that moment, in those several moments.

"God I didn't think I would ever get enough of her," Knowles said wistfully. "And she liked me, too, well enough anyway, at first. You should believe that. We had this ambition thing in common, you see. We really understood one another on that level, and for awhile it was plenty good enough. The change was good for both of us. We made it work."

After a moment he added, "A couple years later I asked her did she ever think about Wes, about how she broke his heart. Because that's what she did, you know. I saw it. They'd run fence together, camped in the meadow next to the creek, rode them ponies all along the ridges, raised foals, built the kitchen cabinets, planted a garden. . . . That garden was in full bloom when we went out to get her stuff. Wesley, by the way, he couldn't handle that, our visit. He knew we were coming because she called to tell him. So Wes got on a horse and rode straight up into the mountains before we got there, and he stayed gone, I'm sure, until long after we'd left.

"And I watched her manipulate this guy. She called and told him we were coming, and invited him to stick around and meet me, and to say goodbye to her, too. She came on real civilized. This just twisted the knife she'd already got into him when she'd earnestly told him that what she was doing was for his own good. And, well, I couldn't hear the other end of the conversation, but he was outraged, I'm sure, if not completely broke down by this attitude. So that when we got out there and he wasn't there, see, she could lay the whole trip on him. As if this breakdown in civilized behavior was all his fault, see. Not hers. No blame on her.

"And I watched her do this. Now, I was crazy about her at the time—" he took a quick sip from his drink, "—still am, really. Though the fuckin' bloom is off the fuckin' rose, I'll tell ya. I knew her well by the time last week rolled around. And part of it was because I watched her do this to this guy. And crazy for her as I was at the time, I was still able to tell myself, Knowles, pay attention, boy. Cause when the time comes, she's going to do it to you, too. Just exactly this. When she's ready, you're next. So have your good time while the sun shines, Knowles. Cause it's goin' to get dark one day, as dark as you ever seen it."

He took up the remote. A seagull skidded above a rooftop across the street, angling sharply in the wind. Knowles flipped through fifty or sixty channels until he'd returned to the football.

"That time she told me about Wesley, I said to her, Hawaii? Are you kidding me? He gave up that little corner of paradise for Hawaii? Did he come out okay? And you know what she said to me?"

"No," I said. "I don't."

"'Oh,'" she said, "'Wes is *fine*. He's *always* fine.'"

The door behind me opened. I heard the rustle of silk and smelled perfume.

"Sir?" said Alfred. "Your six o'clock."

This one was a blonde.

Knowles ignored him. "She didn't say nothing about any of this to you?" he asked testily, annoyed by the interruption.

What was I supposed to say? That'd I'd only spent the one night with his wife?

"It took me a little while," Knowles continued. "But. . . ." He stood up, brushing cashew crumbs and salt off the front of his shirt. "I finally realized the truth of the matter. It was simple. But then, so am I." He looked at the girl in the doorway, then looked at me. "The fact was, Danny, I'd fallen madly in love with a woman I didn't like. I couldn't like her. She wasn't likable."

He finished his drink. "She got right square between me

and that silence, though." He set his glass on the table. "Alfred, bring the soldier another drink." He headed for the door. "And one for you, Miss–?"

"Tara," the blonde said, turning to go with him. "Vodka Collins?"

Alfred inclined his head almost imperceptibly in her direction.

"Ah yes," Knowles said appreciatively, taking her arm. "Tara."

ACQUAINTANCE
RENEWED
NINE

Over the next few days, my protracted speculation over her husband's motives inevitably circled back to the real subject, Renée herself.

You have to learn how to talk to me. Talk means trust. Tell me everything. Expect reciprocity. Start with a kiss. Pucker up. . . .

I'm not given to a lot of fantasy, but Renée's voice began to assert itself often, in my reverie. I'd don the gun muffs and there she'd be, well inside the audio perimeter of distantly snarling miters.

How could a chance encounter, even highly charged, have such an effect?

Well, the simple answer is, chop saws don't have all that much charm. They help you do a job you've done a thousand times before. There's a cranial module that watches out for your fingers, analogous to the one that allows a zebra to graze in spite of nearby hyenas. Beyond that, there's only so much concentration necessary to the task.

An old salt, of the type you don't see around San Francisco so much anymore, used to say that the most dangerous job on pre-war tug boats was the wiper's, whose duty was to wipe with a rag huge connecting rods going up and down alongside the engine in the hold of the ship. The trick was to find the dumbest guy in port for this job, a guy who had to focus every synapse to accomplish it. A smart guy couldn't keep up with it. The task was so repetitive, so stupid, that a guy with even half a brain would forget what he was doing, start thinking about something else, get a good fantasy going—and find himself maimed for life.

There's something to that story.

A moral.

Let's see: Maybe it doesn't pay to be smart?

Perhaps it would be more accurate to say that I, in my reverie, was the one addressing Renée, rather than the other way around. She remained inscrutable. I could remember her eyes, the gleam of perspiration along her sternum, the down along her forearms. But I couldn't remember her voice. That's not accurate. Though her voice implied intimacy, there hadn't been time to say much at all. So I made up these conversations we might have had, or replayed the ones we did have, and, finally, it's a wonder I didn't cut my hand off.

No matter how feral the painting, in color and style of frame I'm conservative. For contrast, you see. It's non-competitive. Subtle. The frame's there to do a job, not to assert itself. Similarly, the frame around my imagined or replayed conversations with Renée, the woman I never knew, whom I wanted to know and never would, was my routine. Work, eat, sleep. Read the paper, make a batch of quesadillas, walk the streets and beaches of San Francisco. And indulgently fantasize about Renée.

A tough mistress herself is San Francisco. The light, utterly lucid, shows everything. The air is clean, dry, capricious, and it can be violent; yet thunder, lightning and snow, for instance, are extremely rare. The place hovers, beautiful, on the edge of the continent, year in and year out. Fog envelopes it, sure, but that just makes it damp and cozy. And when a fog burns off midmorning, the town is that much more spectacular. You get every hue, value, shade, and saturation between blue and violet; between yellow and orange, too—tangerine for example. Cerulean. Parrish blue. Then comes *terremoto*. Ordinary people, driving home from work, get killed. Or the mayor gets shot. Or it rains for forty days straight. Expensive houses collapse into the sea.

Framed by this natural beauty, failure is lurid. Despair is palpable, as are success and achievement. This environment is that dichotomy of extremes peculiar to the American West. The frame of beauty provides a contrast to every human endeavor. A stone groove can switch to palpitant horror mid-diastole, like a reversal of the poles of the earth. While your life is going over the spillway, you'll catch yourself admiring the god-like serenity of the lake that's expelling you. I mean, I presume socialites jump on ordinary guys in the cabs of their pickup trucks in other cities of the world, but I don't want to take the time to ferret them out. I found one already.

Socialite. There's an interesting term. In Boston, if you don't belong to a Mayflower family, you're dirt, socially speaking. I actually met one grand dame there, in whose home I was installing a painting, who refused to speak to me because (a) we hadn't been properly introduced, (b) I was the help, and (c) I wasn't related to any "decent" people. She lived within a glass bell of reasons she couldn't deal with me, wherein she silently sipped sherry and watched me as if I had designs on the silver. But San Francisco is in the West, and the West is different. There are at least two fabulous mountain ranges between San Francisco and Boston, plus Indiana and Nebraska—plenty of distance between the old white ways and the ones peculiar to the eastern shore of the Pacific Rim. It's true that if your great granddaddy came here in the Gold Rush and did well, that counts for something. But that was only 150 years ago, after all, as opposed to 400, and more power to him, and this mentality prevails over blueness of blood. Thus, what people can do to make them-

92

selves prominent in San Francisco society is virtually unlimited. You can be a financier or a rock star. You can be a scion of the family that brought the railroad to California, and so much the better if you managed to hang on to some of the money. Sally Stanford, notably prominent by the time she died, was, in reverse chronological order, a mayor, a restaurateur, a madam, and a hooker. You can be a preacher's daughter from Arkansas and marry in at the top. There's a club whose membership is exclusive to gay millionaires; most of their money made in real estate, and every last one of them *parvenu*. In this light the Silicon Rush and its sister, the Dotcom Boom, are all of a piece. And in this light you can even be a picture-frame magnate, like me.

I've framed stuff for museums, and this in turn has brought work from a lot of socially prominent people. It's never translated into very much money, but it affords me a living and I enjoy the work. Museum-quality framing is an interesting trade; there's genuine craft involved, plus if you hang the stuff you've framed, you get to punch holes in some really expensive walls.

The resulting connections once led to a pair of tickets to the opera, very pleasing, bequeathed me for the season by a matriarch who spent it in Geneva getting new kidneys instead. She was—is—a life-long boxholder. The seats were spectacular.

I wondered if Renée might have liked that.

Perfect! Kramer hates opera. Macy's has this little black dress on sale, but I don't have any shoes to go with it. Don't worry, I'll get some. The nice thing about the mini is, it disappears very easily – that's if we bother to take it off at all. Come to think of it, you say these are box seats? Have you seen them? Do you think, if it's dark enough, we could. . . .

So there I was in my shop on Folsom Street, talking to myself. It was in the middle of a long, chopsawy (the local Chinese cafe spells it that way, in my honor; get it with long beans and beef) day, when I looked up from my bench to find Marissa James watching.

"Oh, no," I said.

"I hear you're a murderer," she said, "too."

"Too?" I shucked the gun muffs. "Whom did you murder?"

"Husband number three—or was it number four?" Her kiss was generous and wet. "Anyway, I'm here to renew your certificate of innocence." She'd already been at the chardonnay. "And it's about time."

"You always mix up the husbands when you're drinking, Missy. Probably gets embarrassing, in the dark."

"I've yet to meet one that minded."

"I'd mind."

She cornered me against the saw bench. "Enough to kill me?"

"That's not funny."

Mea culpa. In return for absolution, I'll buy you lunch."

I hung the gun muffs on the saw handle. "Closed for lunch."

She smiled. "Money changes everything, doesn't it, Danny. Chins up," she added, chucking me under mine, "I might marry you yet."

"You're single again?"

"Single again."

"Are you trying to frighten me?"

Missy was a looker, though, and in her youth she'd, as it were, husbanded this resource, refusing to have anything to do with any man who didn't have a lot of money and couldn't be driven to despair when it became necessary. Missy's motto was that it's just as easy to marry a rich man as a poor one. Pushing fifty, Missy's hair was perfectly cut and hennaed, and she remained trim despite booze and idleness and four or five husbands. At least two of these latter had been strictly the worst kind of tennis-playing, secretary-boffing, vodka-swilling, shiftless upper-class 'zero-work' gigolo types she favored because, when either of them put their minds to it, they were good in the sack, and a vacation from the seriousness of the other kinds of husbands, those dumb enough to think a rich marriage means something other than business. With Missy, they all had to put their minds to her needs regularly. She thought of it as a kind of rent.

I'd been framing pictures for Missy and her various husbands and miscellaneous houses for years. She flew me to Hawaii once, just to hang a picture. It was in between husbands two and three, twelve or fifteen years ago, and we had our moment. Show me the picture-framer who would forget snorting cocaine out of the palm of Missy's hand through a cocktail straw, while seated in a very fine restaurant at a balcony table overlooking a moon-lit Waikiki Beach. The evening was unseasonably cool, and she'd worn an ankle-length mink coat with very little under it. The owner of the restaurant appeared wearing a small frown. But before he said anything, Missy ordered a $250 bottle of wine, over-priced, as she observed; but as it was her birthday could he bring it right away? He did, all smiles.

Now, still trim, still wearing a perfume I remembered, she kissed me again.

So impetuous. So rich. So troubled.

She knew how to kiss and she tasted better than sawdust, so I stood still for it, rigid as a blue-collar caryatid in a peristyle labeled *Industry,* and let her slum. I was preoccupied, after all, by the kiss of a dead woman I'd hardly known, and felt altogether too strange to move suddenly. Some sawdust drifted down from my eyebrow into one of Missy's eyes.

"You should have married me when you had the chance," she winced, plucking her eyelid over the offending mote.

I stepped back to brush at my hair and eyebrows, squinting through the descending dust. "It's one thing to be married to a sex object. But isn't it kind of drastic to be married to one who hasn't learned to sail or play tennis?"

She turned loose the eyelid and blinked cautiously. "All of my clubs retain excellent instructors in both."

"Your clubs retain excellent instructors in all three."

She pouted. "Aren't you just a *little* sorry you didn't marry me?"

"I'll settle for the lunch."

"Good. All this talk about sex is making me hungry, not to mention thirsty."

I locked up and steered her toward the chopsawy joint. But Missy's radar was on–"There's penance and there's *penance*" –and before I knew it a valet was driving away in her immaculate Jaguar, stranding us under the awning of a cozy little bistro far out on Sacramento Street, halfway across the city.

Moments after we'd been seated, a glass of chardonnay appeared in front of her. "Here's to murder." She tasted the dewy rim. "And thanks so much for taking the time to lunch with little old me."

I returned the toast with my five-dollar glass of mineral water. "That's not funny."

"Danny, people who drink are ever so much more fun than those who don't. Couldn't you have just a single glass of wine with lunch, for godsakes?"

"Booze and power tools don't mix. That's probably the only homily I ever laid on you. It's more or less imperative. Why can't you remember it?"

"Honey," she drawled, "homily grits comes in cans, and nothing's imperative 'cept gittin' 'em out."

It was either smile or throw the arugula to the floor in a fit of pique.

"Why'd you do it?"

"Do what?"

"Kill Renée Knowles."

My smile faded.

"The cops and the *Chronicle* and the Tee Vee"—she said it just like that, Tee Vee—"all are *intimating* that your arrest is *imminent.*"

"That's sheer, hopeful speculation."

"No, no," she hastily insisted, "the news media aren't allowed to make things up."

"Hey," I said, brightening, "you're amusing again."

A waiter materialized to take our orders. Then we waited for his swivel-hipped retreat through the banquets.

"Okay, Missy. Spill it."

When I heard the glass turn over, I didn't even bother to look. I just jumped.

"Missy missed," Missy said, using her most childish voice.

The stream of wine cascaded onto the seat of my chair before I could move it aside. "Don't sound so disappointed."

"Oh, my," she laughed. "Are we angry?"

"Merely exasperated. It's simply beyond me how a grown woman can act like you do and expect anyone to take her seriously at all."

"Darling," she counseled. "I don't want anybody ever to take me seriously. Except the odd fellow at the altar."

"Why change at fifty?" I grumbled.

"Oh," she shrieked. "Below the belt!"

"Chins up," I reminded her.

The management cleaned the premises, refreshed her glass, and brought me another chair, all with nary a discouraging word.

Missy watched me over her new glass of wine, a mischievous glint in her eyes.

"Now what?"

"Some of the people I normally lunch with have suggested to me that, if it turns out you killed Renée Knowles for the same reason several of them might have killed her, it will be terribly amusing."

"To think that I might have anything at all in common with the people you normally have lunch with would depress me worse than finding myself on a desert island with nothing to read but the *Chronicle.*"

"There are fates more terrible," she said. "What if you were marooned with only its book review section?"

I winced. "Always turning the optimistic screw, aren't you Missy."

"Given that you count among my friends many of your best customers, not to mention where you wouldn't be without me, you should take a bite out of your lunch instead of the hands that feed you. I mean, *really.*"

I began to wish I had ordered a drink. "Life is full of little compromises."

She smiled hugely. "So I'm told."

I could only reflect on this ruefully. What would a compromise be to somebody like Marissa James? To me it meant forking over half my income for the privilege of living in a small room in a beautiful city, or having to go to the VA hospital when I cut off a finger because I won't be able to afford the best surgeon in town. To my Missy, however, compromise meant living without care, so long as she observed certain rules. Try not to drink yourself to death, for example, so as not to foul up a good thing. Don't fall in love, for another example, because love often leads to marriage and marriage, sooner or later, one way or another, will certainly cost you a considerable portion of your net worth.

Of the two of us, which had engaged the greater compromise? I might have posted this impertinent query, but I'd bicycled along that tactless route before, only to be passed on the right by many a Jaguar. Besides, in Missy I had discovered another rule I hadn't known about, which was, don't fall in love with a woman who has and always will have millions in proportion to your thousands, unless one of your chief objects in that union is to help her spend it.

Christ, I thought, watching my lovely friend beyond multiple pairs of hands delivering bread, olives, oil, two Caesar salads, another glass of white wine, and granules of pepper: I could open cans of homily grits all day long.

In fact, yet another compromise I'd learned to make in company with Missy was that of holding my tongue among her friends. Money—more accurately I should say, fortune—comes with a lot of its own rules, of which, depending upon how small a brain accompanies it, and how much self-pity, the subset of regulations involving compromise is very small.

I plucked a tuft of sourdough off the warm loaf. "What might I possibly have in common with your other lunch dates? Other than admiration for your lovely person, that is. Have you found another guy with a chop saw?"

"On the contrary. I've only seen one of those nasty things in my entire life. No, my friends were jocularly suggesting that Renée might have taken you for thirty or forty thousand in one of her horrid little investment schemes."

"Oh, my. They were having their fun, weren't they."

"Not so much as they're going to have when they find I've been lunching with her suspected murderer."

"Missy," I said, leaning toward her as if in confidence. "That you've seen only one chop saw in your life, I can believe. But that you've lunched with only one murder suspect?" I fluttered a palm over the table top. "My credulity falters."

"Oh, well," she admitted, "one denies oneself so little."

"Then my certificate of innocence is redeemed?"

"Danny, really," she said, suddenly earnest. "I believe in you absolutely."

"Thank you."

"I mean, we all know that, as usual, money isn't your problem." She laughed gaily.

See what I mean? Since I had no money, money wasn't my problem. With her, it was just the opposite: since she had money, money *was* her problem.

"Thank you," I said. "I think."

She leaned over the table, exposing a white V of flesh atop her breasts, well below the line of her freckled tan, that demarcated the youth lent her face by cosmetic surgery. "So tell me," she whispered conspiratorially. "Why did you kill her?"

I didn't mind this childish levity; more accurately, I was used to it. And certainly it served to remind me of why, though we'd had our fun, I'd never been able to stay angry with Missy or to remain in her company for very long. It was only the sessions with her investment brokers and accountants that she took seriously. She had two or three of each, by the way, for, in fact, she was no fool when it came to the management of her money. Missy approached investment strategy with the same religiosity of mien as other people approach the IRS or sigmoidoscopy or the gas pedal on a nuclear submarine.

But, as she often could, Missy surprised me. I'd been twisting the tuft of bread, and now she covered my fidgeting hands with her own, and apologized.

Her hands had always been very beautiful, and finely drawn these hands remained, untrammeled despite age and untoward numbers of wedding rings.

"What sort of schemes?" I asked quietly.

She withdrew the hands, arranged the table napkin on her lap, and began to toy with her salad. "Mrs. Knowles would decorate somebody's home, furnish it, provide works of art. This of course involved getting to know the people she was working for, so as to understand their taste–if they had any– to develop or cover for it if they didn't."

100

"You mean she resold them their own ideas?"

"Exactly. Still, they needed to be comfortable with the results."

"Or at least think they're comfortable with the results."

She sighed. "Yes, yes. You're so tiring. We're not all idiots, you know."

I said nothing.

"Anyway, if you're any good at all, and socialize with the right people, and the economy's healthy too, it's a nice little business."

"A good economy being one in which the rich get richer."

"Yes, yes! And the poor get poorer. Naturally."

"I didn't provide that premise of the syllogism. It's not necessarily the bumper-sticker paradigm. I just meant that if someone with money says the economy is good, it means their money's putting on weight in all the right places."

"Jesus," she said. "I feel a cocktail coming on. This wine's not strong enough to deflect your proletarian sentiments."

"May they pierce like bullets. I presume that Renée's arrange-ment was everybody's arrangement? That is, whatever mater-ials she provided her customer, from drapes to antiques, from paintings to bathroom fixtures, she bought thrifty and sold dear?"

Missy waved a hand. "Doubling or tripling the purchase price is standard. Everybody knows that's how it works. It's accepted. She spent a lot of time at estate sales, parties, antique shops, even traveling around Provence or Ecuador or China, always looking for marketable pieces."

"Sometimes the client went with her?"

"Sometimes the client paid for the whole trip. Sometimes they became best friends."

"Or lovers?"

"Renée did make at least one trip with a certain socially prominent lesbian. But usually it was with straight women, often older, with whom she became very buddy-buddy. And then there was the one gay man."

"What gay man?"

"His name is Tommy Wong."

The name was familiar. "The architect?" Missy nodded. Taking some salad, I said, "How's his financial condition?"

"You mean, before-and-after-Renée? That financial condition?"

I frowned. "Is this gossip or information?"

"Well," Missy said, leaning toward me as if in confidence, "it's considered rude to discuss these things, but he's been overheard to claim she cost him about a hundred thousand." She sat up straight again.

"Dollars?"

"No: paper clips, you dolt."

"That's a lot of money."

"For some," she agreed.

"What's her trick?"

Missy smiled sweetly. "You tell me."

I managed a shrug. "All she cost me was two nights' sleep and an interview with a nasty cop." But there was a catch in my voice.

She noted the little blow and moved on. "According to Tommy her m.o.–isn't that what they call it?–was simple. Once she'd gotten to know somebody well, she'd start to make them little propositions. She'd call from New York, for example, very excited. She'd just come from a preview at Christie's where she'd found this lovely Louis Quinze enamel clock, something like that, and definitely underpriced but still way beyond her budget. But she could sell it out west, she was sure, to any of two or three people in Santa Barbara or Carmel or San Francisco or Napa and so forth. Did the friend want to go partners? That was the offer. No pressure.

"Now, Renée wasn't stupid about this setup. She knew a lot

of people, and when she had targeted someone, she got to know them well indeed. She had a real knack for finding individuals who were out to prove themselves, willing to take a chance in order to show themselves capable of making a little money on their own. Another type she could identify simply wouldn't care if a few thousand dollars were to evaporate in a flimsy deal; they might look at the whole thing as a lark. Easy come, easy go–up to a point. But Renée didn't hustle these until later. She was also adroit at avoiding people merely eager to help her, as well as people who were obvious suckers, not to mention people who are sharp or paranoid about their money, or operators overly interested in it.

"She used her dealer/decorator status to work this scam without spending her own money. She would take a partner's money, add it to her own or not, buy a piece–a chair, a rug, an armoire–and turn it over to her customer at twice the purchase price. Many dealers ship inventory on credit, if they know you. Hell, half the time, they haven't paid for it themselves. If you pay attention, you can really get some margins going.

"So she ships the piece with an invoice. Sympathetic to this scrappy girl, the customer pays right away. Then Renée studies the bottom line. She deducts shipping and handling, plane tickets and hotels, a little dough for her time, even good old sales tax, which she dutifully reported, and, finally, the amount of the original investment. What's left she divides by two, adds the partner's investment back in, and writes him a check. Often the investor has completely forgotten about this little deal, and the check comes as a pleasant surprise. It all looks official, and so it is. Profitable, too. In fact, it's a very sweet deal for everybody involved."

"After a while," I surmised, "Renée comes back with a new deal."

"And for a little more money."

103

"And a little more risk?"

"They're primed, of course. A single transaction doubles your money, and you don't even have to know anything about the internet. It even sounds legal. It *is* legal. Perfectly legitimate."

"Why screw it up? What happened?"

Missy shrugged. "The Wong wisdom would have it that your girl got greedy. He quotes the French expression for somebody consumed with avarice. Know it?"

Missy's world view only pitied people who hadn't been to Paris lately; but pity doesn't imply mercy. "No," I said. "I don't know it."

"Of course you don't. I'm here to help you."

"Thanks. What do the goddamn French call somebody who's greedy?"

"Well," she continued pedantically. "The evolution of the slang is very interesting. In the past they might have said *Elle a les dents longues*–she has the long teeth." She dangled two forefingers in front of her upper lip. "Now they say *La salope ci les qui rayent le parquet*–the bitch's teeth are dragging the floor."

"How pleasant."

"Evocative, isn't it? You know, French has a functional vocabulary of approximately 200,000 words. American English on the other hand has nearly 600,000. But French colloquialisms make up for–"

"Did you ever hear it said about Renée Knowles?"

"What," replied Missy, as if frankly astonished, "that she had a bilingual vocabulary of 800,000 words?" She pressed a hand to her breast. "Like me?"

"No, Missy," I said patiently. "That her teeth dragged the floor. That she'd become greedy. Or dishonest."

"Only from Tommy. Never from anyone else. If the word had gotten around, that would have been the end. What I heard from everybody else was that she was honest, hard-working, ambitious and, well. . . ."

"And well. . . ?"

"Well. . . ."

I pointed at her glass. "Give your loquacity a jolt. As if it needs one."

Missy took up the glass with both hands and held it to her lips but didn't drink. "I heard that she liked rough trade," she said over the rim, batting her lashes. "Would you know anything about that?"

TEN

Abruptly abandoning the navigation of our chatter, between exasperation and titillation, Missy produced a cellphone, made the appointment, and we quickly finished lunch. She let me drive the Jaguar downtown while she chatted on the phone with one of her brokers.

That's a real car, that Jaguar convertible. It's powered by a sixteen-cylinder engine. Pedestrians were so taken with the machine's beauty they forgot to spit on it. Don't get me wrong, though; just the other day somebody graffitied the tailgate on my twelve-year-old truck. Ours is an egalitarian society.

Tommy Wong had a whole floor of offices ten stories above the northwest corner of Mission and Fourth. A sleek hood ornament of a blond model in sweater vest, tie, khakis, and tasseled loafers with argyle socks led us through a sea of CADD stations to Wong's office.

"As surely as God made little fishes for sushi," Missy said, wrinkling her nose as the assistant closed the door behind us, "that guy's wearing Chanel No. 5."

"You think it's to cloak his moral turpitude, or to advertise it?"

"I think if he wanted a cloak, he'd wear one."

It was a corner office, facing east, and you could see the entirety of the Yerba Buena Gardens from up there, or what was left of them; for, by that time, the Sony Metreon had defiled their northwestern corner. But the waterfall and café and expanses of walkways and lawn remained, which attracted the office workers now littering the landscaped grounds, smoking or reading or hugging their own knees, eyes closed against their forty-five minutes of lunchtime sun. Here and there amongst them, homeless people lounged in twos and threes, with dogs and shopping carts. Across Third Street loomed the Museum of Modern Art.

Tommy Wong and Missy exchanged a warm greeting. Wong appeared a very smooth character. Of sixty or so years, immaculately groomed and dressed, he projected accomplishment and success and cringed imperceptibly at any but very specific tastes.

I was aware he'd submitted a design for the MOMA building and, like dozens of other candidates, had lost the contest to Mario Botta. When Missy introduced us, I tweaked him on his view as including some of the most exciting municipal architecture in San Francisco.

"That damned museum," Tommy Wong said, shaking his head toward the MOMA.

Missy jumped in. "I like that building, Tommy. Don't be such a sourpuss. Anyone would think you're a sore loser. It doesn't become you. Besides, that whole deal was over and done with ten years ago. And who can forget," she added dreamily, "Signore Botta delivering his speech, at the groundbreaking ceremony, entirely in Italian. My goodness, I just wanted to take him home and eat him with a spoon."

"Certainly, darling," said Tommy Wong, smiling dreamily himself, a man who allowed heterosexual goings-on to amuse him, but distantly. "He would have been thrilled, I'm sure."

"The problem with that building," Missy continued, "is that it dwarfs the so-called permanent collection it's designed to house. We've got a world-class building full of second-class art."

Missy was co-chair of a committee whose purpose in life was to raise enough money to do something about just this quandary, and her segue from the subject of architecture to that of testiculating the permanent collection struck me as a pretty deft ramp-up to putting the bite on Wong for a donation.

But Wong was pretty adroit himself. "Our esteemed and lamented late friend and colleague, Hanfield Braddock III, used to say it was a shame to house such a second-rate collection in a third-rate building."

"As opposed to housing it for free, you mean," Missy replied, "in his beloved Veterans Memorial Building." As Wong didn't rise to the bait, Missy pointed out rather sententiously that "Nothing worth having comes for free, Tommy. You of all people—"

At this exact moment Blondie stuck his head in the door and said, "London on the line, sir."

Wong glanced ruefully at the telephone.

Missy gestured toward the door. "Impeccable timing, as usual. Should we—?"

Wong shook his head as he took up the receiver. After listening for a moment, he launched into thoughtful Chinese.

I took a look around. Two of the walls were entirely of glass, X'd by the thick tubular steel diagonals so common to a seismic retrofit. One entire wall consisted of art books surrounding audio/visual presentation apparatus, the fourth wall consisted entirely of architecture books surrounding the entrance door. Neither collection contained anything technical. No *Gray's Anatomy* or *Artist's Handbook* or *Guide to Color,* no copy of *Architectural Graphic Standards* or *Wood Structural Design Data,* nor any of the scores of volumes of the *Sweet's Manual.* At first I assumed that all the volumes present, and there must have been a thousand or fifteen hundred of them, were so-called coffee table books, containing pictures and a little text focusing on a particular artist's work, on a particular museum's collection, on a particular architect's buildings. Indeed, an entire shelf was given over to books devoted to the structures of Tommy Wong himself.

I had pulled down one of these and was reading the copy on the jacket flap when Missy plucked at my sleeve to distract me into perusing a volume of Giambattista Piranesi's drawings of Rome. They were striking, certainly. After a moment, however, I realized the book was an old one. Then I realized that the reproductions might not be reproductions. "Is this. . . ?"

"Yes," Missy whispered. "He's a collector."

After studying the binding of the large folio I took a closer look at the books around us. With the notable exception of those concerned with the contemporary architecture of Tommy Wong, nearly every book in the room was, for one reason or another, rare.

Wong rang off. Reverting to English he apologized, then shot a cuff to get a look at his watch. "I don't want to rush you, Missy, but–"

"I understand, Tommy. I haven't even gotten around to introducing you to Mr. Kestrel."

"Danny," I added.

Wong frowned as we shook hands. "Have we. . . ?"

"You saw his name in the paper a few days ago," Missy said. "He was the first suspect the cops grilled in the Renée Knowles case."

Wong withdrew his hand. "Poor Renée," he said evenly.

"Yes," I agreed.

"Since he's with me," Missy suggested, "I suppose it goes without saying that Danny had nothing to do with Renée's death?"

Wong looked at her.

"I've known him a long time," she added. "He frames pictures, and he's very good at it."

"Well, of course," Wong said evenly, "any number of people

might have killed her. Even though most of them," he added wryly, not without a trace of bitterness, "have much better things to do."

"Yes," said Missy. "But whoever went so far as to kill her probably had an excellent motive."

"You think?" Wong said sarcastically.

"Danny, here, on the other hand, hardly knew Renée. In fact, so little did Danny know Renée that he actually claims to have liked her."

Wong smiled. "She makes—made—a great first impression."

"Not so much great," I corrected, "as intriguing."

Wong sucked a tooth.

"Well, Tommy," Missy said abruptly, "I know you've got many things to do, and that Renée isn't one of them. But I'd appreciate it if you would take the trouble to run down your experience with her for Danny's edification."

Wong frowned.

"Please," Missy added.

Wong paced to the east window, put his hands in his trouser pockets, and looked down on Fourth Street. "It wasn't sexual, of course. Though Renée was very attractive to men. And, I might add, attracted by them."

Missy caught my eye and winked.

"I think that was one of the reasons she did her deals only with other women and gay men. Straight men could pose a threat, let's say, a threat to her. . . . Let's call it her . . . concentration."

"Were men such a bother?" I asked, rather surprised.

"No, not at all," Wong said. "On the contrary, men were a challenge to her. She'd get around an interesting man and just have to seduce him, or at least insist on getting him to admit that he was attracted to her."

"Did this include married men?"

"Well, yes, of course it did, with one exception—men married to women with whom Renée perceived herself as in competition. In that case, a husband would become a . . . trophy."

Missy smiled.

As goes reluctant dish, I thought, it's not bad. "I appreciate your delicacy," I said, in a most neutral tone, "but you make her sound rapacious."

Wong turned to me. "You found Mrs. Knowles very attractive, Mr. Kestrel?"

I probably turned a color. "Yes."

Wong turned back to the window. "Many men found her attractive, Mr. Kestrel. She was a lovely woman, on the surface."

I didn't like hearing this. I almost felt compelled to defend Renée. But why? I'd not known her at all. "This . . . trophy business . . . to which you refer, Mr. Wong. You mean she'd seduce a rival's husband just to see if it could be done?"

"No. I mean she'd seduce a rival's husband in order to trounce or one-up or at least insult her rival."

"That's not very nice."

Wong daintily cleared his throat.

"Tell Danny what Renée did for a living, Tommy."

"That's an interesting question. The obvious answer would be that she was a 'picker,' as the antiques trade refers to them."

"A 'picker'?"

Missy supplied a clarification. "That's a buyer who scouts estate and garage sales, second-hand, junk and antique shops, flea markets, and private, off-market collections solely in order to identify items that are unrecognized and therefore, usually, undervalued."

"Ah so," I nodded. "I have a friend who comes by my shop to collect odd scraps of exotic wood species. He's a classical guitarist who picks up Spanish and classical guitars at garage sales to refinish and resell at a profit—or to keep and play, if he likes them. Last year he bought a small-bodied Spanish guitar in immaculate condition, including its hard-shell case, for twenty dollars. The owner had no idea what it was, but my friend recognized the instrument as a finely crafted *requinto*. He carved a bridge for it out of a scrap of *bobinga*. It's—"

"A *requinto?*" Missy repeated abruptly.

"Yes," I said, annoyed.

"Oh," Missy said dreamily, with a genuine note of nostalgia, "I just love a man who can handle the *requinto*."

"Yeah. It turned out to be worth a couple thousand dollars."

"Well," said Missy, "he's an ace picker, then." She looked from one to the other of us, expectantly.

Wong smiled indulgently.

"I'm laughing on the inside," I said testily.

Wong said, "Mr. Kestrel, may I ask you something?"

"Sure."

"How well did you, ah, like Mrs. Knowles?"

A moment passed. I said, "I don't know."

"As you observed, she did things that weren't very 'nice.'"

"Well, her . . . adventures aside, what was there that might have been really harmful, or illegal, about her activities? What happened to you, for example? If I may turn the question around, how well did you like Renée, Mr. Wong?"

Wong pursed his lips. "I liked her a great deal, Danny, at first. She was a lot of fun. Also, in a short time she achieved a pretty grasp of certain things that interest me."

I indicated the shelves surrounding us. "Antiquarian books, for instance?"

"Yes, books. It was only much later that I realized that, perceiving my interests, she cultivated her own so as, in turn, to cultivate me. She was quite good at that. For a small example, if something came up that she didn't understand, she'd say so. She was not so stupid as to attempt faking her knowledge before an expert. Which was," he sighed, "flattering in its turn."

"Was she able to turn this into money?"

"Simply. She asked a lot of questions about books–books on art and architecture in particular. The art books of course I could understand, as she had an interest in art herself. But then she started to turn up with architectural items for me to look at, to judge. Eventually I bought a couple of them. That she made money on these deals was fine by me. If I purchased an item, it was because I was interested in, first, the subject, and, second, the coherence of my collection. Relative to these considerations price was tertiary. You understand, however, that only a very extravagant collector wants it known that price is no object. But Renée quickly understood that I am passionate about architecture, and that my collection of books and drawings and manuscripts on the subject is correspondingly important to me."

Wong turned from the window and began to pace the perimeter of his office.

"She began to turn up the odd interesting item. At first it was material that I already had; she merely wanted my opinion as to price and importance. Then she began to show me things I didn't have, but occasionally wanted. I began to acquire from her." He approached a bookcase and pulled down a slipcased volume. "This monograph on Kurt Schwitters, for example." He turned it one way and another, as if inspecting for a frayed corner. From where I sat, the book seemed to have no such defect; but Wong didn't offer it to me or to Missy. Rather, Wong held onto it, visibly consumed by pride of possession, almost to the exclusion of the subject of our conversation.

Blondie stuck his head in the door. "Sir–?"

"Just a moment," Wong said sharply, not looking up.

Blondie disappeared without a word.

"You've heard of the Mertzbau?" Wong asked. I had. I glanced at Missy, who nodded. Wong continued, "Schwitters built it before the war, of course. And because he was a Jew and "degenerate" and so forth, the Nazis destroyed it. Only photographs and some of Schwitters' drawings remain. This," and, without so much as removing the book from its slipcase, Wong replaced the volume on the shelf from which it came, "is the most comprehensive anthology of that material in existence." He turned to us with a complacent sigh. "I don't know how Renée turned it up. And, so long as it's not hot, I don't care."

"Have you looked into its provenance, Tommy?" Missy asked.

Wong sighed. "At the time it came into my possession, I asked for and was given a bill of sale. Now that we know what we know about Renée," he waved one hand vaguely, "I suppose I'll have to do something about verifying its provenance."

Wong was all but calling Renée a thief or, at the very least, a dealer in stolen goods. But I let that pass for the moment and asked, "Did you ever travel with Renée, Mr. Wong?"

"Oh, sure. We went to Europe together a couple of times, to browse antiquarian book dealers, *brocanteurs,* junk shops and so forth. On our last trip she discovered a Chinese chest– almost like a steamer trunk in size, but of tooled leather and lacquered wood, with marquetry and hand-forged hinges and fastenings. Certainly it was very old. I had no interest at all, but Renée loved it. She said she had a customer in Tiburon who would pay instantly for it, and pay well."

Wong paced back to the view behind his desk and passed a careful hand over his carefully groomed hair.

"This chest was extremely expensive and Renée didn't have sufficient funds to make the purchase. Or so she said. I imme- diately offered her a loan. She, note, did not ask me for this

114

favor. I proposed it. And you know what?" He turned to face, not me, but Missy.

"What?" Missy prompted.

"She refused outright. 'Oh, no, Tommy,' she said. 'We're friends. Borrowing and lending money isn't a good practice between friends. Okay?' 'But what about your friend in Tiburon?' I reminded her. 'It's true,' Renée answered, 'Mrs. So-and-so would be thrilled to possess this Chinese trunk.' Then she bit her lip. She looked very cute, biting her lip."

I knew that quirk.

"Well, I didn't care about this woman in Tiburon. And Renée wouldn't tell me who she was, either. Which I thought was odd. But, just as I had become willing to drop the subject, she suggested we do a little deal. I told her I was listening. 'Let's go fifty-fifty on this thing,' she said; 'I can afford that much. In exchange for your participation, I'll manage the project—negotiations, shipping, customs, delivery, final price— everything. When it's all over, I'll split the profit with you. That way, we can still be friends and have this little business deal on the side. Maybe we'll make a little money to take each other out to lunch with.'"

Now Wong had his hands back in his pockets and was pacing a circle behind his desk. "I readily agreed. We were in Rouen at the time."

"Rouen," I repeated.

"France," Missy said.

"I know that," I snapped.

"Hush," she said.

"Renée closed with the dealer on the spot. Fifty thousand francs, w hich at the time was almost exactly $10,000. She gave him a five thousand franc cash deposit and got a receipt. But her credit card didn't have the headroom to cover her half of the trunk deal while still affording creature comforts for the rest of her European trip—or so she said—so I offered

115

to put the whole deal on one of my credit cards. She accepted, but pointed out that cash would fetch us a better price. I agreed, and she cut the deal. Next day we went to a bank and I used my card to get cash. Thus I was in for fifty thousand francs, the whole price of the trunk. Renée offered a stack of traveler's checks against her part of the investment, but I couldn't be bothered. She actually dragged me to a bar, ordered *pastis,* produced two or three folders of hundred-dollar traveler's checks, and made ready to get writer's cramp with fifty endorsements. Ridiculous. I turned her down. I snatched the pen from her hand! What was I going to do with all those traveler's checks? I just laughed and told her to pay me when she got the money.

"But it wasn't that easy. Renée got all upset and we started to argue and ordered two more drinks, and then I began to realize that she was serious about giving me her share of the deal right then and there.

"So I came up with a brilliant compromise. I had her write me a personal check for five thousand dollars, which she did. The cafe owner gave us an envelope. I put my San Francisco address on the front, and she put her return address on the flap, crossing out the name of the cafe. I put the check in envelope, sealed it, and handed it back to her, jokingly suggesting she mail it with her postcards. Better yet, she should keep it until it came time to write me the one that went with it, covering my share of the profit. And that was the next-to-last time I saw that check.

"The next day Renée got up early, to see to the proper crating of the Chinese chest. She hired a trucking company to take it to Marseilles, where, she told me later, it was to sit in a warehouse until a container bound for Oakland had room for it, which might take weeks or even months. But this was cost-effective shipping. I said fine, fine, hardly even listening. There's a cathedral at Rouen, you know, of considerable majesty, not to mention Joan of Arc was burned at the stake there, and shipping a trunk to California or anywhere else doesn't require two people to manage. More interestingly, Rouen is a port—it's sixty or seventy kilometers up the Seine from Le Havre, for gosh sakes. Why go clear across the country to send the damn thing from Marseilles? But I didn't even think about that. For two or three days we went our separate ways in the morning and convened in the hotel bar late in the afternoon.

"By and by, we arrived home. Months passed. I had received a major commission in Tokyo. The Pachinko Maze. You may have heard of it."

Missy had enough wit about herself to clear her throat and say yes, she certainly had, and from the photographs it looked fabulous.

"One hundred million, that project. We're just finishing it. I didn't see Renée for nearly a year. Only once, in the course of a brief phone conversation, had I remembered to ask her about the Chinese trunk. She said something like, 'Oh, yes! I've been meaning to—oh! There's another call. I'm sure I know who it is. Let me call you back,' and she rang off, just like that. She never called and I forgot about it.

"Finally, fourteen months later, I got her on the phone and asked her point blank what the heck was going on with the trunk deal. And still—might I point out?—I had not a clue. *I* was teasing *her.*

"Renée was beautiful. Gravely she asked for an appointment, someplace quiet, so we could talk. I named various places; she declined them all. I finally said, okay then: where? For some reason she named the bar in the Palace Hotel."

Wong pointed at his east window. "There's Botta's building. Behind it's the Phleuger Building. A block north, up New Montgomery, is the Palace Hotel."

117

"I haven't been there in fifteen years," Missy noted. "Not since they finished restoring the Parrish painting behind the bar."

"The Pied Piper of Hamlin," I said.

"Exactly," said Wong, turning toward me. "That's the last time I'd been in there, too: to have a look at the job they'd done restoring the Parrish painting."

"It's worth a look," Missy said.

"I think Renée's point was anonymity," Wong said. "It's a hotel bar, and the Parrish painting is very popular with tourists."

"Obviously," Missy said.

"Obviously," Wong repeated, almost to himself, shaking his head. "Anyway, I fell for it."

"Fell for what?"

"Renée was waiting when I got there. She knew I like a Man-hattan made with Old Overholt and Peychaud bitters, ice cold. Before I was properly seated, two appeared on the table, and between them lay the envelope. It still bore the address of the house I'd sold and moved out of eight months before. In the envelope was the check for $5,000."

"No profit," I guessed.

Wong wearily agreed. "So I supposed. But there was more to it than that. Or less, you might say. Renée thanked me, rather hesitantly, then abruptly toasted to a better deal the next time. I let it go. We exchanged some idle chitchat about the Parrish. Then I came right out and asked what had happened.

"She didn't want to talk about it. I coaxed her. She wouldn't say. Finally I demanded to know what had happened. I didn't care about the money. Did the deal come out bust? Had the Tiburon woman beaten her down on the price? Worse—and here I thought I'd stumbled on the truth—had the Tiburon woman not wanted the trunk at all, leaving Renée stuck with

118

the goods? Was Renée attempting to make good on her half of the bargain, in other words, while taking a bath for the purchase price of this goddamn Chinese trunk?

"All she had to do was let me do the talking. Then, toward the end of the first drink, she let me have the so-called real story, which was that the trunk had never arrived in the United States at all!

"This news called for a second round of drinks. I had a thousand questions. And Renée had some pretty good answers. Bottom line? The trunk had disappeared in shipment. Stolen, undoubtedly. She had receipts from the dealer in Rouen, from the trucking company that took the trunk to Marseilles, and from the warehouse where it had been stored to await shipment. She had the name of the vessel it shipped on, the pier it had left from, she had dates and times, she had a copy of the bill of lading for the container, which otherwise had contained some G.I.'s household goods; there was even a Volkswagen in there. In fact, the container had showed up in Long Beach—which had been a mistake— and been unloaded there. It took a while for her to find this out—the original port of entry was supposed to have been Oakland. She rented a truck and drove down to Long Beach herself. Nine hundred miles, round trip. What the hell. She had all this paperwork. But when she got there—no Chinese trunk. It subsequently developed that the trunk never got into the container in the first place. Which pretty well explained why it never got *out* of the container once it arrived in Long Beach."

Wong sat down at his desk and sighed heavily. A silence ensued, during which Blondie stuck his head in the door again.

"Sir—?"

"In a minute!" Wong snapped, throwing the guy a sharp glance. Blondie evaporated.

"Now, I didn't give a damn about this trunk. So it was gone.

119

So what? And the five thousand?" He shrugged philosophically. "It's not the end of the world. I made some noises
about what a pity and so forth. I ordered two *more* drinks.
Renée was obviously upset about the whole thing. She said
she had spent at least two thousand dollars trying to figure
out what had happened: phone calls to Europe, the rental
truck, a week in a hotel in Long Beach, for godsakes. It was
only after about three months of spinning her wheels that
she realized what must have happened. 'What do you mean,'
I asked, not following her at first, 'what *must* have happened?'"

Wong looked down at the floor. When he looked up, he
repeated his conversation with Renée as clearly as if it had
occurred just yesterday.

"'No insurance,' Renée said simply. 'A mistake they were
waiting for.'

"'Mistake?' I asked. *'They?'*

"She made her voice very small, but even then, or so I
thought, it was suffused with anger. 'I should have insured
the trunk against theft and loss, but I forgot to do it.'

"Right away I knew what this meant. If there was no insurance and the trunk was indeed gone—lost or stolen, it made
no difference—its value was not recoverable. Simple. Open
and shut.

"This was a surprise, however, for I knew Renée as a very
dependable, level-headed businesswoman. She was buying
and selling and delivering and decorating and importing all
kinds of stuff for all kinds of prominent people. 'You forgot,'
I repeated. 'You forgot to insure the trunk?'

"'Yes,' she said, and looked me directly in the eye. 'I forgot to buy a lousy two-hundred franc insurance policy.'

"'And the shipper knew that?'

"'Absolutely,' she said. 'I can't prove it, but I have no doubt
they knew it and acted on it. I don't think the dealer was in

on it. I got Missy James, who speaks excellent French, to talk to him.'"

Here Wong glanced at Missy, as did I. "Oh, yes," Missy nodded ruefully, "I got right into it."

"'Although the dealer evinced a convincing dismay on our behalf,'" Wong continued Renée's tale, "'he also was very clear about whose fault it was. Without an insurance policy, representing a potential fiscal loss to an insurer, nobody would properly investigate the disappearance. What's the incentive? Who else but an insurance company would have the resources to look into it? But without a claim to defend themselves against, why would they bother? Case closed. Hell, the case was never opened! Poof! It's clean as a whistle. Believe me,' she said, 'I've tried everything.'

"Poor Renée was despondent. I asked her how long she'd known about the situation. 'Five months', came the reply. After coming to the conclusion that someone had gotten clean away with stealing our Chinese chest, she'd set about reconstituting my half of the $10,000 purchase price.

"And there it was, on the table between us. Her original check for $5,000. Her bank account was now good for it."

Wong swiveled his chair and stretched his legs toward the view, his back to us, hands clasped behind his head. "Renée was my friend," he said. "I had plenty of money in the bank. I ordered a fourth round of drinks."

"Oh my," Missy said mildly.

Wong sighed a consensual sigh and slowly spun the chair until he faced us. "With the greatest of pleasure, I tore Renée's check into teensy little pieces." He briefly held one hand aloft, its thumb and forefinger just millimeters apart. "And then. . . ." Wong dropped his hand, "I burned the pieces in the ashtray like they were lucky money and it was New Year's Day." After a pause he sadly added, *"Gung hay fat choy,"* and fell silent.

121

Perhaps a minute later Missy prompted him. "Well?"

Wong shook his head. "I asked her whether she might have a little something else going on, another deal, some means by which we might recoup our losses. Notice the possessive plural–*our* losses." He propped his elbows on his desk and sank his forehead into his hands.

"Like an idiot, I raised my glass. And like an idiot I said, 'Here's to next time.'"

FRAME BOY

ELEVEN

O nce in a while, I get the chance to carve a frame. In this endeavor I find a chief satisfaction of my vocation, and with it come many of the venerable atavisms of the trade. Wood selection, for example, and mortise-and-tenon joinery. Odd tools like scorps and spoons and dental picks and rifflers appear on the bench. The aroma of an exotic hardwood replaces the toxic reek of chopsawed polyvinyl chloride. The phone goes unanswered. The day passes quietly, its rhythm punctuated with noises made by hand rather than machine. Routing is the audio exception, to bevel or ogee or rabbet an edge. The rap of the mallet, the whisper of the whetstone – these retard the mad entropy of a chronophagous world.

I heard once of a Japanese carpenter's apprentice achieving the pinnacle of his novitiate when he produced a woodshaving of such continuity and amplitude as to enable him to wrap a sandwich in it. The painter John Plenty, himself a formidable taper of sheetrock, and a Philistine as well, declared in amazement, "Time to go on a fucking diet."

Still, there's great satisfaction in coaxing a planing blade to such sharpness that it skims a nearly molecular layer off the surface of a board, its shaving interrupted only when the blade is lifted from the work. There's skill involved, and it's a privilege to get paid to have this much fun with your hands.

And utterly anachronistic, of course. They say that sixty

percent of the American work force deals only with information, in its daily breadearning. Even so, few among the other
forty per cent carve wood for a living.

So I'd laminated a stripe of a reddish-auburn species called
bloodwood, *Brosimim paraense,* between two blond thicknesses
of bird's-eye maple; thickness-planed it; routed a couple of
flutes along its outer edge; and rabbeted the backside to accept
canvas, the stretcher bar, and the edge of the glass.

Then I mitered, mortised, tenoned, glued up, and squared
the four corner joints. In the end I had a rigid rectangle,
ready to carve. After the carving would come filing and
sanding and a couple of treatments of tung oil, each buffed
with wet garnet paper. Then it dries a day or so. Then come
five or six spray-coats of clear lacquer, with a half-hour of
drying time between each coat. *Then* the picture gets mounted.

Nothing complex in this particular carving, a grape-cluster
motif, viny tendrils, a few leaves. But it's a big frame, four by
five feet, so there are a few days' worth of carving to be done.

I was just brightening the edge of a 10-millimeter bent spoon
when I remembered the name.

Manny, she'd said.

Aside from the fact that Renée was a beauty who would
have no trouble getting whomever she fancied to hop in the
passenger seat with her, she'd obviously had a lot on her
mind. As I saw it, she was more or less desperate to forget
her troubles for a while, and if a few hours of drunken sex
could manage this, so much the better.

Some unspoken glitch in the program had brought her to
tears. I held her for a while. She calmed down sufficiently to
restart her plan, and Bowditch was certain he knew what
happened after that. But in fact, when she was sobbing quietly,
I'd offered to listen if she wanted to talk.

She'd pulled back sufficiently to look at me, in the shadows
of the cab. "You're sweet." She traced my mouth with a finger-

tip. "But it's a mess. A lot of players, a lot of . . . stuff. Manny told me there'd be days–" She stopped.

"Stuff and players," I murmured. "You mean you're moving a lot of dope around the country? Or is it a movie deal?"

Her laugh began as a dismissive one; but eventually it convinced me that something was truly funny.

"Dope and movies," she repeated at last. "No." She pushed the forefinger through my hair. "Dope and movies aren't my problem. But I wish they were."

She kissed me gently. I kissed her back. "Can I be your problem?" I must have said.

The fragment drifted away. In the context of the evening, it had been just that–a fragment. Minor and unimportant.

Or had it?

I put the spoon on the bench and called Bowditch.

A female computer put me on hold, with the complimentary audio of a traffic report broadcast from a helicopter somewhere over Tracy. A big-rig had jackknifed on an overpass at the 580/5 split and flipped over a guardrail, falling across seven of the eight lanes below, crushing that many cars, backing up the early rush-hour traffic for two-and-a-half miles in four directions. . . .

The female computer came back to say that "Officer," followed by Bowditch's recorded growl: "Charles Bowditch"– followed by the computer cheerfully appending, "is not available. Please leave a message at the tone, or press zero for an operator, or press one for further options." I left a message and hung up.

After a little thought I dialed a second number.

"Missy, is this really you? You're not a machine or a clone?"

"Can't you tell the difference?"

"No. I must test you. How are the 49ers doing?"

"Two and one."

"That's two wins or two losses?"

125

"Don't be an ass."

"This must be you. No machine could bring itself to express a coherent sentiment about something so meaningless."

"Oh," she replied, "you're really very alone, you know, tapping away with your little chisels." Missy's father had held six season tickets since the football team was franchised, since something like 1949. Missy had inherited them and rarely missed a game. While the team was winning in the eighties, more than one suitor had tried to marry her for those season tickets.

"Manny," I said.

"What?"

"A guy named Manny. He had some kind of influence over Renée."

"Hmmmmm. . . ."

"Yes?"

"Did Bowditch ask you about a Manny?"

"No. Just now I remembered his name."

"I might know who he is. But I'm not sure. There is more than one Manny in this world."

"What world?"

"My world. Surely you didn't call to talk about your world? Some tawdry place where people work?"

"That's true. I use a saw-sharpener named Manny."

"It's probably not him."

"So name another one."

"Not until I know a little more about him."

"Missy, are you being discreet?"

"Welllll. . . . Let's say that it would be unfortunate if Bowditch were to be nosing around certain law offices, just for one example–"

"A lawyer named Manny?"

"He inhabits a very tall building downtown. If word got around that a socially prominent, over-the-hill babe were

126

pointing her liver-spotted fingers indiscriminately in his direction, it might have decidedly unpleasant long-term effects on her alimony payments. I wish it were him though, the prick."

"Since when do you worry about alimony?"

"Cash flow is where you find it. Besides, I worry about plenty of things, thank you. Certain inattentive men dictate that I sometimes don't have much else to do."

"Oh, Missy. Are we feeling neglected?"

"We were," she said sweetly, "until you called."

"I'm so glad to have cheered you up."

"At least you didn't ask me about a woman."

"What would you know about women?"

"Show me a woman's man, and I'll tell you all about her."

"Let's try it the other way around. What sort of Manny would Renée hang out with? Did she need a divorce lawyer?"

Missy sighed. "Renée never knew the pleasures of divorce."

"Does this Manny shoot people?"

"He's a very good lawyer. He doesn't need to shoot people."

"This is beginning to sound like your complication instead of Renée's."

Missy thought about it. Behind me, the big frame waited.

"Manny Djector," she said finally, "is a big art and antiques dealer."

"This sounds much more promising."

"There are all kinds of stories about him. He produced a TV movie at one point. He's owned race horses; he's lived here and in LA, New York, Europe; he speaks three or four languages; he's been married at least as many times as I have—he's old school like that."

"Like how?"

"If he's sleeping with them, he likes to be married to them, which automatically introduces the possibility of adultery."

"What about control?"

"What about slavery? All of the wives are rich. But none of the horses or movies ever quite pans out."

"So his real gig is marrying rich women?"

"Oh, he moves quite a lot of European antiques, pre-Colombian artifacts, Oriental screens and scroll paintings and whatnot. If it sells, he's interested. Gems, for example. He particularly likes gems."

"Why?"

"They're valuable, portable, easy to hide, hard to find or trace or tax, and they zip right through customs, rarely scrutinized."

"Why's he bother with the other stuff?"

"Well, horses and rich women are fun, for one thing. Equally important, they keep him connected to other people with money, among whom he cuts a certain figure. He's broken most of the bones in his body playing polo, and to walk he needs a cane of which he has an impressive collection. He has been known to get drunk and threaten one or another of his wives with one or another of his canes."

"Is this what you mean by 'cuts a certain figure'?"

"Daniel," Missy said patiently, "people are impressed by all kinds of things."

"Is he a hustler? Yes or no."

"He's a hustler. He's made it go a long way."

"He doesn't sound like Renée's type."

"Not as a husband, that's true."

"There's the antiquities angle."

"Which is obvious. But Manny has plenty of his own action there."

"Maybe Renée had a line on something he was interested in?"

"On somebody, more likely."

"A woman?"

"Woman, man. . . . It wouldn't make any difference to either Manny Djector or Renée Knowles."

"Could it be that he was after Renée just for . . . you know. . . ."

"Sport? No. Manny's pretty butch, but that's exactly what he is. Sex with a . . . a. . . ."

"A fox."

"Did you think so?" Missy's laugh was perceptibly brittle. "She was really very common, Danny."

After a moment I said, "What I think isn't important. What would Manny think?"

"Sex with a fox, as you would have it, wouldn't interest him. He's a predator who sleeps with the women he's preying on. It's a tool. He uses it to control them. Furthermore, since on the whole he hates having sex with most women, he can blame them for forcing him into distasteful acts. When it comes time to put the screws to them, he can work himself up to doing it with that much more proficiency and relish."

"Whoa, Missy. What do you mean by 'distasteful'?"

"Manny keeps an open account with a dungeon in Oakland."

"How the hell do you possess that bit of dirt?"

"Darling, do you think I sit around all day reading Proust?"

"Leather and chains and nipple clamps and stuff?"

"All of that, along with begging to have his tongue pinned to a filthy floor by a stiletto heel."

"You're making this up," I said hopefully.

"Sorry, but no. But since you mention it, I do have an imagination."

"Dare I ask what 'imagination' means, in this context?"

"So far as I'm concerned, it means if you can imagine something, you don't actually have to go through with it."

"Let's skip ahead," I suggested brusquely. "This Djector sounds like a creep."

"Piffle," said Missy. "He's run-of-the-mill. Really."

"Missy, are you sure you're not making this stuff up?"

"What for? To titillate you?"

I pinched my eyes closed. "I languish, unmoved."

"Oh, darling. Nothing's secret in this town. Manny Djector, for just one bad example, is far too visible to keep his dirty little secrets secret for long. He's had too many wives; he's defrauded too many people; he's been in the papers, in court cases, in law suits; he goes to all the parties. . . . Everybody knows about Manny Djector."

"And people continue to deal with him?"

"If you're a collector who spends money, sooner or later Manny Djector will come up with something you want. At that point, all bets are off. If he can do his job, who cares about his personal life? Say your daddy left you a little collection of banks or some oil and gas wells, for example, so you've never had to work a day in your life. Day in and night out, your entire challenge consists of how not to drink yourself to death. When everything life has to offer is at your fingertips, one of the things it offers every day is cocktails at noon."

"Let's stick to the guy in question."

"Oh, him. Well, people like Manny tend to develop interests. Race horses, for example. He knows a lot about them. He had fifty or sixty horses, once, when he was married to Ellena Thatcher. If she hadn't gotten bored with the whole thing and left him, he probably wouldn't be the flamboyant little *thief* he is tod– Oh, my. Missy's speaking out of school. You didn't hear it from me."

"A little bird mentioned something about a thief."

"The little bird meant to say *crook*. He doesn't steal, really, not *per se.*"

"What's he do, then?"

"He cheats."

"Oh."

"It's a fine distinction when you're facing the law. But generally Manny Djector can turn up one-of-a-kind stuff for fabulous prices and knows just who to shop them to when the time comes. No theft necessary. He's an excellent picker."

"Isn't that what Renée was doing?"

"Exactly. Face it, Danny, Djector was her mentor. And back to the point, cheap or sleazy or disgusting as people might find him or her, if either of them has the goods, people will do business with them. Moreover, as you may have noticed, certain people get a thrill out of a brush with sleaze. Like actors who hang out with mobsters."

"At some point, of course, they go home and pull up the drawbridge."

"Sooner than later."

"You got any more Mannys on your dance card?"

"Two's plenty."

"We're forgetting the lawyer?"

"No amount of Prozac could make me forget that fellow; but Renée didn't know him at all."

"Djector does sound very promising."

"That's an unfortunate way to put it."

"So now what?"

"Well, let's see." She rustled papers. "I think that there's an opening tonight."

I glanced at the calendar over the desk. Empty. Just the way I liked it. "Is it a client of mine?"

"A lot of people will be there. It's for whathisname. The guy who does refrigerators."

"Refrigerators?"

"Yes. Da-Gums, Gumz. . . . Here it is. Henry Dodd-Gumpson."

"Henry Dodd-Gumpson? You're not serious."

"No, of course not. Serious has something to do with gravity. Show me the girl who wants to think about gravity."

"He does refrigerators!"

"Danny," she said patiently, "everybody needs a refrigerator."

"That guy couldn't paint numbers on boxcars with a stencil."

"He's having his vogue. There will be lots of people."

"I wouldn't darken the door of that show if –"

"If Djector were to be there?"

"How do you know that?"

"Darling," Missy chuckled, making no effort to hide the tinkle of ice, "Manny Djector is Henry Dodd-Gumpson's European agent. If he's in town, he's bound to be at his client's opening."

"Is he in town?"

"Wellll. . . . Let's put it this way. He had an appointment with the Oakland dominatrix just two nights ago. What do you think?"

A small unopened parcel on my desk contained a new nozzle for the trim sprayer. I fiddled with it for a moment, then set it aside. "Missy, are you sure you've never read Proust?"

"Darling," she replied, amused. "Why should I read Proust when I'm living him?"

TWELVE

The gallery was thronged. Sloan-Pickering were classy enough to have valet parking, though I remembered a time when the two women who ran the place didn't have enough money to tape the sheetrock. Back when John Plenty was doing giant abstractions and getting nowhere, they'd traded him the drywall job for his first one-man show.

Times had changed. Guys with red logos on white jackets with hand-held radios shuttled cars from the curb out front to a parking lot on the Embarcadero, ten blocks away, jogging back and forth and looking pretty fleet about it. Twenty-dollar tips were normal, and a kid got to drive these giant jeeps he could barely see out of, vehicles that had evolved into something more than the two-seat buggies of WW II, and something less than the armored personnel carriers they pretended to be, belligerent gas hogs, nonetheless, that wreak double or even treble the emissions havoc of ordinary transportation, despite California's strict pollution laws. Each is a yuppie tank, expensive to maintain and operate; each is an enameled Let-Them-Eat-Cake with gold fittings. But in a pinch its owner might put the beast in four-wheel drive and surmount any barrier the peasants might erect between murderous anarchy and the gated community. The first step to victory is blow up the gas stations.

A valet took the Jaguar but Missy kept the phone, slipping it into my jacket pocket. "The help tend to make calls," she explained as we joined the crush at the door.

"If you're worried about how much it costs, you can't afford it."

"Danny, you little clichémonger. The problem is, these kids phone these sex-chat numbers. You wind up with weird billings and all kinds of lascivious solicitations that take months to sort out. It's really inconvenient."

"You sort them by hand?"

I glanced sideways at her. Her mouth had assumed a cute little pout, drawing toward its corner a mild erosion of tiny lines, and her surgically tautened cheek assumed a bit of color.

"Don't," she said, pushing me ahead of her. "That's my bad side."

A woman in a faux-cheetah jacket said, "Missy, Darling," passed between us and disappeared without waiting for an answer.

Quite a number of people were milling about the gallery. The four bartenders couldn't have poured drinks faster if they'd been dispensing water in Rwanda. The air was filled with the commingled reeks of white wine and turpentine. Once a spacious second-floor warehouse, with wooden trusses two stories above our heads, cinderblock walls holding them up, and a grid of nine-foot partitions below them and all of it painted white, the gallery's design only encouraged an already considerable din.

For this exhibition the management had acted on the bright idea of chainsawing holes through the various partitions sufficiently large to display Dodd-Gumpson's refrigerators, most of which appeared to have been excavated from the Colma dump to make room for new graves. Mangled, rusted, crushed, they'd been garishly painted in teams of primary colors interloped by antinomian slashes, combinations straight from the color wheel.

"Refrigerators," a woman was saying incredulously, as we gained the head of the stairs.

"That's it," her companion laughed. He waved his plastic wineglass toward a large banner hanging over the stairhead.

Henry Dodd-Gumpson

::

The Rage of Convenience

"Truth in advertising," he observed.
"At least they don't call it art," said his friend.
"Art's *implied.*"
"How's the wine?"
"Delicious."
"Do we really have to linger?"
"Catherine's buying one."
"*What?*"
"I wasn't supposed to tell. But I think she intends to give it to you."
"She wouldn't dare embarrass me like that."
"I realized you would need time to compose yourself. . . ."
As Missy scanned the crowd and said hello to every third person, I skimmed a twenty-four point *raison d'être* posted next to the bar.

> . . .Ruined appliances as synecdoches of throw-away technology / Artifacts of middle-class comfort in a comfortless age / Whiff of freon tinged with nostalgia and spoiled food / Mother bought block ice in the August wreck of Queens / A yard of dripping canvas, odd bits of manure and straw / Travail and Material of Art / Utter permeability of the gelatinous membrane between structural Pragmatism and eviscerated Form / Rotted elk in junked prototype catalyzed a new aesthetic—

"Sir?"

A young woman in a tuxedo eyed me expectantly from behind the bar.

"These New Yorkers think they can come out west and just make monkeys out of us," I said.

She looked beyond me. "Next, please."

"Two wines," I said hastily. "One white, one red."

"We have Chardonnay, Chablis, cabernet, merlot, pinot, zinfandel. . . ."

I shook my head. "One white, one red."

She poured double-handed. "Next, please."

I shunted the plastic glasses through the mob to Missy, who said: "He's here."

"Djector?"

"Over there, talking to the blonde."

Djector had a shaved head, a gold and black striped vest buttoned under a Chesterfield, a maroon scarf, highly polished black shoes, and an ebony cane. He seemed to be an animated talker.

"Let's go."

Moving from group to group, most of them with their backs to the art, Missy began the peculiar halting waltz of the gallery-goer. There were squeals of recognition, air kisses, handshakes, and nervous laughter. The noise was terrific. And then, between us and our quarry, a mob intervened that included the gallery co-owner, Olivia Sloane, the artist Dodd-Gumpson, and a half-dozen others. Ms. Sloane carried her clipboard of price listings and a roll of adhesive red dots.

The little party had paused to consider a battered refrigerator veneered with various sizes of plastic french curves, layer upon layer of them, the whole then slathered in chrome yellow and randomly slashed by strokes of flat black.

"This one's called *Diana on Ice*," Ms. Sloane was saying.

"Um," said a woman standing next to her.

136

"Don't you just love it? If Henry hadn't sold me one already, I'd take it home myself."

"There's another one like it?" the second woman said, sensing her escape.

"Oh, no, not at all," Ms. Sloane said indulgently. She cradled her office supplies against her breast and gazed upon the work with evident satisfaction. "All of Henry's designs are unique. It's just that he's tried many, many ideas, and if you pay attention, you can see the chronology of a given motif as his work evolves from thought to thought."

"Oh," said the woman, disappointed. She seemed a little too drunk to get out of this purchase without being rude, but not so inebriated as to be unprepared to do so.

The artist stood near by, somewhat aloof, with one hand in the back pocket of the designer jeans of a tall brunette standing next to him. Both of them manifested the post-coital smile of the momentarily sated cocaine user.

"Is . . . is it signed?" the potential customer asked.

Ms. Sloane smiled hugely. In the pinball of art-deal call and response, the answer to this question was foreordained. "Mr. Dodd-Gumpson prefers to become acquainted with the owner before he signs his work. Knowing exactly to whom the work is going, and, preferably, having consulted on its siting, he can personalize the inscription."

Dodd-Gumpson, lips drawn back over clenched teeth, nodded insanely.

"Oh," said the prospective buyer. "Perhaps we can arrange a reception. But what if the ultimate owner isn't the buyer? I mean, what if it's a gift, or, or–yes–a donation? Yes. . . ."

Missy steered us around this little scene, but our quarry had vanished into the crowd.

"Damn," she said. "Come on."

She plunged into the throng, spilling a drink or two and politely but firmly pushing people out of our way.

137

"There he is." She stopped so abruptly that I plowed into her.

"Oh, darling," she said, squirming against me. "You're so impetuous."

"Me? Impetuous?"

She took my hand and stepped forward. "Manny, here's someone you've absolutely got to meet."

Djector turned his gaze and smiled hugely. Although Missy wasn't the twenty-something blonde he had cornered between himself and a bullet-riddled Kelvinator, she was still very attractive.

"And where do I know you from, young lady?" He smiled benignly. "The nut house?"

"Oh stop it, Manny. This is Danny Kestrel, framer to the stars."

She didn't quite have to put my hand into his, but she would have. Djector showed no compunction in allowing boredom to wrinkle his false smile as we shook hands. I could be of no use to him, so why expend the neurons?

Missy eyed the blonde. "I'm Marissa James."

"Tawna," the girl said, taking Missy's proffered hand with just a hint of relief. "Tawna Spelling."

"Is your grandfather in TV?" Missy asked.

The young woman blushed. "Oh, no. That's another branch of the family. My dad's a goat farmer."

She looked at me and laughed.

I laughed with her.

Missy and Djector didn't laugh.

"Actually," Djector said, "Miss Spelling studies art next door."

"The Academy of Art?" I concluded.

"She's quite accomplished," Djector added.

Tawna's smiled vanished. "You haven't even seen my work."

"Oh, but I can tell," Djector continued, unembarrassed. "You're very serious, and your art will not be inferior. If it were, you'd be doing something else entirely, something better suited to your sense of higher purpose."

Tawna hesitated.

"It's always a question of whether to run or hold your nose," I observed mildly, "when facing a tsunami of bullshit."

Tawna tried not to, but she smiled again.

Djector allowed a look to escape his features that said a great deal more about himself than he'd just revealed to us about Tawna, before he mastered his impulse and said, "A little, as you say, *bullshit,* Mr. . . . ."

"Kestrel," I supplied, but I wasn't looking at him. Tawna was blushing again.

"Kestrel," Djector repeated. "Framer to the stars. Just a little framing goes a very long way, I find."

I took a little time off from enjoying the smile of Ms. Spelling to take a look at Djector. His aging features carried less menace than his tone, but he was no cream puff, either.

"Manny is a man of great intuition," Missy put in.

"You can't judge a person's work the same way you judge a person," said Tawna.

"Ah," I piped up, "perhaps you've read Proust's *Contre Sainte-Beuve?*"

Missy slowly rolled her eyes my way before she rolled them back toward Tawna, who listened, frowning, as Missy said, very politely so as, I presumed, not to laugh, "That's very true, Tawna. Have you seen the refrigerator over in the corner that Dodd-Gumpson set off the grenade in?"

"Of course I have," Tawna said. "Why?"

"Simply because you'd never know by looking at Dodd-Gumpson that he was that stupid," Missy said, dulcetly earnest. "Would you?" she asked Djector. When Djector smiled thinly, Missy looked to me.

"Oh," I said, nodding toward the group that included the cocainized artist. "He looks the part to me, all right."

Tawna Spelling took umbrage at this and wrinkled her brow accordingly. She was so cute she might have leeched the malice out of a normal conversation. "I study the figure with Hank," she said forthrightly. "He's a very talented, knowledgeable man. And a great teacher, too."

"You didn't say anything about smart," Missy observed.

"He's very smart," Tawna snapped. "This is one of the best galleries in town. Look at all these people. Look at the tremendous amount of work he gets done. Look at his prices. And all the awards he's won. There are a lot of artists here tonight, too. They respect him, and they respect his work."

"How did we get onto this subject?" I asked.

Tawna shrugged. "I don't know. We're only standing in the middle of a one-man show by Henry Dodd-Gumpson."

"Yes, but how much can we find to say about despoiled refrigerators?" Missy wondered.

"Well," said Djector, speaking mostly to Tawna, "I sold two in Europe just a couple of months ago, from his last collection. We did quite well, as a matter of fact. The shipping alone—"

"Don't forget to insure it," I suggested.

Djector, who had been about to expand on his subject, favored me with a look designed to indicate that he retained no memory of our having been introduced. Unfortunately or not, it also indicated that he had no idea what I was talking about.

"You see?" said Tawna.

Missy, who had been frowning at me, now favored Tawna with a slightly cross "No."

"Miss Spelling perceives that Europeans love their Dodd-Gumpsons," Djector continued urbanely. "As a matter of fact,

I wasn't even the principal agent on either sale. Still, I made out very well. Very well indeed."

"You had a sub-agent or something?" Missy asked.

"That's a very good way of describing her," Djector smirked, not a little condescension creeping into his voice.

"Would that description include brunette hair, about five foot five, a little black dress?" I asked.

Djector stopped smiling.

"Did you get paid?"

"I got paid," he said quietly.

Tawna was looking from one to the other of us uncertainly.

"Danny was a friend of hers," Missy said.

Djector looked at me; then he looked at Missy. "And you, Ms. James? Were you a friend of Renée's?"

Missy said nothing.

"Because if you knew Renée at all, Ms. James, you knew that she didn't have any friends."

"Is this the Renée that's been in the papers lately?" Tawna asked, looking from one face to another. "The murdered woman?"

"Yes, darling," answered Missy, "the murdered woman. The very one."

Instead of keeping my mouth shut, I said to Djector, "That's a pretty cold thing to say about somebody who's been dead less than two weeks."

"Excuse me," Djector replied, with an air of strained patience, "but exactly what would you know about it?"

Damn little, I had to admit.

"Everybody loves somebody," said Tawna hopefully.

"I didn't attend the funeral," said Djector matter-of-factly. "Did no one spit on her grave?"

Tawna made a little gasp. Missy made a little laugh.

"Nobody," I said. "A couple of women were pretty upset."

"A couple of them were the opposite of upset, I'll wager."

"That's true," I admitted. "It was a strange event."

"That's more like it," said Djector. "More like the Renée I remember." He chuckled dryly. "I'm sorry I missed it."

"Why did you miss it?"

"You were in town," Missy pointed out helpfully. "I saw you at that auction on Townsend Street."

Djector bowed slightly in her direction. "You should have said hello." He turned to me and said, "Frankly, Mister–"

"Kestrel."

"Yes. Interesting name. A small falcon, is it not?"

I shrugged. "My grandfather adopted it on Ellis Island in favor of the unAmericanizable Hungarian surname he was born with. He was a bird-watcher."

"I didn't know that," Missy said. "One learns the most amazing things in one's pursuit of art." She looked at Tawna. "Don't you think?"

But by now Tawna had assumed her adults-are-so-weird face.

"You were about to speak of your feelings for Renée," I reminded Djector.

He looked toward Tawna, not really seeing her. "I thought for the longest time she had it coming," he said, with careful but frank certainty. "Judging by the way she behaved, by the way she treated other people, by the people she was associating with, I thought it was just a matter of time." He looked at me. "If you'd known Renée, you'd know what I'm talking about. Don't get me wrong. We live in a world where one gets away with what one can get away with. But. . . ." he clenched his fist and added quietly, "Renée *burned* people."

Tawna made a little frown.

"Did she ever burn you?" I asked.

Djector smiled faintly. "Oh, Renée had to try. Kill the father/ teacher and all that. That's the way she was. That's the way everybody is. She tried, but she didn't succeed."

"What did she try?"

He opened the fist slowly and shook his head. "She didn't get away with it. If she'd sent me a flowchart ahead of time the ploy couldn't have been more obvious. I merely waited. When she stumbled, as I'd foreseen, I was there to catch her. After that—for a while anyway—" he slowly closed the hand until it was a fist again, "she was mine."

Despite herself Tawna had been listening closely; now she started visibly, with a little gasp. Nobody spoke. We all looked at Djector. The noise of gallery-goers seemed to have faded, as if they had retreated to a respectful distance.

"Mine," Djector whispered.

"Ah. . . ." Tawna said after a moment, "I have to go find a . . . a friend?" She shook Missy's hand. "Nice to have met you," she said quickly. And just as quickly she walked away.

Djector watched her go.

Another moment and I persisted. "What was it Renée accomplished while she was 'yours,' Manny?"

Djector neither moved nor spoke. Soon he blinked abruptly, as if we'd just that moment appeared in front of him.

"Nothing," he said, so quietly I almost didn't hear him. "In the end, Renée Knowles didn't accomplish a goddamned thing."

ThIRTEEN

To whet a nick off the edge of a V-gouge, you have to hone the paired edges symmetrically. I was just about there when the phone interrupted.

"Kestrel?"

"That depends," I said cautiously, "on what you're not selling."

"Don't fuck with me, wise-ass. Where is it?"

"I beg your pardon?"

"Don't fuck with me, wise-ass. Where is it?"

Instead of taking this advice, I said, "Listen, dickhead. Why don't you hoof it back to Rewrite and get a fresh script? Either that, or go get yourself a job you can handle."

On his end of the line, a cash register rang up a sale. "Kestrel," the voice said, "you just fucked yourself in the ass."

A phrase of *All Along the Watch Tower* escaped the jukebox near the cash register, and my caller hung up.

The clock over the desk said four forty-five.

I called Bowditch. "How come you don't call back? You find somebody else to love onto death row?"

"You're on my list," he breathed laboriously, as if he'd just sprinted up a flight of stairs, "but there's any number of blighted lives ahead of you. What's up?"

"Two things. In reverse order, I just got a call from a guy telling me I have fucked myself in the ass."

"I could have told you that."

"Can you trace the call?"

144

"Not without probable cause."

"What's that mean?"

"Various things. Let's say right after he calls, somebody takes a shot at you. Before you lapse into a coma, you mention the call to a beautiful nurse. Since Evans' wife has left him, he takes the nurse to lunch to debrief her. It might take two or three lunches to get enough information to swear out a warrant."

"Jesus Christ and the Brownian motions of justice."

"The law is there to protect people, Kestrel."

"Hey." I glanced over my shoulder. As usual, the street door was wide open. "I'm people."

"Says you." Bowditch took a loud sip of something. It sounded like a broom sweeping a flooded gutter.

"Bowditch," I said impatiently, "you and I know I didn't kill Renée Knowles. So who was this call from?"

Bowditch belched. "I can't help you. You said there was two things."

"Unbelievable. You ever heard of Manny Djector?"

"Yeah. The guy's clean."

"That creep is clean?"

"As far as this case is concerned, Djector is clean. He was all tied up in his mistress' dungeon the night the Knowles woman got it. It was fun getting him to admit it." Bowditch made a noise that might pass for a laugh among his friends.

I said, "I guess I'm the last person in town to hear about Manny Djector and his Oakland dominatrix. Listen—"

"How did you know it was Oakland? Was it Djector that called?"

"No way. But he—"

"Okay. Look, Kestrel. Don't play cop. Renée Knowles had dealings with all kinds of people. But unlike you, most of them move in a nether world of high-flying pickers and dealers who deal almost exclusively in cash, don't pay all their taxes,

145

and have more than one bank account in more than one country. In general they are a bunch of mendacious hustlers with two things in common: they will do almost anything to keep from working for a living, and they share an uncommon love of money and the things money can buy. And while as a sociological phenomenon they may rank high on the scam-meter, they also have a correspondingly low murder rate. Very low. As in nil. They might fuck each other, but don't shoot each other."

"Who said this guy accusing me of having 'it' has anything to do with pickers and dealers?"

"You must have figured out by now that picking was what Renée knew, and pickers and dealers and their customers were the only people who would talk to her. My god, her own husband didn't like her."

"You figured that out too, huh."

"It wasn't difficult."

"But Knowles didn't hate her, either. Certainly not enough to kill her."

"All the pieces aren't all in place yet but no, it doesn't look that way." He thought for a moment. "Are you telling me that guy who called sounded like Knowles?"

"No. He had some kind of southern drawl. I'd never heard the voice before."

"L.A.?"

"No, no. Louisiana. East Texas."

"You pay Knowles that courtesy call after the funeral?"

"It was passing strange. He misses Renée, but he's not exactly saying Kaddish."

As we were talking, I'd been digging absently into the desktop with the V-gouge, turning up a little curl of plywood veneer with a tiny triangular cross-section. Now the vertex of the gouge hit the buried head of a brad and stopped. A

146

direct hit. The vertex was ruined. It would require an hour of honing to fix it. I dropped the tool in disgust.

"There's not much to say about him," Bowditch continued. "The butler and Knowles alibi each other. There's no murder weapon. You were the last person to see her alive."

"Wrong. The person who shot her was the last person to see her alive."

"In any case, you were also the last person to fuck her."

This was not going well. "How do you know?" I shouted. "Are your tests back?"

"All in good time, Kestrel," he replied calmly.

"You don't know any more than I do."

"Ever have, you know, flashbacks? Ever get dosed with that Agent Orange?"

I offered him advice similar to that which my anonymous caller had offered me, and hung up.

After a turn around the block to cool off, I settled in over the sharpening stone to work the V-gouge back toward something I could use. Behind me on the carpeted bench the big frame waited. No carving had been done. In a large cupboard in the back of the shop the painting destined for the frame waited, wrapped in polyethylene. Two dealers, one patron, an artist, and a lot of money were waiting for me to finish this frame. I was contracted to install it, too. The patron's picture gallery was a long hall between his library and dining room, traversing the front of a 9,000 square foot Spanish-style villa in Atherton. A veritable constellation of receivables would be in orbit until I finished the job.

The devil caused my phone to ring again. Likely he caused me to answer it, too.

"Danny," said a sharp voice. "This is Michelle Canton."

"Yes, Michelle," I said pleasantly. "I was just this minute attacking your frame."

"Not to hassle you, Danny. But that's what you said the last time I called."

"True," I agreed, forcing a pleasant tone into my voice. "But the last time you called me was a mere four days ago. We artisans take time."

"Danny," she said, not bothering to mask her impatience, "I called you at least a week ago."

I glanced at the calendar. Michelle was a high-strung item who made a lot of money dealing art. A day or two in her shoes, buffeted by the weather generated by hundred-thousand dollar paintings, one might indeed accumulate much of the stress attributable to a month of ordinary life. Against the temporal elasticities of just such clients as herself, I had long since developed the defensive habit of logging calls. Each active client was associated with a particular color. Michelle's was taupe.

"Michelle," I said, "you called me at 1:45 P.M. on Tuesday. To put it charitably, you were traveling a little faster than usual. But still, Tuesday was only four days ago."

"That's impossible. What time?"

I repeated it. "That's Pacific Daylight Time," I added. "For a change." I heard the rustle of pages.

"No way. I was on the Concorde for most of the afternoon."

"So? They don't have phones on the Concorde?"

"Are you out of your mind? It's five dollars a minute to call from the Concorde."

"Since when does that stop you?"

"Besides," she added coyly, "you're not allowed to use a phone in the hot tub."

"I'm sure they're working on the problem. You were in the hot tub all the way to London?"

"It's only two-and-a-half hours from Washington."

"It's just that I didn't hear any splashing."

"There was too splashing," she said petulantly. "Going and coming."

"Michelle. Did you call me up just to tell me in your ever-so-subtle way that you got laid in a hot tub on the Concorde on Tuesday?"

"And this morning," she said dreamily. "Coming back."

"Congratulations," I sighed.

"Do you think you could have the frame ready by tomorrow, Danny?"

I made a taupe note of the present call. "Today's Friday, Michelle."

"So? Aren't you nearly finished?"

I didn't even cast a glance toward the carpeted bench. "The species are glued up. The frame's assembled and routed. The motif is sketched. The carving's barely started. I've been accused of murder. There you have it."

"You see? If you work all weekend. . . ."

"What's the matter, Michelle, are we a little short of cash?"

"You don't know the half of it."

"Is that your Day-Runner you're riffling through?"

"Yes."

"Make a note. You called me today, Friday. Got it?'

"Okay," she lied. "Why?"

"Page forward to next Friday." I waited. Silence. "You there?"

"I'm there," she said stubbornly.

"Make a note: *Call Danny re Steinmetz job.* Okay? Got it?"

"Got it," she said icily, and hung up.

I myself made a taupe note in next Friday's box. *Call Michelle.* Then I replaced her pencil in the coffee can and took up the maimed V-gouge.

Each wing of the gouge is ten millimeters of Solingen steel. This material will hold an edge through a fair piece of work, but it takes a fair piece of work to sharpen the edge in the first place, let alone shape it. You can hone the outside of the V with a regular flat stone, which means you can put your back into it and get quick results. But working the inside of the V requires narrow water stones, and on these you can apply no more pressure than fingertips can bring to bear. Sharpening whole sets of these gouges requires concentration and time well beyond most modern conceptions of either. It is this aspect of tool-sharpening, a subversion of temporality itself, that is so appreciated by the traditions of English and Japanese carpentry; and while professing great admiration for it, and while in fact paying good money for the results ultimately accruing to such effort, it is precisely people like Michelle Canton who have absolutely no capacity to understand it.

After about an hour the re-honed gouge cut as cleanly as I could hope. Soon shavings were piling up alongside the frame. But the renewed reverie evoked the troubled awkwardnesses of an archetypal dream. Amid the click of her two bracelets, the sighs, the imagined conversations, Renée's smile revealed a pair of fangs—long teeth. I pondered the emerging portrait of her character as I worked the wood, and only gradually became aware that I was no longer alone in the shop.

Their presence wasn't difficult to detect. One of them was smoking a cigarette. The other was chewing clove-scented gum.

I didn't look up or stop working. There wasn't much I could do except stretch out the time between my realization and their next move, and abruptly I remembered the last place I'd had a similar feeling, along a vine-entangled cirque above a waterfall. Then, as now, it was just before dark. I'd gone out second with a full compliment of gear but didn't have the radio, and that's part of what saved me. That, and I acted like I didn't know they were there. It was a bad place, and that's why the radio had been consigned to the middle of the squad. You couldn't see and you couldn't hear, for the waterfall filled the air with mist and pink noise. The trail was over-grown, steep, and wet, so it took both hands and careful attention to climb it. Anyway, there was no point in looking around. There would be nothing to see.

I climbed a hundred yards without stopping. Corporal John-son, the only other guy up top, already knew. He grimly ordered me to keep going. If we didn't secure a ridge above the river before dark, our position wouldn't be one. They would wait for the radio, then come after the rest of us. I was half a mile away before the shooting started. Before it was over, they'd picked off two guys caught on the slope and shot the radio to pieces, but the Lieutenant had figured out the play and fooled them. He called in support ahead of time, before the shooting started, then put the radio on the last guy—the Lieutenant himself. It was a good move that cost him his life.

The two in the shop were different. I was so caught up in analyzing Renée that they'd had plenty of time to kill me. But they didn't. They smoked in the line of duty, but they probably didn't carry automatic rifles. Nor would they be as tough as those four guys in the jungle—it was only four guys, manning that ambush. But I wasn't so tough anymore, either. It was thirty years later and my troop strength amounted to a V-gouge and a bad back. Not counting my brain, of course.

"No smoking," I finally announced. I studied the edge of the gouge. "Can't you guys read?"

A cigarette butt ticked onto the shavings beside the frame, trailing smoke. I flicked it to the floor and ground it out as I stood to face them.

One was a little tall and the other was a little short. The smoker wore one hand bunched up in the pocket of his leather jacket, obviously fondling a gun. The tall guy smoked, too; he held an unlit cigarette and a red butane lighter in one hand and chewed the gum, but appeared to be unarmed. He wore a tweedy suit jacket over a pineapple shirt, khaki slacks, no socks, and scuffed loafers. On the whole he looked the type to sell used cars and spend the profits along with the sales tax at the track. An altogether different occupation than the one practiced by his buddy, who looked as if he'd been X-ing all night and was headed for a repeat as soon as he took care of a little business.

"Guy wants to see ya," said the car-salesman.

"So? Where is he?"

The little guy smiled with pointy brown teeth to make a frankfurter cringe.

His partner sighed. "So lock up, frame-boy. We got a short waitin out front."

With just two nouns, contracted into one, this car salesman had managed to denigrate who I was and what I did.

"Yeah," said Ecstasy. "It's inna yellow zone and we don't want no ticket." His scofflaw laugh filled the air between us with swamp gas.

I took a step toward them.

"Leave the chisel where we can see it," advised the car salesman.

Once I might have tried to take these guys with or without a chisel. Whether or not I was equal to the task would have made no difference at all to me.

But now I actually took the time to reflect. This gave Ecstasy a chance to haul out a cute little powder-black 7.65 automatic. Its hexagonal barrel was no bigger than the handle on the gouge I was holding.

"I'm up all night," he said wearily. "No trouble."

I laid the tool alongside the frame. "Probably your conscience is bothering you."

Car Salesman thought this was funny.

The phone began to ring.

152

I looked at them.

They looked at me.

After four rings it stopped.

"That'll be my mother," I said. "Now she's worried."

"She shoulda thought of that before she had ya," the guy with the gun said.

"Before we go," Car Salesman said, "is there anything you'd like to show us?"

"Is there anything you guys are particularly interested in?" I indicated the materials around me. "Aluminum? Hardwoods? Paint-grade quarter-round in deceased-gunsel gray?"

The little guy squeezed his eyes shut and rotated his head atop his spinal column, apparently an uncomfortable thing for his neck, for a vertebra popped audibly, and he winced.

"You know what we want," Car Salesman said. "Figure it this way." He pointed his lighter. "Bring along the goods since we're going anyway. Save us a trip. Who knows?" He smiled sadly. "Maybe you'll make it home in time for supper."

"Sure," I said. "What time is it, anyway?"

Car Salesman cocked an eye directly at the clock over the desk behind me. So where in hell had I been while they cased the place? "Six-fifteen," he said. His eyes fell back on me. "What time's Momma puttin on the nosh?"

"Oh," I shrugged, "seven o'clock?"

He raised his eyebrows. "Momma's jumping the gun, I'd say."

fOURTEEN

They were driving a Humvee, the military vehicle popula-
rized by America's war in Iraq. The Humvee is wide,
long, tall, low-geared, big-tired, bulletproof, uncomfortable,
expensive, ridiculous, and an ostentatious pig, even by
American standards.

"Hey," I said, "this is inconspicuous."

"Get in," Ecstasy said.

"No, really. Everybody's looking at us." I waved at a clus-
ter of tourists gawking from the other side of Folsom street.
They waved back. "Let's grab a cable car to Fisherman's
Wharf."

Ecstasy gave me a nudge in the ribs with the muzzle of his
concealed pistol. From across the street it probably didn't
appear like anything more than two guys hustling a third
into a Humvee at gunpoint, just like in a movie. Everybody
was probably wondering where the cameras were. We have
a Film Commission, you know.

But if the two delivery boys certainly had their aversion to
publicity, I was curious as to their employer, so everybody
stayed calm. I climbed into the back seat with Ecstasy, whence
about ten yards of open country stretched between us and
the driver's seat. In between was a prairie of pure trash—
newspapers, styrofoam cups, Chinese take-out cartons, CDs
in and out of their boxes, a flannel shirt, a pair of striped
boxer shorts, pages torn from a pornographic magazine.

154

Forward of this mess were the vacant .50-caliber machine gun mount, a telephone, a high-end AM/FM CD player, and an LCD screen let into each seat-back, one of which looked like it had been head-butted. The leather upholstery was the color of a gassed caterpillar, a peculiar green which, despite the contiguous odors of cigarettes, coffee, rotting fruit, and uncertain digestion, retained some redolence of the tanning vat.

Once underway, Car Salesman caused a hidden speaker-phone to dial a number. We all heard the voice that answered, and I had heard it once before, at four forty-five, but now the bar ambiance was missing. Car Salesman told him we were on our way and hung up.

Ecstasy lit a cigarette.

"Hey," I said. "Offer me one."

When he looked at me, I made the backwards peace sign.

"That means fuck you in certain parts of the world," Ecstasy observed.

"But you and me, we're brothers in addiction–right?"

He showed me the backwards peace sign. "Shut up."

"Come on, let's have a smoke. I left mine on the bench."

He shook out a mentholated Kool and lit it for me. It tasted like a hooker's earlobe. I hadn't smoked a cigarette in thirty years, but it had been nearly that long since I'd seen the business end of a gun, too. I guess there are certain things you have to do twice.

Car Salesman drove east, which was good, because Folsom is a one-way street. But nobody put a bag over my head. While riding in the back seat of a Humvee with a bag over your head wouldn't be particularly conspicuous in San Francisco, the absence of that precaution meant that nobody was worried about concealing the route from me.

This was probably cause for concern.

At the Embarcadero Car Salesman turned right and drove

to Third Street. Lo and behold, the drawbridge was up. He closed with the last in a line of cars and stopped. Two cars ahead of us a police car waited, too.

"Hey," I said, leaning forward and pointing the cigarette toward the windshield. "Honk so I can wave."

Ecstasy pulled me back by my collar, but I kept right on talking. "I don't blame you for being nervous. You got important things on your mind. Like, what if that Beretta went off in your pocket? It happens, you know." I held up a thumb and forefinger. "Guy goes for his rod in a hurry. Because he's ready for anything, a round is chambered and the safety is off. He even keeps his finger on the trigger. But when he drags the pistol backwards, it hangs up in the upholstery— bang: a rocket in his pocket. Where its goes is anybody's guess. Plus the slide rips the webbing between his thumb and forefinger." I showed him mine. "Strictly a bonus. Powder burns at the very least. Cheap jacket? Up in flames. An expensive one melts. But now the lining's snagged in the slide, too. So your gun's jammed, you're wounded, and you're on fire. Know what I'd do?"

"I heard this one before," said Car Salesman, watching the rearview mirror. "Go ahead; tell him."

"To put out the fire and disinfect the burn," I said, "I'd piss all over you."

Ecstasy didn't think this was funny. Car Salesman yucked it up like he hadn't had a good laugh since the Edsel.

I jabbed my cigarette Ecstasy's way. Just perceptibly, he jumped. "Quick-draw artists screw up all the time. They snatch the pistol out of the holster—" I slapped my thigh and pointed a finger. Ecstasy twitched and made a mess of rooting out the gun. By the time he got it aimed at me, Car Salesman and I were both laughing. "Same deal. The sight hangs on the leather and boom, a .44-caliber crease, right down the

156

thigh. You're lucky if you don't kneecap yourself. I knew a guy who let it happen twice. He still limps."

"Aw, bullshit," Ecstasy said. "Alla goombah hadda do was file off the sight."

I shrugged. "Think of it as an I.Q. test."

Car Salesman laughed. Ecstasy stuck out his lower jaw. I made as if to touch his jacket. When he batted my hand with the pistol, a long rayon thread trailed after the barrel.

Ecstasy angrily snapped it off while Car Salesman made fun of him. "Frame-boy's right. You gotta think about that stuff."

"Nice piece, though," I said. "You got a permit for it?"

Car Salesman snorted and went back to his driving.

"Don't need one," Ecstasy leered, "on account it's disposable."

"How's that?"

His eyes rose from a fond glance at the pistol until they settled on me like a pair of flies on a sandwich. "Use it once, throw it away."

Car Salesman inhaled mucus through his nose, cleared his throat, and spit out the window.

"Oh, well," I said, "so I guess it's not the same gun that killed the Knowles woman."

"Huh?" Ecstasy considered the gun from various angles as if he were studying the color of wine in a glass. "She's a sweetheart, and she don't make so much noise."

"Indoors or outdoors make a difference?" I asked. What the hell. He might accidentally confess, like in the movies.

Ecstasy ignored me. "Trouble is, I can't get a steady supply of them. I have to hang on to this one until I can score the next one." He showed me the brown teeth. "Ya see."

So indeed there was a chance Ecstasy had used this weapon lately. Maybe when Clarence Ing digs the bullet out of the back of my head, his ballistics will be able to tie my murder to the Renée Knowles case and exonerate me as the perpetrator in it, too.

"Cool," I admitted aloud.

Having allowed a tall mast to slip down Mission Creek toward the Bay, the massive Lefty O'Doul counterweight thudded back into its bed. The alarm bells ceased, the crossbars lifted, and traffic began to flow over the bridge.

Car Salesman turned left off the bridge onto China Basin and continued south along the edge of the bay. On either side of us were ruined piers and warehouses, many of them surrounded by chainlink fencing. A lot of trash was blowing around. Scraps of sun-faded polyethylene fluttered in the breeze, impaled on the shark's teeth of hundreds of yards of spiraling concertina wire. Carcasses of burned-out vehicles appeared regularly, a number of them inhabited. One provided a vivisection of personal possessions: a hockey stick, a box fan, a surfboard, a basket stuffed with clothing, stacks of newspapers, a dashboard collection of rubber dinosaurs grazing along the dashboard. A lean dog lay in the shade of the rocker panel, leashed to the back door handle by a threadbare length of green garden hose.

"Are there no ashtrays in this preposterous rig?" I asked.

Ecstasy snorted. "Ain'tcha heard? The fuckin army is fuckin smoke-free." He demonstratively flicked his ash onto various *Chronicle* pages wadded up at his feet. I did likewise. But a moment later, when Ecstasy turned to flick his cigarette butt out the window, I merely let mine drop. He lit another only a moment later, and I pestered him for one, too.

"Gotta watch it," he leered, hiking the pack in my direction. "Might get the cancer."

"Life is short."

His eyes flicked up to meet mine. "The fuck you say."

Thus comforted, I parked one cigarette over my ear and accepted a light for the second one. Ecstasy pocketed his lighter and settled back into his seat, the filter tip of his Kool clenched between his teeth. "Two, three, four nails in the coffin," he muttered, "what the hell."

Car Salesman took a left at Illinois. At Twentieth he turned east past a derelict guardhouse at the entrance to the old Union Iron Works, and clattered down the cobbles onto Pier 70. Railroad spurs came and went below us, and dilapidated brick walls with thousands of shattered windows towered on either side. As Car Salesman turned onto the broad, deserted dock, he touched a remote control above the passenger sunshade. A garage door swung up and out of the side of a cavernous wooden pier shed, its cupped boards unpainted for a generation. Deep windrows of wind-blown trash lay along its sides. Plywood or wire mesh covered its windows.

The door swung to behind us. Car Salesman switched off the engine and turned in his seat, smiling in the semi-darkness. "Home sweet home." Ecstasy pointed his gun at my door handle.

A chill tang of salt air carried with it the pungency of old pilings, rotting despite their creosote. With it came the creak of the sagging pier, the purl of tidal waters, the reeks of diesel fuel and of barnacles exposed to the sun, the stale scent of scaling iron, the crepitations of the sheet metal roof high over our heads as it contracted with the evening chill. Beyond the front end of the grotesque HumVee, one odor overwhelmed all the others.

"Gumbo again," the Car Salesman muttered. "Goddamn it."

"Let's saw this job off and go find a nice, thick steak for a change," Ecstasy suggested.

"That's a damn good idea," Car Salesman replied. A heavy maroon theatrical curtain hung before us, transverse to the length of warehouse, separating the garage entry from the rest of the building. Car Salesman beat the folds until they parted, revealing one of those hip domiciles you see pictures of in magazines like *Design Unlimited,* along with articles about the places software entrepreneurs go in order to decompress after inventing the future. The corrugated metal ceiling was also the building's uninsulated roof, maybe three stories above us. Along the perimeter of the building a row of concrete mushroom columns shot up from a three-inch wooden deck designed to hold much more equipment than a HumVee or even the one-hundred-per-cent copper restaurant kitchen or the complementary big-screen entertainment center. A fourteen-ton overhead crane spanned parallel rails topping the columns, an artifact from the building's industrial past, its motor parked high against the far gable. In the gloom below it a Christmas tree hung from the massive pulley block, with a full compliment of colored lights. Above the tree the crane's tonnage was plainly visible as the numeral 14, stenciled onto the pulley sheave. Wooden scissor-trusses spanned the entire space, sixty or seventy feet, bearing wall to bearing wall, and marched on eight-foot centers perhaps two hundred feet, gable to gable. Two symmetrical rows of skylights were set along each pitch of the roof, way up there in the gloom, obscured by a half-century of grit and soot.

We walked into the kitchen, an area designated by large roll-around stainless wire shelving units, the kind you might see in any restaurant or hotel. Two ovens and an eight-burner gas range stood under a sheet-metal hood, facing a three-by-twelve-foot butcher-block countertop, also on casters. You could roll everything but the ovens and stove out of the way so as to host a party, light a photo shoot, stage an orchestra rehearsal, or maybe hose down your elephant. A large cylindrical pot simmered on the stove. From thirty feet away it smelled of crawdads and black-strap molasses, okra and onions, cumin and peppers, celery and shrimp, pole shacks and dysentery.

Beyond the counter were clusters of furniture which, along with the lighting, defined various otherwise more or less traditional spaces. There was a dining area, a living room, the entertainment center. Further back, a shaded lamp overhung a pool table. Beyond that were an old-fashioned pinball machine and a jukebox, their winking lights reflected in glasses hanging from a rack over a bar. Just short of the bar, against the eastern wall of the building, a cozy fire blazed in the mouth of a wood-burning stove.

Between the new arrivals and the butcher block counter, a lamp dropped a cone of light over a circular dining table, sufficient to seat six. On its far side a man waited, his features obscure in the shadows above the lamp. As we approached, just to show his alpha dog which of us was running dead last, Ecstasy administered a rude shove to my shoulder.

"Mr. Kestrel," said the fourth man, in a drawl I recognized, "set a spell."

Car Salesman slammed the rim of a chair seat into the backs of my knees. I sat down.

The table top was littered with interesting items. A drinking glass, a bottle of gin, a small clasp knife, a map of San Francisco, a ballpoint pen, a pink note pad, a pager, a cell phone, a key-chain tamagotchi, an open bindle of dope, and a black truncheon two inches in diameter and eighteen inches long, one end of which had a handle like a billy club.

The other end had a head like a circumcised penis.

The man with the drawl sat down, too.

"Drink, Mr. Kestrel?"

FIFTEEN

I'm not thirsty," I lied.

The man's thin coppery hair was pulled back into a short ponytail, his eyebrows were plucked, and his eyelashes were long. Several small gold hoops were threaded through the rim of his left ear. *"Mon vieux,* you are a guest in my," he made a little circle in the air with the blade of the knife, "house." He took up the paper bindle and smiled. His hands were pudgy and looked soft. "My guests are always thirsty." He aligned the V of the bindle's fold along his extended forefinger and began to tap one edge with the knife. Grains of the brownish powder with the lavender blush hopped along the longitudinal crease until they dropped into the empty glass. The man glanced up from his task. "Get it?"

I assumed the powder was heroin, although it could have been crushed book reviews. I'd seen plenty of junk in Vietnam, along with the origami squares of magazine pages it usually came in, up to an eight-ball or seven grams; if so, this particular heroin was a different color than I remembered. "Powders aren't noted for quenching the thirst," I observed.

The tamagotchi peeped.

The man glanced at it, sighed, and laid bindle and knife aside to pick up the toy. His tongue moistened his lips as he manipulated the buttons on the tamgotchi's face with his fat thumbs.

As I watched him, a green light briefly glided through the gloom beyond his right shoulder and disappeared, and for a

162

moment I thought there must have been somebody else in the back of the warehouse. But then the light appeared and disappeared again, further to my left, and I realized that it must have been on a boat coasting past the warehouse windows.

"There, there, *ma petite Zou-Zou.*" The man put the tamagotchi on the table and took up the bottle of gin. "Now she'll sleep," he said fondly.

"How much she weigh?" the Car Salesman asked in a bored voice.

"Fifty-six pounds," the man proudly answered, as he half-filled the glass with gin.

"Wow, I think. Wow?"

"*Zou-Zou est formidable,*" the man agreed, setting the bottle aside. "*Vraiment.*"

"The bayou meets the opposable thumb," I sniped.

The man looked up at me. "*Tu as raison,*" he laughed affably.

"Let's see," I mused, "French plus gumbo plus self-effacing humor equals . . . Cajun?"

He stirred the cocktail with the blade of the knife, unperturbed. "Gin plus junk plus Cajun plus Frame Boy equals big night in Frisco." Removing the wet blade from the cocktail, he passed each side of it over his tongue, and smacked his lips. "Big night in Frisco," he repeated.

Hard by my right ear, the Car Salesman's stomach growled.

"*Parlez le patois?*" the Cajun asked me.

"Not even enough to play pinochle," I said.

The Cajun pushed the cocktail across the table. "Drink it all." He sat back in his chair and folded the knife with a click. "Then we'll see who pees the farthest."

I looked at the drink. Motes revolved slowly in the clear fluid.

I looked at my host.

He looked at me.

"Before we get too blotto," I suggested, "maybe you can explain why I, of all people, deserve your hospitality?"

"That seems redundant, *mon vieux.*" The knife unfolded in his chubby fists. "You had your chance to make nice on the phone." The knife closed with a click. "Now we try in person."

I cast my eyes toward the roof. "Did I miss something, motherfucker?" Then I leaned forward and said, "I must have missed something."

Ecstasy and the Car Salesman each pulled my shoulders back until I sat up straight.

The Cajun propped his elbows on the table and opened the knife, balancing it between two fingertips. Above the blade, his eyes were strangely moist.

Far out on the bay, a foghorn emitted a long moan.

"Well," I said, shifting in my seat. "Do you want to know anything special? Like for instance, how to miter aluminum channel without leaving a burr? Or, let's see, why you deserve a discount from Joe Bishop, who sells the best double-sided tape in the world?"

Ecstasy brought the butt of the Beretta down on my head just so. A little tap. I didn't see it coming. But it wasn't unexpected, either. A dial tone appeared in my ears, and the horizontal scan of my optic nerve sawtoothed momentarily. Since they were going to tune me up whether I fought back or not, I started with an elbow to Car Salesman's nuts. Ecstasy had to settle for one to his knee. In return I got one ear flattened by the pistol butt, against the side of my head, along with an expertly leveraged choke-hold and a sharp bootheel to my instep. These adjustments took only a few seconds. I didn't even have to stand up.

The Cajun merely watched. The Car Salesman tilted the chair back on its legs, away from the table, at about a forty-five degree angle, so Ecstasy could pop me one in the solar plexus. While I was gasping for air, they got most of the cocktail down my throat, some of it by way of my nose. Altogether, it sounded like ten A.M. at the espresso bar.

Ecstasy and the Car Salesman sat the chair back up, straightened their clothes, and got fresh cigarettes going while I finished gagging. After a while I noticed the Kool parked over my ear had fallen onto the table and grunted pathetically toward it. Ecstasy, my brother in addiction, understood. He thoughtfully laid the filter on my lower lip and set fire to the other end.

Then we waited. About halfway along its length, the Kool began to taste luxurious. A few puffs later the rest of me did, too. "Lenny Bruce was right," I slurred to nobody in particular,

The Cajun, who had made a little shelf under his chin with his fingertips, now pointed the penknife at me and said, "'I'll die young, but it's like kissing God.'"

I nodded, as it were, by way of signaling agreement, and smacked my lips. "That's some cosmopolitan downtown you got there, *mon vieux.*"

The Cajun seemed content to watch my head loll so far to one side that my ear nearly touched my shoulder, so I milked the effect. It wasn't difficult. Seventy-five percent of me wanted to do nothing else. The cigarette fell off my lip onto my shirt. "Tsk, tsk," Ecstasy said. He brushed it to the floor and stepped on it.

Now the Cajun, judging me medium rare, set aside the penknife and took up the ebony truncheon. His fingers traced its length until they reached the circumcised tip, where they lingered with the attentive pride of a queer *mohel* inspecting his work of seventeen years before.

"Renée gave it to you, Danny. So now you give it to us. See? It's simple."

"Renée," I whispered.

"Not an hour before she died," the Cajun added. "So tell us where it is," he pushed the head of the truncheon through

165

the circle of his thumb and forefinger, "and save yourself a split rectum."

I looked at the truncheon in wonder. The light glinting off it was almost tactile. No bamboo shoots under the fingernails for this tribe. I slowly nodded my head, up and down, gradually changing its orbit until it wobbled back and forth. "Look, *mon vieux,* you . . . gotta tell me . . . what . . . it . . . cause other . . . *wise* . . . Sheee. . . ." I was sliding off the chair.

Ecstasy pocketed his gun to help Car Salesman right me. "Sit up, you sack of shit."

I happily agreed that this was most necessary. And by then, a gleam of doubt had appeared in the Cajun's eye.

"I'm just a . . . what am I? Oh yeah. A frame-maker. Frame-boy." I laughed. "'It' don't mean anything . . . sub*stan*tive to. . . . What the hey 'it' is, any-the . . . hey way. . . ? Huh?"

"You were the last person," the Cajun said carefully, "to see her alive."

My eyes closed. "No!" I feebly struck at the table and missed. "I've heard that . . . before. The last person who . . . killed her . . . I . . . I. . . ."

"Yes?"

"Snot. Snot true. . . ."

"Snot true?" the Cajun shook his head. Even Ecstasy sighed disgustedly, while Car Salesman chuckled.

"Snot me. Me. Last person her. . . . Snot. . . . I didn't. . . ."

"Shoulda used crank," the Car Salesman observed.

Then the tamagotchi peeped. With an intuition for destroying suspense usually reserved by commercial interruptions of televised movies, the Cajun set aside the truncheon and took up his tamagotchi. "Oh, Zou-Zou," he said, "my little pest." And he fretfully thumbed Zou-Zou's buttons.

Six inches from my right ear, the Car Salesman's stomach rumbled like distant summer thunder. "She's hungry already?"

166

"Fifty-eight pounds," the Cajun squinted studiously. "I got a hundred and five points."

Bored out of his mind, the Car Salesman whistled approvingly.

"Next thing ya know," said Ecstasy, "she'll be goin ta college."

"Zou-Zou, *ma petite,*" the Cajun said, "brought into this world, only to die." He set the toy aside and cocked an eye at me. "And how do you feel, Brother Kestrel? Suffused by probity? Or we feelin ass-trial. Get it, Brother Kestrel?" He patted the truncheon. "Ass-trial?"

Ecstasy sniggered.

My eyes had become slits. "Heroin I can take," I whispered, lifting my head a little. "Gin, I never liked."

The Cajun took up the truncheon and patted it into his palm. One two, one two three. . . .

I permitted myself a lazy, depraved leer–easy enough to do. I was pretty stoned. My lips had become as numb as pair of dead snakes. A thin skein of saliva rolled over the lower one, slid down my chin, and depended to the breast of my shirt.

The Cajun's eyes darted to the half-empty bindle. One never knows the strength of street heroin. When they legalize it, one will be better able to judge such things. In the meantime, had one fed Kestrel too much junk?

"Give me that baby," I blurted, spraying saliva over the table. "Gimme that big black dick."

The Cajun's eyes snapped back to me, wide with disbelief.

"The whole thing."

The atmosphere palpably warped. Brooding idly to my left, hands in his pockets and a cigarette on his lip, Ecstasy stiffened. Car Salesman, hungry and fey and aloof, probably hadn't been paying attention; but he sensed the change and paused his cigarette halfway to his mouth.

167

The Cajun, too, was taken aback. I was supposed to be intimidated, cowed and terrorized–a nervous wreck, made pliable by this homemade truth serum, anxious to spill the beans.

Lascivious wasn't in the program.

The Cajun hesitated. Had he misjudged? His uncertainty ticked by, measured in seconds. The truncheon had worked before, no doubt. Before, all he'd had to do was show the thing, and the squawking began. Had he ever gone so far as to actually sodomize a recalcitrant hero, savaged him–or her– until they were reduced to a gibbering fink?

At any rate, no one had ever begged him for it. Until now.

Here, now, sagged turpitude beyond his experience.

Far down the waterfront, a container ship blew three short blasts on its horn, and they echoed among the surrounding hills, the signal for imminent departure. The waters of the bay lapped the pilings that supported the building. Occasionally the shifting tons of listless brine made the whole structure shudder. Waterlogged timber, wire rope gone slack with age, seized turnbuckles, rusted iron rods and railings creaked and groaned all around us. At the far end of the room, the fire crackled in its grate. The gumbo bubbled on the stove. A seagull landed on the roof with a faint thump.

The Cajun had been counting on disorientation and fear, and now he was deprived of them, his most valuable inquisitorial tools. How could the leverage have shifted so? He had his victim all hopped up on junk; it was three guys to one; he had this great damn truncheon, and no lubricant in sight. Frame-boy was a wildcard. Frame-boy was the one guy out of ten thousand who could handle heroin and gin and rape, too?

Slumped in my chair, eyes glazed slits, a stupid grin on my face, drool on my shirt, poised behind my guise of doped pervert, I watched the wheels turning beneath the Cajun's

168

thinning hair—his dyed hair, I abruptly realized; his hair was dyed that lustrous copper.

Then he moved a pawn. The Cajun said, "Not yet, Brother Kestrel," and patted the truncheon. "Not till you tell us."

"Ohhh," I said, audibly disappointed.

"As far as we know," he continued, "which is pretty far, you were the last person to see Renée Knowles in possession of . . . a certain *precious object.*"

"Precious," I repeated, as if thoughtfully desperate. "Could you be a *little bit* more specific? Was it *small?* Was it *round?* Was it *big?* Was it *three-dimensional* at all. . . ?"

The Cajun's features tightened. "Goddamn it, Brother Kestrel, you'd try the patience of a dog-eatin' gator."

"But the only things I saw in her possession were a cell phone and a bottle of booze," I sniveled. "You got to believe me."

And the Cajun lost it. He suddenly screamed, "You fuck, *it don't belong to you!*" and he rose out of his chair sufficiently to swing the truncheon at arm's length, parallel to the floor, a counterclockwise sidearm haymaker aimed at my head that could have killed me. I ducked. The truncheon skipped up off my shoulder and glanced onto my ear, the same ear that had been boxed bloody already, and hit the Car Salesman in his left elbow. Dildo or no dildo, it was a weapon too, as viperous as any length of rubber hose or a braided sap. If I hadn't thrown myself toward the Car Salesman, if that thing had hit me squarely in the side of the head, I surely would have awakened listening to a different drummer, if I awoke at all. Ecstasy himself spun out of its way, and just in time, or the truncheon might have raked one or another of the vital organs at the bottom of his ribcage. The back of my sideways-tilting chair caught the reeling Car Salesman on the hip, and he and I and the chair went over altogether. His left ankle, caught between the edge of the chair seat and the floor,

169

snapped like a wet chopstick. We both heard it. The Car Salesman just had time to yelp before the heel of my hand caused his septum to visit one of his maxillary sinuses.

"Give!" raged the Cajun, oblivious to the mistake he had made, and with a formidable backhand he brought the entire length of the truncheon smashing down on the table top, crushing the gin glass.

"Holy shit!" Ecstasy screamed, "the Hummer's on fire! The Hummer's burning!"

The Cajun's eyes bulged toward the Humvee, parked no more than twenty-five feet behind us, just beyond the gap in the theater curtain. The smoldering cigarette butts had done their job. The HumVee's interior now glowed like the maw of a Bessemer furnace, and its two-piece windshield, two narrow rectangles framing the flames, gave it a demonic cast. Smoke and debris and tendrils of fire whirled in its interior, and the air feeding through the slits of its barely opened windows made determined whistling noises. The coiled phone antenna on its roof was beginning to list to one side, like the staff of a pennant drooping over a melting snowbank.

"Motherfucker," the Cajun screamed, "that bitch cost a hundred grand!"

Ecstasy had sprinted halfway to the car before he put it together and turned on the heels of his leather-soled loafers, simultaneously trying to get the gun out of the pocket of his leather jacket. One of his shoes came off and clattered toward the HumVee without him, while Ecstasy slid lengthwise to the floor with a muffled pop. His gun had gone off in his jacket.

I stood straight up under the edge of the table, upending it. The bulb in the hanging lamp exploded and the Cajun fell forward as the table turned over on top of him. A nice oak table it was, too. Heavy and dark and possibly Stickley. Conscious of the slim chance of Ecstasy's being tangled up forever, even if he was wounded, I planted a foot on the side of my fallen chair, leaped as high as I could, and came down dead center onto the bottom of the upturned table with both feet. There was a satisfying crunch and a brief, deflating screech. I descended into a full knee bend, then sprang up and away, toward the back of the warehouse.

Passing the stove I yanked the tureen off the burner and turned it loose, slathering the floor with smoking gumbo. Scalded screams erupted from beneath the oak table. I vaulted the butcher-block counter and made for the far end of the building. My left kneecap just nicked a sofa arm in the dark. But I homed in on the glow of the wood stove and, as soon as I got there, upended it in a roar of adrenalin. Smoking stubs of mesquite and a lot of orange coals spilled over the brick hearth and onto an oriental rug beyond. Next to the stove a pile of magazines and newspapers teetered atop a woven basket full of kindling, and I levered the whole of it over the scattered coals.

The first shot pierced what was left of the stovepipe, which hung over where the stove had been. I dove behind the stove as a second round caromed off it. A third shot shattered the plastic bubble over the jukebox selections. I came up with a chair and flailed at a window with it. The glass fell out of the frame, but there was expanded wire mesh screwed to the sash on the outside of the building. In two blows I had dashed the chair to pieces against it. I threw the tangle of shattered legs and rungs toward the front of the building. A bullet clipped the calf of my left leg, but I barely felt it. I retrieved a stool from the bar, and the mesh yielded to it. I threw the stool toward the yelling at the front of the building and pitched myself sideways through the window.

Outside it was black. I fell for a longer time than I thought I should have, and just as I was thinking I'd seriously misjudged the drop to the pier, it slammed my left shoulder,

171

hard, almost exactly where the truncheon had already whaled it. Then my head hit the pier a ringing blow even as I tried to let the momentum carry me end over end, which it did, twice. Step by step, I thought, crumpling to a halt, I will increase the distance between that handgun and my back. Ever cut heroin with adrenaline? You'll love it, baby. Accruing these injuries was like watching a screaming mob through a double thickness of bulletproof glass; the injuries were very distant; they were happening to somebody else. I rolled until I found my feet and stood up running.

The sprint lasted a good sixty or seventy yards in total darkness. I could only perceive the lights of Oakland in front of me, eight miles across the bay. There must have been the sounds of my footsteps, but I couldn't hear them. Despite the crease in the calf, which probed the opiate buffer like a point of steel, I hardly stumbled. I ran swiftly, like an Olympian, like a fleeing thief, like I'd just lit a short fuse to a whole box of dynamite, and I was just getting my arms pumping when I ran straight off the end of the pier.

DEATH OF A PRINCE

SIXTEEN

I awoke to find myself draped over the crotch of an X-brace and sodden as Irish peat. It was still dark. From the knees down my legs floated in water on one side of the brace, my forearms trailed in the brine on the other side. Eventually I realized that I was underneath the eastern end of Pier 70 and a foot or two above sea level.

Who could know what forces had been at work in the night? I found that I couldn't move freely and in turn remembered, as if from a dream, that before passing out I had managed to lash two front loops of my jeans to the thrubolt at the vertex of the brace with my belt. One of the loops had snapped. But for the other, I might not have been above sea level at all.

Warm enough to know I was still alive, too cold to believe it, I opted for another nap.

Something touched my shoulder, and a voice spoke. The intrusion had an annoying ring to it, like a stone hitting a propane tank. I opened one eye. A gaff hook hovered before my face for a moment, then went away. The other eye refused to open.

Daylight. Thick ridges of mist drifted beyond the shadow of the pier. Water lapped the pilings, and the pilings creaked. There were odors of rotting kelp, drying barnacles, creosote, wet ashes, and mildewed laundry.

173

The head of an old man rose into sight and fell, as a swell advanced among the pilings.

"Big waterfront lightning last night," the old man said. "Took out the whole pier shed."

"Gck," I submitted.

The head rose into sight again. In advance of it came a paint-daubed watch cap atop a nest of white hair. There followed a gray moustache, thick and untrimmed and stained with nicotine ochres, and finally a week's growth of whiskers scattered over a face tanned madrone by wind, sun, and alcohol. The rheumy eyes were a brilliant blue that almost matched the violets of the burst capillaries teeming on the nose.

"You okay up there, skipper? Not too chilly? Argh hargh harg."

"Ch-ch-ch. . . ."

"Well, look at her positive. If you're cold, you're not dead. Argh hargh harg." He pointed the gaff. "I bunk just around the corner." The head sank out of sight again. "Got propane, salmon, eggs. . . ." The head came back. ". . .and a hot shower, dock-side."

"Time zwit," I managed to ask.

"You got invertebrates measuring your ass for a picnic and you want to know what time it is?" He used the gaff to flick a hermit crab off my shoulder. "It's fuckin late, skipper, argh. . . ."

He steadied himself against the brace. A distinct odor, half diesel fuel and half acetylene, rose and fell with him. "You wanna stay here, or what?"

I shook my head, indicating the negative.

"Well come on down then."

I peered over the edge of the three-by-twelve. The unplaned surface tore at my cheek, which pulled the closed eye open.

The salt stung, the light was painful, and I was stiffer than primed canvas.

The old man stood in an aluminum dinghy a few feet below me. Its bottom was strewn with a variety of gear, which I set to inventorying as lackadaisically as an insurance adjuster on chlorpromazine. Rubber waders, red plastic jerry can, one-gallon milk-jug floats, various lengths of line, hanked and otherwise. Rusted crescent wrench, bent screwdriver, the head of a ballpeen hammer. A grease-streaked army sweater, one wooden oar, a quart of Pennzoil. Two fishing rods, one small anchor, a crab pot; a coil of yellow nylon line in a galvanized tub; an inch of brackish water sheened by oil, in which floated pieces of styrofoam bait cups. A lidless cooler contained a crab, two fish, and four long-necked bottles of Budweiser, all of them adrift in a listless dirty slush.

One touch from me, I reflected, and that slush would be ice again.

"Hey you skipper. Gonna make it?"

I tried to fledge the nest, but the belt only let about a third of me fall off the brace and hang there. Flailing feebly I couldn't reach the belt, my hands were frozen anyway, and I was too incoherent to explain the problem.

The old man pulled himself and his boat along by his hands, following the timbers until he could peer up between them. "Oughta show that knot to the Sea Scouts." He produced a cork-handled sheath knife, thin and curved from much sharpening, and darted the blade between the timbers. The belt parted and I dropped the four or five feet into the dinghy. The middle third of me fit neatly into the washtub. One ankle cracked against a gunwale, but my head rebounded safely off the plastic jerry can. The boat wallowed uncertainly, but the old man rode it out with ease.

Pain was far beyond proportion to whatever injury might have generated it, a symptom, it turns out, of hypothermia.

175

Stay out all night, you learn stuff. For a long minute my heart beat wildly and irregularly, another symptom. I began to hyperventilate, too, but then the arrhythmia stopped—the whole heart stopped—and I couldn't breathe at all. Existentially speaking, this was worse than anything that had happened all night. The old man could only watch these convulsions. I could only experience them. The situation was out of our hands. When the palpitations passed, the heart started again, and I was left gasping.

"You might be okay; you might not," the old man said comfortingly. "It's up to you."

I tried to speak but my lungs convulsed. The air that moaned past the larynx sounded like hinges on a dumpster lid.

"Hypothermia's a motherfucker," the old man agreed. "Can't even drink when ya got it."

He pulled us piling to piling. At the outer edge of the pier he sat down and tugged alive the tiny outboard. "You gonna make it?" I choked a little bile over the side. "There's a sign of life," he said.

The little craft circled under its own power while her captain twisted the cap off a bottle of beer. When he straightened the tiller, we arced out over the bay. Athwart the gunwales I had a seal's-eye view of the waterfront as it slid past us.

At two hundred yards, Pier 70 presented a scene of devastation. Charred spars stood at skew angles amid a blackened wreckage whose original purpose had been rendered indiscernible. Although fire equipment certainly must have drenched the pier in both fresh and salt water, the wreckage still smoldered. A temporary chain link fence blocked access from the street. Long yellow ribbons fluttered over the entrance, marking the place as a crime scene, and a police car was parked in front of the gate. Probably the debris would have to cool a while before the arson investigators could excavate whatever might be left of, for example, three hoods and a HumVee.

The sun had just cleared the Oakland Hills to the east of us, across the bay. It couldn't have been much later than seven in the morning. Six inches below my nose, the brine rolled by. My mind momentarily worked again: I'd gone to a lot of trouble to find that warehouse. "Phone?" I whispered.

"What's this look like, a fuckin Range Rover? You're hanging out in the intertidal, skipper. Ahrgh hargh hrgh," and the captain took a swallow of beer.

He asked my name. I told him and asked his.

"Dave—they call me Two Boat." He lifted two fingers off the bottle. "On account I got two boats."

"Th-thanks, D-Dave."

"No problem. Been pulled out myself."

"This is my f-first t-time."

He chuckled. "I thought you was a sea lion. They like to haul out in them timbers and take a little rest. Get away from the harem. That what you was doin?" He eyed me closely. "Gettin away from the harem?"

I tried to smile but bit the inside of my cheek instead.

He gestured toward the cooler. "Want a beer?"

"N-no. H-hot t-tub."

This delighted him. "A hot tub would kill you, Danny. So might would a beer, for that matter."

"You around that p-pier often?"

"Every couple of days." He snatched the crab out of the cooler. "There's good crabbin under there." A claw came up to nip his hand, and he dropped it back into the cooler.

"You k-keep p-pots under there?"

"Some say it's not such a good idea to be eatin out of the bay. Heavy metals, you know. Toxins. The red tide. Intestinal parasites. Industrial solvents. Selenium. Bacteria.

Sewage. . . ."

"J-Jesus."

"It's the end of the world, no doubt about it. I'm ready, though. Come an git me, man. Ahrgh argh argh." He upended the beer and finished it.

"What b-burned up last night?"

"Big pier shed. Total loss." He dropped the empty into the cooler. "Only the one tenant, though. Some kind of antique business. Obviously an insurance deal." He rummaged for a fresh beer and opened it. "Old furniture and stuff burn real good, but a failing business burns better." He took a sip. "Ahrgh hargh hrgh."

"You remember the name of the company?"

"Never knew it."

"How do you know it was antiques?"

"Know a teamster hauls containers there for a drayage company, out of Alameda. He likes to pass an hour at the Forward Hatch on Third Street, have a couple snorts before he sits in traffic back to the East Bay. I drink there, too, when I can afford it."

I knew the Forward Hatch. An atavism. Life-rings from scrapped ships on the wall, a cargo net covers the ceiling, there's always a bottomless bowl of chili, with salad, for $3.95, a draft of beer with a shot of the well tequila for a dollar-fifty, a lingerie show every Friday at quitting time, for free. In the days Neal Cassady was a brakeman, rails criss-crossed the acreage around the Forward Hatch, a large area bound by Townsend Street on the north, Seventh Street on the west, Mariposa Street on the south, and the cargo terminals lining the bay east of Third Street. The rails had once run considerably north, right into the heart of San Francisco, all the way to Spear and Market, and the Southern Pacific Railroad once owned all the land under them. But high rise buildings and changing times—in short, money far bigger than that to be had from hauling cattle and pig iron—have pared the rails back, along with the longshoremen and railroad men who had contributed to most of the Forward Hatch's receipts. Now many of the piers were mere clusters of rotted pilings jutting raggedly out of the Bay, hazards to navigation and development alike. The rails had been torn up. The former freight yards were shoulder deep in fennel and stacked railroad ties, deserted but for the odd encampment of homeless people, awaiting the massive urban development, pending construction of the new baseball park at 3rd and Townsend, just as surely as typhus follows a tidal wave.

"Ever seen any people on that pier?"

"Sure. One time they had a whole living room arranged outside the mouth of a forty foot container—lamps, chairs, rugs, even a barbecue grill. People sitting around having cocktails. Which reminds me." From the hip pocket under his flannel shirt he produced a pint of dark rum. "Smoking, watching the sunset, catching rays. Looked real civilized. Ersatz living room. Want some?"

"N-no thanks."

"Probably kill ya anyway," Dave said, "Argh hargh hrg. From now on, it's soup and sleeping bags for you, Danny."

"H-hot t-tub," I bleated.

Dave took a sip of rum and chased it with beer. "No. Death trap. What you need is a hooker for the sleeping bag. You budgeted for hookers?" He capped the pint.

"Isn't it kind of early for that?"

"Not if you're an alcoholic," he said, fitting the bottle into his pocket.

"It's n-none of my b-business."

"It ain't a business. It's a vocation. Argh harg hrgh."

I tried to laugh but it sounded like I was gargling marbles. "You live aboard?"

"Home sweet home on the buoy ball." He pointed. "Other side of the dry docks."

"Ever get to know any of those antique dealers?"

"Not my kinda people."

"What kind's that?"

"Other alcoholics." He shrugged.

"There're plenty of alcoholics dealing antiques."

He shook his head stubbornly. "Opposite end of the canapé table."

"Which end is that?"

"Whichever end I'm not. It could just as well be you or me trussed up on that central platter with our little feets tied together with little white socks on them and an apple in your mouth. Bunch a wild rice an' sage an' raisins stuffed up your ass, too. Them people don't care who they eat, so long as they're eatin. That's the world according to Two-Boat."

"How could you tell that about those people?"

"Hell, I can spot 'em a mile away in the dark without an odor to go by. There's the ones that fit in, see, and then there's the rest of us. There's some good ones, mind you; don't get me wrong. But these folks on that pier, well, let's put it this way." He leaned toward me. "They never fuckin waved hello." He waved his beer. "Hellooo, motherfucker. It's that simple. They fuckin never fuckin waved hello. They're too good for Two-Boat. Fuck 'em."

"Fair enough. What else didn't they do?"

"Hell, I don't know. They didn't even look at me. I was drivin right up under 'em to get to my pots. Right up under 'em. They didn't care. Just kept on smokin and drinkin and jabberin. I could hear everything."

"Everything?"

"Sure. I was straight down under 'em."

"Couldn't they hear the motor running?"

"I use the oars up under the pier. Too much wire rope and

180

stuff under there. Foul the prop. They paid old Dave no attention whatsoever."

"What did they talk about?"

When he flared the arm holding the bottle, a little beer went aft with the breeze. "Nothin."

"They must have talking about something."

"They talked about the same stuff that everybody else talks about. El Niño. The short-comings of the President. The new ballpark. Price of real estate. Probably why they burned the building down, for the real estate."

I knew better than that. But I said, "They burned down their own building? Why?"

"Waterfront lightning. With this new ballpark going in, land's worth a fortune down here."

"That's football, right?"

"What? No, that's the Giants."

"Basketball, right?"

"No, the *baseball* ballpark." He frowned. "You from around here?"

"Sure."

"That's all a real native cares about, you know."

"What? Baseball?"

"Well, sure. If you've lost interest in baseball, you've lost interest in life."

"Speak for yourself."

"Anyway, speakin for them other folks, the Port Commission controls everything on the waterfront, see, piers and all. All this development down here's got a lot of money flying around. So before these people could get evicted, they burned themselves out. That way they collect the insurance. It's simple."

A fish leaped straight up out of the cooler and fell back into the two or three inches of bilge water in the bottom of the boat. Dave adroitly hooked a forefinger into the fish's gills and held it up. "No you don't, sweetheart; you're mine now. You're about to meet your purpose in life. Although I don't know how I'm gonna get them raisins up your ass. Ahrgh argh hargh." He corrected course slightly. "You like salmon, Danny? How about rock cod? Bass? Anyway, think you could hold down solid food? Two-Boat's hell in the galley."

"N-no."

He dropped the fish back into the cooler. "Well, whatcha wanna do? Watch television?"

I made a face and it hurt.

"Picky bastard. Well, you can watch me eat. Poached rock cod, crab salad, hot coffee with rum in it. Man!" He rubbed the beer bottle over his belly. "Ain't we livin?"

"That c-coffee sounds good."

"A little rum might do you some good, too. But ya gotta be careful."

"I'm a c-careful m-man."

"I can see that. What you really need, though, is a hooker in a sleeping bag."

A navy hospital ship, talcum white with a red cross on every side of it, was hauled up in the ways of the Bethlehem dry docks. The clamor of air hammers, welders, and gantries rattled within the spray curtains billowing around her.

"What kind of c-cars do they drive?"

"I see a clean Beamer out there a lot. But it's the HumVee you'd notice."

"One of those army things?"

"Looks like a metal lunchbox, painted black."

"Who drove it?"

"Guys. Ever seen a woman drive one of those things?"

"I g-guess not."

"Women're too smart to drive 'em. But there's this cute broad who drives the Beamer."

"What's cute?"

"Brunette, small. But, you know. . . ." He made sinusoidal gestures with his beer hand. "Cute. Always dresses nice, a lot nicer than the guys with the Hummer."

"These guys. One taller than the other?"

"Yeah, but who ain't? I mean, you take any two people –"

"Ever see the woman close up?"

"Only through binoculars, argh hrgh."

"What color was the BMW?"

"Black, with tinted glass all the way around."

"Anything else? Anything unusual?"

"Yeah. One of the HumVee guys pulled a gun on her once."

"A gun? What was that about?"

"Beats me. I was getting up pots about half a mile away, minding my own business."

"On this thing?"

"Nah." We had rounded the dry docks by now and he pointed at a wooden boat of about thirty feet. "I was out and about on *Rummy Nation*. Only looking cause I seen the broad was there."

"The brunette saw you?"

"Probably not. I was in the wheelhouse. Anyway, the guy put away the heater and they went about their business. The broad did a funny thing, though."

"I n-need a l-laugh."

"Happy to oblige. When she pointed out my boat, the guy with the gun looked my way, saw the boat, then looked back at her. His gun was kinda drooping. And you know what that little girl did? She laughed in his face.

"Really? She laughed at a guy holding a gun on her?"

"Calm as you please. I'd say she was genuinely amused and didn't give a shit what that guy thought. Plucky little thing."

"You ever see her in the Forward Hatch?"

"No. But the two guys in the HumVee stop in for a pop once in a while."

"Seen them lately?"

"Yesterday," he nodded. "They drove past the bar just as I was gettin there." As if scanning for hazards, Dave peered ahead intently. "Had another guy with 'em."

"D-do tell."

Dave told nothing.

"What time was that?" I finally asked. "Do you remember?"

"Sure," Dave narrowed his eyes, "it was right around Vodka-thirty."

"When's that?"

"When the rum runs out, ahrgh hargh hrgh. . . ."

SEVENTEEN

Aboard *Rummy Nation*, Dave stirred a spoonful of honey into a cup of tea. While he fed of it to me a spoonful at a time, he recalled a fisherman who'd spent a night clinging to a styrofoam cooler. "He was five miles off Muir Beach by the time the Coast Guard found him. He'd been in the water fourteen hours. You know how he got warm again?"

"N-no."

"He moved to Costa Rica. Argh hargh hrgh."

Based on the Mediterranean felucca, brought to California by Sicilian fishermen, the so-called Monterey design of *Rummy Nation* had lost few of her ancient lines. But her lateen rig had been replaced by a single-cylinder Hicks diesel, which left just enough room below for a foetid sleeping bag and a kerosene stove. The boat appeared ship-shape on the outside and derelict within. The reek of mildew suffused the air below deck, where pocket bilge pumps whirred often. Cricket cages, bait buckets, beer bottles, and all manner of fishing gear were in evidence, along with a crusty ketchup bottle and an empty restaurant napkin dispenser. The rusted pot-pulling davit, aft at the starboard gunwale, looked like it had seen 75 years of service. The only amenities were the sleeping bag, which looked like it had been fragged more than once, a 49ers stadium cushion that Dave used as a pillow, a portable TV, and two large ice chests. Squirreled away in cubby holes were canned goods, medicines, clothing, and books to do with the

185

sea. There was a formidable array of tools as well, for Dave was a waterfront mechanic specializing in anything diesel. Hanging on the door of the companionway, a drugstore frame contained a reproduction of a painting of Donald Crowhurst's infamous *Teignmouth Electron*. She was nosing into a gnarly sea with halyards flailing, nobody visible on deck.

Head down in the companionway I easily surveyed this demesne, as its lord drizzled iodine into the lacerations on my legs, which in turn lent me glimmers of a return to sensation. But it was when Dave debrised the bullet hole in my calf with a Q-tip and a hot razor blade that I rediscovered the absolute present.

"These scratches would be from the barnacles on them pilings you went shimmying up," Dave said. "Same thing that happened to your hands. Course it's news to me that a barnacle carries a gun—but hey, there's a million stories in the intertidal."

I changed the subject. "Is the dinghy your other boat?"

"Nah," Dave said, blotting the iodine with a rag that reeked of diesel. "Notice them buoys on the way in?"

I had noticed the buoys. But what really stood out was the ten feet of rigged mast, including spreaders and a radar reflector, encircled by them. "*The Stripéd-Ass Bass*," Dave said, reaming the bullet wound with a twisted tip of the rag. "She's havin' a little submarine vacation."

"Your other boat's on the bottom?"

"That's a nice, clean hole," he said, squinting at the wound. "The round must have been jacketed. At least somebody's respecting the Geneva Convention."

"Why don't you raise her?" I asked through clenched teeth.

"What for? She'd just go down again."

About nine-thirty we rowed in, and I stood in the lukewarm trickle of a dockside shower until I couldn't stand up anymore. Then I dressed and Dave loaded us into his pickup truck, which was a land-based version of the rest of his fleet, a salt-corroded three-quarter-ton GMC purchased at a municipal auction. Two tones of brown—three including the rust—and one of cream, it had full utility lockers, a gas-powered arc welder, and two feet of trash in the bed, including the ubiquitous oar. There were also an angle-iron materials rack, an engine derrick with winch, a pipe vise on the rear bumper, a trailer hitch, and a revolving orange caution light on top of the cab.

Getting out on Folsom street, I leaned on Dave like a drunk, weak, unthawed, and cursing. Bearing most of my weight, Dave cursed heartily, too. The shredded legs of my jeans dangled below my knees like fetlocks, vividly stained by blood and iodine. My hair was matted and streaked with salt. Direct sunlight was so painful to my eyes that Dave had parked a pair of very dark wraparound sunglasses over them. Pedestrians gave us a wide berth.

Still too numb to do little more than keep melons cool, I had to allow Dave to get the keys out of my front pocket. As he was rooting around, he said, "Any reason a cop should be parked across the street?"

"Probably the vice squad."

"He's making a call."

Dave barely had the door unlocked before a second unmarked car boxed in the pickup and Bowditch boiled out from under the driver's wheel. "Kestrel!"

"Oh no," I said, "*insalata mista.*"

"I hope there ain't no shootin'," Dave said. "I'm plumb out of iodine."

Though he clearly had other things on his mind, Bowditch pulled up short when he got a look at us. "Jesus Christ, what in the fuck's happened to you?" I was touched. He yelled it like he cared, and his face turned nearly as purple as the ribs in an organic cabbage.

187

"A mere caress from only one of the seven seas, with prejudice," Dave said. "Otherwise he'd look like me. Argh hargh hrg."

"Come on in," I said, as Dave carted me through the door.

"Fuckin' cop," Dave muttered, as he dragged me up the stairs.

"Dave," I winced, as he dropped me on the bed, "where's the percentage in insulting the police?"

"If he didn't like bein insulted, he wouldn't be a cop." After he got my boots off, he said, "You got any soup around here?"

"No."

"Got any cash?"

I dug a saturated twenty out of my jeans. Bowditch appeared at the top of the stairs and leaned against the doorpost, clutching a briefcase and huffing like the athlete he wasn't. "Don't they have physical requirements on the police force?" Dave said, wringing water out of the soaked bill.

"That's Lieutenant Inspector Bowditch," I said. "Lieutenant, this is Dave."

Dave showed Bowditch the twenty. "Can I get you a doughnut or something, Officer?"

Bowditch's eyes brightened. "That your truck, out front?"

"Argh. . . ."

"Registration's two years out of date."

"Can't get the sonofabitch to smog," Dave said immediately. "It needs a new carburetor and it can't be a rebuilt, see? You can only get it to smog with a factory original." He held up five fingers. "I'm tryin to do the right thing, Lieutenant, but the factory cocksucker costs twice the rebuild. Five hundred bills, and that's un-fuckin-installed."

Nobody spoke.

"I can install it myself, no problem. But hey," Dave spread his arms, my Social Security's only six thirty-seven a month."

We waited.

"Make it a bagel," Bowditch said.

Dave showed a lot of missing teeth. "For sure, Lieutenant. Ya want cream cheese with that? Lox? A blowjob?"

"Just a large regular coffee," Bowditch said testily.

Dave left. Bowditch said, "Who's the rummy?"

"He pulled me out of the bay this morning. I'm in love with him."

"He smells like a life preserver."

"Tell you what, Lieutenant. Let me catch my wind, here, and that old man and I will hand you a month's work. Until then, just shut up and let me be cold. Okay?"

Bowditch patted the briefcase. "Today it's strictly information." He squinted at my leg. "Is that a bullet hole? Inflicted, perhaps, by discharge of a firearm? Or did the teredo worms get a head start?"

"Your eyes don't deceive you."

Bowditch grunted, but otherwise shut up and took the opportunity to case the apartment—which didn't take long because it was two rooms and he'd gone over them already, the night he'd picked me up for questioning. His curiosity befell the bookcases lining the walls.

"Lot of books."

"What am I supposed to do, disagree?" It was just about then that I realized I was fresh out of patience. A weariness I hadn't experienced since the war was blosso-ming, from which the banter with Bowditch seemed distracting.

Bowditch pulled a book from a shelf and looked at the cover. "You read all these?"

"No," I snapped, "they're just insulation. There's a whore-house bathroom on the other side of that wall, there, see, and if there's one thing I can't stand, it's the sound of gargling at four in the morning. It's worse than television."

He replaced the book on the shelf and opened his briefcase. "Yeah, well, whores brings up the subject of today's sermon."

"Why not live and let live?" I groaned.

"Ever heard of a Queen called Theodora?"

"I kn-know a lot of q-queens."

"This one's dead."

"That h-hardly n-narrows it d-d—" I couldn't finish the sentence. My entire musculature began to convulse.

If Bowditch noticed, he ignored it. "Think sixth century, A.D., Danny. If you know any queens from the sixth century, you know this Theodora broad."

"Lieutenant, my body's on f-fire, my legs are c-cut to rib-bons, there's a b-bullet hole in one of them, and I haven't even told you about the giant d-dildo. But I n-never heard of a q-queen called Theordora."

Bowditch looked at me strangely. "Giant dildo?"

"God d-damn it, I thought p-people didn't st-stutter when they g-got angry."

"No, no, I'm interested. If you'd prefer to discuss current events or even physiology, far be it from me —"

"It's g-got to wait. Wait'll Dave gets b-back."

Bowditch shook his head. "Danny," he persisted, "time is money. One way or another somebody's going to do some talking. Me or you?"

"Okay okay—you. I q-quit."

He produced a book from his briefcase. "Ready for a bedtime story?"

"I'm passing out on my own just fine, thanks."

He opened the book to a place marked by a pink While-You-Were-Out memo slip. "They tell me this book is a great one."

Curiosity got the better of me. "What's the n-name of it?"

"The Decline and Fall of the Roman Empire."

"I'll be d-damned. It is a g-good one. Since when do c-cops read Edward G-Gibbon?"

"Since we switched from doughnuts to bagels."

The street door slammed. Dave made his way up the stairs, and it wasn't until we watched him cross the room that I realized Dave walked with a limp. He deposited my keys and a plastic shopping bag on the countertop. "Them Chinese insisted on throwing in an order of chopsawy. Don't worry, I got won-ton soup, too, hot and sour. And a cup a joe for the Lieutenant, cup a joe for Dave, a hot bagel for the Lieutenant." He paused and said hopefully, "They was out a sesame so I hadda get onion." Bowditch rolled his eyes. "I knew you wouldn't know the difference," Dave continued. "Cream cheese, marmalade, soy sauce. . . ." He lined up packages along the sink. ". . .Chopsticks for the soup, can a sardines for Dave, and," he set a festively labeled brown bottle on the tile with a clank, "one pint a cheap rum." He held up a register receipt. "Nineteen dollars and sixty-four cents."

"I'll write it off somehow," I said.

"I'll leave it right on the—hey, how come you got no magnets on your refrigerator?" He removed the tops from the coffee cups. "Nudge, Lieutenant?" Bowditch nodded. Dave slopped an inch of coffee out of a cup into the sink, topped it off with rum, and handed it to Bowditch. He spilled two inches of coffee into the sink out of his own cup, topped it off, and toasted us: "At least twice a day may the tides of beauty efface the footprints of life off the beach of your mind." He took a long, loud sip. It sounded like eight inches of Velcro separating.

Bowditch sipped the coffee experimentally and made a face. "Christ, that's good." He displayed a pack of Vantages. "Mind if I smoke?"

"I'll join you," said Dave. "Got a spare?"

191

"Hey," I protested, "this is intensive care."

"Vantages ain't smoking," Dave said, accepting a light.

"It's just like quitting," Bowditch agreed, lighting his own.

I punched two pillows against the wall and pulled myself into a half-sitting position. "What about that soup?"

Someone began pounding on the street door. Filter clenched between his teeth and his doctored coffee in one hand, Dave was opening drawers with his other hand, looking for a spoon. "Want to get that, Lieutenant?"

Bowditch shrugged and headed downstairs, chewing a mouthful of bagel.

After watching me try to hold the spoon by myself, Dave said, "I'm gonna have to feed you."

"I'm not hungry," I said disgustedly, dropping the spoon into the bowl.

Dave pulled a chair up to the bed and poised a spoonful of soup in front of my face. "Open wide, goddammit."

"What's going on in here?"

Missy stood at the top of the stairs with one hand on her hip and a quizzical expression on her face. She wore a silk blouse the color of tea roses under a black jacket, a kilt with a big safety pin low down on its seam, black stockings, and black elf boots. She looked like a million dollars, but that was probably an underestimate. Bowditch stood a couple of steps down the staircase, wheezing.

Dave stood up off the chair, the bowl of soup in one hand, a cloth napkin in the other, and a confused look on his face, laughing uncertainly. The spoon clattered to the floor.

"M-Missy, this is D-Dave. And v-vice v-versa."

"Argh. . . ." Dave said uncertainly.

"I'm sure," Missy said. "What's with the sunglasses?" Then she saw my legs. "Daniel, what's happened to you?"

"A little sw-swimming mishap."

192

Glibness did nothing to conceal my chattering teeth. I'd thought Dave's tea had shaped me up, but I seemed to be regressing. Tremors rippled my frame from one end to the other, and my teeth clacked audibly.

Missy dropped whatever pose or pretense of amusement she'd been assuming and pushed Dave out of the way. "You're trembling. Let me —" She removed the sunglasses and laid her hand on my forehead. "My god! You're as cold as Daddy's annulment!"

"H-how c-cold is th-th. . . ?"

"Yeah," Dave wanted to know. "How cold is that?"

She turned on him. "What have you done to Danny? Who are you?"

"Now now, little lady," Dave began.

"What have you done to Danny!" Missy shouted.

"Hey, take it easy," Dave shouted. "I'm the guy who pulled him out of the drink."

I attempted introductions. "Lieuten-tenant B-Bowditch, M-Marissa J-James. I'm g-getting f-fucked up h-here. . . ."

Missy didn't even look at Bowditch. "We've met." She glanced at Dave and wrinkled her nose. "Plainclothes detail?"

Dave choked on his plainclothes coffee.

"Hey," Bowditch said, "don't impugn the luster of the force."

"Danny, what's wrong?" Missy looked from one face to another. "What's wrong with Danny?"

"I fished him out from under Pier 70 this morning," Dave said. "He spent the night there."

Bowditch started visibly.

"All night?" Missy repeated, appalled. "Is that true?"

"W-well, I g-got s-started k-k-k—shit—k-*kind* of l-*late*. . . ."

"Hypothermia," said Dave. "Core temperature's gotta be down below ninety for the symptoms to start. Gets below 78," he sucked a tooth, "it's the Big Enchilada."

"What about that goddamn fire?" Bowditch said.

193

Missy said, "Hypothermia. My God. Haven't you tried to warm him up?"

"Sure, but you gotta take it slow. Sometimes they can't keep nothin down. Tea, soup." Dave lamely showed her the bowl. Missy sniffed it suspiciously. "Can't warm 'em up too fast though, ma'am. You gotta be careful."

Missy applied her palm to my forehead. Her hand felt hot. "He's like ice!"

"Nah," Dave pursed his lips, "the bay's pretty shoal where I found him. He shouldn't be colder'n, oh, sixty, sixty-five degrees.

Missy stood up. "Danny, listen," she said, taking off her jacket. "Do you have a sleeping bag? An eiderdown? A duvet?"

Dave looked puzzled. "What the fuck's a duvet?"

I motioned toward the only closet.

Missy hustled over there and pulled the door open. "The top shelf," she said, standing on tiptoe. "Damn it, hurry up." She turned to Dave. "Help me help Danny." But Dave had the soup in one hand and his coffee in the other. "Lieutenant. Hand me that stuff bag." Bowditch, clearly more interested in what I knew about the fire, reluctantly complied. Missy tucked the stuffbag beneath one arm and pointed. "That quilt as well."

She whisked the sleeping bag out of its nylon bag, unzipped it, and laid it over me. Then she snatched the quilt out of Bowditch's hands and flung it expertly, so that it settled perfectly over the sleeping bag. Then she frowned.

"Y-yes," I said. "Y-you g-gave it t-to me after that m-magic n-night—"

"I don't recall the first thing you're talking about," she primly interrupted. "How flattering you should make up stories after all these years. Does hypothermia include hallucinations?"

"F-Fifteen years."

"Don't try to talk. You're delirious and you might embarrass me." She steadied herself with one hand on the kitchen counter, cocked a knee, and removed one of her elf boots.

"Ahrg hargh hrgh," said Dave, backing around the counter, thoroughly disconcerted.

"Hey." Bowditch looked as if he were going to panic, too. "I gotta talk to this guy."

"When he feels like talking to you, you can talk to him," Missy said, unbuttoning her blouse. "Turn around, you two. Close your eyes."

Bowditch looked like a butterfly about to be flattened between the pages of a book.

"M-Missy," I protested.

"Shut up, Daniel. Conserve your strength."

Dave, for some reason, was blinking uncontrollably.

"Turn around, turn around." Missy tugged the tails of the blouse out of the waist of the kilt.

"Mrs. James," Bowditch tried again. "This is a police matter. I—"

"A police matter? Good. Do as you're told or I'll have Mayor Brown down on you so fast you, your. . . ." She stamped her bare foot impatiently. "Your badge will look like it spent the night on the cable car tracks!"

Bowditch turned pale. He actually reached for the place on his chest where his badge would have been pinned when he walked a beat, twenty-five years before. Without another word he turned his back on us.

"I saw Willie just last night," Missy added. "He was with that model, whatshername." The blouse unbuttoned, she had both hands working on two buttons on the hip of the skirt. "To tell you the truth, the last time I even so much as heard about a Borsalino, let alone saw one, it was on Moose Malloy in *The Big Sleep*."

"'About as inconspicuous as a tarantula on a slice of angel food,'" Dave quoted to the kitchen window.

"That just about sums Willie up," Missy said. "But I must say, that model's legs are longer than a bookie's memory."

Dave half-turned at this and she snapped, "Watch the street. Everybody's eyes closed?" and she stepped out of the skirt.

Missy's still a woman, I thought to myself, as she folded the skirt, placed it on the seat of the chair, and draped the blouse over the back. Then, as gracefully unaffected as if she were thirty and I were twenty-seven and we'd been lovers since college, she slipped under the quilt and began undressing me.

"I-I-I-I. . . ."

"Just another minute or two, gentlemen," she said to the room; and to me, "You're doing very well. Try to husband your strength." As the shredded jeans peeled past my equally shredded shins she said, "Jesus Christ."

"Barnacles," Dave said to the kitchen window, "sharp as grandma's opinions."

Bowditch muttered at the staircase.

My clothes on the floor, Missy put her arms around me. "Daniel!" she shrieked, "you're *freezing!*"

"Not q-quite. . . ."

Missy met my eyes with her own and she bravely engaged as much skin between us as possible. The sleeping bag and the quilt and even my own skin began to capture her warmth. She rubbed the tip of my nose with her own. "Can you feel anything?"

I could feel a great deal, but my tongue refused to form coherent syllables.

She picked up the hem of the sleeping bag and smiled. "Chins up." I raised my head, and she tucked the bedclothes snugly up to my neck.

196

ЄIGDTEEN

"One of you jerks should have thought of this already," Missy said.

"I'd rather d-die," I said.

"Argh. . . ."

"I didn't know people got cold at fires," Bowditch commented, by way of inviting an explanation.

"Stories." Missy snuggled deeper into the bedding. "Just like summer camp."

I stuttered my way though an account of the previous evening: what the three guys looked like, that they drove a HumVee, that it had something to do with Renée, that it had a lot to do with why I'd called Bowditch yesterday, that Dave had seen Renée with her BMW, and Ecstasy and the Car Salesman with their HumVee, all at Pier 70 at one time or another, and that Car Salesman's body might be found in the rubble.

When I'd finished, Missy said, "That's appalling."

Bowditch was thoughtful. "Let's see what Clarence makes out of that mess. Maybe it'll add up."

"To what?"

"There's a lot to catch up on." He flashed his copy of *The Decline and Fall of the Roman Empire.* "You have a copy, too. Ever read it?"

"Have I ever read it?" I asked incredulously. "Nobody's ever read it. Not in its entirety, anyway."

"Au contaire," said Dave.

We all looked at him.

"The which," Bowditch continued, "Sergeant Maysle tells me is too bad."

We all looked at him.

"She's read it?" I asked.

"True," Dave nodded. "It's one of the great books."

We looked back at Dave.

Bowditch thumbed the book's pages. "Sargent Maysle tells us that there are any number of good stories in it. One of them, towards the end, is especially interesting to those of us gathered here today."

"Stories," said Missy, snuggling. I looked at her. *In summer camp,* her eyes said, *we always shared sleeping bags and stories. Jeeze,* mine replied, *I had a deprived youth.*

"Argh hargh hrgh. I'll prepare more coffee for nudging."

"It's in the f-freezer."

Bowditch parked a pair of half-lens reading glasses on the tip of his nose, angled the book toward the light coming from the kitchen window, and found his place. "Okay. The story is called *Portrait of an Empress.* It's about a Roman queen called Theodora, who lived from about 508 until 548, A.D. Let me note that the capital of the Roman Empire was no longer Rome because Constantine had moved it to Byzantium and renamed it Constantinople, now called Istanbul, some two hundred years prior to Theodora's birth. Theodora was married to the Emperor Justinian, not to be confused with Justin, his predecessor. That's enough preliminaries. Let's plunge in." He cleared his throat.

In the exercise of supreme power, the first act of Justinian was to divide it with the woman whom he loved, the famous Theodora, whose strange elevation cannot be applauded as the triumph of female virtue. Under the reign of Anastasius the care of the wild beasts maintained by the green faction at Constantinople was entrusted to Acacius, a native of the isle of Cyprus, who from his employment was surnamed the master of the bears. This honourable office was given after his death to another candidate, notwithstanding the diligence of his widow, who had already provided a husband and a successor. Acacius had left three daughters, Comito, Theodora, and Anastasia, the eldest of whom did not then exceed the age of seven years. On a solemn festival these helpless orphans were sent by their distressed and indignant mother, in the garb of suppliants, into the midst of the theatre; the green faction received them with contempt, the blues with compassion; and this difference, which sunk deep into the mind of Theodora, was felt long afterwards in the administrations of the empire.

"These bears were used in various staged entertainments in the Hippodrome," Bowditch interjected, "the big sports arena of the era. The Blues and the Greens were political factions—subject to the whims of the monarchy, of course."
"Oh, lamented monarchy," Dave remarked.

As they improved in age and beauty, the three sisters were successively devoted to the public and private pleasures of the Byzantine people; and Theodora, after following Comito on the stage in the dress of a slave, with a stool on her head, was at length permitted to exercise her independent talents. She neither danced, nor sang, nor played on the flute; her skill was confined to the pantomime art; she excelled in buffoon characters; and as often as the comedian swelled her cheeks and complained with a ridiculous tone and gesture of the blows that were inflicted, the whole theater of Constantinople resounded with laughter and applause. The beauty of Theodora was the subject of more flattering praise and the source of more exquisite delight. Her features were delicate and regular; her complexion, though somewhat pale, was tinged with a natural colour; every sensation was instantly expressed by

199

the vivacity of her eyes; her easy motions displayed the graces of a small but elegant figure; and either love or adulation might proclaim that painting and poetry were incapable of delineating the matchless excellence of her form. But this form was degraded by the facility with which it was exposed to the public eye and prostituted to licentious desire. Her venal charms were abandoned to a promiscuous crowd of citizens and strangers of every rank and of every profession; the fortunate lover who had been promised a night of enjoyment was often driven from her bed by a stronger or more wealthy favourite; and when she passed through the streets, her presence was avoided by all who wished to escape either the scandal or the temptation. The satirical historian has not blushed to describe the naked scenes which Theodora was not ashamed to exhibit in the theatre. After exhausting the arts of sensual pleasure. . . .

Bowditch squinted. "There's a footnote."

At a memorable supper thirty slaves waited round the table; ten young men feasted with Theodora. Her charity was *universal.*

He peered over the lenses of his glasses. "Italics his."
Dave, distributing brown sugar among two coffee cups, said softly, "Universal means all forty of them?"
Bowditch continued,

. . .she most ungratefully murmured against the parsimony of Nature. . . .

"Another footnote."

She wished for a *fourth* altar on which she might pour libations to the god of love.

200

Bowditch peered over his lenses. "Italics his."

Missy counted fingers. "One, two, three. . . ."

"Kinda puts a new twist on the term *five-way*," Dave commented. "Italics mine. Argh harg hrgh."

. . .but her murmurs, her pleasures, and her arts must be veiled in the obscurity of a learned language.

"*Ohhhhhh,*" sounded three voices, disappointed. But Bowditch, setting Gibbon aside, dug into his briefcase and produced a second book. "Fortunately, the scholarly Sergeant Maysle has provided us with the source of Gibbon's salacious allegations."

"*Ahhhhh,*" three voices sounded, as one, intrigued.

"The 'satirical historian' cited by Gibbon was called Procopius. He was an exact contemporary of Theodora and Justinian, and he left us a book called *The Secret History.*" Bowditch showed us the cover of a battered Penguin Classic, then opened it to a pink While-You-Were-Out slip. "Though Procopius fabulates he can't be discounted entirely, because he was on the scene—sort of. Here's what he has to say about Theodora when she was a little girl of about twelve, and I'm glad my wife's not listening."

For the time being Theodora was still too undeveloped to be capable of sharing a man's bed or having intercourse like a woman; but she acted as a sort of male prostitute to satisfy customers of the lowest type, and slaves at that, who when accompanying their owners to the theatre seized their opportunity to divert themselves in this revolting manner; and for some considerable time she remained in a brothel, given up to this unnatural bodily commerce. But as soon as she was old enough and fully developed, she joined the women on the stage and promptly became a courtesan, of the type our ancestors called 'the dregs of the army'. For she was not a flautist or harpist; she was not even qualified to join the corps of dancers; but she merely sold her attractions to anyone who came along, putting her whole body at his disposal.

Missy whispered, "What's it mean, Danny, to say 'she acted as a male prostitute to satisfy customers'?"
"I-I-I–"
Dave shushed us.

Later she joined the actors in all the business of the theatre and played a regular part in their stage performances, making herself the butt of their ribald buffoonery. She was extremely clever and had a biting wit, and quickly became popular as a result. There was not a particle of modesty in the little hussy, and no one ever saw her taken aback: she complied with the most outrageous demands without the slightest hesitation, and she was the sort of girl who if somebody walloped her or boxed her ears would make a jest of it and roar with laughter; and she would throw off her clothes and exhibit naked to all and sundry those regions, both in front and behind, which the rules of decency require to be kept veiled and hidden from masculine eyes.

"What's it mean, Danny?" Missy persisted.
"W-will you be q-quiet?"

She used to tease her lovers by keeping them waiting, and by constantly playing about with novel methods of intercourse she could always bring the lascivious to her feet; so far from waiting to be invited by anyone she encountered, she herself by cracking dirty jokes and wiggling her hips suggestively would invite all who came her way, especially if they were in their teens. Never was anyone so completely given up to unlimited self-indulgence. Often she would go to a bring-your-own-food dinner-party with ten young men or

202

more, all at the peak of their physical powers and with fornication as their chief object in life, and would lie with all her fellow-diners in turn the whole night long: when she had reduced them all to a state of exhaustion she would go to their menials, as many as thirty on occasion, and copulate with every one of them; but not even so could she satisfy her lust.

"Her charity was *universal*," Dave reminded us.

One night she went into the house of a distinguished citizen during the drinking, and, it is said, before the eyes of all the guests she stood up on the end of the couch near their feet, pulled up her dress in the most disgusting manner as she stood there, and brazenly displayed her lasciviousness. And though she brought three openings into service, she found fault with Nature, grumbling because Nature had not made the openings in her nipples wider than is normal, so that she could devise another variety of intercourse in that region. . . .

"Four," Missy said, fanning herself with one hand, "plus one makes *five.*" She fanned her face. "Isn't it getting *warm* in here?" She fanned mine. "Aren't you warm, Danny?"

"N-no," I said, "I'm c-cold."

"What's it mean, Danny," Missy said, tickling me, "'libations of Venus'? What's it mean? Huh?"

"M-Missy, p-please, I'm ill."

"There's just a little more of Procopius," said Bowditch.

Three disappointed voices sounded as one. *"Awwwwww."*

Often in the theater, too, in full view of all the people she would throw off her clothes and stand naked in their midst, having only a girdle about her private parts and her groins—not, however, because she was ashamed to expose these also to the public, but because no one is allowed to appear there absolutely naked: a girdle round the groins is compulsory. With this minimum covering she would spread herself out and lie face upwards on the floor. Servants on whom this task had been imposed would sprinkle barley grains over her private parts, and geese trained for the purpose used to pick them off one by one with their bills and swallow them. Theodora, so far from blushing when she stood up again, actually seemed proud of this performance. For she was not only shameless herself, but did more than anyone else to encourage such shamelessness.

"Talk about gettin goosed," Dave remarked. "Argh hargh hrgh."

"There will never be a better advertisement for studying the classics," Bowditch observed, closing Procopius. "There's more along those lines, but everybody gets the idea."

"We haven't learned much since," said Missy.

"Whatcha doin' later, honey?" Dave leered.

Not missing a beat Missy replied, "I'm driving over to City Lights to buy a copy of Procopius."

Bowditch showed the cover of his book. "Be sure you get the Williamson translation. The others are more prudish."

Dave considered this. "Kinda makes you wish you'd paid a little closer attention in Latin One, huh?"

"Actually," Bowditch said, lighting a cigarette, "Procopius wrote in Greek."

"Oh," Dave blustered, "Greek ain't no hill for a highstepper."

Bowditch exhaled a plume of smoke. "Now that I have your undivided attention," he said, and reopened *The Decline and Fall of the Roman Empire.*

After reigning for some time the delight and contempt of the capital, she condescended to accompany Ecebolus, a native of Tyre, who had obtained the government of the African Pentapolis. But this union was frail and transient; Ecebolus soon rejected an expensive or faithless concubine; she was reduced at Alexandria to extreme distress; and in her laborious return to Constantinople every city of the East admired and enjoyed the fair Cyprian, whose merit appeared to justify her descent from the peculiar island of Venus. The vague commerce of Theodora, and the most detestable precautions, preserved her from the danger which she feared; yet once, and once only, she became a mother. The infant was saved and educated in Arabia by his father, who imparted to him on his death-bed that he was the son of an empress. Filled with ambitious hopes, the unsuspecting youth immediately hastened to the palace of Constantinople and was admitted to the presence of his mother. As he was never more seen, even after the decease of Theodora, she deserves the foul imputation of extinguishing with his life a secret so offensive to her imperial virtue.

Pouring coffee, Dave whistled thoughtfully. "Her own kid." "That's important," Bowditch nodded. "We'll pursue Theodora a little further, for background. Then we'll take up the story of her son."

In the most abject state of her fortune and reputation, some vision, either of sleep or fancy, had whispered to Theodora the pleasing assurance that she was destined to become the spouse of a potent monarch. Conscious of her approaching greatness, she returned from Paphlagonia to Constantinople; assumed, like a skillful actress, a more decent character; relieved her poverty by the laudable industry of spinning wool; and affected a life of chastity and solitude in a small house, which she afterwards changed into a magnificent temple. Her beauty, assisted by art or accident, soon attracted, captivated, and fixed the patrician Justinian, who already reigned with absolute sway under the name of his uncle. Perhaps she contrived to enhance the value of a gift which she had so often lavished on the meanest of mankind; perhaps she inflamed, at first by modest delays and at last by sensual allurements, the desires of a lover who, from nature or devotion, was addicted to long vigils and abstemious diet. When his first transports had subsided she still maintained the same ascendant over his mind by the more solid merit of temper and understanding.

"By any other name," said Missy, "it's all the bitch's fault. Her nasty wiles ensnared the ascetic, hapless potentate in her foetid, adhesive web. . . ."

"Gibbon was English," Bowditch pointed out. "And eighteenth century English at that."

"Theodora should have gotten a feminist to write her story," Missy groused.

"Gibbons are where you find them," Bowditch replied officiously. "Hear him out."

"Who," I asked, "c-coaches you l-lately?"

"Sergeant Maysle, definitely. She majored in forensic anthropology with minors in classics and philology—remember?'"

"How c-could I forget?"

"Why isn't this Maysle over here reading Gibbon to us?" Dave asked. "No way she ain't better looking than you are."

"Oh," came the mild response, "Sergeant Maysle is temporarily banished to Park Station for accusing our belovéd chief of sexual harassment. Her duty's not, shall we say, as flexible as it used to be. Otherwise, I assure you, wild horses couldn't have kept her off this case. And I could use her."

"How'd she entice him?" Missy asked dryly.

"I'm sure I don't know. But it seems he gave her a pair of earrings."

"So?"

"So can we get back to the story?" Bowditch suggested testily.

"Yes, do." As Missy sat up to accept the mug of soup and a spoon from Dave, the bedclothes fell from her shoulders. An angel of silence passed over the room.

Dave abruptly handed off the soup and backed away until he could reach the pint of rum on the kitchen counter.

"It's not like I'm a snake or something," Missy said. She looked at me with big innocent eyes. "Is it?"

"S-s-s-s-certainly not."

Bowditch abruptly resumed reading.

Those who believe the female mind is totally depraved by the loss of chastity —

"Oh!" Missy expostulated in exasperation. "In his dreams!"

"Hush, woman," said Dave, hastily adding, "Argh hargh hrgh," as Missy shot him a look.

"Hear the man out," Bowditch insisted.

. . .will eagerly listen to all the invectives of private envy or popular resentment which have dissembled the virtues of Theodora, exaggerated her vices, and condemned with rigour the venal or voluntary sins of the youthful harlot. . . .

But the reproach of cruelty, so repugnant even to her softer vices, has left an indelible stain on the memory of Theodora. Her numerous spies observed and zealously reported every action, or word, or look injurious to their royal mistress. Whomever they accused were cast into her peculiar prisons, inaccessible to the inquiries of justice; and it was rumoured that the torture of the rack or scourge had been inflicted in the presence of a female tyrant insensible to the voice of prayer or of pity. Some of these unhappy victims perished in deep unwholesome dungeons; while others were permitted, after the loss of their limbs, their reason, or their fortune, to appear in the world the living monuments of her vengeance, which was commonly extended to the children of those whom she had suspected or injured. The senator or bishop whose death or exile Theodora had pronounced was delivered to a trusty messenger, and his diligence was quickened by a menace from her own mouth. "If you fail in the execution of my commands, I swear by him who liveth forever that your skin shall be flayed from your body."

"That's a quote," Bowditch noted.

Missy asked, "Was the him who liveth forever the same god Christians call God? Or was it some other deity?"

"Good question," said Bowditch. "If Sergeant Maysle were here, she could answer it for you, although, on the whole, it's an entirely separate lecture." He held up the thick paperback. "I ain't exactly read the whole thing. But this section is called *The Eastern Empire in the Sixth Century*. By then the Romans had boiled God down to a single deity, with Jesus as His son. But there was a lot of argument about what the nature of Jesus was. Was he entirely man? Was he God incarnate? Or was he half man and half God? The Sergeant says it was neck and neck there for a while, heresy versus heresy, but what it ultimately had more to do with was politics rather than theology."

"Nahhh," said Dave. "What a cynical thing to say."

"Or maybe," Missy said thoughtfully, "Theodora being smart, it was the threatened messenger who believed in one god."

We all looked at her.

"Actually," Dave nodded, "Constantine had Christianized the empire about 200 years earlier." Now we all looked at him. "But so what?" he went on. "Fuck up, get skinned. What's God got to do with it?"

"Since when do you know so much?" Bowditch asked unpleasantly.

"I was a merchant seaman for fourteen years, Lieutenant. Before the introduction of the VCR and satellite television, we were the best-read minority on the planet. I probably read two hundred books a year while I was at sea. Ask me anything about Harold Robbins."

Without hesitation Bowditch asked, "Who killed Renée Knowles?"

Without hesitation Dave answered, "Who's Renée Knowles?"

"The brunette on Pier 70," I said.

Now it was Dave's turn to look around, from me to Missy to Bowditch and back to me. "Somebody killed her?"

"Can we get back to the darn story?" Missy interrupted. "It's sexist, it's beautifully written, and I want to know what happened."

"I should point out that I'm skipping bits," said Bowditch. "The odd catalogue of good works and whatnot."

"That's okay," said Missy, "stick to the evil stuff."

The prudence of Theodora is celebrated by Justinian himself; and his laws are attributed to the sage counsels of his most reverend wife, whom he had received as the gift of the Deity. Her courage was displayed amidst the tumult of the people and the terrors of the court.

"Oh, well," said Missy.

"Particularly during the Nika Riots," Dave interjected, "which were comparable to the unrest following the assassination of Caligula. For five hundred years—"

"But you digress," Bowditch interrupted.

"Nobody's read *I, Claudius?*"

Nobody spoke.

"Seen it on television?" Dave asked.

Missy raised her hand.

"It's lonely, being well-read," Dave said sullenly.

Missy asked, "Am I wrong, or is this a love story?"

"Absolutely," Bowditch confirmed.

209

Her chastity, from the moment of her union with Justinian, is founded on the silence of her implacable enemies; and although the daughter of Acacius might be satiated with love, yet some applause is due to the firmness of a mind which could sacrifice pleasure and habit to the stronger sense either of duty or interest. The wishes and prayers of Theodora could never obtain the blessing of a lawful son, and she buried an infant daughter, the sole offspring of her marriage. Notwithstanding this disappointment, her domain was permanent and absolute; she preserved, by art or merit, the affections of Justinian; and their seeming dissensions were always fatal to the courtiers who believed them to be sincere. . . .

Perhaps her health had been impaired by the licentiousness of her youth; but it was always delicate, and she was directed by her physicians to use the Pythian warm-baths. In this journey the empress was followed by the Praetorian praefect, the great treasurer, several counts and patricians, and a splendid train of four thousand attendants. The highways were repaired at her approach; a palace was erected for her reception; and as she passed through Bithynia she distributed liberal alms to the churches, the monasteries, and the hospitals, that they might implore Heaven for the restoration of her health. At length, in the twenty-fourth year of her reign, she was consumed by a cancer; and the irreparable loss was deplored by her husband, who, in the room of a theatrical prostitute, might have selected the purest and most noble virgin of the East.

Bowditch closed the book and peeled his reading glasses from his face. "She was about forty years old when she died."

Missy, posing a spoonful of soup an inch from my mouth, looked at him. "Is that the end of the story?"

Dave and I, too, looked expectantly towards him.

"Not quite," Bowditch said. "Remember the son?"

"Theodora's son?" Missy said.

"The son who was never seen again," Dave said, "even after her death?"

Bowditch pointed at the copy of Gibbon with his spectacles. "The deal is, the son survived."

210

NINETEEN

"Theodora's illegitimate son," Missy repeated, "survived?"
Bowditch nodded. "In a manner of speaking."

"But Gibbon wrote that the son presented himself at the palace and was never seen again. Gibbon must have gotten it from Procopius, who was there. You said he was there."

Bowditch nodded. "Gibbon did get it from Procopius." He produced an audio cassette from the briefcase and squinted at its labels. "Sergeant Maysle's lecture thesis for her master's degree in philology is called *The Syracuse Codex*. She and I have discussed it many times over the past year or so. But," he indicated a boom box tucked into a bookshelf, "I see you have a tape machine. Too bad we can't view the slides, too."

"But," Missy interrupted, "to heck with technology. You tell it to us!"

"Really?" said Bowditch, looking ingenuous.

"You're so good at it."

"Shucks," said Bowditch.

"Why, sure, give it a try," Dave chimed in. "You got us all jacked up on it."

"Well, I suppose I. . . ."

"Come on, Lieutenant."

"Bludgeon us with your erudition, argh hargh hrgh."

"You must have some good reason for boning up on this material. Why not practice it on us?"

Bowditch considered the cassette. "All right. When I lose

211

my bearings or my voice, whichever goes first, we'll go to the tape." He set the cassette atop the boom box and rooted a student's composition book out of the briefcase. "I've got notes, too."

I wanted to ask what this had to do with hypothermia or Renée Knowles, but before I could express myself Missy nudged my shoulder. "Let's hear the story. You're not going anywhere."

Bowditch said, "If anything in this account rings a bell with anybody, speak up. By the time it's over, you'll understand why I'm telling you all this."

Dave said, "Does that include me?"

Bowditch opened the notebook and flattened it onto the kitchen counter. "If you can place the Knowles woman on Pier 70–yes, it includes you. Definitely."

Dave took a stool on the outside of the counter, bumming another cigarette as he passed Bowditch. He placed a saucer on the counter halfway between himself and Bowditch, for an ashtray, and his coffee within easy reach. He hitched his heels on a rung of the stool and leaned both elbows on the counter, the knuckles of one hand curled within those of the other, in which the cigarette dangled loosely. "The most natural position in the world," he said contentedly.

Bowditch leafed back and forth in his notebook, smoothed a page with the side of his hand, and began.

"There's a manuscript. First discovered in the library of a looted chateau at the height of the Terror in France, in 1794, it disappeared again, in 1830, when it was stolen from a display case in the Bibliothèque Nationale, in Paris, along with a trove of Byzantine antiquities–coins, sculpture, pottery, belt buckles, weapons and so forth. Only a few of the lesser items were ever recovered.

"By far the most important item lost to the robbery, the

212

manuscript is called *The Syracuse Codex*. It contains the story of Empress Theodora's son, sometimes called John, whose real name was Theodosus."

"All *right*," exclaimed Missy.

"In her lecture, Sergeant Maysle initially points out what she terms an historical anomaly. John is mentioned by Procopius in his *Anecdota,* called by us *The Secret History;* and Procopius is the authority on Theodora cited by everyone, including Gibbon. There are other authorities, of course; but only Procopius mentions John. Little else is known. Even so, based on a single paragraph in Procopius, one author has gone so far as to create an entire novel about this John. We'll leave this question of names aside, except to note that Sergeant Maysle deals with the Procopian 'John' in an appendix, in which she demonstrates fairly conclusively that, during the moment in which 'John' is supposed to have disappeared from Constantinople—and it was a specific moment—Procopius was in Italy with the General Belisarius, for whom he worked as a secretary. Procopius, therefore, had no direct experience of the story.

"For scholarship's sake, however, Sergeant Maysle quotes the Procopian paragraph in full. As do I." Bowditch reopened his copy of *The Secret History* to yet another pink While-You-Were-Out slip.

Now it happened that while Theodora was still on stage she became pregnant by one of her lovers, and being unusually slow to recognize her unfortunate condition she tried by all her usual means to procure an abortion; but try as she might she could not get rid of the untimely infant, since by now it was not far from acquiring perfect human shape. So as she was achieving nothing, she was compelled to abandon her efforts and give birth to the child. When the baby's father saw that she was upset and annoyed because now that she was a mother she would no longer be able to employ her body as before, he rightly suspected that she would resort to infanticide; so he took up the child in acknowledgement that it was his and named it John, since it was a boy. Then he went off to Arabia for which he was bound. When he himself was on the point of death and John was now in his early teens, the boy learnt from his father's lips the whole story about his mother; and when his father departed this life, performed all the customary rites over him. A little while later he came to Byzantium, and made his arrival known to those who at all times had access to his mother. They, never imagining that she would feel any differently from the generality of mankind, reported to the mother that her son John had arrived. Fearing that the story would come to the ears of her husband, Theodora gave instructions that the boy was to come into her presence. When he appeared, she took one look at him and put him into the hands of one of her personal attendants whom she regularly entrusted with such commissions. By what means the poor lad was removed from the world of the living I am unable to say, but no one to this day has ever set eyes on him, even since the decease of the Empress.

"That's Gibbon, almost word for word," Missy observed.

"True," Bowditch continued, closing *The Secret History*. "And until the turn of the nineteenth century, that was all the world knew about her son, John. Then *The Syracuse Codex* turned up, and specific details of the story were revealed."

"What about that chateau library?" Dave asked.

Bowditch held up a forestalling hand. "It's all to do with a corrupt bookseller and his arrangement with a certain band of castle-looting *sans-culottes*." He indicated the tape. "You can read the rest of the story in Sargent Maysle's book."

"What?"

"We don't have time for it."

"But you—"

But Bowditch would not be distracted from the thread of

214

his story. "Archaeologically speaking," he resumed firmly, "the codex looked pretty genuine, when last it was seen. If we could get our hands on the original today, we could apply a great deal of technology and scholarship to accurately dating it, much more than could possibly have been brought to bear by 1830."

Bowditch ran a finger down his page of notes. "A second appendix to Sergeant Maysle's thesis will zero in on dating the codex in terms of its Greek. It's in a cursive script, she says, with accents, breathings, capital letters and separate words, which represent well-defined historical innovations in written language. Before them, words were run together with no accents or diacritical marks, entirely in capital letters, too. At one point the lines went across the page, left to right, then just dropped down and went back the other way, right to left."

"*Boustrophedon*," Dave interjected. The three of us looked at him. He described flat sinuosities in the air with his cigarette. "As the ox plows, argh hargh hrg. I rarely find an opportunity to use that word," he added modestly. "I tried it out in West Marine once, but–" he shrugged, "–they didn't have any."

"Yes, *The Syracuse Codex* has no boustrophedon," Bowditch continued, stumbling over the pronunciation. "But it's not in what they call *minuscule*, either, a script which came into general use about three hundred years after the presumed date of the Syracuse Codex. Also, it's written on sheets of parchment instead of scrolls of papyrus or vellum. This counted heavily toward its authentication. The historical transition from scrolled vellum to *quires* of paper, actual leaves cut to uniform size, is distinct. A *codex* is a bound set of these quires. The Syracuse Codex, in other words, is a book. Not that anybody alive has ever admitted to seeing the thing, not publicly anyway. Sergeant Maysle made her translation from a transcription of the Greek produced by the Biblioteque Nationale."

"This cop translated the codex from Greek?" Dave asked, astonished.

"Sister's doing it for herself," Missy pointed out.

"Okay. The boy. . . . Well, Theodosus wasn't a boy; he was a young man. Procopius says he was in his early teens when he turned up at the palace, but the codex puts him at seventeen. He was named Theodosus by his father, called Manar, who doted on the boy's mother despite her fierce rejection of them both. John the Baptist was a big star in Constantinople at the time, and Manar had given the child this placatory name only long enough to get him away from his mother in one piece. Manar, in fact, was not a Christian at all.

"Like his parents, Theodosus was 'well-favored'—good look-ing, resourceful, intelligent, and, not surprisingly, ambitious. His father, as Gibbon hinted, had been well off. He was a Damascene merchant. This is why, when the boy showed up in Constantinople to claim the attentions of his mother, he was hardly without resources, having both money and a personal servant. This is as much as to say that nobody in the drama was either completely helpless or completely naive. Theodora's reputation was known throughout the Orient, well beyond the borders of her own empire. She was feared at least as much as she was admired, and only Justinian trusted her.

"The servant's name was Ali. He it was who saved Theodosus' life, only to watch as the boy—well, we'll get to that. And years later it was Ali, not without resources himself but dying by then, who dictated his version of the story of Theodosus to a Greek scribe in the city of Syracuse on the island of Sicily. It should be mentioned that for a very long time almost every citizen of the Roman Empire communi-

216

cated in Greek. Latin was the language of the law, of the courts, and of the western or Roman partition of the Christian church. We might also note that, even though the Empire was still called Roman, its capital and the seat of government had been in Byzantium since Constantine moved it there and renamed it for himself in 330 A.D. Two hundred years later what we now call Italy was in constantly changing hands, mainly those of the Ostrogoths, and this flux persisted for the entire thirty-eight years of Justinian's reign. The city of Rome was sacked three times while he was emperor, once by his own army, and the guy we now know as the Pope was a relatively minor character who spent most of his career besieged in Ravenna.

"Thus the text of Ali's story came down to us in Greek instead of Latin or Arabic or, I don't know, Coptic? This in turn is one of the many reasons the Codex stayed hidden from Gibbon, who, while as informed an historian as the eighteenth century could hope to produce, had to make do with sources which, though vast and varied, could not be entirely comprehensive, and did in fact include a great deal of conjecture and misinformation."

"Especially," Dave interrupted, "the latter half of the original *Rise and Fall*—which includes the Theodora story, does it not? Much of it was discounted by later scholarship, particularly those chapters dealing with so-called Araby."

We all looked at Dave.

"When I signed onto *Tantric Bypass* out of New Orleans," he explained, "with a load of shoe polish and macaroons bound for the Mekong Delta, she had 2500 LPs and 5000 books aboard. The skipper always said to hell with going down with his ship; he was going down with his library—as, sad to say, came to pass."

After a brief, stunned silence, Missy said, as if miffed, "That's fine for you, but nobody else has time to read ancient history."

"Certainly not the people so busily living it," I sniped.

"Oh!" she squealed, *"low blow."*

"Not to mention," Dave added, "that one of the driving wheels of Gibbon's historicity was the ascendancy of Christianity; which focus, by its very nature, tended to exclude developments in Arabia, particularly after the rise of Islam."

Silence.

"Islam dates, as I recall, to Medina, after Muhammad fled Mecca in, oh, about 622."

Nobody spoke.

"A mere seventy-five years," Dave added helpfully, "after Theodora cashed in her chips."

Silence.

"Ya think I'm just a rummy, doncha."

"No," said Bowditch, "I think you're a drunk. How old are you?"

"Sixty-three."

Bowditch looked shocked. "You're two years older than I am."

Dave squinted. "You should check yourself in the mirror some time, Lieutenant. That bluish tint to your lips indicates a shortage of oxygen in your blood."

Bowditch touched one hand to his mouth.

"Antioxidants might help," Dave added solicitously. "Try doubling up on the olives in your martinis. Olives are loaded with Vitamin E, argh hargh hrg."

"I th-thought I was the one with the b-blue lips," I said.

"There's a catalogue of Gibbon's library," Dave continued. "Did you know that, Lieutenant?"

"As a matter of fact," nodded Bowditch, "Sergeant Maysle conducted a search of its index in order to check some stuff for this story I'm *trying* to tell you."

"And?" Missy asked.

"Nothing," Bowditch said. "Obviously, if Gibbon had

known of Theodosus or Ali or the Syracuse Codex, he'd have cited them."

"Now," Missy said thoughtfully, "if I may extrapolate the thread here. . . . Has this Syracuse Codex turned up again?"

"Aha," said Bowditch.

"Are you going to tell us what happened?"

"All in good time." He turned a page in the notebook. "The kid had a lot of trouble getting in to see Theodora, on account of her fanatic retinue. As could be expected, all kinds of rivalries and cliques and schemers existed among these people, and they amounted to a veritable throng. Finally, however, Ali connected with a distant cousin, who was a lady-in-waiting to Theodora.

"Intrigue followed intrigue. Just to get to first base, for example, Ali had to sleep with the retainer, his own cousin. He wasn't particularly averse to this, he recorded, because she was very attractive. On the other hand, neither he nor Theodosus could be sure of what they were getting into. All they knew for certain was that Theodora was Theodosus' mother, and that Theodosus could prove it."

"Prove it?" Missy asked, startled. "How?"

"His father had bequeathed him a piece of jewelry, a ring. That ring was—and remains—the source of a lot of trouble. The Codex suggests but does not confirm that Theodora herself possessed such a ring, and there's an interestingly twisted apocryphal story, from another source, that she used it to reveal herself to Justinian, who then married her because of it. Although this account obliquely dovetails with what we find in the codex, it seems to stem from the same confusion as that of Theodosus' being named John. Not that there weren't a bunch of guys named John running around at that time—there were lots of them. Like their namesake the Baptist, these Johns most often bore a qualifier. John the Scissors, for example, was a tax collector, who got his name from his habit of trimming the edges off such coins as passed through his hands. There were John of Capodocia and John the Hunchback, too—all of whom, by the way, figure in the story of Theodora. But I digress.

"In his codex Ali mentions not one and not two but *three* rings, and says that Manar on his deathbed bequeathed one of them to Theodosus, along with the bombshell that the Empress of the Roman Empire, the infamous Theodora, was the boy's mother.

"Ali describes this ring in great detail as consisting of a small but spectacular amethyst of exceptionally deep reddish purple, "wine-dark," as the Greek scribe inserted, obviously preferring the Homeric epithet to whatever term Ali used. The stone was modest in size, but the cut was unusual, what jewelers now call *cabochon*, which means the stone is not faceted but rounded or dome-like. Its setting was gold, modest too, but exquisitely wrought and at great cost by the hand of a Dravidian-speaking craftsman who worked for one of Manar's trading partners in southern India."

"How," interrupted Missy, "could Manar be sure that Theodora would recognize this ring after so much time had passed?"

"A good question, for which there's an even better answer."

"Which was?"

"Manar knew that Theodora possessed, or had once possessed, an exact duplicate."

"How did he know that?" Dave asked.

"Because he gave it to her," Missy and I guessed simultaneously.

"Exactly," said Bowditch. "He had the two rings made at the same time. Ironically, Theodora's copy was the price of their son's life in the first place. Manar had the rings made while she was pregnant, but showed her only one of them. When she'd brought the child to term, they traded."

"A ring for a child. There must be a name for that kind of bargain," said Missy.

"Yuppie adoption?" I suggested.

"Did Theodora know about the second ring?"

"Very sharp of you to ask, Miss James, and the answer seems to have been no," Bowditch confirmed. "Not, that is, until Theodosus turned up and showed it to her."

"Seventeen years later."

"Correct."

"This guy Manar sounds pretty sharp himself," Missy said.

Dave nodded. "He engineered and delivered a whammy seventeen years into the future."

"Well," said Bowditch, "as Sergeant Maysle has pointed out, Manar was one of the very few people we know of, man or woman, to have put one over on Theodora. She was widely and still is regarded as one of the most cunning and Machiavellian personages in all of Western history."

"That didn't stop Manar from making the mistake of revealing to Theodosus his mother's identity," Dave pointed out.

"True," Bowditch nodded. "Still, he must have been a pretty interesting guy. Unfortunately, like a lot of people in this tale, Manar remains lost to history, a tantalizing unknown. But bribing Theodora to go full term with a pregnancy couldn't have been that difficult. She was a circus girl. All she likely required was a roof over her head, two or three meals a day, maybe an allowance. A very valuable piece of jewelry would have been a sweetener for her, and insurance for Manar. Perhaps, as well, we can assume that Manar assured Theodora that the child would never be a burden."

"So there are—or were—two amethyst rings," Missy concluded. "But you mentioned three."

"Hang on." Bowditch sipped his coffee, turned another page in his notebook, and read, "'The Audience with Theodora'."

221

TWENTY

A li didn't go. Theodosus forbade him to attend in order to forestall any treachery from Theodora. They were sure that any liaison could not proceed undetected, not to mention unsanctioned, in Theodora's court. Both realized that, in allowing Ali to sleep with his cousin, the Empress was merely indulging her retainer. Any heir-to-the-throne business, they were certain, would be another matter altogether.

"Sure enough, after a couple of weeks of dalliance, Ali sensed a change in his cousin's demeanor toward him, which nominally proceeded, he records, from a conflict between his sense of propriety and the lady's lack of delicacy."

"In bed, he means—meant?" Missy asked. "As regards sexual requests?"

"Almost certainly."

"No details?"

"No details."

"Awwwwww." Three disappointed voices sounded as one.

"Ali was a converted Christian and he misbehaved with his cousin only insofar as he understood it as in his line of duty. Theodosus, Ali says, was informed of the liaison every step of the way—as was Theodora, no doubt. The cousin's flagging interest signaled the initiation of machinations that would culminate in the boy's meeting his mother at last. So it's conceivable that Ali's prudery was more a matter of intrigue rather than principle."

"Argh hargh hrgh."

"I love it!" Missy said.

"J-Jesus. Is n-nothing simple in this story?"

"More!" Missy demanded.

"Theodosus got his audience with the empress. Insuring that he had a chance of getting out of it alive, however, was tricky. Theodora was surrounded by hundreds of fanatic loyalists. Ali was particularly wary of a cadre of," Bowditch referred to his notebook, "one hundred and twelve dyke assassins."

"That's in the Greek?" Missy asked.

Bowditch shrugged. "The purpose of translation is to unlock the secrets of a culture sequestered by its language, in order to divulge them to another culture *via* its own language." He fastidiously pinched an imaginary secret up off one page of the notebook and transferred it to the facing one.

We stared at him. "Are you sure you're a cop?" Missy said finally, squinting as if at a bright light.

"Look at his shoes," Dave said. "Of course he's a cop."

"The female guards were culled from the ranks of reformed prostitutes living in a Theodora-sponsored cloister across the Golden Horn, and were fanatically devoted to their liberator."

"So how exactly did two yahoos from Alexandria get around a hundred and twelve so-called dyke assassins?"

"Theodora waved a hand," said Bowditch. "But, and this is important, when Theodosus went to the palace, he went alone. In the meantime he had ordered Ali to disappear and to take the amethyst ring with him."

"Ahhhh so," said Dave.

"Good m-move."

"But without the ring, how could Theodora recognize Theodosus as the real McCoy?" Missy asked. Then she looked at me and we both said: "The third ring!"

Bowditch nodded. "Theodosus was the spitting image of

his father, as like Manar as 'two draughts of wine drawn from the same jar,' as Ali's scribe so helpfully put it. Theodosus must have looked very much as his father had about the time the boy was conceived, seventeen years before. Theodora could not—would not—have missed the likeness."

"What about the third ring?" Missy persisted.

"That's the chip off the old block. For, you see, when Theodosus passed through the big bronze gate to the palace, he carried a copy of the amethyst ring."

Dave whistled appreciatively.

"A duplicate of the duplicate!" exclaimed Missy.

"It's p-positively B-Byzantine."

Bowditch held up two fingers. "An exact duplicate, save two key details. The shape of the stone and the working of the setting were reproduced exactly. That was tricky, concerning which there's a whole back-story in Ali's dictation, telling how he and Theodosus went about finding the guy capable both of copying the ring and of keeping his mouth shut."

"How did they do it?"

"They journeyed to Madras and found Manar's old partner, who also had been Manar's best friend. I forgot to write down the son-of-a-bitch's name." Bowditch made a note. "Anyway, this guy knew the whole story. It further developed that it was he who first turned up Theodora, when she was still a hooker working the Hippodrome. Commerce-wise they simply hadn't liked one another. After a while he found someone else and handed off Theodora to Manar, who made the mistake of falling in love with her."

"This is better than *A Thousand and One Nights*," Missy marveled. She looked at me significantly. "And much better than Proust."

"I b-beg your p-pardon."

Bowditch nodded. "If you like stories, this one's got it all. The Indian merchant, who by then was an old man, had en-

224

joyed life in Alexandria. It was through his family that Manar had been able to open up trade connections to India, enriching both of them. But the minute the partner began to hear rumours about Justinian and Theodora, which spread throughout the empire so quickly as to belie the period's lack of telegraphy, not to mention email, he found that life 10,000 miles from home was suddenly not so interesting as it once had been. He wound up his affairs, bid Manar adieu, and headed back to India in the certainty that, sooner or later, the move would prove good for his health."

"A prudent man," Dave observed.

Bowditch agreed. "Manar's old partner wisely tried to dissuade Theodosus from making the attempt on his legacy. He agonized aloud, wondering why in the hell Manar had even told Theodosus who his mother was. He called in an astrologer who, Ali testifies, having cast the boy's horoscope, refused to tell him its predictions and departed in great haste. The old man was despondent. He even offered to take Theodosus into his business. The young man politely but firmly declined. Theodosus was not to be swayed from the path to his destiny, as Ali put it in the codex. He wouldn't listen. He couldn't listen. His plans were laid, and mere intimations of mortality weren't going to stop him. The former partner finally agreed, despite his reservations, to have the ring duplicated. Only then did Theodosus tell Ali that what they were really going to attempt was an ambitious plan to get a piece of Theodora's action. Theodosus didn't see how she could bring herself to deny her own son."

"Silly boy," Missy observed. "All he really wanted was to meet his real mother."

"Maybe so. But just because he was ambitious didn't mean he was foolhardy. He designed in a couple of safety valves. The near-duplicate of his ring was an important step. Ali wasn't a bad ally, either."

"'Near-duplicate', you say?" Missy stretched out her left hand, palm down, and considered her arched fingers. She still wore three of her wedding rings, plus a couple of others. "What was 'near' about the near-duplicate?"

"Theodosus had his father's amethyst ring copied, all right. He had the goldsmith pay particular attention to details in the setting and the rounding of the stone. But the setting wasn't gold; it was brass. And the stone wasn't amethyst; it was garnet. This was deliberate. The result was very accurate but relatively worthless. The colors and craftsmanship matched so precisely as to be unmistakable to anyone who had closely observed either of the originals. Yet it was worth nowhere near as much—" Bowditch's voice disintegrated into a fit of coughing.

"Damn," said Dave, taking a sip from his pint, nearly empty now. "This story reminds me of that time a hurricane blew me and Cap'n Josh all the way to Cuba, in nineteen hundred and sev–."

"Quiet," Bowditch said. "This is police business."

"It was then, too," Dave said, "argh. . . ."

"David," Missy said impatiently, "shut up. Can't you see that Theodosus and Ali are walking into the jaws of death?"

"Havana's nicer than that," Dave admitted.

"Death was in the cards." Bowditch confirmed. "There are day-books and other material from Justinian's court records that hint at the arrival of Theodosus. While the lady-in-waiting was having her fun and stalling the meeting, the Empress formulated plans of her own. Theodora's object was very simple. A son by any man other than the emperor could do nothing but screw things up for her. She was particularly worried about Justinian's reaction. Though he'd wanted a son of course—as in, what monarch doesn't?—Theodora had been unable to provide him with one. Devoted to her as he was, Justinian had resigned himself to having no progeny.

226

Theodosus would only rock the boat. In addition, Justinian and Theodora were extremely close. They discussed every-thing–or almost everything. Everything accrued to them—both were extremely avaricious. They were devious and they were cold. Letting a son by another man share the power, the riches, the pomp, the delicate equilibrium–it was out of the question.

"The name John, by the way, was adapted by Theodosus as a pseudonym most likely to be recognized by his mother, the name she would remember him by. In the end it confused Procopius, who, as I said, was at the time in Italy with his boss, the General Belisarius, and the Roman army. John was the name he later heard, and John it became in *The Secret History.* Which itself, by the way, remained undiscovered–in the west at least–until thirteen hundred years after it was written.

"Theodora recognized her son immediately, of course; and but for the boy's conniving prudence she would have had him killed immediately. It was the amethyst ring, beyond his mother's grasp, that saved him. Had he not deliberately gone to lunch without that absolute proof of her past and his paternity, presenting instead the false ring as proof of the genuine ring's existence, Theodora would have had him exterminated on the spot. Her snare was set. A surviving day-book of Justinian's court doesn't say why, but it notes that the bronze doors, usually left open, were closed behind a certain visitor. In anticipation of his arrival, two of the palace lions had been starved for three days.

"Aside from its intrinsic threat, however, the genuine ring was exceedingly valuable, and Theodora never passed up an opportunity to accrue riches. She wanted that ring. Theodosus was counting on this. A third detail prolonged the boy's survival as well: the empress knew of the existence of Ali. Ali, the Empress recognized, was a loose end. Since the city

227

was rife with her spies and she'd heard nothing about him, she proceeded with caution. To pounce on Theodosus and, subsequently, by torture and dragnet attempt to bring the unwilling servant to light, might give Ali time to escape. Therefore, exuding all her considerable charm, along with a good meal and some dancing girls, she casually as if spontaneously struck a deal with Theodosus.

"While the proof of his paternity looked good, she told him, without examining the amethyst ring and comparing it to its mate, she was hesitant to bring the boy's case before the Emperor. It took a minute for this to sink in. Its mate? Theodosus asked. Why, yes, his mother replied, the mate survives. It's long been the sole and secret emblem of my maternity. I couldn't bear to part with it. She went on to plainly state that if Theodosus were to prove his case by the formality of merely presenting the original ring to be indisputably matched with its mate, then she would welcome her son to her bosom. Immediately she would present him to the emperor Justinian as if he were their own son. It was well-known that she exerted a powerful sway over her husband. The temptation for Theodosus was great, as it was meant to be.

"Yes, the ring's mate. Theodora flatly declared that after seventeen years she was still in possession of her copy of the ring. When Theodosus produced its twin, she would install the pair, she declared, in a certain temple dedicated to relics of the travail previous to her ascendancy.

"Theodosus readily agreed to her proposal. However, he said, so complex were the precautions he'd taken to ensure the safety of ring and of the man who carried it (of whose trustworthiness her majesty already had proof) that it would take him three days to retrieve them from their obscurity. Oh, yes, Theodora confirmed; toward that worthy servant our most magnanimous gratitude is certainly due; and, she appended coyly, there is among us a certain *heart,* to which your man Ali has but to announce his claim.

"I'll be sure to tell him, Theodosus assured her, and he bowed low enough to kiss the porphyry under his mother's feet. Anticipate our return with the vital proof in no less than three days, and no more than five.

"It will be the longest three days of my life, the Empress assured him. And she covered his cheek with her hand."

TWENTY-ONE

J esus!" exclaimed Missy, squirming in her enthusiasm. "Arhg. . . ."

Bowditch shook his head. "My throat's raw. I need a cigarette. Let's let Sergeant Maysle finish the story."

"But you were doing so *well*," Missy protested.

"I was reading straight from her text by the time I got to the end," Bowditch said, ineffectually masking a cough with his gruffness. "We must be on the B side by now." He fed the cassette into the machine and pressed the rewind button. He showed us his cigarettes. "Mind?" Nobody objected. Dave accepted one for himself. By the time the cigarettes were going, the tape was ready. The balance of the narrative was provided by a woman's gently inflected Irish brogue.

"Theodosus had no intention of returning, for the moment he set eyes on the Empress he'd been appalled to recognize, in her own eyes, both his birth and his death. He later told Ali that he'd nearly lost his nerve, and that pursuing the charade took every ounce of concentration he could muster. He could only hope that his subterfuge with the surrogate ring had delayed the end of his life. At any moment he'd expected the Empress to call his bluff and have him done in; or, at the least, to cause inch-wide strips of his skin to be flayed from his torso until the Queen became convinced he didn't know where to find Ali or the amethyst ring: that the

230

two things were beyond his knowledge; at which point she'd kill him anyway.

"His mother really was astoundingly beautiful. Her eyes radiated intelligence, and he felt that they could see right through him. They were the eyes, he told Ali, of a goddess. He played the marveling bumpkin, and that part, at least, wasn't too difficult, for the court was full of wonders. Eunuchs and maidens and 'barbed denizens of Amazonia' exchanged discreet whispers as mother and son conversed. Incense and delicacies vied to fog his senses. A recumbent pair of female lions, the largest he'd ever seen, flanked Theodora's throne. Columns of silk dyed with extract of *porphura,* the purple exclusive to royalty, breathed along the walls. All manner of costumed peoples came and went obsequiously. High in the intricately tiled dome of the chamber shafts of sunlight lanced through an obscurity of smoke. Exotic birds flew to and fro up there, making strange calls, and occasionally one would spiral to the floor, rendered senseless by the exotic fumes. Thickly layered carpets from all of Arabia allowed the bird to alight unhurt, to be retrieved by one or another of the court idlers, who would stroke and coax the creature back into consciousness and renewed flight. And woe betide, Theodosus was told, anyone who happened to harm so much as a feather. In short, he was surrounded by exotica, and it was not difficult to appear dumbfounded.

"Elsewhere we've discussed Monophysitism and its influence on Justinian and Theodora. Ali tells us that it was only Theodosus' trust in a faith superior to whatever heresy this she-daemon, his own mother, might hold sacred, that carried Theodosus through the interview. In the end, ardently reminded of his assignation three and no more than five days' hence, Theodosus was given the gifts of a purse full of gold *solidi,* and a magnificent horse. With multiple assurances of his swift return, egged on by the urgency to kindle the union with his beloved mother, members of the palace retinue set him on the Mesé Road, the western route out of the city.

"She did not kiss her wanderer goodbye, Theodora declared coquettishly, in order that she might kiss a prince when he returned.

"Theodosus later told Ali that, as he mounted the horse, Bellerophon by name, a beautiful, spirited creature worthy of a prince, two ravens flew straight down the road before him, calling raucously, as if urging him to hurry. It was a sign he hardly needed. Never in his life had he been so certain of a thing; that, were he to return to the court of the Empress Theodora, at the very least he would never breathe free air again. How foolish he had been to imagine that he might claim his birthright from that tigress! But such a palace! What luxury! The girls! African birds! Scented eunuchs! Furnishings and jewels and spices. . . . But clearly, all that was unthinkable. Unattainable. A naïve dream. To his credit, however, and with but momentary regret, Theodosus forthwith abandoned his ambitious plan and set his mind to the mechanism of his escape from the clutches of the Empress of Rome.

"The backup scheme was simple. Ali remained in possession of the amethyst ring, and from three days prior to the audience at the palace Theodosus had had no idea of Ali's exact whereabouts. This was the temper of the plan with which Theodora, detecting its volatility, had judged it best not to interfere. Not yet.

"Once through the westernmost gate of the city—called, as it happens, The Golden Gate—Theodosus followed the wall clock-wise, north and east, until he came to the Gate of Charisius, where he turned straight north. This was the road to Anchialos, a small port on the Black Sea, in which he hoped to find a ship. Failing to escape by sea he might regain this same road, and thence quickly reach the Danube River, the nearest frontier of the empire.

"For a day and a half he rode north, looking neither right nor left nor whence he'd come. At some point—Theodosus knew not when—Ali had begun to watch him. The plan was explicit. If Theodosus had not appeared in a day's time, Ali was free to disappear, taking the genuine ring with him as a token of gratitude for his years of service. If Theodosus had turned up showing signs of torture, if he wasn't alone, if he were followed, Ali was to disappear anyway. Only if Ali could assure himself that no interference was possible was he to show himself.

"Almost at once the scheme seemed threatened. Not long after Theodosus left the city, a northbound runner—not on horseback or in a chariot, nor wearing the royal escutcheon: that is to say, a plain-clothes runner—overtook and passed Theodosus. This athlete might have been on any kind of a mission. He could have been delivering a message to a rich merchant, or communicating between armies, or carrying a letter of assignation from a nobleman to his mistress. He may even have been on an unrelated errand for the Empress.

"Theodosus, of course, didn't believe for a minute in the serendipitous appearance of a royal messenger. The runner diminished northward, disappeared into a vale, reappeared as he topped the next hill, and was gone.

"A hour later a second northbound runner passed him. In between, on the half hour, he was passed by a young man jogging south. An hour later he met another southbound messenger. This was the pattern. From then on, it did not deviate.

"Not long after noon on the second day, as Theodosus passed a thick copse of trees, Ali fell in beside him, astride his own horse and trailing two fresh ones.

"'Nice horse,' Ali said.

"'Yes. His name is Bellerophon.'

"'It is by this horse that they know you, Sire.'

"'Yes.'

"Ali had watched the palace. Hours before Theodosus mounted Bellerophon, the messengers had begun to flow. Unable to foresee her son's precautions, the Empress had taken several of her own. In the week preceding her meeting with Theodosus, she had created a legion of foot-messengers specifically dedicated to the idea that if for some unforeseen reason her son managed to leave the palace alive, he would not escape her grasp. The moment Theodosus presented himself at the palace, a poet, concealed behind the throne, possibly one Paulus Silentiarius, known for the fine detail to be found in his verse, had dictated a careful description of the boy's features: his clothing and demeanor, his bearing and age. The horse, too, had been prepared as a contingency. A close description of Ali had been gleaned from his lustful cousin. Before Theodosus departed the palace, hastily memorized information had begun to disseminate along every road leading from the capitol, fanning outward like condensation along the spokes of an accelerating wheel. Even the purse given to Theodosus contained obscure coins, minted not with the visage of Justinian but with that of Justin, his predecessor, and long out of circulation.

"At every relay point—each separated by an hour's run, a matter of some one hundred *stades* or about ten miles—two runners waited. The first, having heard the description of Theodosus, headed back toward Constantinople; likewise, the second set out in the direction away from the capitol. All these eyes were peeled for Theodosus, but especially they sought Bellerophon. Men might disguise themselves. But Bellerophon had won many a holiday sprint in the games at the Hippodrome, and sired many a brilliant foal. So famous a steed could not be disguised.

"These messengers could not read; indeed, as a matter of royal security, they were forbidden the skill. The description

234

of Theodosus was recounted verbally. Having memorized it from his predecessor's recitation, the outbound messenger received the scroll containing the written description and set out. The original runner waited for the next outbound runner, gaining thereby an hour's rest. The pattern was repeated at each succeeding waypoint until, twelve relays out of the capitol, about one hundred and twenty miles, and on every road radiating from it, a pool of runners waited. There a literate *excubitor* took delivery of the scroll and read it aloud. Each hour a runner departed for the capitol. On the half hour, a new runner arrived. Thus the descriptive information radiated centrifugally away from the seat of government, while intelligence collected centripetally towards it. A panel of interviewers at the palace was quickly apprised of the absence of Bellerophon and Theodosus from every road except one, the road to Anchialos.

"So long as there was no sign of deviation from the intent expressed by Theodosus, of retrieving Ali and the amethyst ring, the Empress stayed her hand. She confidently depended on the greed of her son—itself a proof of his heritage—to bring him back to the door of her palace, the very portal of his doom.

"Ali and Theodosus, noticing the messengers, modified their plan accordingly. Agreed that the further they got from the capitol the better, Ali faded back into the scenery, and Theodosus rode north alone.

"Noting the timing of the runners, Ali chose his moment. Late on the evening of the second day the hourly southbound messenger passed Theodosus. Not long after this messenger was out of sight, Ali rejoined his master on the road. Presently, having slowed their horses to a walk, they were overtaken by the next northbound messenger. As the boy passed, Theodosus smote him with the flat of his sword. They dragged the unconscious body into the bush. Out of sight of the road,

Theodosus donned the runner's clothing, and Ali donned the clothing of Theodosus. They then murdered the naked runner and concealed his corpse as well as they hastily could. They stripped and freed the three extra horses, scattering them in the wild country west of the high road in the hope that, intercepting a perfectly good stray horse, with no arms or insigniae to identify it, most peasants would fail to inform the authorities of the animal's existence.

Bellerophon was a different problem, however, and this magnificent creature they retained, along with what little untraceable money they had between them, as well as the two rings. Ali's weapons and the remaining clothing they quickly buried, with the purse of gold *solidi* on top, in the theory that, if found by any persons other than the empress' agents, such evidence might well disappear without a trace.

Then Ali and Theodosus doubled up on Bellerophon and, given his rein, the steed quickly make up for lost ground. When they felt they'd regained the slain runner's pace Theodosus descended from the saddle, bade farewell to Ali, and took to his feet, running north.

"Ali records that it was a difficult thing, dressed and mounted as he was, to restrain Bellerophon while their common master disappeared over the next hill, jogging like an athlete towards, at best, an uncertain fate. While like Ali himself the messengers could not read, they'd all heard the description of the virile Theodosus. What stood in his stead was the fact that, by the nature of their profession, these messengers were in the prime of their health and youth, so that Theodosus, of their age and likewise favored, blended easily with the runners. Bellerophon, on the other hand, by his singularity remained their best decoy. White as a new sail and sixteen hands high—no one would mistake this animal for another.

"The next messenger bound for Constantinople certainly mistook Ali for Theodosus. Five minutes later Ali ventured a backward glance. The messenger had disappeared southward. Immediately he turned Bellerophon and walked him south. A half-hour later, as the next northbound messenger passed, Ali leveled him.

"He dragged the unconscious boy into a ravine out of sight of the road, stripped him of his clothing, dressed him in the clothing of Theodosus, and killed him. Severing the head and taking care to mutilate its features, he concealed it separately from the body.

"Now, himself dressed in a dead messenger's clothing, and retaining only a sharp dagger from his master's effects, Ali re-mounted and spurred Bellerophon north until he judged they'd overrun, by a mile or so, the distance the messenger might have attained unmolested, but not so far as to run headlong into the next southbound runner. And it was here, as the codex tells us, that Ali had to perform a most difficult deed.

"Bellerophon was a magnificent animal: spirited, willing and full of heart—altogether, as Ali records, a mount fit for a king. Accordingly, having led Bellerophon into a grove of trees, Ali recited a king's prayer before he slit the horse's throat.

"After five or six miles afoot, maintaining the steady unflagging pace of the professional runner, Ali heaved into the next relay station to the north where, to his great relief, he found Theodosus sharing olives with two or three men next to a well. Among them waited a southbound messenger. Nobody betrayed the least sign of recognition. Rather, as Ali approached, Theodosus sprung to his feet, as if overeager.

"'Where's Phanos?' Theodosus asked loudly.

"'He stepped on a viper,' Ali replied.

"They tarried only long enough to exchange the passwords each would need to make his way safely north, the passwords which, by then, Theodosus had gleaned from the southbound runner. If nothing had been seen on the most recent leg, a runner was to say *ou-tiz,* the Greek for 'no man' or 'nobody'. . . ."

"Son of a bitch," I blurted.
"How's that?" Bowditch looked up, his lighter poised beneath yet another cigarette.
"Shhh!" Missy hissed.
"Quiet!" growled Dave.
"Stop the tape?" Bowditch asked.
"No!" Missy and Dave said simultaneously.
"No," I echoed softly, and shook my head.

". . .seen Bellerophon by himself," the tape continued, "then *alpha* became the pass-phrase, and *beta,* if Bellerophon with Theodosus. The key password, however, *gamma,* indicated two men with Bellerophon—whether or not there was another horse made no difference. And if *gamma* he was to append the sun's position and the number of the next milestone. Within hours of receiving the code *gamma,* the Empress would strike.

"Pacing around the well, hands on hips and breathing heavily, Ali watched Theodosus, now the northbound messenger, disappear up the road. The southbound messenger, who had been there long enough to regain his wind, was not self-conscious about doing the talking while Ali caught his own breath. His conversation was all about how stupid Theodosus was; about what was going to happen to Theodosus when the Empress decided it was time to reach out and collect him; about how beautiful it would be to see Bellerophon from close up. Conspicuously absent from this gossip was any mention of kinship between the Empress and her quarry. The information had been suppressed.

"It seemed like no time at all before the next southbound

238

runner appeared out of the gathering darkness. The word *outiz* was passed, and the rested runner took off south, toward Constantinople.

"*Outiz.* To Ali this meant that Theodosus, northbound, had passed the southbound runner undetected.

"The new man didn't want to talk. That was fine with Ali. The night air was thick and hot, and, with some sixty or seventy miles of running to look forward to, he would need all the repose he could get.

"A half-hour later the northbound runner appeared. From this man, also, Ali received the word *outiz.* No man to report. No sign of Bellerophon, either. Nor of the servant Ali.

"The messenger tagged him, and Ali set out. He was one hour behind his master in their footrace against death."

TWENTY-TWO

D eath," Missy whispered.
"Death," Dave nodded.
Ou-tiz, I thought.

"They ran all night and all the next day," the tape continued, "Theodosus leading the way. They saw each other every ten miles. At each relay station Ali tagged Theodosus, uttering the word *ou-tiz,* and Theodosus began the next leg north. At each relay point they gossiped with southbound and substitute runners. Their quarry had disappeared. *Ou-tiz* was the word. Neither man nor horse had been seen.

"Word of the sudden disappearance of Bellerophon and his rider would take abut a day to get south to Constantinople or north to Anchialos, the end of the chain where the runners were allowed sleep before starting their return. In other words, by the time the Empress Theodora heard of the abrupt discontinuity in her son's journey, Theodosus and Ali would be tantalizingly close to attaining their freedom.

"They still faced formidable barriers. Two runners were dead, remember. Runners were slaves, and slaves belonged to owners. An abrupt disappearance by the two impostors would be a certain giveaway, against which their head start might prove insufficient to protect them. Ali and Theodosus had no time for rest.

"Arrived in Anchialos the next night, with the smell of the sea in the air tantamount to that of freedom, Ali noticed about

240

the encampment several examples of *Delphinium stavisagria*, and it gave him an idea.

"A medicinal plant native to southern Europe and the shores of the eastern Mediterranean basin, Ali knew it by the Latin name his grandmother gave it, *hierba vomita*: or, literally, pukeweed. Its seeds, we know today, contain an emetic alkaloid guaranteed to induce vomiting. In the ancient world they were commonly used to treat severe indigestion, dysentery, and poisoning. Of course, severe vomiting could appear to be a result of poisoning, too, rather than its remedy, and it was on this knowledge that Ali intended to capitalize.

"As if he had a portent of what was to come, Ali records, Theodosus was reluctant to endorse this measure. He argued against it. He preferred to take their chances with the head start they already had. But Ali pointed out that they had no arms, no conveyance, little money, and the clothing of slaves. Only the two rings stood between them and destitution, but they were also the two things that would instantly give them away. They daren't attempt to convert either ring into cash or a bribe until they were well out of the long reach of the Empress.

"In any case, Theodosus could think of no alternative to Ali's proposed subterfuge. It remained imperative that they contrive two substitute runners for the next day's return trip south; for, without them, Theodosus and Ali would find themselves running right back to Constantinople. Moreover, scarcely sixty miles south of Anchialos, there waited the corpses of two men and a world-famous stallion, which daylight would surely reveal to an army of bounty hunters.

"Theodosus reluctantly agreed to attempt the deceit. Ali quickly chewed a dozen seeds, forestalling any renewed objection by Theodosus. Better he than his master, Ali thought, as he washed down the bitter hulls with a cup of the thin wine provided the slaves. He well knew the debilitating effects of *hierba vomita,* for his grandmother had administered it for almost any reason, and he felt it necessary that his master retain his strength in case something went awry.

"The seeds promptly rendered Ali desperately ill. Theodosus was genuinely alarmed at the violent reaction; and although Ali didn't let on as much, he was frightened as well. To use a modern parlance, he thought he might have overdosed. The seeds soon had him writhing on the ground. Not only was he painfully retching, as expected, but he was convulsing as well. Perhaps, as Ali mused much later in his codex, the seeds were much stronger in Anchialos than they were in Samana, where he grew up.

"Part of the responsibility of a cadre of elite *excubitors,* or Imperial legionnaires, in addition to maintaining a vigilant eye for the Empress' quarry, was to keep order among the bivouacked messengers. It was to a gruff and surly example of this warrior caste that Theodosus, cloaking his noble demeanor by a most obsequious entreaty, appealed for relief. His story was that he and the sickened Ali were owned by the same family in Constantinople. If the legionnaire were to excuse Ali from his duty, as it was obvious he must do, then perhaps he would allow Theodosus to stay behind as well, in order to nurse his fellow back to health sufficient to see him home.

"The *excubitor* refused. Agreeing that Ali looked too enervated to run another hundred and twenty miles, he ordered him shackled to a tree for the balance of the night, or for the balance of the week if that's what it took, until his health improved. This was speedily done. As for Theodosus, the *excubitor* peremptorily declared him fit to begin the run back to Constantinople at daylight, as scheduled, and ordered it so.

"The legionnaire turned to go. Always, as Ali wistfully recalled, one for the broad gesture in their childhood theatrics,

Theodosus determined to proffer a last histrionic entreaty. In doing so, however, he committed the error of forgetting his place. He fell to one knee, with head bowed; but he placed his hand on the *excubitor's* forearm.

"This representative of Rome, recognized throughout the civilized world as a living image of absolute power, was not to be touched. The *excubitor* drew his sword as he wheeled. And, with a precision whetted by a lifetime of war, he struck the head of Theodosus from its shoulders."

"Oh my God!" Missy shouted. She abruptly covered her mouth with one hand, nearly spilling her drink.

"Blow me down," Dave whispered.

Death, I thought.

On the tape, distressed murmurs filled the hall in which Sergeant Maysle was lecturing. But she had foreseen the effect her words must have on her audience; having allowed a few moments for a dismayed reaction, she finished her tale.

"To the Syracusian scribe Ali recounted the moment in excruciating detail. Twisted on his side in the dust, doubled up by abdominal cramps, his ankles in chains, Ali watched in stunned shock as the hope of his future, his friend for life, and the end of all their plans rolled into the untrustworthy shadows cast by the sentry fires. The *excubitor* watched impassively as the head-less corpse twitched out its last blood. Plainly, as Ali observed from the distance of half a lifetime, this soldier had problems unrelated to some pesky, boy-loving slave. Certainly the Empress had threatened to have the *excubitor's* own head if Theodosus, Ali, Bellerophon, the amethyst ring, its garnet copy, and perhaps even the purse of gold *solidi* were to elude her grasp. So much responsibility to drive a man sleepless, and a mere slave had dared not only to question his judgment, but even to touch him. So what if

243

he might have to compensate the owner? A legionnaire would delegate but short shrift to so insignificant an obstruction, impudently arisen in the path of duty at so inopportune a moment."

Missy snuffled. A tear rolled over her cheek, and she absently smoothed a wrinkle in the quilt.

"The throes of Theodosus had barely ceased," the tape concluded, "as the *excubitor* wiped his blade on the dead slave's tunic. Without so much as a backward glance he departed, kicking the severed head out of his path as he went.

"Ali never saw the *excubitor* again.

"'*Ou-tiz*,' Ali dictated to the scribe, some thirty years later. The night of Theodosus' murder he'd said it over and over again, through tears and vomit that plagued him until dawn.

"The last line Ali dictated in Syracuse was, '*Ou-tiz* —No Man—is my Prince.'"

FOUR OR FIVE OTHER DEAD PEOPLE

TWENTY-THREE

O h my God, that's such a," Missy fluttered her hands, "such a *sad story*. Stop the tape! Please stop the tape."

"No problem." Bowditch stopped the tape. "It's over."

Missy's sadness vanished. "What?" she shouted. "It can't be! What happened to the rings?" I'd never seen her in such a tizzy. "Wait," she added quickly. "Don't tell me. Wait. I have to powder my nose." She waved her hands. "Turn around, turn around!"

Dave and Lieutenant Bowditch turned their backs.

"Stay under the covers," she told me. She took her purse, padded into the bathroom, and closed the door.

"How you feeling, Kestrel?" Bowditch asked, lighting yet another cigarette.

This solicitude came as a surprise. Before I could an-swer him, Bowditch sighed a plume of smoke. "Every time I get ready to retire, somebody gets killed in this town."

"It's society's way of saying it needs you," Dave suggested.

Bowditch laughed without mirth. "That night you escorted Renée Knowles home, Kestrel?"

"She knew the story," I interpolated, "and so did you."

Bowditch nodded curtly, but said, "You told us she left her car keys at the gallery."

245

"With Gerald Renquist."

"You never saw them again."

"Him? The keys? No. Neither one of them."

"You told us Renée Knowles pointed out a parked car."

"That's true. A BMW. She said it looked like hers, and she was proud of it."

"Looked like hers or was hers? What color?"

"Black maybe?" I looked at Dave. "It was dark."

Dave said, "The one at Pier 70 was black."

"Go with black," Bowditch agreed. "I've seen the registration. Anything else? What about the windows?"

"The ones on the car she pointed out were tinted."

Dave nodded. "Likewise."

Bowditch produced a ring of keys with an alarm remote and held them up. "Recognize these?"

"No. Where'd you get them?"

"Renquist handed them over when we interviewed him."

"So you already knew about the keys when you talked to me?"

"Sure. We'd already talked to Gerald."

"That's right. So what's the problem?"

Bowditch snorted. "News of Mrs. Knowles' death had him rattled. He volunteered the keys before we asked. He had them in an envelope. While we were talking with him, a messenger showed up."

"To take the keys back to Renée?"

"Correct."

"Gee, that makes Gerald look pretty clean, doesn't it?"

Bowditch shrugged.

"So where's the car?"

"Good question. We got keys and no car."

"Did Renquist move it? Did you ask him?"

Bowditch shook his head. "It's too late for that."

I looked at Dave. Dave blinked.

"Damn it," I said.

Bowditch nodded without enthusiasm.

"Where?"

"A dirt parking lot at Candlestick Point."

"When?"

"Fairly early this morning," Bowditch sighed raggedly. "Very damn early."

"How?"

"They shot him; they cut him open; they set his Mercedes on fire with him in it."

Dave whistled.

"That's pretty thorough," I noted.

Bowditch pitched the keys at the open mouth of his briefcase and missed.

I'd never said as much, but I knew Bowditch for a highly respected cop who had solved a lot of murder cases. His name had been in the papers regularly for years. But up close any vestige of the ambitious crime-stopper had diminished or gone away entirely. No longer would Bowditch see the visitation of justice upon bad behavior as paramount or inevitable–if he ever had. Now he would see only the bad behavior as inevitable, and only staying out of its way as paramount. People were going to keep on killing each other whether he went to work or not. That's the way it was.

The bald spot high up on his head might well have been rubbed there by the countless number of times he'd passed a hand over it in frustration. Perhaps, when he was younger, this gesture had presaged a realization, a step forward in an investigation, a revelation as to a minute fracture in some-body's story. But it had long since failed to be anything but a habit. Some disjunct mechanism now passed the hand over the bald spot for him, automatically; whereas, once, the gesture had anticipated a hunch, now it precluded one. And instead of trailing with it the odd strand of reddish hair, now the palm came away speckled by dandruff and redolent of hair restorer.

Bowditch retrieved the tape from the floor, dropped it into the briefcase, and said matter-of-factly, "Renquist's dentist is diving in Cancún this week. When he gets back, we'll see a positive on the teeth."

"Teeth," Dave said to his coffee.

"At least he had some," Bowditch sniped.

"A lot of fucking good they're doing him now," Dave pointed out.

I said, "That's all you found?"

"All?" Bowditch shrugged. "The fire was pretty thorough. The faggot's own mother won't recognized him."

"Will you show him to her?"

He shook his head.

"Does two make a pattern?" I asked.

Bowditch open a hand, noncommittal. "That warehouse at Pier 70? Gerald Renquist's name was on the lease."

"Wow," I said. "What in the hell is going on?"

The bathroom door opened, and Missy reappeared. Dave and Bowditch both widened their eyes, abruptly closed them, and turned away.

Missy dropped her purse on the floor next to the bed. "You sure have some interesting reading in there." Her stockings whispered almost as loudly as her voice, as she slid under the covers. "Who's Apsley Cherry-Garrard?"

"Another c-cold guy."

She looked around the room. "Am I interrupting something?"

Bowditch had turned around and opened his eyes, but he said nothing.

Missy's eyes showed no sign of the tears she had shed. But when she suggested cocktails to Dave, her cheerfulness was forced.

Dave kept his back turned as he upended the pint rum bottle over his glass. Empty.

"Ohhhh," Missy frowned, disappointed. "Do we have any Chardonnay?"

"Only a bottle of red," I said. "Very ordinary."

Missy pouted. "It's too early for red."

"I don't know," I observed. "It must be at least noon."

"Silly boy," she said, giving me a little push. "You have hypothermia. You can't be in on this discussion. How about vodka?"

"Argh hargh hrgh."

"Missy, for Chrissakes, that guy over there is a homicide inspector. Try to take him seriously."

She favored me with an expression of total seriousness. "Danny Kestrel, do you have any idea how difficult it is to properly manage Prozac?"

Now everybody looked at her. She appeared attractive, fresh, bright-eyed, with good skin and muscle tone and renewed makeup.

"You p-poor thing," I capitulated, "it's in the f-freezer."

"With a twist," Missy smiled.

Dave rubbed his hands together. "Got a lemon?"

"In the basket next to the sink."

"Lieutenant?"

Bowditch ignored him. "So anyway," he addressed me, "since you were tied up last night, we don't make you for the guy who did for Gerald."

"Thanks," I said.

"Did for Gerald?" Missy asked. Her smile collapsed. "Gerald who?"

"Whoever did for him did for the Knowles woman, too. I'd say it's nearly certain."

"It's n-nice to be off the hook and m-merely f-frozen."

249

Missy drew away from me. She looked frightened. "Gerald who?"

To Bowditch I said, "What's the connection? The car keys?"

Bowditch was watching Missy. "Maybe. We don't know. Your guess is as good as anybody's."

"You ready to be serious?" I asked Missy.

"Somebody killed–"

"Gerald Renquist. Yes."

Missy eyes went out of focus. "Gerald Renquist. . . ."

"They found him at Candlestick Point."

Missy didn't reply.

"Are you okay, Missy? Was Gerald a friend of yours?"

Her eyes came back and she said, "Renée took her own chances. But Gerald. . . ?"

"You knew him, Mrs. James?"

"Yes. Not well. But. . . ."

"Did he have any enemies that you know of?"

"He was harmless. He was gay, of course. But so what? Poor Girly." She looked at me, then at Bowditch. "Does Girly know? Have you told her?"

"Mrs. Renquist, you mean? By telephone, yes. We reached her in Glen Ellen."

Missy nodded vaguely. "She keeps a house there."

"I expect to interview her this afternoon." Bowditch cleared his throat. "May I ask your whereabouts last night, Mrs. James?"

"I beg your pardon?" Missy said, startled. She recollected herself and said, rather crossly, "I had dinner at Postrio with about twenty-five of my closest friends. One of whom, as I already told you, is the mayor of San Francisco."

Bowditch didn't turn a hair. "So you did. I should have made a note."

"So much for Missy James setting fire to Gerald Renquist at Candlestick Point," I said.

"Fire?" Missy breathed.

"Shut up," said Bowditch.

Dave handed Missy a twelve-ounce glass half-filled with vodka, a twist of lemon, and ice.

"To Gerald," she said tonelessly, and took a cautious sip. "Delicious," she told Dave. Then she added, "My God," without enthusiasm.

"That Prozac," I asked, "does it smooth the jagged edges, like they say?"

Missy ignored me.

"I'm sorry about your friend," Dave said.

Missy thanked him for his courtesy.

TWENTY-FOUR

Think out loud." Bowditch ejected the tape. "I'm listening."
"What's so interesting about what we think?" I asked.

"You didn't have a direct hand in this business, Kestrel," he pointed the cassette at me, "but you were in the thick of it. Now that you know some of the background, maybe you remember something germane."

"You mean, maybe I noticed a corner of the Syracuse Codex when Renée opened her purse?"

"That'd be nice."

"I'll bet it would. The only thing I see that connects her to the Theodosus story is the word *ou-tiz.* It upset her that I knew it."

"Yeah. When Sargent Maysle mentioned it on the tape, you jumped. What's up?"

"Renée was surprised I knew the word, and I was surprised she knew it. All by itself it's an unusual piece of vocabulary—forget its literary antecedents. Anyway, when Renée found out I learned *ou-tiz* from *The Odyssey* via Ezra Pound, she relaxed. I suppose it's safe to assume that Renée learned it somewhere else, and she was relieved it wasn't the same place I learned it. Certainly she never heard of Ezra Pound. Can we assume she'd never heard of Sergeant Maysle either?"

"This lecture was recorded at Cambridge," Bowditch said, holding up the tape, "England. That's the only time Maysle's presented it, and she hasn't published it yet."

"Where else would she have seen it?" Missy said. "Where else would anybody see it?"

252

"The Odyssey," I said, "if you read Homeric Greek."

"She'd have to read Greek to get it out of the codex, too," Bowditch pointed out. "There are no published English translations of it. A transcription was produced by the Bibliothèque Nationale, with an *en face* translation, into French of course; but that book's been out of print for well over a century. What function does *outiz* serve in *The Odyssey?*"

"After Odysseus has blinded the Cyclops," I answered, "he smuggles himself out of the giant's cave by clinging to the underbelly of one of his prized sheep. Blind Polyphemus sorts through the wool of each animal as the herd is going out to graze, but he misses Odysseus. He wants to know, however, what sort of man has managed to blind him, progeny of the incestuous union of Uranus and Gaea, who has bullied the world for his whole life with impunity. Odysseus answers *ou-tiz*, which means *no man*, or *nobody*. But in Homeric Greek, you see, *ou-tiz* is also a pun on Odysseus' name. So, while blinding the giant to his presence as well as to the truth, Odysseus can't resist giving him a clue by way of a punning riddle to his true identity, while making his escape—and under the cover of not only wool but modesty as well."

They all looked at me as if I had just crawled from under a rock.

"Oh, Danny," Missy sighed, "you were always so smart. How did you ever manage to remain so poor, too?"

"It's quite tricky to do both," I responded crossly. "To the point, given Sargent Maysle's story and the potential money involved, I'll stick my neck out. Find one hundred people who know that the word *ou-tiz* is Greek for 'nobody' or 'no man.' Ninety-seven will know it because the *Syracuse Codex* is worth big money. The other three will be mutants who read Homer."

"Awwww," Dave and Missy said.

"So one of the three mutants met one of the ninety-seven

mercenaries, and that's how Otis came to be attached to your phone number," Bowditch concluded wearily.

"Very likely, that's correct."

"A sweet nothing, in the end."

"A sweet nobody," Missy emended.

"No more, no less," I agreed.

"Wrong." Bowditch gave his briefcase a significant kick. "You've all heard the setup."

"Setup?"

"Think about it."

"Get Sergeant Maysle to think about it."

"She's thought plenty about it. Her annotated translation of the Codex will be published next spring, along with a considerably expanded version of this lecture."

"Yeah, fine. So Danny Kestrel and Sargent Maysle and Renée Knowles and the Syracuse Codex and Ezra Pound and Odysseus and Homer have one word in common. Granted, it's an unusual word."

Missy frowned. "And Gerald Renquist: is he in that loop?"

Bowditch pointed at her. "A most excellent question, Miss James, the answer to which, I'm sorry to say, entails a story."

"You're way more fun than Scheherazade," Missy smiled gleefully.

"Argh, but not so cute."

I dropped my feet to the floor and tried to sit up. The room spun and I toppled across Missy's lap.

"Come to Missy," she said, smoothing my hair. "Which reminds me." She retrieved her purse from the floor. "I almost forgot."

Cellphone in one hand, drink in the other, Missy thumbed a pre-set number. "Jerome? It's Missy James. I absolutely must cancel this week's session," she glanced at her watch, "twenty minutes from now. So sorry. See you next week. Ciao." She hung up. "Darned shrink never answers his telephone. He's afraid of it." She dropped the phone into the purse and the purse on the floor next to the bed. "Sit up, Danny." Still holding her drink, she set about fussing one-handed with the bed-clothes. Things arranged to her satisfaction, she sat up against a pillow, folded her hands around the drink in her lap, and looked expectantly at Bowditch.

"All set?" Bowditch asked unctuously.

"Yes, Lieutenant. Please continue."

"Last year," Bowditch said, obviously controlling his temper, "a house burned in Sea Cliff. A nasty burn in a big, expensive house. Good accelerants, as the arson investigators say, contributed to the fire's speed and tenacity. Only after the flames broke through the roof did a neighbor notice. The fire department took six hours to bring it under control.

"Two interesting things were discovered in the rubble. The first was a dead man. He was a male Caucasian, tortured and shot to death, and we've never been able to identify him."

"Tortured and shot?" Missy repeated, aghast.

"The other interesting thing was a photo album," Bowditch continued. "In and of itself, this photo album was of sufficient quality that we were able to trace it to Flax, a big art supply store, at Valencia and Market; but that trail ended right there."

"This album, however, wasn't on the coffee table or in the library where you might expect to find it. Quite the contrary, it was in the goddamn oven in the kitchen. We're reasonably certain that this was a spontaneous hiding place selected on the spur of the moment, a matter of opportunity, and perhaps inadvertently forgotten there. It was only by virtue of this coincidence that the album survived."

Bowditch had not ceased to search out reactions. "Does any of this ring a bell?"

"Was this in the *Chronicle?*" I asked.

Bowditch wearily shook his head. "You know how it is when

you're having sex. It's a higher plane of existence. Or so they tell me," he added morosely.

I was uncertain why this was being directed at me, however obliquely. But goddamn if at that moment I didn't remember something Renée had said–sighed, rather–*Sex makes everything better.* An unguarded sentiment with which few would disagree, perhaps; but I had found the implied anonymity disconcerting. Sure, Renée and I hadn't known each other at all; our sex had been virtually anonymous. But I would have preferred a less democratic formula. Something a little more personal.

Missy chimed in. "Sharpened perceptions, acute sensibility, increased blood flow, clarity of vision. . . . Maybe even an orgasm. These things give an edge to life."

"You forgot a balanced checkbook," I sullenly quipped.

"Ohhhh," said Missy, "you *really* got off."

Brusquely I asked, "Who owned the house?"

"A good question for which there's too easy an answer. The house was rented. The owner of record was legitimate. He's sold the place since. An agency managed the rental, and they're legitimate, too–legitimate enough to get sued for their mistake. Because everything about the dead tenant, and I mean everything, was phony. Previous landlords, employers, his financial records–it was all fake, right down to his passport and mother's maiden name. His rent checks were real enough, to the tune of seventy-five hundred a month not to mention first and last month plus a deposit just to get in there, so, despite what everybody says, nobody looked too closely at the rest of him."

"Hey," Dave said appreciatively, "that's my annual Social Security income."

Without thinking Missy declared, "You can't live on that."

"I only smell like I'm dead," Dave shot back.

"Didn't you successfully sue your second husband for your monthly flower bill?" I asked her.

256

"A thousand dollars a month." Missy took a sip of her drink. "It wasn't enough either," Missy sniffed, somewhat petulantly.

"Yes," I recalled. "That *was* in the *Chronicle.*"

All that could be heard for a moment was the traffic on Folsom Street.

"Oh, hell," Dave said, "maybe you can buy the next bottle of rum . . . or something."

"Using the name Melanofski," Bowditch abruptly continued, "this renter waltzed right through a process specifically designed to screen tenants by their financial references. You, for example," Bowditch said to Dave, "wouldn't have gotten to first base. But credit-wise you're probably rock-solid next to what we know about this anonymous dead guy and his bogus *curriculum vitae.*"

"With Social Security and two boats," Dave asked, "am I not fuckin' fiscally impeccable?"

"The sole purpose of this Melanofski's bank account was to pay his rent and incidental expenses in San Francisco. Beyond that?" Bowditch made a whipping sound by forcing air between his clenched front teeth with the top of his tongue: "Phwwt."

Dave imitated it perfectly.

Bowditch nodded. "He skirted the normal screening process by coming at the rental agency through a Swiss tenant-referral service. Everything about the guy was bullshit. Outside his paper shell he didn't exist."

"What about fingerprints? What about his phone bill? What about laundry stamps in his underwear? Or his teeth?"

"The fingerprints and his laundry were all burned up. We got DNA, but without something to match it to, DNA means nothing. It's the same problem with dental profiling. You have to know where to look. The Swiss don't give regular cops the time of day with this stuff. Not to mention we couldn't even prove he was Swiss. Melanofski's phone was cellular, and that's about what you would say for his dry goods, too. Generic and untraceable. You bought a cellphone lately?"

"Who the hell wants one?" I said defensively.

"Yeah," said Dave.

Missy laughed.

"The point is they're easy to get. This guy bought his cellphone from a head shop on Market Street. End of lead." Bowditch scratched his day's whiskers with the audio cassette. It sounded like a dog's forepaw on a screen door.

"So the photo album," Dave concluded, "is all you have."

"Exactly."

"Well?" Missy said. "What was in it?"

"Whoever burned down the house and killed this Melanofski—did I mention he was murdered?"

"No," I confirmed. "You said he was tortured, shot, and incinerated."

Bowditch nodded. "Somebody shot him in the head, face first. They also hurt him quite a bit before they killed him. There was blunt trauma to each knee and one elbow, three fractured ribs, and internal bleeding—very painful. But whoever killed him missed the photo album. Maybe they didn't know it was there, maybe they didn't think it was important, maybe they weren't even looking for it."

"Had the guy been gutted?" I queried.

"No," Bowditch said.

"Thank God," Missy said.

"Then goddamn it, what's so interesting about these photographs?"

Bowditch gave his briefcase another kick. "Each photograph is an eight by ten, in color. Each was shot from a tripod. Careful attention was given to ensure the proper film, lens, lighting, focus, and exposure. Each is a little smaller, by maybe eighty percent, than the actual size of its subject, which is the reproduction of a single page; taken altogether, the photographs reproduce the entire Syracuse Codex."

TWENTY-FIVE

Everybody started talking at once.

"But it's been missing since 1830!"

"Even Sergeant Maysle has never seen it!"

I racked my thawing brain. "Doesn't 1830 predate photography itself. Not to mention, color photography?"

"Aha," said Bowditch. "We'll have to give you a decoder ring and little badge, Danny."

"Argh harg hrgh. . . ."

Missy was so excited she was having trouble speaking, for a change. "That means. . . . That means. . . ."

"That means, forget the photographs," I concluded. "That means, the original is alive among us. So where is it?"

Missy looked at me, then turned on Bowditch. "Where is it? Where's the original?"

Bowditch jabbed a finger my way. "Danny always knows what questions to ask."

"That's because he never has the answers," Missy pointed out. "There must be reproductions of this codex in books, right? Even if the books are out of print? In libraries? In museums?"

Bowditch shook his head. "Kestrel is right. The 1830 theft predated photography, though just barely. However, the Bibliothèque Nationale did make something called an electrograph of a wax seal on the back of the codex before the theft. So a photograph of this same seal amounts to almost certain authentication."

"Do you mean to say," Missy concluded, "that there are no *legitimate* photographic reproductions?"

"That's correct."

"The photo album itself has intrinsic value?" I asked.

"Insofar as the album's unique—maybe so. But it's probably not unique."

"In any event, the photo album is not the big fish."

"No."

"But whoever made the photos has been swimming with the big fish," Missy inferred.

Bowditch nodded. "The photographs are of the original Codex. They're high quality and recent."

"You can tell how old they are?" Dave asked.

Bowditch nodded. "Oh, yeah."

"Then this photo album, it's kind of like. . . ." Missy mused. "What do the real estate people call it?"

"A prospectus," Bowditch suggested.

"A prospectus," Missy agreed.

"So it would appear."

"So this Melanofski was a salesman? Working on commission?" Dave speculated.

"A salesman," Bowditch shrugged, "or a buyer."

"When, again, was the original heist?" I asked.

"1830."

"And nobody's seen the codex or the other loot since?"

"I didn't say that. Some of the artifacts have been recovered, in the interim, in far-flung parts of the world. On the other hand there's a medallion, of which there's also an electrograph. It's a disc of solid gold, depicting Justinian triumphant over the Vandals, and it has never resurfaced. Neither has the codex, officially. Unofficially, however, it has been seen—" he consulted his notebook "—in Hong Kong, Monte Carlo, Basel. . . ." He looked up. "Which brings us to Iraq."

"It's trying to go home to Byzantium," Missy said dreamily.

"Sergeant Maysle begins her treatise by explaining how the Syracuse Codex wound up Iraqi state property. She sketches its illegal history until it surfaced in Baghdad, not long after the assassination of Faisal II, in 1958." Bowditch pinched the bridge of his nose between the fingers of one hand. "Let's flash forward. Anybody know how the Iraqis treat someone caught smuggling their national artifacts?"

"Slap on the wrist?" Dave suggested.

"The slap is applied to both wrists by a sharp edge. Then the convicted thief, now a double amputee, wanders the streets of Baghdad all day, every day, for a month, wearing his severed hands as a necklace."

"Sub-copacetic," Missy said.

"Argh. . . ."

"In extreme cases the sharp edge is applied to the neck."

"But," I interrupted, "doesn't that merely serve to inflate prices on smuggled artifacts?"

"Most astute," Bowditch nodded.

"So how much is the codex worth?"

Bowditch fished a cigarette out of his jacket pocket. "The figure we've heard is ten million bucks."

"That's a lot of rent on the old buoy ball," Dave observed.

"Iraq has been there a long time," I mused. "It used to be Mesopotamia. The Garden of Eden was there—no?"

"So the good book tells us."

"They must have national artifacts they haven't even excavated yet."

"That's true. If they ever get their politics straightened out, with a narrow-gauge railroad and good management, cruise-ship terminals, and air-conditioned malls and whatnot, they'd have the hottest tourist trap in the Mideast."

"Oh, joy of commerce," Dave commented.

"The point is, they're sitting on antiquities and archaeology the likes of which haven't been seen since Napoleon redis-covered Egypt."

"Let's see." Dave rubbed his whiskers. "Why am I thinking Gulf War?"

"Maybe you have a criminal mind. I don't want to make a short story long or anything, but in a blacked-out hotel bar during the bombing of Baghdad, an American TV newsman was offered the chance to purchase the Syracuse Codex."

"Wait a minute," Missy complained. "I'm getting confused. What about the guy in Sea Cliff?"

"He comes in later. Dave's right about the Gulf War. The First Gulf War, that is. It's quite a story. The newsman tried to turn it into a book." Bow-ditch made a face. "The writing is dreadful."

"He got it published?"

"No, it remains in manuscript—it's a printout, actually. We first discovered it as raw data on the hard drive of the news-man's incinerated Powerbook."

"Did you say incinerated?" I interrupted. "Again?"

Bowditch nodded. "The data was recovered by an expert in burned-up hard drives. It was encrypted, too. The password was 'Shirer.'"

Dave frowned. "As in William L.?"

Missy and I looked at Dave.

"The Rise and Fall of the Third Reich?"

"Yes. Newsguy didn't have a backup disk or even a paper copy—none that survived the fire, at any rate. But we got to read it anyway. If his screed is to be believed—which it often isn't—his Iraqi connection took him up an alley, down ancient stone steps, through a dank basement, and into the sewer system. His connection carried an automatic weapon and a ninja star, disarmed a booby trap, and so on and so fucking forth. There's even a bat-infested catacomb."

"Sounds like he strayed pretty far from the evening news."

262

"Physically, and mentally. Detail-wise, it's a bunch of hooey. His most vivid paragraph concerns tearing the pocket of his Brioni jacket on a nail."

"That's *terrible*," Missy confirmed.

"To give him credit for self-awareness, he also wrote a long and rambling deliberation on the difficulty of finding the correct tone for his story, which he envisioned as an historical novel; he never found it. Altogether, it's a tough read," Bowditch sighed. "It seems he took certain risks, at any rate. For one example, he expensed the hundred-thousand dollar purchase price of the codex as part of his TV crew's hotel bill."

"Wait a minute. He paid a hundred thousand dollars for something worth ten million? That's a major discount."

"You speak with utter clarity, Kestrel, and we'll get to that figure in a minute. There were twenty-five people on the news crew, they all ate, drank and slept in that hotel for four or five months, so embezzling the purchase price didn't present too much of a problem. There was the moral issue, of course." Bowditch cleared his throat. "He smuggled the codex out of Iraq and into the United States in a footlocker full of technical manuals and documentation appurtenant to satellite uplinking, data compression, signal processing, and whatnot. In his manuscript—which, by the way, is called *The Baghdad Connection—*"

The room, as one voice, said, *"Awwwww."*

"—Newsguy swears he made the purchase only in the interest of rescuing the Syracuse Codex for posterity. He was torn between taking it to the Museum of Natural History, the Frick, the Smithsonian, the National Geographic Society, the Getty, the British Museum, Time-Warner, and about fifty other places. He made a chart of the advantages and dis-advantages of each—that's personal advantages and personal disadvantages. The most logical recipient of them all, the

263

Bibliothèque Nationale, occurred to him, but he dismissed it on the principle that a diplomatic uproar over a domestic donation would be better for his career. He frankly admitted that he would ink a book deal before he allowed anybody to so much as glimpse the codex. He'd always wanted to write a book. Ever since Newsguy read *The Rise and Fall of the Third Reich,* he felt that all he'd ever lacked was an historic opportunity equal to his talent. The Syracuse Codex was his ticket."

"Bowditch." I eyed him narrowly. "Are you making this up?"

"No, and the Newsguy wasn't either. He detailed a marketing plan: bookstore appearances, signings, readings, preferred talk-show hosts for interviews, publishers – he even named a publicist. Newsguy listed people in the media who owed him a favor, arms he could twist for interviews or profiles or fourteen-carat blurbs. He listed agents and book editors he could jawbone into getting the thing properly published and reviewed. He named an old girlfriend, a magazine editor, who could be relied upon, as he wrote, 'to dot the i's, to cross the t's, to render this cascade of jumbled impressions coherent and readable–in short, to shape and tame this Leviathan, that shadows my days and haunts my nights.'"

"Thar she blows," said Dave.

"Another girlfriend, an art director, could be relied upon to plant a timely 'Lost Antiquities' feature in her Sunday Magazine. In anticipation of the demand he composed three *curricula vitae*–of one hundred words, one thousand words, and twenty-five hundred words. Anything longer, he declared, they'd have to pay him to write."

"Is there anything substantive to this story?"

"Oh sure, plenty. You just have to dig for it. The narrative begins with Newsguy holed up in Mill Valley. He planned to tell the story as a series of episodic vignettes, flashed back from the bucolic nocturne of his scented garden. There've been guests, see. They've eaten well and drunk better and now they're gone. Newsguy is sitting with a bottle of Cognac once given William L. Shirer by Henri Pétain's *attaché de presse.* He stares into the barbecue pit: as glow its briquettes, likewise his memories. Crickets elide into the ticking of the beaded chain that hangs from the ceiling fan above the bar in the Baghdad Hilton. Sporadic coughs of distant anti-aircraft fire can't benight the fractious conviviality of the correspondents gathered there. From around the world they've come, every stripe of journalist and jackal. . . ."

As Bowditch waxed enthusiastic in the depths of his story, so I began to catch hints of the young cop he once had been. It was like glimpsing the face of an old friend in the features of an obese stranger. He paused to suck at his cigarette. When it delivered no nicotine, he took it out of his mouth and looked at it. He'd forgotten to light it. He smiled tiredly.

"Did this news reporter have a name?" Dave asked.

Bowditch scratched his lighter alive. "His name is—was— Kenneth Haypeak."

"Gosh almighty!" declared Missy, startling all of us, "I remember that guy. He was a nobody on one of the all-news networks until he became a SCUD-stud, one of the talking heads trapped in Baghdad when the bombing began. He looked like something deliberately cloned from generations of halfbacks and fashion models."

Bowditch coughed. "They're called telejournalists."

"He died in a . . . a big fire. It was on the news. . . . Wait a minute: *Ken Haypeak* stole the Syracuse Codex?"

"No," I reminded her, "he bought it."

Missy screeched, "But the man came across as an *idiot.*"

"No," I reminded her, "he bought it cheap."

"Too cheap," Dave pointed out.

Bowditch pointed his cigarette at Dave. "Right in one." He looked at me. "You never heard of Haypeak?"

"Look around. Do you see a television?"

Not taking his eyes off me, Bowditch said, "Nope."

"I never heard of him."

"Never heard about what happened to him?"

"No."

Dave prodded the air in front of him with his forefinger, as Missy snapped her fingers at him. "Wait. . . . He . . . I remember. He . . . Oh! What *was* her name?" Dave said, "Myra, Manta, Minna, Minola—?"

"Carrington!" Missy exclaimed, pointing back. "The weather woman."

Dave snapped his fingers. "Moira Carrington."

"That's it!"

"Weather woman?" I looked from Dave to Missy to Bowditch. "Weather woman?"

Bowditch shrugged.

"What about her?"

"Same thing as Haypeak," Dave said.

"They perished in a fire," said Missy. "Awful."

"Another fire? How many fires are in this goddamn story?"

"Four," Bowditch said, "if you count Pier 70. In Newsguy's and Weatherwoman's instance, it was his cozy Mill Valley bungalow that lit the night sky." He watched the smoke rise off the end of his cigarette. "They and it burned to the ground."

"You were able to identify them? As opposed to the mystery tenant in Sea Cliff?"

Bowditch said, "At the time it was difficult to find anybody who didn't know who they were."

"Let me guess: there was no Syracuse Codex in the oven?"

Bowditch pursed his lips. "Not that we noticed."

"How about an album of photographs?"

"Funny you should mention that."

266

"Haypeak took the pictures," Dave concluded.

Bowditch nodded. "The Mill Valley fire started in a closet at the back of the house, which Haypeak had been using as a darkroom. Along with the photographic chemicals," he added caustically, "he stored a lot of gasoline in there."

Dave silently drew a finger over his throat.

Missy shivered. "I was weekending with the Caplins at the time. They have a big house at the top of Cleveland Avenue, above Tamalpais Junction. The television played it up as a home-invasion robbery and made everybody nervous. They reported that Haypeak and Carrington had guests for drinks and dinner that night. The security system was still turned off when they went to bed. . . ."

"You heard it on the news," Dave pointed out, "so it must be true."

I said, "This is complicated."

Bowditch shrugged. "Way I figure it, Haypeak was a patsy."

"He was set up?"

"By this other guy?"

"The one in Sea Cliff?"

"That's possible, but I don't think so. We did learn from phone records that Melanofski and Haypeak had plenty to talk about. Whoever killed them was a step ahead of us. They did their half-assed best to make both hits look like robbery. All of the weather-girl's jewelry was stolen, for example. But she didn't really live with Haypeak, and her townhouse in Manhattan was full of jewelry. Choice stuff. Jewelry was her hedge against the day she would no longer look young enough to announce the weather unthreateningly. We found a gem dealer who told us that jewelry was Ms. Carrington's fun but serious investment. Her taste for jewelry was noted when the gossip columns itemed her romance with Haypeak."

"So if they were after her collection, they hit her at the wrong time?"

Bowditch dismissed this. "That goddamn Syracuse Codex is worth ten million bucks. It's of scholarly and historical significance, so there's a prestige factor. The two puffballs were bringing down three hundred thou a year between them— and so what? Next to the codex it's nothing. Sure they took what rocks she had with her. They stole Haypeak's Rolex and his Jeep, too. We found the car two weeks later in long-term parking at the Oakland airport. This fit with the idea of a home-invasion robbery.

"The Mill Valley fire gave us the phone records that sent us back to Sea Cliff. Throw in the dark room, which we were able to tie to the photo album. The Powerbook hard drive gave us the Baghdad story. The codex had to be the prize.

"Haypeak was set up, no doubt about it. He was dumb enough, vain enough, ambitious enough—just what somebody needed—but more importantly, he could leave Iraq and re-enter the United States with little or no official scrutiny. Who else could do that? Saddam Hussein wanted the media there, the Allies wanted the media there, the media wanted the media there—everybody on the planet with a television wanted them there. It was perfect. A good con man could finger this Haypeak guy at midnight on Halloween at Castro and 18th. They really nailed him. They got Haypeak to *pay* them to let *him* smuggle *their* codex out of Iraq and into the U.S. It was beautiful. A hundred thousand bucks! *The Rise and Fall of the Third Reich*, my ass."

"Argh," Dave muttered.

Bowditch shook his head. "According to the draft on the hard drive, the Baghdad connection gave Haypeak the story that the Syracuse Codex had disappeared off a bombed truck while it was being transported with a bunch of other antiquities away from one of Saddam Hussein's palaces, which had been targeted by Desert Storm. Because surely he remembered the palace? When a missile blew it up, he'd covered it. He'd stood before the smoking wreckage on global television. He'd observed how precise the bombing had been, to have missed the hospital just up the street!

"Haypeak wrote that, by pure happenstance—not that I, an Inspector of Homicide, believe in *happenstance*—he knew exactly what was being offered him by his 'Baghdad connection.' Had he not been given a tour just a few weeks before? Did he not recall seeing the codex in its display case?"

"If he knew that much," Dave said, "you'd think he would have known enough to take one look at the deal and run all the way back to the makeup trailer."

"Egg-fucking-zactly," Bowditch confirmed. He nodded toward Missy. "Pardon my French."

Missy was looking puzzled. "I don't get it."

"Sure you do," said Bowditch. "Haypeak thought he was holding cards because he was the guy who could get the codex out of the country. Why else bring him in on it? But that was his only card. *He* should have charged *them* for the service. Get the thing out of the country, give it back to them, make a hundred thou or whatever, end of story. Then he'd have been okay. But at some point he got ambitious. Then, just to prove what a dumb-bell he really was, he refused to turn over the codex when they came to get it. Maybe he even put up a fight for a refund on his network's hundred grand. But for some strange reason these people thought the codex was rightfully theirs and that Haypeak was just a sucker and an errand boy. These people probably had guns for sure, but they came calling with matches and gasoline, too. Bad people. Haypeak was in over his head from square one."

"You mean," said Missy, "it wasn't just some common thief he was dealing with? Haypeak was a . . . a dead man . . . from, as you would say, square one?"

"You're sweet," Dave said, "Argh harg hrgh."

"From the moment he said yes," Bowditch confirmed, "he was toast."

"So who stole the codex in the first place?" Missy asked, somewhat bewildered.

Dave said, "Could it have been that guy in Sea Cliff?"

"The guy in Sea Cliff was the Baghdad connection?" Missy frowned, thoroughly confused.

"I don't think so, Miss James," Bowditch said.

Dave raised an eyebrow.

"So who did Haypeak buy the codex from?" Missy looked from one to another of us. "Who was the Baghdad connection?"

"Gerald Renquist," I said.

Missy screamed.

Dave laughed.

Bowditch almost smiled.

TWENTY-SIX

I'm losing my mind," Missy frowned. "Is hypothermia contagious?"

"The one straight thing about this story," Bowditch declared, "is that everybody in it is bent. People get around this Syracuse Codex, their reality gets distorted."

"Haypeak smuggled the codex out of Iraq," Missy persisted, "Because he was hornswoggled into it by Gerald Renquist? Is that what you're telling us?"

Bowditch nodded. "It's pretty certain. Renquist spoke Arabic, English, French, Farsi, and a little Russian. Did you know that?"

"Actually, I do know it," Missy said. "He was a language major at Stanford. A bright guy."

"What was he doing serving drinks at his mother's art openings?"

"It went hand in hand. Girly sold a lot of art to rich Iranians in the early seventies. After the revolution she repurchased many pieces from them, cheap. Remember all those guys colonizing Beverly Hills after Khomeini?" She snapped her fingers and moved her forearms from side to side, in parallel, and sang, "Ya, ya, ya, ya–stayin' alive. . . ."

"Jesus Christ, Missy," I said. "I'm trying to get well."

"How come you know so much?" asked Bowditch.

"About Iranians?"

"No, about the Renquists. Tell us about Girly."

271

"That's Arlene's nickname. Renquist was her second husband."

Bowditch extracted a small notebook from the breast pocket of his jacket. "Harold Renquist? The real estate developer?" Bowditch pointed his pencil at Missy. "The guy who owned the land under SquireBank headquarters?"

"That's true, Lieutenant. I'd forgotten that." She turned to me. "In fact, Tommy Wong designed the building. It was one of his first big commissions."

Bowditch narrowed his eyes. "Tommy Wong?"

"The architect. I introduced him to Danny just the other— was that *yesterday?*"

I thought about it. "No idea."

"Danny wanted to ask Tommy a few questions about Renée Knowles, see—" She stopped.

"Yes?" said Bowditch, evincing an insidious, expectant patience. "And what, exactly, were you trying to discover about Ms. Knowles, Kestrel?"

"Ahm, nothing specific, Inspector. I figured since you were after me, and Missy knows I'm innocent, and Missy and Renée run—ran—in similar circles. . . ."

"I beg your pardon," Missy said. "I did not *run,* as you put it, with that guttersnipe."

"What makes you say that, Mrs. James?"

"Say what?"

"Guttersnipe."

"Well," Missy sniffed. "It's a matter of class, isn't it?"

"As in, you have it, and she didn't?"

"In a word? Definitely."

"I see. Would you like to go on record with some of your distinctions?"

"I, for one, am among the living, and Renée Knowles is not."

Bowditch raised an eyebrow.

"Missy," I said tiredly, "you're exhibiting one of your less endearing traits to the Inspector."

"Oh, I get it," she said archly. "No sooner than I breathe life back into your frozen corpse than you bite the breast that suckled you."

"I'll mix the metaphors around here," Bowditch said.

"Hey, hey, little lady," said Dave. "Have a metaphor on the rocks with a twist. Shaken, not mixed. Argh harg hrgh."

Missy pouted.

"Come on," Dave cajoled.

She petulantly beaked up a little vodka.

"How often do you take that Prozac?" I asked.

"Every day," Missy said, not looking at anyone.

"Does it work?"

"They'll have to pry that prescription from my cold dead hand."

Dave regarded her a moment, then laughed uncertainly.

Missy continued. "Tommy Wong knew the Renquists well. As long as Girly was married to Harold Renquist, she decorated for Wong. This was no small potatoes. She rented and sold paintings and sculpture to Tommy Wong's various clients both before and after they took occupancy of big commercial buildings. She must have done a dozen of them with Tommy and Harold. SquireBank Headquarters, for example, is sixty stories, and every elevator lobby displays an oil painting. The main lobby has something like ten pieces of art on permanent display. Every one of those works passed through Girly's hands.

"When she divorced Harold—which happened, oh, maybe half-way through the SquireBank project—her phone stopped ringing. Tommy never hired her again."

"The husband told Wong to dump her?" Bowditch asked.

"Oh, no." Missy looked up. "Of course not. Harold was

only too happy to go into divorce court and show that, due to her extensive decorating career, his soon-to-be-ex-wife had plenty of her own money. Tommy waited until the divorce contract was final; then he dropped her. Just like that. As far as Tommy was concerned, the decorator's job was a plum to dispense as he saw fit. Girly had been in the picture because she was his biggest client's wife. Once she was out of Harold's life, she was off Tommy Wong's list of subcontractors."

"Was it a shock to her?"

"It was. Girly's not all that smart. She'd convinced herself she'd been getting all that business on the merits of her work and not on those of her husband's connections."

"Would it be fair to say there was residual enmity?"

Missy smiled. "Residual enmity."

Bowditch poised his pen above the spiral notebook.

"As I recall," Missy sighed, "the Squirebank building was worth something like 250 million dollars. This was back when a million dollars meant something. Not like now."

"That's true," Dave said. "A million dollars don't mean shit today."

"Tommy's commission was three percent, I think. Something like that."

"That's seven and a half million dollars," Dave promptly calculated.

Missy nodded. "The job made his reputation and his fortune."

"How did all this affect Gerald Renquist?" Bowditch asked.

"Gerald was at Stanford at the time. Pending the divorce settlement, his mother was taking a big financial hit. Stanford is very expensive. Gerald had to go to work. It was very embarrassing for him."

"What," growled Bowditch. "The kid was embarrassed that he had to get a job?"

"I'm always embarrassed when I have to get one," Dave pointed out.

"He'd never had one," Missy shrugged. "The poor thing hardly knew how to go about it."

"*Awwwwww.*" Three voices sounded as one.

"But he learned fast."

"What'd he do?"

"He went straight to Tommy Wong."

"I'll be a son of a bitch." Bowditch made a note.

"He said, look, Tommy. I know you've been putting up with mother's dreadful taste for years, and that it's been strictly because of my stepfather, right? Tommy said, Gerald, you're very perceptive. After I saw how she handled that *Corduroy Terrapin* debacle in Burlingame, I knew it was just a matter of moments, so far as Girly's taste and my buildings were concerned. So Gerald reminded Tommy of a Victorian bed-and-breakfast Girly had decorated for him, very posh, two years before. Tommy remembered it, of course, and readily admitted it was well done, adding that Girly had bought herself some time with that job. I'm glad you think so, said Gerald, because, from the hand-carved Hector Guimard escritoire in the library to the die-cast floral patterns of the lock strikes, *I* did the whole thing—under Mother's name, of course, because Mother was in detox the whole time.

"Naturally Tommy was incredulous—and delighted. Tommy has an eye; you can't fault him that. And his eye had recognized immediately that the Victorian remodel had been a quantum above Girly's usual work. He'd suspected at the time that Girly had secretly sub-contracted it in order to achieve a quality otherwise beyond her ability. It didn't take much to convince him that it was Gerald's work and not Girly's. And from that day forward it was deal after deal for Tommy Wong and Gerald Renquist. I'm not sure that Girly ever realized what happened. Tommy and Gerald were lovers,

275

briefly, too. But that soon gave way to a chaste professionalism. Meanwhile, Girly blamed everything on her ex-husband. After Harold died of a stroke in that bathhouse on Geary, there was nobody willing to set her straight."

"Can you beat that?" Dave said. "He stole the job from his own mother."

"Bathhouse on Geary," Bowditch nodded, writing it down.

"I'm aghast, as usual," I said.

Missy focused her eyes on a middle distance. "That's nothing. How much time do you have?"

"This is very interesting, Mrs. James," said Bowditch.

Missy smiled winningly. "Miss."

Bowditch inclined his head politely. "I have all the time in the world."

"Does this means there's a connection between Renée, Tommy Wong, Gerald Renquist, and...?"

"Baghdad?" said Bowditch. "I don't know. But there's little doubt that the man Haypeak heard speaking at least three languages without accent, who sold him the Codex, was Gerald Renquist."

"You can prove that?"

"Due to his interest in gray market antiquities, the Treasury Department has files on Gerald. Also, we know for certain that the war marooned Gerald in Iraq. What you've told us just now about his opportunism," he nodded toward Missy, "indicates that he was certainly brazen enough to manipulate a little thing like the Gulf War to his own ends. Which is precisely what we believe he did. But, of course, there's no proof."

"We. . . ?"

"SFPD and let's not forget the Iraqis. Unofficially, of course."

"What can they do about it?"

Bowditch shrugged. "Very little. With, I must mention, one exception."

"Well?" Missy asked impatiently.

"Bounty hunters." Bowditch leveled his gaze directly at me. Everybody else looked at me, too.

"Ohhhh," I said. "Bounty hunters. That's *wonderful*. What is this? A video game?"

"You wish. Professionals are commissioned all the time to recover stolen art and antiquities—not to mention, to procure components for biological warfare. But then there are the free-lancers who monitor these contracts so they can go after them on their own."

"Freelancers," I repeated stupidly.

"Which type do you think took you for a ride, Danny?"

"Uh. . . . Freelancers?"

"I'm asking you."

"They were clumsy. Does that help?"

"The professionals make very few mistakes. Which reminds me. How hard did you hit that guy?"

Everybody looked at me. After a minute I said, "Pretty hard."

Bowditch pulled a Polaroid from the briefcase and handed it to me. I tried not to let Missy see it, but she did, and she recoiled with a gasp.

The lighting was merciless. What little clothing remained had melded with what little flesh remained. All the hair was gone, including not only the eyebrows and eyelashes but the eye-lids, too. The eyeballs had boiled out of their sockets. Ears, nose and other fleshly appendages were gone. The sightless skull stared up at the photographer, and at us.

Around the corpse were bits of charred wood, pieces of a chair, the legs of a table. Had he expired before the flames reached him? Or was he conscious?

Either way, the Car Salesman had come to a horrible end.

277

"Well?" Bowditch wanted to know.

"That might be the guy." I held out the photo. "It's hard to tell."

"He certainly got himself dead," said Bowditch mildly.

"That black thing?" I said after a moment.

He looked at the picture without touching it. "In the upper left-hand corner?"

"It's a dildo."

"What?" Missy said, snatching the photo. "Let me see that."

"Do tell," Bowditch nodded, just perceptibly. I wondered when he'd last been surprised in the line of duty.

Missy handed the photo to Dave. He looked at it, then at her. They both nodded. Dave handed the picture back to Bowditch.

"If you ever get a decent picture of this guy," I said, "you could try showing it to Dave."

Bowditch didn't quibble. "If he was a freelancer, it would be a good bet that this wasn't his first loss of yardage."

"Just his last," I observed.

Bowditch made a note. "There'll be a mugshot somewhere."

"A dildo," said Dave.

"I'm shocked," said Missy.

"I'm charmed," Bowditch said.

BOTTOMFEEDERS

TWENTY-SEVEN

John Plenty's studio was a converted garage on Potrero Hill, with a loft built across the back third of it.

You could drive right in, if he let you. But his 4x4 Ford Explorer, as big as my apartment, was usually hogging the parking space. Sometimes at night, drunk, with the studio dark, John would turn the Explorer's headlights onto whatever portrait of whatever society waif he was currently painting. He'd sit in the driver's seat blasting his artistic sensibilities with whiskey by the quart and rock and roll as loud as the radio could make it. For an hour or even two he'd watch his work look back at him through the windshield and hate himself.

Society portraiture was what John did, and he did it well. He commanded big prices, each a little bigger than the last, and he made a practice of grousing about how insufficient the compensation was, about how each portrait cost him more than it cost its owner. And Dorian Gray help the comely subject who declined to sleep with John, lest the dark side of John's artistry envelop her portrait like a pestilence, lest he paint the subject as if she were dead, with truly spooky results. Thanatoses, death as a philosophical notion, death as a way of life, living death, became the subject of the portrait, with the sitter the latest metaphor, an armature for the theme. In

279

his exegesis of this frustration, which most people would call rage, John Plenty's talent prevailed, and these portraits were prized by the people who had the nerve to recognize what he was capable of accomplishing in them. Most of his customers, of course, were merely outraged, if uncuckolded. Occasionally one would pay off the commission solely for the right to destroy the work. This generated publicity, and John's prices soared.

The problem was that John, who seemed the very embodiment of a Renaissance if minor genius, whoring himself to the pope or the Medici, proved irresistible to these women. Minor or not, he was as close as most of them would ever get to that certain force of nature, a genuine creative impetus. Most of them knew it, and many acted on it the only way they knew how: they slept with it. Accurate, detailed, delicate, tender, rendered with great sublimity, it was these portraits, of those who had submitted to him, that drove John nearly mad. Alcohol, of which he consumed great quantities, didn't help. Nor did certain psychological factors. His father, for example, had been a career Marine who despised his son for being an artist. John, a delicate boy, had spent his entire youth listening to the father disparage the mother for defending, let alone nurturing, their only child's obvious talent. When a kindly local portraitist, who happened to be homosexual, took John under his wing, giving him lessons and art materials for free or at cost, the family rift took an abrupt turn into a full-blown rupture. John's father, severely and genuinely embarrassed by the company his son was keeping, conceived and promulgated the bizarre notion that the boy he'd raised as his own could not possibly be—was not, in fact—his own flesh and blood.

A mere side-effect of all this was that, by virtue of a severe and seldom-violated regimen, John strove to remain at fifty-three years old as fit as his father had been at twenty, when the latter had jumped off an LST at Iwo Jima carrying fifty-five pounds of gear. But age and drink were taking their toll. John's customers didn't know what to do with an unframed picture. Thus, a Kestrel frame had come to be part of his price: "Portraits by John Plenty," read the display type; smaller type continued with "varnished, framed, delivered, installed." These frames varied from fairly straightforward moldings to elaborately carved ones, price negotiated by John or his agents, based on my own pricing and John's aesthetic judgment. It was a satisfactory scheme for both of us. For one thing, unless they wanted to visit my shop and inspect the real thing, I didn't have to deal with any of John's customers, most of whom, in my view, were difficult, spoiled, and uninformed. I saw these traits as undesirable, but John took delight in thwarting and even taunting them. His predatory ways were no business of mine, however; just as my modest finances were none of his. Over the years, between the generous checks and extraordinary bottles of wine, we had become friends, of sorts.

It was long after dark by the time I was banging on the corrugated sheet-iron facade of John Plenty's studio, and he was long past sober.

He greeted me with no more than a growl, along with the distinct odor of gunpowder. Closing the door he waved me to a pair of chairs in a corner of the studio while he fetched a glass and ice. Between the chairs stood a low table and on it, next to half a fifth of Jameson, lay a box of cartridges and a long-barreled .25 automatic. Spent shells littered the table and the floor around the chairs. There was even one in the glass of whiskey, gleaming without luster under the ice.

At the far end of the studio, a floodlamp clipped to the ceiling angled its beam onto an unframed portrait hung head-high on the wall. I walked up there to have a look. The picture was a good fifty feet from where John had been sitting to shoot at it. If his aim had been to stitch an outline of the lovely face in the picture, he was about a third of the way along and doing pretty well. The subject of the portrait was Renée Knowles.

"Ice," John said dully. "Glass." He was pretty far gone.

"Thanks." I walked back to the chairs and John handed me the drink. There were two ice cubes in it. The rest was whiskey. "That's a stiff one."

He filled his own glass, which left the bottle three-quarters empty, and fell into his chair. "You won't get much for seconds." A little whiskey slopped out of the glass onto his blousy Italian shirt unnoticed. "Unless we venture out for another one."

"I'll drive," I cheerfully assured him, and took the other chair.

John took a pull on his drink, set it on the table, and took up the pistol. Without a word he leveled it at the target and squeezed the trigger. There was a snap, but no discharge.

"Son of a bitch."

"I hate when that happens," I said pleasantly.

"I was reloading," he rolled his eyes as he pulled the empty clip, "when I was rudely interrupted."

He began to finger slugs out of the styrofoam liner of the ammo box and into the clip. "What, no hollow-points?" I commented mildly.

"More's the pity."

"Can you still get hollow-points?"

"Danny," said John tiredly, "you can get anything you want. Haven't you noticed that?"

"No," I replied thoughtfully. "I haven't."

He palmed the clip into the grip of the pistol, jacked a shell into the chamber, and squeezed off a round. A little dust drifted down from the cinder-block wall behind the portrait. The spent shell clinked to the concrete floor.

"That a .25?" I asked. "It looks like a target piece."

"That it is."

"Shoots straight?'

He shot. "Very." He shot again and a third time. After a short pause he emptied the clip—five or six more rounds—at the portrait.

"Have a look," he said, taking a sip of whiskey.

"I don't give a shit," I said.

"Yeah," he said. "There's that."

I looked down the long room. "Do you?"

He thought about it. "It's hard to paint something that no longer exists."

John had never been able to paint from his imagination, for the simple reason that all of his imagination had been used up by his Vietnam experience, another side effect of the conflict with his father. What he painted, therefore, had to be sitting in front of him. It took time to paint it, too. This necessity kindled the intimacy that almost always arose between himself and the women who sat for him.

"You've painted Renée before."

"I've painted her before."

"Two or three times."

"True."

"Knowles paid for the pictures?"

"Not this one."

"It's not finished."

John put down his drink and released the empty clip. "Not yet it isn't."

I considered this. "Why not just put a slug into the forehead?"

He looked at me.

I looked at him. "Get it over with."

His eyes flared with menace, but he mastered the impulse and the eyes became dull again. "I'm an artist, not a butcher."

And he meant it. He knew what he was talking about. The distinction formed the threshold of his sanity.

I waited. When it became clear that nothing more was forthcoming, I said, "That's it?"

He fumbled at the box of ammo.

"Who killed her?"

He fingered a slug against the spring of the clip. "Guy with a gun."

"Guy?"

He shrugged.

"Tell me about her."

"What do you care?"

"Haven't you heard? I might've killed her. I'd like to know why."

He laughed abruptly. "Renée Knowles wouldn't look twice at you."

"Why not?"

"Because you don't have anything she needs—needed—that's why not."

"Is it that simple?"

"That friggin simple, Danny boy." He snapped the clip back into the grip and tossed the pistol to me. "Locked and loaded."

I caught it and tossed it back to him without even looking at it.

He caught it. "That friggin simple."

"Where's that leave you?"

"Ahead of you, Danny."

"Which way's ahead?"

He sighted the pistol at the picture. "Now, Danny, you've asked a damn good question." He fired a round. "But it's the wrong question." He fired again. "As usual, you're asking the wrong questions at the wrong time and in the wrong place." He fired two more. "And while you're asking the wrong questions," he fired, "at the wrong time," he fired, "and in

284

the wrong place," he fired, "people are getting killed." He fired until the slide locked.

"Gee," I said into the silence. "What do the neighbors think?"

He dropped the smoking gun onto the table top with a curse. He took up the bottle and said to it, "The neighbors are scared to fucking death of me."

"This is getting nowhere in style," I commented as he poured. He offered me the bottle. I declined. He inverted it over his glass. A sliver of whiskey slipped out of the neck and the bottle was done. "What was Renée to you, John, to get you this upset?"

He placed the bottle on the floor. "She was a babe, Danny. I know you noticed that much."

"And so what? Since when do you care about any of the women you paint? All I've ever heard you do is complain about them."

"That's true," he said. "Morphologically speaking, they're all inferior copies of Mary."

Mary had been John's first and only wife, and the stylus had stuck here more than once. I knew the tune by heart.

He waved the glass. "Big house, big cars, big travel. Big family, big pool, big another house, big another travel. Try not to drink yourself to death, live in style without making too many waves, keep an eye on the dough, don't piss it away, try to incubate the nest egg, don't get played for a sucker, trust no one, and stay clear of the press." He looked at me. "Not drinking yourself to death is the high hurdle. There's all that time on your hands, see. And nothing to do. It only takes an hour or two to look after the money, even if you're serious about it. How much tennis can you play? How many meetings of the Cousteau Society can you attend? How many Borneos can you kayak?"

"It seems to me," I said pointedly, "that it wouldn't take so much money to drink yourself to death."

He toasted me with his glass, then finished it in one go. "No, but it helps." He set the empty glass on the table and took up the pistol. "The nice and scary thing is that after the sauce drives you crazy or ruins your kidneys, the money will not only keep you out of the madhouse but also buy you new kidneys to ruin all over again. With a little smart investing," he chuckled distractedly, "you can *drink forever.*" He racked the slide, pulled the trigger dry, racked it again, snapped the firing pin a second time.

"You fell in love with her."

The smile faded. "Who," he said, his voice cracking uncomfortably. "Mary?"

"Renée."

A full minute went by. "Renée?" he asked. "Renée. . . ."

John peered down the empty firing chamber, into the barrel of the pistol. "Oh, I dunno. Love is kind of. . . ." He let his voice trail off. He put the gun down on the table, carefully, and passed the empty hand over his face. "I guess so." He looked at the palm of the hand. "You know there's a species of mite specific to the furrows of the human brow?" He looked at my glass. "You got any of that drink left?"

"Other than that," I said, handing it over, "it was pretty much like you said, wasn't it?"

He looked into the glass and nodded. "I got $75,000 for the two pictures I managed to deliver. You framed them."

I shrugged. "I didn't know who she was, then. Just another job. Good work, though," I added too hastily.

"Exactly," he almost laughed. "Just another job." He inclined the edge of the glass toward the pistol target. "There was another thirty coming for that one. You know what?"

"You'd have done it all for free?"

This seemed to strike him as a startling intuition. He half sat up, then sat back in the chair. "I'd have done it all for free."

"Why?"

He made a face. "It started out as just another job, like you said. Rich guy wants a portrait of his pretty young wife, makes no bones about the terms. So much down, so much upon completion." He shrugged. "Didn't want too fancy a frame. . . ."

"Don't let it get you down."

"Man," he said, "don't you ever worry about money?"

"Sure."

"Then why don't you do something about it?"

"I go to work."

"Yeah. That's just it. You go to work."

I could have said something like, if you're so worried about money, why didn't you stay with Mary? But I already knew the answer.

"Fucking Buddhist," John grumbled.

"So the job turned into a dream assignment."

"Yes. That's what it was. She came over here two days a week and sat for me. After a while it was three days, then four. She began to bring a bottle of wine and some groceries. I told her old man—what's his name?"

"Kramer Knowles."

"Sure. Kramer. That's it. I told Kramer the picture was giving me a little trouble, but not to worry. It wasn't going to cost him anything extra, it was just going to take a little longer. I offered to throw the sketches into the deal. I suggested the results might be worth the wait. He bit. Pretty soon Renée was over here all the time. She was even taking her calls here."

"Calls? What calls?"

"Business calls. She had all kinds of scams going on."

"Which was it? Scams or business?"

He laughed. "What's the difference? Buy cheap if you have to buy at all; sell dear no matter what. That was the gist of it. There was a lot of action from an architect guy."

"Tommy Wong."

"That's him. They had a lot going."

"He plays it down."

John frowned. "Oh yeah?"

"Oh yeah."

"Well, what with her being murdered and all. . . ."

I indicated the far wall. "Doesn't seem to have inhibited your reaction."

"Yeah, well . . . I liked her."

"And Wong?"

"I don't know. I never met him. But I don't care what he says, they had all kinds of scams going on."

"Why do you say scams?"

"Scams, business," he said impatiently. "It's not like they were actually *making* anything."

"Like art, you mean?"

"Yeah," he said bitterly. "Like art."

"Okay. So?"

"So nothing. After a while it seemed like things were getting obvious. I felt like I had to come up with something for the husband."

"What did Renée feel like?"

"Renée didn't care."

"Since when do you care about a husband?"

John squirmed in his chair.

"Hey, John. You weren't feeling a little guilty–" I frowned. "Were you?"

"Guilt's the wrong word. I wanted . . . I wanted to show somebody, everybody–how should I put it? That I was doing my part? That I'd done fair work for fair recompense? Nah.

288

I wanted to paint a picture that showed what I felt for Renée. That it was real. That it was beyond the money. Beyond cheating and lying. That it. . . ." He stopped. "Man," he finally said, "I had it bad."

That made two of us. "So you went to the husband. . . ?"

"The picture was finished. I showed it to him and he liked it. Then I offered him a deal. Kramer, I said, this picture's okay. But if you don't mind my saying so, there's something about your wife's look that intrigues me. Aesthetically, I mean. How about another shot at it? I'll cut my price in half. I'll go one step further. If you don't like the picture, I'll keep it, and you won't owe me a dime."

"He bit again?"

"Right away. He liked a deal. Girly Renquist was always whispering in his ear about what a good investment my pictures are. Here was one for half price."

"I've got to ask you something. Did any of this look fishy to you?"

He looked at me, then looked away. "Not at the time."

"It was good?"

"Good?" He nodded. "It was hot, Danny. I was like . . . I was like a kid around her. I felt I could do anything. I even started talking about quitting the portrait game, leaving town, getting a place in the mountains, getting down to some *real* painting." He laughed without mirth. "Some real painting. . . ."

"That's if she'd give it all up and go with you, I presume."

"Oh yeah. Had to have Renée with me. Had to be right next to my sweet inspiration. Wouldn't be the same without my . . . my sweet inspiration."

Thinking of Wes, Renée's cowboy, I said, "She laughed in your face? No?"

"No." He sighed. "She strung me out."

"Aha. Why?"

John shook his head. "That might have been the second worst part of the deal. I never found out. Not exactly, anyway."

"What happened?"

"We got into the discount portrait—which, by the way, turned out to be a good picture. The trouble was, I painted it in two weeks. Two weeks! I've never done that. Not bad, though. I worked on it whether she was here or not. That bullshit I usually hide behind went right out the window."

"About pacing yourself? About the light being just right?"

"Yeah. All that business with the chair or the sofa being spiked with the curtains draped just so in the light, and working only between 11:30 in the morning and two in the afternoon, even less in winter but always with a north light— all of it. I got some balanced-temperature lights and painted and painted and painted. . . . That picture was in my head, man. I could study it anytime I wanted. It was a gas. You know, Danny?" He sat up in his chair. "If she had gone to the mountains with me—" He stopped.

I just watched him.

John settled back in his chair. After a moment be began to tap his fingers against the side of his glass.

"What else?"

He wagged his head back and forth atop his spine, as if seeking relief from extreme weariness. "I didn't even show it to the husband. I set it against the wall, right next to my bed." He pointed at the loft. "Whether she was up there with me or not, I saw her picture every night when I went to sleep, and every morning when I woke up. It was my favorite painting. A picture like I'd never done before. Without missing a beat I got Renée to start sitting for another one." He nodded toward the far wall. "That one. I don't even know if I told her how pleased I was. No doubt I did, though. No doubt I went on and on about it." He retrieved a piece of ice from his glass and cracked it between his teeth. "Like now."

"Meanwhile, what was Renée up to?"

He waved a hand. "Hell, Renée got to where she was posing with the cellphone in her hand. Buck naked; freezing, even; holding the pose; but holding the phone, too. I sketched her holding the phone. Awful. She laughed when I showed it to her. I laughed too. I guess the point is that I paid no attention to what she was doing. None whatever. The bitch."

"Is that how it ended?"

He looked into the empty glass. "One day she just stopped coming. By then I'd shown the second picture to Knowles, and he'd snapped it up. It was in that show the other night, the night she—"

"That doesn't sound like you, John."

"What doesn't sound like me?"

"You've got this all-time ultimate work and you not only sold it, you sold it for half price?"

"That's right, Danny. I was not my normal self. I would have done anything for Renée. But all of a sudden I wasn't paying attention. I felt like I owed that guy something. Hell, my normal self was grateful to him for letting me ball his beautiful wife all those months. My new self wanted that picture the hell out of here, along with everything else that reminded me of her. It seemed like the least I could do was deliver on the work I'd promised. Knowles may be a hick, but he took one look at that second picture and had the checkbook out faster than a LERP can cut a—" He stopped. Drunk or sober, John was disciplined about his Vietnam references. He refused to use them.

"But not as fast as Renée got away from you."

"That's correct," he said. "One day she was practically living here. Putting on clothes fresh from the dry cleaner while she was talking to that guy Wong on the phone. Next thing I knew I couldn't find her. The cellphone number had been disconnected. I burned her damn clothes and used the drawings for kindling." He jerked his head toward the front of the building. "Right out there in the street." He nodded toward the painting he'd been shooting at. "I saved only this last painting."

"Why?"

He didn't answer.

"You saw her again?"

He shook his head. "The next time I saw her was the last time I saw her. You were there, too."

"At your opening. You spoke to her."

"She was drunk. So was I."

"Did she say anything memorable?"

"Not much. I didn't know what to expect, and no matter what she said, I didn't know if I could handle it. In the moment I was shocked. I'd never seen her that drunk. I got the strong impression she needed help. I think she wanted to ask me for it, too. Of course, I had no interest in helping her. Once bitten, twice masochistic—right? I already knew her as well as I ever would. Once she had dropped me, with no explanation, with the third picture only half completed, the scales fell from my eyes and it was about fucking time. I saw almost everything she said or did in an entirely different light. It was all lies, Danny. It was all. . . . But a funny thing happened.

"That night as you know there was a big crowd and business to attend to. I like to tell myself I would have said no to anything she might have suggested. But I can't deny that I was drawn to her.

"I imagined that I could see her assessing whether or not she might manipulate me into whatever it was she had on her mind. I was telling myself that if she wanted to try, I'd set her up before I said no. I'd hang her out to dry somehow. I could have used a little revenge, after what she put me through. But just as she was about to pitch me, someone or something changed her mind. I could see it. The uncertainty showed on her face. I knew her well enough to read it there."

"What changed her mind? Somebody in the gallery? What did she want?"

"I don't know. We were locked into this thing, alone in the crowd so to speak, just for that moment. I don't think it was another person's presence, but it could have been. And I don't think it had to do with her overcoming her habit of getting men to do things for her, or anything corny like that. And I don't think it was her wariness of my being on to her, either."

"So what was it?"

He drew a careful breath. "I think Renée knew she was into something over her head. And I think she knew that whoever she dragged into it was going to find himself in over his head too."

"No matter who it was?"

"No matter who it was."

I thought about the Cajun and his two helpers.

"You could have protected her. Physically, I mean."

He shook his head. "Before I got a chance to find out what was going on, Renée opted out."

"You didn't want to know what was going on anyway."

"That's true."

"But given the right circumstances, you might have tried to help her?"

"Maybe."

"What if her life had been in danger, simple as that?"

He nodded. "I would have tried to help her. Simple as that."

"May we conclude," I suggested carefully, "that by not asking for your help, Renée might have saved your life?"

"That's exactly right," he said without looking at me, and continuing to nod thoughtfully. "And lost her own."

I did not express the idea that, while John might readily

have saved Renée's life or even died in her place, he might prefer that they had died together.

He stopped nodding and looked up, but not at me. His gaze followed the floor of his studio to the far wall, then lifted through the lingering tendrils of powder smoke until it found the bullet-riddled, unfinished portrait of Renée Knowles. Multiple perforations showed that John's aim had long since faltered in its attempt to outline her features.

"Danny," he said softly, "will you drive me to a liquor store?"

TWENTY-EIGHT

John got his whiskey. I dropped him and it at his studio and drove north across town until I hit the beach. From there I headed west, past Fort Mason and Gas House Cove, past the Harbor Master's office and the St. Francis Yacht Club, past Crissy Field to the entrance to Fort Point. The gate to the road along the seawall was locked. The sign read, "Park Closed from Dusk to Dawn." Now, why would a government care about interdicting nocturnal introspection?

Or is it that the authorities can't stand the idea of citizens going down to the beach to seek an hour's relief in stargazing? There's so much to see. Orion, Betelgeuse, Taurus, Polaris, the Dippers and the Milky Way, sometimes a comet, once a year the Perseid Meteor Shower, the black holes you can't see but want to be there, and always enough satellites to remind the amateur astronomer to weed those telecommunication stocks when he gets home.

It's getting so there aren't any real detours anymore except in your own mind, all of which, however, you need to be told, lead directly to sociopathy. Either that or there is only one, which is the Big Detour, the one they make you take all your life, the one that keeps you from having a life—in which case the result is the same. Alcohol fumes in your brain? Inhale deeply. Satellites in the eyes? Close them. Savor a foghorn in fresh salt air. Is this what they call useful cognitive dissonance?

295

The barrier leaped, I followed the catenaries of ancient anchor chain along the seawall, its iron links so salt-corroded they were fissured like petrified wood.

It was after midnight. As the sign promised, I had the quarter mile of Marine Drive all to myself. The Alcatraz light winked. Traffic on the Golden Gate Bridge, high above, was at a minimum; despite the big moaner only tendrils of fog drifted through the ochers of the mercury lights up there. In the darkness below the span the cyclic inexorability of ton after metric ton of restless, seething brine heaved through the Gate, leaden, godlike, adamantine.

In order to move its volume through a narrow passage in the same amount of time as it has been accustomed to moving unconstricted, a traveling planetary mantle of water must increase its velocity. This is the venturi effect. But it is precisely in the throat of this Golden Carburetor that the Pacific Ocean encounters the freshwater outflows of both the San Joaquin and Sacramento Rivers. The collision of these and other forces in so confined a chute often makes for 'fat' surfing conditions.

So it was, this night. The surf was booming. Wave phosphorescence, wave height, wave spray, wave curl, all were fat. The heavy combers exploded against the seawall, throwing head-high skeins of salt water clear over the two lanes of Marine Drive. This was the real reason the road was closed. The park service doesn't give a damn whether you're introspective or not. It's liability that makes the bureaucratic wheels spin, not mental health; far from it.

Little I know of, on this earth, that can make a man forget his troubles so quickly as the sights and sounds of the Pacific Ocean. But for once this balm didn't work its magic.

I'd heard a lot about Renée Knowles over the last two weeks. While even in death she had managed to infuse John Plenty with fresh romantic notions, it seemed that he, too, along with everybody else, wanted me to face the fact that Renée

Knowles had been somebody I could not have trusted or even liked, that she was a case of great ambition fueled by little or no talent. While even humanness might be considered a token in the crap shoot of talent, can any humanity at all come solely from greed?

Was this moral posturing naive? Merely fastidious? I wasn't sure. If in theory it is hard to stand aside while ugliness wins, in practice it can be quite dangerous. Likewise, a Bartleby-like fastidiousness might easily be put to the test. The Vietnam years presented an excellent example. Not specifically indifferent to the manifestations of the war but certainly behaving Bartleby-like toward the politics supporting it, I'd found myself well and truly drafted. Not only had I defactoed myself into witnessing the biggest military fiasco since the first month of World War One, but I had an E ticket to getting myself killed by it.

And now here I was, locked in a micro-climatic synecdoche, if I may be allowed to invent a category right here on the beach—the world of Renée Knowles; a nasty ecology populated almost entirely by people I'd just as soon have nothing to do with. But it seemed clear that if I didn't admit that I'd become involved in something I didn't understand from the very moment I'd met the woman, then, just as surely as if I were trying to get across a highway by pretending there's no traffic on it, I was going to get myself run over.

A stone skipped down the dark face of the bluff behind me, across the road.

Maybe walking around a deserted and fenced-off beach at one in the morning hadn't been such a hot idea after all. I turned and slowly scanned the obscurity behind me, turning my back on the surf. If evil stalks on jet skis, so be it.

But there was nobody around. It was true I couldn't hear a thing above the noise of the surf except the cypresses, gossiping in the wind, to which I listened. They seemed to be saying that the reason we were all alone down here was that the rest of the population of San Francisco was too busy looking for the Syracuse Codex to join us.

No sooner had I articulated this comforting thought than I sensed movement a few yards down the seawall, and a shadow clipped the edge of my peripheral vision.

I hit the asphalt. Hard.

The shadow glided slowly overhead, flared up, then perched on a stanchion thirty yards down the road.

A night heron.

Good bird, my father would have said.

I stood up and dusted off the salt-seasoned grit. Better road-rashed than fragged, but now I could admit to myself that, whatever the situation was, it was having its way with my nerves. It wasn't often that I jumped at the sight of a night heron.

Checking for my keys, I remembered hers.

Right away it seemed too obvious. But the prime directive was, everything that had seemed natural that night at the Renquist Gallery—everything—had turned out otherwise.

The talk of suicide, the drunkenness, the caresses, the kisses, those all-too-brief hours in the cab of the truck—forget them. Right. At any rate, that stuff was too distracting. The need was to get simple, to establish the truth of some simple, substantive detail. So solve the car keys. Then we'll graduate to greater theories.

As reluctantly as any drunk, who had been embarrassed into admitting that she was too drunk to drive, Renée had yielded her keys to Gerald.

But what if Renée *really* hadn't wanted to give Gerald the keys to her car?

What if she'd had a better reason than mere inebriation?

Come to think of it, was she genuinely drunk?

Had even her drunkenness been a deception?

Suppose it had been a matter of life and death—not that she didn't drive drunk, but that she didn't drive at all?

What if Gerald knew all about it?

What if he only *thought* he knew all about it?

Had Renée and Gerald died because of those keys? Or in spite of them?

At any rate, Bowditch now had the keys. So where was the car?

The events of the night of Renée's death realigned themselves around this question. Just the thought that there was something besides common courtesy behind the exchange of keys threw a whole series of details into a different light. For example, now that I knew that she had considered enlisting John Plenty's help, before changing her mind, before letting him off the hook—as he saw it at least—and before allowing herself to get too drunk—or pretending to be too drunk—to make any ostensibly worthwhile decisions. . . . In light of that moment, it seemed that Renée must have had a much better reason for going to that opening than merely to revisit two nudes com-missioned by her husband and painted by a former lover; two nudes that normally hung in her own home anyway; and a former lover she hadn't seen since she'd broken off the affair.

I sat on a section of damp anchor chain and considered these things.

Fifty yards west a big swell threw up a copious tower of spume and rolled away.

The night heron took flight with a croak and glided back the way it had come.

I headed for the truck.

By two A.M. I was driving through the parking lot behind the Renquist Gallery. Only three or four cars were scattered among two parallel rows of empty slots that flanked a bed of geraniums across the block. A demographic fluke for that neighborhood, there was not a single BMW in sight.

Okay. Just checking.

They'd found Gerald out by Candlestick Point, about as far as you can get from Steiner and Greenwich without leaving the city. But there'd been no sign of Renée's BMW. Bowditch had been in possession of the keys since the morning after Renée's murder.

Had someone killed Gerald for keys he couldn't produce?

Or had they killed him for a car he couldn't produce?

I turned south on Steiner toward Union.

If the cops had found the Beamer, it would now be languishing in the impound garage at Eleventh and Mission. German shepherds would be keeping an eye on it. Clarence Ing would already have vacuumed it for pubic hair and shirt buttons. And, surely, Bowditch would have told me about it?

I turned east on Union, drove a block, turned south on Fillmore.

The cops had found my phone number in Renée's hand and picked me up immediately. The next morning they'd interviewed Gerald Renquist to verify that he'd seen me leave the opening with Renée, and, incidentally, to ask for her car keys. Gerald immediately handed them over. Why wouldn't he? For that matter, what else could he do?–but that wasn't the question. The question was, what had he already done? Or, perhaps more importantly, what had he not done?

Could it be that he wasn't able to do whatever it was he was supposed to have done because he ran out of time? If so, was it because Renée had pulled a fast one on him?

What if (a) the initial handoff of the keys had been insidious? What if (b) one way or another Gerald was supposed to get the keys because (c) there was something that needed to be done with the car but (d) he couldn't find the car because

(e) Renée lied about where she'd parked it so that (f) Gerald, unable to accomplish his mission, (g) got himself killed, (h) just like Renée did.

So, when Gerald told Bowditch he didn't know where the car was, he wasn't lying at all. Still, he must have been a pretty cool customer not to let on how scared he was.

I luxuriated in my paranoiac scenario and embroidered it effortlessly.

Gerald had intended to get those keys all along, and whether Renée liked it or not could cut either way. But the more I thought about it, the more it seemed probable that, whether or not Renée was fighting the idea, the handoff had been planned.

Maybe Gerald was a repo man on the side?

Now you're thinking, Danny.

Across Filbert and halfway to Greenwich, I came across the mouth of Pixley, the southern boundary of the parking lot. I turned and followed it past the gallery parking lot to its end, a block away. Nothing.

I U-turned and drove back down Pixley the way I had come, double checking. It continues for two more blocks beyond Fillmore, heading east, and so did I. Still nothing. Nothing, that is, except no less than eight BMWs, certainly a more accurate reflection of the demography of the neighborhood; and nothing, that is, except all the time in the world to make sure none of these Beamers was the one I was looking for.

When paranoia thinks it's onto something, it hums like an old radio. Humming determinedly, I drove a grid with the Renquist Gallery at its center. I took Pixley back to the gallery, turned right on Steiner, drove a block past Union to Greenwich, took a right, turned back up Fillmore to Filbert, took a right past Steiner to Pierce, took a right, drove to Filbert, caught the block of Filbert back to Steiner, took a right on Steiner and headed across Union to Green, took another left.

301

My disguise was perfect: I looked exactly the hapless home-coming neighborhood resident, woozy from a late-night programming session and absolutely unable to find a parking spot. Appearance is everything.

Forty-five minutes later I was driving down Laguna three blocks east of Fillmore and passed the mouth of Harris Place.

On the map, Harris looks like a discontinuous, eastern extension of Pixley. Pixley stops on the west side of Webster Street and does not go through to Laguna. One block east, on the opposite side of Laguna, there's a half-block cul-de-sac called Harris Place.

And there, on the north side, three parked cars off Laguna, between two garage entrances, in a perfectly legal parking space, sat a brand-new black BMW with tinted windows.

There was a small rectangular sticker, blue with black letters, dead center on its rear bumper.

Look at Me When I'm Hitting You

Maybe Renée had parked it there. Maybe she hadn't.
Maybe Gerald had parked it there. Maybe not.
Gerald and Renée were dead.
Nobody knew where this car was except me.

TWENTY-NINE

Just to remind myself I wasn't home-free or anything like that, I parallel-parked into the driveway directly in front of the Beamer, nudging its front bumper with the rear bumper of the pickup. The BMW began to cry rape.

These particular cars posses a klaxonic device at least as annoying as the one employed by Mercedes. They sound like spine surgery with a reciprocal saw and no anesthetic. The Beamer's lights pulsed with regulated shrieks as if it were having the wrong sins tattooed upon its lacquered flesh by the mechanical needles of *The Penal Colony*. How reactionary. I only wanted to break into it. A thief might work up a dudgeon.

Just because some BMW is getting diddled, a neighborhood has to suffer aural necrosis. Not to mention that, thus disturbed, each and every Beamer cohort lying in bed puts a pillow over his head and waits for the noise to go away. Nobody was going to call the police. The Yuppie Credo is: All for none and none for all.

Not to mention, I would have been mighty embarrassed to be the one person in history to be caught breaking into a car just because its alarm was going off.

I unparked the truck and backed out of Harris Place to the corner of Laguna. There I waited, thinking.

After sixty seconds the BMW shook off the fit and resumed its armed/parade-rest mode.

Not far away, on Lombard Street, there's an all-night dough-

303

nut shop. Buy a box of doughnuts and a thermos, they fill the thermos with bilious coffee for free. And well may you ask why anyone should treat himself to a cup of joe *ordinaire* in San Francisco, a city whose molecular constitution mandates an espresso cafe every forty Ångstroms or so, featuring coffees of sufficient virulence to jerk the consumer quantum-wise, valence to valence—not to mention unleash the tigers of insomnia. The answer is, since they're able to charge three or four dollars a cup for their rocket fuel, espresso parlors don't have to stay open all night. Whereas, you sell chocolate-covered doughnuts by the dozen for a dollar, you have to work 24 hours a day. It's the law. It's the taser of capitalism.

Forty-five minutes later I was again parking in front of John Plenty's studio. By now it was five in the morning, with no sign of daylight.

Two fifths of whiskey is a lot of booze, and I determined to pound loudly on his door to get John's attention. But at the first blow the door swung wide open.

It hadn't been locked. It hadn't even been closed.

The hinges creaked, though.

I thought, John must have shaken off his melancholy sufficiently to call up one of his many girlfriends and invite her over to chase his blues away, and he left the door open for her while he took camphor injections and an ice bath to sober up. Simple, no?

No.

There'd been a good fight. After the fight there'd been a thorough search. The destruction was considerable.

It would be difficult to determine what John had lost to the search: but it was obvious what he'd lost to the fight.

He lay where he had fallen, half out of the chair I'd last seen him in, and half on the floor. Blood on his knuckles gleamed wetly in the dim light. This and a tuft of hair clenched in his left fist would give Clarence Ing something to gloat over.

John Plenty was one of those guys who had wanted to fight in Vietnam. Not unlike other kids in other times, he thought he'd be good at war. John volunteered for the Marines because his dad had been one. Then he volunteered for hazardous duty, and for a while he specialized in long-range reconnaissance. He blew up stuff, killed people, saw many others die. To John, politics was something that happened elsewhere. Whatever the brass called duty, John called duty, too. He followed through to the best of his ability, which was considerable.

Halfway through his second tour, things changed. You could say that it was all the publicity that was beginning to leak in-country from the States, where anti-war protests had become news. Guys coming back from leave began suggesting to their buddies that they might want to go elsewhere other than home when their time came. Pot and heroin began to show up in places hardly anybody thought appropriate— perimeter foxholes, for example. People stopped caring about what happened to themselves and the people around them.

John began to do a lot of sketching. Quick, rapid portraits of friends, villagers, burned-out tanks, ruined buildings, but mostly of people. Kids and women, old folks, soldiers and civilians. He did a number of portraits of prisoners. If he heard about somebody getting killed whom he'd drawn, he'd page back through his sketchbooks and put a second date on the portrait with a cross next to it. The crosses started out simple, just two lines. By the time his tour ended, the crosses had become much more elaborate: Maltese crosses with exaggerated serifs, like he'd seen on comic-book Stukas and Fokkerwulfs when he was a kid; Celtic crosses with the circle over them, carefully drawn to look as if they were of weathered stone.

305

One day, John was drawing a grunt he'd talked into sitting for him. Sitting subjects, posing them, was relatively new. The kid was going to send the portrait to his family. They'd made a few attempts, but John couldn't get what he wanted. The kid was up for the work of sitting still for an hour at a time in the jungle, because, what the hell, he was stoned anyway. John's skill had become well known in the regiment. His sketches decorated the canteen, and beer was free for him there. He'd published a few drawings in *Stars and Stripes*.

They'd gotten a pose and a sketch they both liked. Another sitting or two and it would be finished. In fact, as John, quite drunk, had once told me, the portrait part was finished. He was only fiddling with the background foliage, getting it accurate, and his concentration was such that he never heard the round dropping in. It arrived, however, and evaporated the subject of his drawing. Just erased the kid. A direct hit.

The detonation merely lifted John up and set him down again, a few yards away, with a concussion and temporarily deaf. Bleeding from his ears, disoriented, his fatigues a little torn, and unconscious, he was otherwise unscathed.

By the time they medevaced John to the rear, he was conscious and drawing. Somebody had loaded the sketchpad in with the rest of his gear. He'd quit on the portrait and the background flora, however, and started in on the cross.

Cleaned up, he wasn't obviously injured. Everybody knew who he was so he didn't have to make a big fuss in order to keep his sketchpad. Triaged for lack of immediate medical need, John wandered the rear area, asking if anybody knew what the date was. Most of them could tell him and did, but he couldn't bring himself to actually write it next to the cross. As soon as the charcoal hit the paper, his mind stopped. He couldn't remember anything. When he came to his senses, he only knew it had become time to put the second date to the kid's cross. So he'd add a few strokes to the cross and ask

306

the next passerby for the day's date. And the cycle would begin again.

After a week or two he settled down. They gave him tranquilizers and kept him around the psychiatric unit for a while, and it wasn't until a guy came to tell him to get ready to go back forward that he became violent and tried to kill the messenger. A new lieutenant had sent another new guy to tell him. Everybody else knew better. And so, it was in the Fayetteville stockade that John learned enough about painting to do oil portraits; along with, not incidentally, enough locksmithing to break into any kind of a car, a BMW for example.

A lot of good that was going to do me now.

He'd taken as good as he dished out—worse, I suppose, if you count that he got killed doing it. Many abrasions showed on his face and skull. His shirt was shredded, a shoe was missing, he'd been shot in the left leg, but what killed him was a bullet to the chest. Ballistics would reveal whether it was the same slug that had passed through the palm of his right hand.

So now we were up to how many? Renée, the Car Salesman, Gerald Renquist—that's three. John Plenty made four.

And I wasn't even sure why.

And what about the two newscasters? Or the unidentified guy in Sea Cliff? That made seven.

And still I didn't know why.

I stood looking down at John's body and thought, I should have turned around and gone back for that Cajun son of a bitch. Him and his trigger-happy gofer. I couldn't be sure it had been them, of course; it was just that they were the only punks who'd shot at me lately. That, and John's place was a mess. It had been heavy-handedly turned out. He'd been savagely beaten and clumsily murdered. Ecstasy and that Cajun seemed likely suspects. I'd seen their clumsiness and stupidity up close.

The conclusion troubled me though. Those guys had seemed less than professional. In any case there remained the question of their employer. Who would have hired low-octane leg-breakers yet been willing to countenance a great deal of mayhem? They weren't much more than cheap thugs, and they were in over their heads with some of the people they were being sent out to attend to. Killing was a lot of bother. It attracted attention. In matters of such delicacy, a professional sends out other professionals, people with skills. So who was sending clowns to do a guerrilla's work?

Another clown?

Just two hours earlier and I would have been here with John. Together, John and I could certainly have taken the Cajun and Ecstasy, guns or no guns; from the look of things John, drunk, had nearly taken them by himself.

Perhaps they had waited for me to leave?

The chair he'd been sitting in was overturned, as was the table next to it. Spent cartridges littered the floor. There was a pool of spilled whiskey.

They'd snuck up on him, or tried to, though it was hard to tell; for the destruction ranged over most of the studio, a matter of some fifteen hundred square feet. It appeared that they'd caught him nearly passed out in his chair with his back to the front door—which, quite possibly, he hadn't even bothered to secure.

Still, blind drunk and three decades removed from the jungle, the instincts that had kept John alive for the better part of two tours must have alerted him. Here and there I trod on shards of a whiskey bottle. Its neck turned up at the foot of a big easel. I inserted the shank of a paintbrush into it and picked it up. One or two inches of jagged spikes flared from the neck like a splash of glass. Blood darkened their edges.

308

In the silent shadows cast by light from the loft a scenario developed. Scared, enraged, fighting again after years of self-control and, if the truth were ever known, taking not a little pleasure in the combat, John Plenty would have come up from sheer instinct, a formidable foe, killing right and left.

Only an unusual foe might have withstood John's reaction unaided. Much more likely there had been two of them, possibly three or even four. Slumped in his chair, the bottle may already have been in his hand. Arcing upwards as he stood, coming at least a hundred and eighty degrees around him, traveling quite fast by then, the bottle had hit something and exploded. A head? A shoulder? A gun barrel?

But that wasn't the end of it. John had used the shattered neck before he went down. His reaction with the bottle had forced the intruders to defend themselves. There had been a direct blow to meat. Somewhere tonight there was a circle, two inches in diameter that the jagged bottleneck had jammed and twisted into flesh like a key into a mortal lock. Shreds of meat remained with the blood on the points of glass. Whoever had sustained this injury was marked for life. Here was something for a good forensic anthropologist like Clarence Ing to study. Clarence would recreate the scene with remarkable precision. Clarence was an actively employed guy, lately.

The scream must have been formidable. John would have recognized it for what it was–if he heard it at all, in his adrenalized rage: success. It would have made him fight that much harder.

Killing John wasn't in the plan, however, and in that regard he had won the fight. They'd had to kill him before they could conduct the search. Perhaps, once again, they had killed without getting what they wanted.

No doubt John's alacrity had hastened his own death. One

could hope that his instincts had added exponentially to the Cajun's burden. Perhaps knowledge of this deed had informed the smile to be seen, even now, hardening on John's face. Perhaps he knew, in surrendering to death, that at least one of the enemy was badly hurt.

The big easel, originally to the left of where John and I had been sitting, was still upright, though it had been spun on its casters. On the floor near it I found a clip for the .25, fully loaded. I lifted the upturned chair and found the cartridge box, crushed and empty. Shell casings, crushed paint tubes, clothes, sketchbook pages, and broken glass littered the floor. I myself was leaving plenty of sign. There would be footprints in blood, fibers in the whiskey, fingerprints everywhere. Clarence would sort it out. But by the time Bowditch caught up with me, it wasn't going to make any difference. By then things were going to be settled, one way or another.

Under the chair that remained upright, the one I'd been sitting in when I visited, I found the target pistol. Its clip was empty. I exchanged it for the full one and chambered a round. Not a cannon, exactly, but cannons are for people who can't shoot straight. I put the gun in my belt. Call me simple; it made me feel better. Then I took a different kind of turn around the place.

They'd torn up everything. In the loft all the clothes had been turned out of an armoire and bureau; the mattress was slashed, the bedsprings turned over. John's entire collection of compact disks was on the floor; the screen of his TV was smashed. They'd ripped the curtain off the shower rod and the soap-dish out of the tile. The lid of the toilet tank lay in pieces on the floor. What few sheetrock partitions there were in the place had been kicked in.

Downstairs, the light of the looted refrigerator showed they'd gone so far as to tear the P-trap out from under the kitchen sink. Boxes of scouring agents and detergent were upended on the floor. The back panel was off the microwave. Two wire grills lay on the floor in front of the open door of the broiler oven. Spices and mayonnaise jars and foil-wrapped leftovers had been opened and dumped on the butcher-block counter. All the drawers hung open; the floor was strewn with silverware and broken crockery. There was quite a bit of blood around, too. Somebody with a two-inch gouge in his infrastructure had been putting extra hemoglobin into his work.

In the studio they'd gone through portfolios, tools, paints, slide carousels, and the books, too, of which there were a considerable number. Furniture cushions had been slashed, along with the upholstery and even the spare tire on the back of John's Explorer.

Had they managed to take him alive, John may have told his visitors where to look.

Maybe not.

John's lips had pulled away from his teeth.

Nope, the rictus seemed to leer, they didn't get what they came for. Got a hurt put on them, too. Not bad for a dissolute middle-aged drunk, huh Danny?

Huh?

Huh Danny. . . ?

311

Tb]IR-Ty

Though *Rummy Nation* was moored a mere twenty blocks from John Plenty's studio, it was a world removed. At a quarter to six in the morning, John's studio lay in darkness on a west-facing slope of Potrero Hill. But the five meager piers of Mike's Boatyard looked straight at the Oakland hills, ten miles east across the bay. Over this uninterrupted expanse of placid water the rays of the barely-risen sun skipped up and off a peeling plywood sign, like a ricochet of glass.

Fuzz on Your Bottom?
Call
Mike's Bottom Service
We Dive
We Scrape
We Cheap
>>Props, Bottoms, Leaks<<
>>Haulouts, Parts, Repairs<<
Call 1-800-WET-BUTT
FREE GUESSTIMATES!

Its graphic showed two fish watching a diver, in mask and snorkel, goose a startled mermaid.

Propped and disassembled, abandoned in various states of restoration or repair, dismasted, disemboweled, holed, stove, lap-straked, ferrocemented, fiberglassed, or just plain sinking, perhaps twenty boats were hauled out at Mike's at any given moment, some for a week, some forever. Yellow and orange dropcords trailed down ladders and scaffoldings and criss-crossed the pitted macadam. At each of their female ends waited a lead-choked disk or palm sander, a drill motor, a paint-streaked bucket of hand tools, and three or four empty long-necked beer bottles, one of them a terrarium of cigarette butts.

It was six in the morning but Dave already had something disassembled on a rusted sheet-iron table in the shadow of the crane cradle, and he was glad to see two quarts of coffee and a box of doughnuts. "Arhg," was all he said when I put them down on the table, and he produced two cups, swabbing their rims with a corner of his shirttail. Without ceremony he drained coffee from the thermos into both cups, taking care to leave room for a gout of dark rum.

We sipped. The iron carcass clenched in the jaws of the welder's vise was freshly painted bright red. "Fuckin' injector pump." Dave pointed into the sunlight. "Off that thing out there."

I shielded my eyes. There were several "things" out there, bobbing on the morning swell. Most of them looked like they could use an injector pump at the very least.

Dave plucked a package of Camels and a butane lighter off the shoulder-high cleat of a crane tire. "Fuckin' thing." He took a noisy pull on his coffee.

"Why fuckin'?"

"It's a fuckin' relic. They stopped makin 'em in 1948."

I considered it. "This is a rebuild?"

He nodded. "Have to hand-fabricate every part on it."

"That's a lot of work for somebody."

"And a nice piece of change for Dave, argh hargh hrgh."

"Why bother?"

"Restoration. Has to be exact. Otherwise it ain't," he cocked the wrist of his cigarette hand, *"concourse d'elegance.* Argh hargh hrgh."

The emphysemic bleat of a shift whistle floated over the water from the drydocks, where the hospital ship was still hauled out. Tiny hardhatted men stood under her stern, looking up at a half-dozen chainfalls hooked at various angles to one of her two massive helical propellers.

"That prop must be a hundred feet across," I observed.

"At that scale it's called a screw," Dave said. He made a circle with his two hands. "Props only get about this big. Unless you're talkin' airplanes. They'll have it off before we switch to beer."

"Right," I said, uncertain how soon that might be. "They always pull the screws?"

Dave exhaled cigarette smoke around the jelly doughnut he was eating. "Only when they been up on a reef."

"Somebody drove that thing up on a reef?"

"Ex-captain," Dave confirmed. "Argh hargh hrgh."

"Is the shaft bent?" From where we stood, the shaft looked to be a round piece of solid steel about twenty feet in diameter.

"It should be bent. They rammed it right up that ex-captain's ass." His laughter disintegrated into a fit of coughing.

We watched the shipyard workers study the manipulation of the chains. After a while I was ready for that beer. Dave slid his hand under the lid of a styrofoam cooler beneath the welder's bench and came up with a frosty longneck. When he twisted the cap off, a curl of mist rose from the mouth of the bottle like a snake from a basket.

It tasted a lot better than the coffee. After a few sips the sun cleared the Piedmont hills and I broached the subject: "Ever outfoxed the alarm on a BMW?"

Without hesitation Dave asked, "Is it stock?"

"I don't know. Don't all of them come from the factory with alarms now?"

"Usually. What model?"

"Almost new. In fact," I snapped my fingers, "you've seen the car. It's the same one that used to show up at Pier 70."

"Late nineties 365i. The alarm, huh?" He thought about it. "How bad you want inside?"

"What's that mean?"

"You care if the car gets hurt?"

"Not at all. I just don't want it yammering while I go through it."

Dave minded his business. "Where is it?"

I described Harris Place.

"You need to take it apart?"

"I don't know. I don't even know what I'm looking for."

"That alley doesn't sound like a good place to find out."

"It's not even a good neighborhood for it."

"So you should move the car first."

"That's all right by me."

Dave jerked a thumb over his shoulder. "Boatyard's got plenty of fresh air, sunlight, tools, cold beer–" He patted the threadbare sidewall of the huge tire. "Even got a crane." He started coughing. "People are always working on their cars around here."

"Yeah? How bad does Mike want a stolen car on his scene?"

Dave thought this was funny. He dismissed my compunction with a wave of his hand, and managed to say we could always take the car back when we were through with it, before his laughter turned into a coughing fit. Leaning both hands on the bench, the coffee cup in one hand and the cigarette in the other, he cleared his throat two or three times, each scour reaching deeper and deeper. It sounded like he was dragging chain out of a locker, three feet, five feet, then seven feet at a time. At last he corralled and ejected an elongated bolus of

315

mucous about the size and color of a small screwdriver handle, lazuritic green shot through with coffee-colored strands. We watched it twirl over the iron bench and arc down to the edge of the bay, fifteen feet below the grade of the crane dock, where it bobbed on the eddies of a mild swell dissipating among the pilings. Just as our fascination waned, a sleek, olive-drab fish launched straight through the surface of the brine, arched one way, then the opposite way, then fell back to the water with a smack and disappeared, taking the expectorant with it.

I watched the ripples diminish to nothing, then looked at Dave.

His eyes gleamed. "Argh hargh hrgh, I love the fuckin' sea. Never a dull moment." He pointed to where we'd last seen the bolus. "And that's why I don't never swim in it, neither."

"Never?"

He made a face. "Here." He rooted about among the tools and parts on the iron bench until he came up with a spring clamp, about eight inches long.

"What's that?"

"It's a 200-amp alligator clamp."

"So?"

"So look at this." Using both hands he squeezed open the clamp to show a metal spike inside one of the two jaws. It looked like a misplaced tooth. "Know what that's for?'

"Looks like that spike would go right through anything you clamped onto. A finger, for example."

"That's right. What if you clamped an electrical cable?"

"Same deal."

Freeing one hand, so the jaws closed with a snap, he pointed to one of the handles. "What if there was a wire—here?"

"You could put juice into the pierced cable, or take juice out of it."

"Right again. Movie guy gave it to me. Gaffers, they call 'em."

"Where'd you run into a gaffer?"

He waved the clamp. "They're always shooting movies around here. Art directors think this joint looks like a real boatyard, argh hargh hrgh." He raised a didactic finger. "Always get friendly with nuts-and-bolts guys. They got a lot of cool equipment."

"Like 200-amp alligator clamps?"

"They use them to poach electricity. It takes a lot of juice to run them lights they got. If you plug a hurricane fan into a fifteen amp wall socket, the breaker just goes pow. So a gaffer goes upstream and taps the juice between the breakers and the pole, see. Leaves the meter out, too. Then they got all the amps they want. Hell, I've seen them light up this whole boatyard with just one of these clamps. Espresso machines, makeup trailers, and everything. It's free, too."

"Okay," I said slowly. "Now that we know what this thing's for, what's it for?"

Dave's eyes twinkled. "Where'd you say that Beamer was at?"

Half an hour later, Dave paralleled his Jimmy into the driveway in front of the black BMW without touching it. Then he dropped an orange cone in the street behind the Beamer, and another one in front of the truck.

"That looks very official," I observed.

"It's an insurance deal," Dave replied.

A double-hung window rattled open a few feet above the cab.

"Hey, Mister," said a woman's voice. "That's a private driveway."

We looked up. A woman in iridescent sweat-fashions

clutching a cordless phone glared down at us. She was obviously sitting on something.

"Private property," she repeated, pointing straight down. "Can't you read?"

There was a sign nailed to the garage door.

Don't Even THINK of Parking Here

"Excuse us, ma'am," I said, pointing at the BMW. "My car won't start. This guy's going to try to give it a boost. If that doesn't work, he's going to tow it back to the dealer. This is the third time since I bought the car, I might add. If it was paid for, they wouldn't even return my calls."

"Bummer." She squinted at the trash in the bed of Dave's truck. "Sounds expensive," she said dubiously.

"Five hundred a month," I said. "That's the only reason they fix it for me."

"That sucks," she sympathized.

"Yeah," I agreed, as lugubriously as I thought tenable. "Either way, though, we'll only be a few minutes."

"I'm retired," she said. "Mind if I watch?"

I slid my eyes toward Dave. He'd uncoiled one of the welder's leads and run it down the sidewalk to the driver's door. "Always enjoy an audience," he said, as he lay down next to the car. "It's people make the world go round, I always say," he added, speaking to the underside of the rocker panel.

"That's all I ever get to do," I said. "Join the club."

"What," she said absently.

"Watch," I repeated, wondering whether she had ever jump-started a car before, imagining that she and her deceased husband had owned a towing service for thirty-five years. To say the least, it was a job not ordinarily done with welding leads. But for the time being she seemed content to observe uncritically.

318

Having attached the ground lead to bare metal on the chassis just under the driver's door, Dave returned to the truck for the hot lead. He unscrewed its rod clip and threaded on the copper shank of the spiked alligator clamp. Whistling, he uncoiled enough lead off the stanchion to reach down the alley to the passenger side of the BMW, onto which the lady upstairs happened to have a bad angle.

"Where's he going?" She leaned an inch or two out the window.

"I don't know, lady. Triple-A said he was the best. Said he was funny, too."

"Oh," she said, interested. "They have Comedy Towing Service now? Like Comedy Driving School?"

"Argh hargh hrgh," Dave said beneath the car.

"I guess so," I replied vaguely.

Lying face-up on the pavement, Dave rooted one hand blindly under the Beamer's front fender, just behind the wheel, cursing cheerfully. The woman in the window watched him like she'd watch a television.

In almost any car, a cable connects the battery to the starter motor. Dave found the BMW's and closed the serrated jaws of the alligator clamp over it. Out of the bib of his coveralls he produced a small C-clamp. He screwed this down on the clamp until the spike completely penetrated the cable. Replacing the C-clamp into his bib pocket he stood up, brushed himself off, and returned to the back of the one-ton, whistling again. I paced back and forth, trying to look as much like an impatient BMW owner as possible. "Should I mention my appointment with my broker?"

"Not unless ya want to rattle me," Dave replied.

I shrugged helplessly.

Just as Dave was about to punch the starter button on the welder, the woman's phone rang. She let it ring, as if unwilling to be distracted, but finally she answered it. Dave made close-

319

the-window semaphores with his free hand. The woman clearly saw him do this, and just as clearly she ignored him. Dave titled his head to one side and wagged his eyebrows toward the exhaust stack atop the welder, which reached to within a foot of the windowsill. Still she ignored him. He pulled out the choke and hit the starter button but did not turn on the ignition switch. The engine turned over without starting, and soon we smelled gas. He stopped cranking the flooded engine.

"Pretty day," he said.

"You don't own a BMW," I groused.

"That's true," he agreed. "But I do own two boats."

He depressed the choke, turned on the ignition switch, and tried the starter. The engine caught immediately, and its stack belched a thick plume of blue-black smoke straight into the open window. The woman screamed and slammed down the sash with the butt of the cordless handset.

"Whaddya think," Dave yelled over the sound of the motor. He placed his hand over the big amperage dial. "Two hundred? Two-and-a-quarter? The full dose?"

"Give it the works."

"I'm a little worried about the gas tank."

"What?"

"The gas tank!"

I pointed my index finger straight up and circled it in the air.

Dave shrugged, cranked the dial all the way up to 240 amperes, and engaged the clutch. The RPMs died way down, but the governor quickly revved them back up, way beyond the idle rate, obviously pulling a heavy load.

"Thar she blows!" Dave yelled.

The BMW alarm yelped once and quickly ascended in pitch, right past supersonic, then ceased to exist. What sounded like four kids trying to break a tie in a foos-ball tournament turned out to be the automatic door locks jacking up and down in their sockets to an erratic, samba-like tempo until they, too, stopped. Every light on the car lit up too, inside and out: turn signals, and parking lights, fog lamps and dome lights, map lights and headlamps. They lit, and they lit, and they lit—that is to say, the lights waxed to an incredible brilliance, an impossible incandescence, glowing brightly despite the broad daylight until, the welder pulsing hundreds of amperes through every circuit in the vehicle, every bulb, computer chip, instrument, step-motor and sensor evaporated in a puff of copper atoms, like a single overworked plug fuse that just happened to cost seventy thousand dollars.

The welder's engine suddenly revved up, free of its load. The governor kicked in and returned the RPMs to a pleasant idle. The rain-cap on the exhaust stack rattled merrily, mission accomplished. Dave shut it down.

We stood for a moment, somewhat awed by the acrid wisps of bluish smoke rising from the continuous seam defining the Beamer's hood.

"Notice the locks," Dave whispered.

We approached cautiously. Inside the car the lock handles showed their orange tabs. Dave tried the outside handle on the passenger door. When it opened, no alarm sounded. He closed it again.

"Argh hargh hrgh."

As Dave reached under the rocker panel to unclip the alligator clamp, the double-hung window rasped open. "Hang on, Shirley. Young man?" The woman, not bothering to place her palm over the phone's mouthpiece, coughed theatrically. "I'll have you know, I have the asthma."

"I tried to warn you, lady," Dave said, rolling up the positive welding lead. "But you'll be glad to know that this here motor runs on soy-diesel exclusively. Totally fuckin' organic. That puff of smoke didn't hurt ya no more'n a pipeful o' opium would." He slung the coil over the stanchion on the passenger side of the pickup bed. "It's just not as much fun."

"He says it's organic," the woman told the phone.

"If I had time, I'd drink a cup of it just to show you," Dave said over his shoulder. As he yanked the ground lead out from under the driver's side, he made a show of handing me a huge bundle of keys and saying, "Try the recalcitrant sonofabitch."

The woman put a hand over her phone's mouthpiece. "Young man, what's the name of your company?"

I opened the door and sat into the driver's seat. The interior reeked of fried electronics. I pretended to insert a key and turn it. "Nothing," I yelled, though Dave was standing right there.

"Dead?" he shouted.

"Completely," I yelled back.

He backed up the sidewalk, coiling the ground lead. "Pop the hood." I found the hood latch under the dash and pulled it.

"Young man!" the lady said.

Dave looked up at her. "I ain't no young man," he said sternly.

She stopped coughing.

"But I'm not so old," Dave added, "that I might not wanta buy a lady a drink. I'm talkin about somethin a little stronger than soya-diesel, too. Even if she is too sick to smoke."

Unconsciously, she touched her hair. "Well."

"Name's Bob," Dave said. When he'd thrown several loops of ground lead over a stanchion, he returned to the BMW and raised the hood. "Whew," he said, recoiling. "That ain't exactly comely."

"It's not very loud, either," I agreed, rounding the front fender.

"Looks like the battery's gone," Dave said. "Argh hargh hrgh."

"Jesus Christ," I said, when I got a look at it.

"He can't help you now," Dave said, and, raising his voice, "We'll have to take the bastard downtown."

"Damn it," I agreed.

Within a few minutes we had the BMW's front end dangling from the truck's motor hoist, its bumper fendered off the tailgate by a bald tire. I threw the plastic cones into the bed and walked alongside without a word as Dave backed the awkward rig out of the alley as pretty as you please, like he'd been doing it all his life. Once he got it to Steiner I climbed in with him. Dave sounded the horn and waved at the lady in the window. "I'll be back for that cocktail," he shouted. She waved uncertainly, and we drove away.

Forty-five minutes later the two vehicles were parked in the boatyard about twenty feet from Dave's workbench. A five-yard dumpster, ten boats, and a slatted chain-link fence occluded us from the street. Nobody seemed to be around.

"Where's Mike?"

"He'll be in around noon," Dave said, "if he ain't too hung-over."

We didn't even drop the car off the hook. We took each seat out of it, slashed its upholstery, and threw the remains into the dumpster. We tore out the carpet and threw that away, too. Dave removed the radio, the air conditioner, the glove box, the center console. We looked in the air filter and under the exploded battery and behind the fried dashboard. Dave got his fingers into every crevice of the transmission tunnel from underneath the car. I took the grills off all four speakers and cut the cones out of them. Dave set to work unscrewing the interior door panels. There was a spare tire loose in the trunk. I cut it longitudinally, stuck my arm all the way up it in both directions, and threw it in the dumpster. The trunk's carpet followed. Under the carpet was a lidded compartment, which I opened.

And there it was.

"Hey."

Dave came around the back of the car with sweat running off the end of his nose. "Shoulda looked here first."

No attempt had been made to conceal it, but steps had been taken to ensure its preservation. The box was fourteen inches wide, twenty-four inches high, and three inches deep, of mildly-tinted Lexan or some similar, tough material. The edges of the sides were epoxied or siliconed to the back, and a half-inch thick so they could be tapped and threaded. Black washer-head Allen bolts studded every three inches around the perimeter of the lid. Some kind of gasket material was squeezed by the bolts between the underside of the lid and the four edges of the sides. On the back were a bar code label and two other labels with serial or inventory numbers. Along the two long sides of the box were three duplicate labels in Arabic, Greek, and English. The English one read:

Tighten fasteners in diagonal steps
with torque wrench only,
incrementing 2 ft-lbs per step,
not to exceed 24 ft-lbs.
Always replace gasket material!

The nipple of what looked like a tire valve protruded out of one side of the box. Teed at right angles to the stem of the valve and built into edge of the box was a round, white-faced gauge with black demarcations covering a range of two hundred somethings, indicated by the finely tapered arrow of a telltale.

"This box is airtight?"

"Vacuum-tight," Dave said. "That *mic* stands for microns." He tapped the gauge with a fingertip. The needle moved a degree or two, but not much. "You use the valve to pull air out of the box with a vacuum pump." The Lexan was tinted but you could see through it. Dave swabbed the lid with a rag. "What the hell is it?"

It looked like a stack of wrinkled paper, each leaf so thick it might have been cloth. The top sheet had stamped insignias, a couple of signatures, and many hand-inked Greek characters on it, a few lines of which were arranged symmetrically. Greek is a language I don't read. But there was no doubt in my mind that we had found the Syracuse Codex.

CHUM

Th1RTY-ONE

It was early enough to catch Tommy Wong at home, so I looked him up in the phonebook. No listing, no surprise.

Half asleep, Missy picked up when she heard my voice on her machine. And though half asleep, she refused to tell me where Tommy Wong lived until I told her why I wanted to see him. I told her it was none of her business.

"We have to talk," she insisted.

I capitulated. I hung up thinking, *Well, we may as well get it over with.*

We met in a Russian tea house, way out Clement Street, at the foot of the Legion of Honor. I got there first, ordered coffee, took a table in the back, and fell asleep. I awoke to discover Missy looking down on me, as usual, but solicitously. "You look unwell."

I felt unwell, too. It had been a couple of days since I'd slept, bathed, shaved, or eaten anything other than whisky, coffee, or doughnuts. Missy, on the other hand, looked great. Perfectly cut jeans, a silk blouse under a woolen jacket, a scarf and a beret. The picture of mental and physical health. I told her so. "Thanks," she said. "Now I know something's Wong—I mean, wrong."

"Very funny."

"Nothing's funny about Tommy. He's an architect, remember?"

"Is he a killer, too?"

"Now who's being funny?" She sat down. "What the heck's going on?"

I showed her three fingers. "Renée Knowles. The guy in the warehouse. Gerald Renquist."

"Yes?"

I lofted a fourth digit. "Add John Plenty to your list."

Missy turned pale enough to display twenty thousand dollars worth of plastic surgery as clearly as if it were on a map. I'd known about their affair of course—I'd framed the damn painting.

"Is this a small world," I asked, "or is it merely achieving infinite density?"

She dully asked if I knew who had killed John, but she wasn't looking at me or even listening for an answer. I didn't bother to respond. A little while later she said, "Was it the same people who killed Gerald?"

"Nah," I said, watching her. "It was the same people who killed Karen Silkwood."

She looked away. "What's with the service in here?"

"What's the matter, Missy? Not feeling banterly? We were making a list of who's been killed lately. Don't worry," I patted her hand. "The list doesn't have to be comprehensive. Let's just name the ones killed in, say, the last two or three years." She took the hand away. I resisted the urge to grab it and squeeze until she gave up the name of her plastic surgeon. "You've been around since the beginning, Missy, since long before I got dragged into it. What's it been for us—fifteen years? And all of a sudden you show up on my doorstep because my name in the newspapers reminds you that you're in between husbands?"

She shook her head. "Danny, you're—"

"Don't bullshit me; just answer one question. Does Wong want the Syracuse Codex so badly he's killing people for it?"

I'd rarely seen Missy at a loss, but for once she couldn't seem to find anything to say, let alone tell a simple lie.

"I know you know what I don't know, Honey." I gently pinched her remodeled chin between my thumb and middle finger. "Maybe you'd like to hear it this way–ready?–I'm next. Okay? Me, Danny Kestrel, your erstwhile compadre, the old frame carver. Whoever's killing people, if they're not after me by now, they will be by the end of the day. Hell, I'm the only one left. Sooner than later my brains are going to be scattered all over that carpeted bench you once happily perched on to watch me work. I'm not stupid enough to think my getting killed might mean anything to you, Missy. But Darling," I tapped her nose with the tip of my index finger, "don't you be so stupid as to think it doesn't mean anything to me."

She batted my hand away just as the waitress appeared. Missy ordered vervain tea–for her nerves, she said. I asked for more coffee.

"Wong's address, Missy. Then you should go home and wait for the evening news. What time does he leave for work? And if you don't know, spare me the coy."

So, instead of a simple lie, she as if reluctantly told me a simple truth. "He lives at the end of 29th Avenue, just beyond El Camino del Mar, in Sea Cliff."

"Sea Cliff? That's just a coincidence–right?"

"I don't know, Danny. You're the answer-man, this morning. It's a big sienna-colored villa, with dark green doors and shutters and trim. You can't miss it. He leaves for work six days a week at eight-thirty, as predictable as a wind-up duck. But today, I happen to know, he'll be hanging around the house."

"Thanks. Now give me the why of it."

Our beverages appeared. Missy stared at her tea and didn't taste it, lost in thought. A clock on the wall said it was nine forty-five. I asked the girl for a scone, to soak up the acid. A slug of Dave's rum might have done well, too. I wished to be warm again. I wished to be rereading all of Chekhov. I wished I was an anteater who worked for an exterminator in Bolivia.

At five minutes to ten, Missy got loquacious. "The story goes back to my second husband, whom you knew."

"Yeah, I remember him. Carnes. He seemed all right."

"Don't be judgmental. Kevin had plenty of problems."

"His wife being one of them."

"He never remarried." She smiled thinly. "We had our fun, but Kevin couldn't keep up. He lived in his father's shadow, for one thing, and he never got over inheriting that twenty million dollars when he turned twenty-one. The specter of all that money haunted him through his youth."

I shook my head. "Jesus Christ."

"No, really. He'd been afraid to marry until he met me. There were plenty of women, of course. But what with the fortune and the, let's say, *permeability* of pre-nuptial agreements, he'd never been able to make the commitment. Aside from that he was good with money. Despite a high standard of living, he made his money grow."

"How grown was it when you got through with him? Or have we strayed from the subject?"

She shrugged. "I wasn't greedy. Not like some people might have been—are. I got a nice settlement and that was that. It was almost amicable. And in spite of the divorce, Kevin wound up with more money than he started with."

"More than twenty million dollars?"

She nodded.

"And you, if I may ask?"

She smiled ruefully. "I wound up with a nice settlement and no husband."

"That's our Missy. Always even-handed. Always the balanced point of view. What's the point?"

"The point is that Kevin did very well with the cards God dealt him"

"First it's Kevin, now it's God. How many characters are in this story?"

"The story you are asking for," Missy said evenly, "is this. Do you have any idea how Kevin increased his fortune?"

I did not. Kevin Carnes was another person you saw in the social columns, when he was in town. Always in a tuxedo, always with an ingénue on his arm, always just passing through from London to Sydney, or from Hong Kong to Paris. "I have no idea what he does. As a matter of fact, I've always assumed he doesn't work at all. Also, for some reason, I can't remember why, I have the impression he's gay. Doesn't he live in New York?"

"Bangkok, at the moment. He's not gay, by the way. I just said that in an interview when I was mad at him. It's like it was written in stone from that day to this."

"Even dumber than spilling your drink."

"Pardon?"

I waved it aside. "You were telling me how Kevin increased his fortune."

"You're aware of a thing called celebrity-worship?"

"How sordid does this get?"

"There are people," she persisted, "who maintain shrines. Usually the shrines are in their homes, but sometimes a collection becomes so extensive the collectors have to dedicate an entire building to it, which they fill with things relevant to the object of their reverence. I'm sure that even you, Danny, have noticed that Elvis Presley ephemera, for example, are hugely popular. Graceland is a national shrine. Posters and photographs are coveted. But there is somebody out there who owns that little black Gibson Elvis is usually holding in those photos, and they paid a lot of money for it. Even little things can be costly. Let's see. How about something fairly

330

esoteric, like, say, a handbill advertising Elvis' very first appearance on a radio program called *Louisiana Hayride?* That's worth a pretty sum. Stage costumes, hand-written mash notes, a tear-stained prescription for painkillers, the bill of sale for his bullet-proof Cadillac, even the Cadillac itself. . . . Get it?"

"Why are you telling me this?"

"Kevin, who had always wanted to succeed far beyond his father's low expectations of him, put much of his inheritance into the market for celebrity ephemera. But he didn't just go out and buy a few records. He sought out respectable collectors and purchased complete discographies. He knew how to bargain for them, and he knew enough to store and forget them after he bought them. Two or three or five years later he would sell for ten or fifteen times what he paid. That's what you call a good rate of return.

"Soon enough, he was wheeling and dealing. He compiled quite an inventory of this stuff. He got into celebrity musical instruments for a while, especially electric guitars, but soon discovered that it was a wildly volatile and inflated marketplace. So he got out. Even so, he always made money."

Missy sipped her tea. "He had money to begin with, which helped. But he did smart things with it. Ready cash in the world of ephemera can make a tremendous difference. Wherever we went, people would turn up to offer Kevin choice articles. Items for the connoisseur. And it wasn't long before he'd branched out of pop music and into really esoteric stuff."

"I detect a relevant thread—at last."

"Let's see. There's high-demand stuff that's relatively obscure. For example, how about one of Bob Simmons' hydrodynamic planing hulls?"

"The early surfboard?"

"Hand-carved in 1948."

331

"They're still around?"

"One or two."

"Are they expensive?"

She held her hand over the table and wagged it port to starboard.

"Not the big money?"

"No, but not negligible either, And then, let's see. Perhaps you heard about the movie star who recently paid a pretty sum for an item billed as 'Jack Kerouac's Raincoat'?"

"No, I hadn't."

"You must have been reading Proust on an asteroid at the time. How about the movie director who paid $25,000 for one of the three Rosebud snow sleds used in *Citizen Kane?*"

"That was news."

"How about the wreckage of James Dean's Porsche?"

"I'm a little vague on that. But . . . really?"

"How about. . . ." Missy toyed with her teaspoon, "John Lennon's shoe?"

"I beg your pardon?"

"When John Lennon was killed," she said carefully, "he threw a shoe."

I've seen any number of thrown shoes. John Plenty threw one. My face must have gone quite blank.

"There's a bloodstain on it," Missy added.

"Indeed," I said coldly. "You've seen this . . . ghastly item?"

She didn't say.

"Okay. More to the point I suppose, how much did it go for?"

She shrugged. "The rule of thumb is, double your cost to the next buyer, or don't sell." She smiled coyly. "But with some of these items, darling, the sky's the limit."

"It sounds like the sky's the limit on the depravity factor, too. Darling."

"That all depends on how you look at it."

332

"How do you look at it?"

"I look—looked—at it as my clever husband's lucrative and highly successful business."

"And how did he look at it?"

"The same."

"He had no sentimental attachment to his inventory?"

"None."

"What about the customers?"

"For some it was strictly business. Others were what Kevin called *end users.*"

"They bought to savor."

She nodded. "Take the guy who bought Jim Morrison's bathtub, for example."

"Say that again?"

"Jim Morrison's bathtub?"

"Jim Morrison? We're back to rock and roll. You mean the Jim Morrison whose career with The Doors lasted all of three years?"

"Four," she corrected. "That's the boy. Surely you know, Danny, that Jim Morrison died in his bathtub in Paris?"

I nodded vaguely. "For some goddamn reason, I know he's buried in Père Lachaise."

"You see?" She pointed her spoon at the center of my forehead. "Celebrity awareness penetrates the *darkest crannies.*" She smiled. "Most of them, anyway. I can't believe you haven't heard about Kerouac's raincoat. It's so literary. Anyway, let me assure you, that bathtub makes that particular end user feel very *special,* Danny."

"Just as long as he doesn't get any on me, he can feel special all he wants."

"Oh, Danny. Don't you understand? People are desperate to be part of the excitement. It's an identity thing. They—"

"Bottle it. Jim Morrison's bathtub does about as much for me as a Republican tax cut. Where in the hell did it come from, anyway? Is there one chance in ten thousand that it's really the bathtub Morrison died in?"

"Well, it came from Paris, of course. As you may or may not recall, my culturally deprived friend, whether he overdosed or drowned or was murdered by Lee Harvey Oswald, everybody agrees that Morrison died in his hotel bathtub. Kevin used to buy hashish from a guy—strictly for personal consumption, you understand—who met another guy in an Algerian bar in Montmartre who knew the plumber hired to remodel the bathroom in the hotel suite, *tout de suite,* so it could be rented out again, minus the opprobrium."

"It sounds like the least they could do. Subtract the opprobrium, I mean."

"It shows a distinct want of imagination, if you ask me. That particular opprobrium reads as infamy. Infamy is marketable. It's static, and you can cash in on static infamy because it fits in a nice little box that doesn't scare people, on account of its lack of dynamic potential. That is to say, they can stare at it all they want because it's not going to bite them back."

I stared at her. "Promise?"

"Kind of like the little thrills folks get with their kiddies at Madame Tussaud's Wax Museum looking at Edward Teach or Jack the Ripper or Gilles de Rais or Andrew Lloyd Webber—"

"Okay, okay, the bathtub is static infamy; I'm convinced."

"As soon as the police inquiry was over, the plumber swapped out the tub, overnight. He trucked it back to his shop in some *banlieue* and sat on it for ten years."

"Are you about to tell me that you and your ex-husband shared a personal experience with, or in, this useless bathtub?"

She smiled. "There wasn't time. And useless? When Kevin gave him fifty thousand francs for it, please assure yourself that our plumber was confirmed in his opinion that his bathtub was very far from *useless."*

"Fifty thousand francs?" I said incredulously.

"At the time the franc was about five to the dollar," she converted proudly.

"Ten thousand dollars?" I had to whistle. "And Kevin managed to sell it for twice that?"

Missy drew back. "You're learning, Danny, but you're behind the curve. Kevin sold it for fifty thousand dollars *three months later.*" She patted the table top, once. "Five times what he paid for it."

I blinked. "I'm in the wrong business."

"Of course you are, darling. He never even had to lift it. The plumber was happy to make another two thousand francs to crate it up and ship it off to America."

"Was it insured?"

Missy smiled and nodded. "Do not doubt it."

"But how could the customer be certain this was the bathtub Morrison died in?"

"That's the beauty of–how would you say?–that racket?"

"Definitely I would say racket. But you would call it sour grapes."

"Indeed. We had a letter and a receipt from the plumber, of course. But at the time of the tragedy, photos of the bathtub were in every newspaper in the world. The media can be fertile as well as barren; I have reason to know. Under the right circumstances, it's like having your very own publicity firm–except it's free."

"Same deal with Lennon's shoe, I gather."

She nodded. "Excellent photographs. Every angle. Exhaustive."

"And Kerouac's raincoat. No doubt there's a photo of him wearing it?"

"Oh, exactly. And that brings up a point: it's a very special photograph, taken by Allen Ginsberg."

"I might have guessed. Which makes the raincoat more valuable, which makes the photograph more valuable, then the raincoat, now the photograph again. . . ."

"You're catching on, Danny. It's called an association item. Between the two you have a feedback loop."

"Each item validates the inflated value of the other."

"Book collectors love to have a book signed by its famous author," she nodded. "But what they really like is a book inscribed by its famous author to some other famous author. Or to a famous painter or to a famous musician or to the ruined noble-woman who shot the *arriviste* Emperor."

"Always the hope of a Restoration, eh Missy?"

"Something like that, my Bolshevist caterpillar."

"So these items just get more and more valuable."

"In terms of the rate of return," she smiled sweetly, "it's better than a whole refrigerator full of Krugerrands." Missy's expression changed. "Which brings up another point." She reached for her purse. "Take a look." She slid an envelope over the table. Nine by twelve, manila paper, metal clip with a grommetted hole, the envelope bore no address, stamps, or wine rings, nor any hint of little wooden parts. It was innocuous. Inside was a single photo.

I studied it for a while. When I looked up, Missy was watching me.

Flanking her, Ecstasy and the Cajun watched me, too. Each with his hands clasped in front of him, they looked like two unshaven seraphim with their flies open, forming a proscenium for their urban Magdalene. They had materialized out of the teahouse scenery like a hologram of giant, prehistoric lice, as silently as an image thrown from a hidden projector in your local under-funded tarpit diorama.

This time both of them were armed.

Missy tapped the photo and said, "Where is it, Danny?"

336

Thirty-two

H ello, boys. Lose your way to the border?"
The boys said nothing. Still, I wasn't unhappy to see them. I just wished I had something to shoot them with. Maybe I could get one of them to run out to the truck and get John's gun for me? The trouble with guns is they're never around when you need them. They're only around when other people need them.

The Cajun wore one now, probably to reassure himself against the reddish gumbo burns on the left side of his face. Ecstasy had been working on presentation. His pistol no longer waited in the pocket of his jacket, which had a suspicious-looking exit wound midway up the zipper; his gun now lived up his left sleeve in some kind of spring rig. The trick had probably looked good in the instructional video, but Ecstasy's sleeve bulged like a snake that has just swallowed a rat.

"Hey, Missy, where'd you find these two action figures? At the toy store?"

The Cajun's memory was working, so he stayed respectful. But Ecstasy wasn't up on his food chain *politesse* so he tried bluffing. "The last guy who toyed with me—" he began.

"Shut up," the Cajun snapped.

"That's right," I said. "Silence and introspection might get you out of this. Since neither of you looks any more cut up than usual this morning, may I assume you've been keeping

337

your muzzles clean?" It was true. Neither of them had lately confronted the wrong end of a broken bottle. My disappointment puzzled Ecstasy almost as much as it did me. "Th' fuck's he talkin about?"

Missy wanted to interrupt. "Hold on," I stopped her. "We can save a lot of bother if everybody tells where they were about two-thirty this morning. Individually, collectively—it makes no difference. If the story is straight, we won't need to get riled with each other at all."

Ecstasy frowned like he couldn't remember what happened five minutes ago. The Cajun smiled dreamily, as if he couldn't remember anything else. Missy, annoyed, said, "They're supposed be asking you the questions."

"They're too busy getting themselves killed to ask questions."

"Yeah," said Ecstasy, frowning.

"So now there's a fourth guy dead, up on Potrero Hill," I told them.

"Where the fuck's Portrero Hill?" Having learned no doubt from the editorial page of the *Wall Street Journal* to cloak uncertainty in belligerence, Ecstasy raised the lump in his jacket. It looked like the arm of a catapult. One of the early meanings of *catapult* was *brandish.* Etymology often makes me smile; my wayward smile made Ecstasy snarl.

But the Cajun was smart and taking raps wasn't in his line. He stayed Ecstasy's hand and said, "Two-thirty this A.M. I am proceeding tongue-wise around the world in the Hotel Chambourg, Eddy at Taylor, Room 605, upstairs in the front. About eight-thirty the trick is bailing because the blow is gone when I get a call to make it way out Clement Street to here, to this joint. The sum-total of my knowledge is, with a little cash I get to ring the gong again. You wanna talk to her? You can talk to her. It ain't so much fun as talkin to Einstein, though, and her nose runs *all* the time." He jerked a thumb

338

at Ecstasy and rolled an eyeball toward Missy. "About these two, I'm sure I don't know."

"Thank you, my friend, that's more than we needed to know. What about you?" Ecstasy shook off the Cajun's hand, and smoothed the sleeve over his weapon, as if hopefully kneading a cancerous growth. "Not that I think you'd go off half-cocked," I added. "Not without being told."

"Go on. Break the sordid news," the Cajun urged him.

Ecstasy scowled. "I am having a private moment with my football team in my hotel room, not far enough up the hall from him." He twitched a cheek muscle toward the Cajun. "Same joint, same floor, different room. On account the walls are thin I am watchin' the 'Niners win the Superbowl again with headphones on, at least until my third of the eight-ball is gone. I never did get to sleep."

"The fuck you say," the Cajun said. "You got any left?"

"Fat chance." Ecstasy yawned. "Next thing, it's time to go to work. Maybe an hour ago."

I looked from one to the other. "A dump at Eddy and Taylor has VCRs in the rooms? What are they, welded to the radiators?"

Ecstasy looked pugnacious. "I always got my VCR." He framed a rectangle with his hands. "Hi-res screen, stereo headphone jack, you put the tape right inna bottom. We boosted it last—"

"Who won?" the Cajun asked suddenly.

"Huh? The fuckin' 'Niners, of course."

"Again? Don't you love it when that happens?"

Ecstasy shrugged. "That's the cool thing about tape. Plus, after the game, there's about an hour of blowjobs."

"You know," I said, "I think you're off the hook."

Ecstasy looked uncertain. "What hook?" He frowned. "We ain't on no hook." He scowled. "You're the guy on a hook."

"Who? Me? For what?"

339

Impatient to get in on the conversation, Missy tapped the photograph. "For this."

I looked at it, then at her. "What are you going to do, Missy? Have me blown away? Right here in front of the samovar? Like the guy on Potrero Hill?"

Missy blinked.

"Who got blown away?" Ecstasy wanted to know. "Where's this Potrero Hill?"

The Cajun said, "We didn't blow nobody away."

"Just our own blow," Ecstasy insisted, "is all that got blown away."

They turned to Missy. The color had drained from her face. "Is this true, Miss James? Somebody else is working for you?"

For once in her life, Missy James was at a loss for words. She was thinking hard, though. You could see it.

"Missy," I said.

She shook her head, distantly.

Missy had always been one of those wealthy people, not so rare as one might wish or think, who had never doubted her place in the world. Not for an instant had she questioned the suitors, the husbands, the chauffeured automobiles, the restaurants and hotels, the multiple homes, the boxes at the football stadium, the three-month sojourns in Europe—unless, of course, she deemed one or another of them substandard or deficient.

Now, however, she was questioning her judgment. It was about time, too. I had assumed it was John Plenty's infatuation with Renée that had gotten him killed. But it was plain that Missy was in the equation, too. The difference was, even dead, Renée Knowles knew more about what had happened to John Plenty than Missy ever would. Missy had suddenly realized that, like Renée, she was in over her head. Something was officially out of control.

What took her so long? If the story of Jim Morrison's god-

340

damn bathtub were true, hadn't Carnes had the sense to carry a gun when he accompanied a stranger in the middle of the night to the suburbs of Paris with fifty thousand francs in his pocket? Had he concealed the gun from Missy? Had he been stupid enough to take her along for the ride? Or was it all just a lark that their mutual dumb luck had enabled them to get away with?

In any case, nobody around the table in the back of the little Russian cafe on Clement Street that morning had experienced the wrong end of a broken bottle while killing John Plenty. Judging by the wreckage of his studio, John had proved a tough guy to the bitter end. Looked at that way, maybe all four of us were playing over our heads.

Missy's thoughts revealed themselves in her eyes. She was finished. She wanted somebody to tell her what to do.

I said, "Tell these guys to beat it."

The Cajun relaxed his jaw a little too soon, I thought, for a guy who was looking to scoot out from under a murder rap. But he was ready to scoot.

Missy hesitated.

"For chrissakes, Missy, pay the clowns what you owe them, tip well, send them on their way."

She looked at me.

"Chop chop," I added, "we've got an appointment."

She looked at them. They watched her synchronously, like two dogs waiting for their biscuits.

"It's all over," I said patiently. "People are getting killed. These guys don't have what it takes."

Ecstasy and the Cajun didn't even bother to take offense. Missy gave up. She retrieved a kidskin wallet from her purse and counted out five one-hundred dollar bills. The Cajun took the money and re-counted it. Ecstasy watched the count and shuffled his feet.

"I had a talk with my friend Lieutenant Bowditch," I mused

aloud, "–down to homicide?–just, let me see, it must have been yesterday afternoon, right before my nap. He mentioned that his lab had pulled quite a few latents from that big fire on Pier 70. 'Pellucid,' I think he called them, 'pellucid latents.' He seemed very pleased with the laboratory work, and–that big computer they have down there?–it was happy, too. Bowditch expected to be interviewing suspects as soon as tomorrow. Perhaps I should point out, to you boys especially, that tomorrow is today?"

Ecstasy blustered. "He can't pin that shit on us. You're the one who set the–"

"Shut the fuck up," the Cajun advised him in a mild tone, as he slapped two bills against his partner's chest. "Count your blessings." Ecstasy counted them–one, two–and smiled sleepily.

The Cajun shoved him toward Clement Street.

"Make it last till Mardi Gras," I called after them.

As he pulled open the door, Ecstasy turned and hefted his basket in my direction. The Cajun pushed him out to the street.

"Who owned the HumVee?" I asked, as the door closed behind them.

"Tommy," Missy said, still distracted. "It was so tacky that he figured nobody in a million years would think it was his."

The waitress reappeared to ask if we wanted our check, her eyes darting nervously toward the street. We asked for refills and she went away, disappointed.

I considered the photograph. It was grainy, black and white, possibly a copy of another photograph. "Where's a girl get hold of two, originally three, such ready-made idiots?"

Missy chewed her lip.

"What's the matter, darling? Prozac wearing off?"

She tried to smile. "I'm afraid it wore off quite some time ago, Danny."

"I'll bet. So the baggage handlers come from Tommy, too?"

"Tommy, too," she confirmed.

"This is getting serious. How deep are you into this Wong guy?"

She shook her head. "I'm not sure anymore."

"Does he know we're here?"

She made no reply.

"Son of a bitch." I cast a glance toward the street door. "Are those two guys. . . ?"

"No," she said. "They don't have the faintest idea what's going on. Tommy put me in touch with them through one of his construction foremen. That's the last he heard of it."

"For some reason I don't believe that."

"That part about the Tenderloin hotel was true," she said quickly. Her voice was beginning to quiver a little. "I called Emil right after you called me."

"Emil? That Cajun guy's name is Emil?"

"Yes."

"When did you call Tommy?"

"After I called him."

"What did you tell him?"

"That I was going to meet you, and that you were asking for him."

"Goddammit," I said, bringing my fist down on the table.

"Is everything all right, sir?"

The consternated face of the waitress peered around a corner of the cafe counter.

"Just dandy," I growled. "Bring us a check."

"Not to worry," Missy said in an undertone. "He's waiting for me."

"At home?"

"Yes."

"To do what?"

"Bring you to him."

I looked at her. "You were going to do that?"

She looked at me imploringly. "He has only one interest—"

"*Right,*" I said. "Did he say something quaint? Like, nobody's going to get hurt? Didn't you hear the first thing out of my mouth? John Plenty's been murdered. And this," I stabbed a finger at the photograph, "is what he was murdered for. You know what?"

"Ah. . . ." Missy replied tremulously. "What?"

"He didn't have it, that's what. He didn't even know what it was. Just like me. I didn't know what it was until Bowditch appeared with that insane story he got from his scholarly Sergeant. What's her name?"

"Maysle," Missy said miserably. "She's famous."

"Sergeant Maysle is famous? For what?"

"For her translation of the Syracuse Codex," Missy said, somewhat astonished. "It's been widely excerpted in anticipation of the Bollingen edition."

"*What?*"

"I'm not lying," Missy wailed. "Please believe me."

"Never. Calm down. We'll get this sorted out, one way or another. Leaving aside that this brilliant scholar is a sergeant in the San Francisco police department who has been exiled to Park Station because she had the guts to file a sexual harassment suit against her chief—the existence of which doesn't seem to have derailed the Bollingen edition of her translation of the Syracuse Codex—why in the hell do you know any of this stuff, which you obviously have known all along, even while you were in bed with me listening to Bowditch explain everything you knew already? And why in the hell does Tommy Wong care enough about it to kill people over it?"

Missy declared flatly, "Somebody else is killing people. Tommy would never hurt anybody."

"That takes the cake. He puts you onto a triumvirate of

bowling-alley leg-breakers and whatever the hell else they are, who carry guns and kidnap people, and you don't think Tommy Wong won't hurt anybody? The real question is, how does he get them to *not* hurt people?"

"Not Tommy," she said stubbornly. "He's a collector and a gentleman and that's all."

"A collector of what?"

She moved her chin toward the photo. "He owned that, once."

"He owned this, once?" I flicked it across the table. "Good. Maybe now you'll tell me what the hell it is?"

She looked from the photo to me, back and at me again, in frank astonishment. "You really don't know?"

I shook my head. "I really don't know."

"That's a close-up of a garnet stone."

This raised an eyebrow.

"It's the gem," she declared, "in the Ring of Theodosus."

tDiRTY-tDRee

"Y ou don't say." I took up the photograph and studied it with renewed interest.

Missy watched me closely. Now that we were discussing one of her favorite subjects, she had regained a little of her composure. "Danny, are you telling me the truth? Do you really know less than nothing about any of this? Really really really?"

I dropped the photo on the table. "I've never seen this ring in my life. I'm completely in the dark." I sat back in my chair. "And who knows, Missy? If you leave me in the dark I just might ripen, as the poet Philip Whalen once wrote, like a tomato or a madman."

She pursed her lips. "Left in the dark," she observed ruefully, "you might see your three score and ten."

"You're not following the logic of contemporary events. Left in the dark, my three score and ten is contraindicated. And not only that," I tapped the photograph, "everybody says that the damn codex went missing after the fire in Mill Valley, but nobody ever actually saw it there. In the meantime, the Weathergirl collected jewelry. Was this ring part of her collection? Was this ring the object of all that mayhem all along?"

"Okay okay," she sighed. She lifted the photograph until it was perpendicular to the table, looked at it for a moment, then let it fall.

346

"The Syracuse Codex has been missing from the Bibliothèque Nationale for a hundred and seventy years or so."

"Since 1830."

"That's certain. But the underground art world has known its whereabouts for at least fifty years. Ever since it disappeared from a villa on the coast of Greece during World War Two."

"A Greek museum?"

"Did I say it was a museum?"

"But I thought that television guy—"

"Ken Haypeak."

"Right. Jesus, what a name."

Missy shrugged. "It was his stage name. Don't worry about it."

"Newscasters have stage names?"

"Danny," Missy smiled, "you poor dear, you really do inhabit a uniquely tiny world."

"If newscasters have stage names," I repeated stupidly, "is nothing sacred?"

"Certainly not the news," Missy pointed out.

"Anyway, I thought he stole—"

"Bought," Missy corrected.

"Bought, then stole, the codex from Gerald Renquist. Where did Gerald get it?"

"It's just semantics. Forget Haypeak. That whole story is true, but it's also a red herring."

"A red herring? The guy and his girlfriend get burned alive in his—"

"Listen to me. Haypeak was shown the codex in a *private* museum. Not a municipal museum, not a state museum, not a national museum, but a private museum. It was in a private collection."

"You mean like the Getty? The Guggenheim? What difference—?"

"No, no, Danny. A private collection. A special collection. A collection that's open to no one, let alone the public. A collection owned by an individual, specifically for the amusement of that individual."

"Not open to regulation, inspection, taxation?"

She nodded assent.

"Not subject to *legal protections,* either."

"That's correct."

"Which is as much as to say, pirates and thieves and larcenous collectors were buying and selling the Syracuse Codex from and to each other. . . ."

"Many times over."

"Since the original theft? Out of the Bibliothèque Nationale, I mean?"

"There's even some question about the authenticity of the Bibliothèque Nationale's acquisition. But at least that purchase was public."

"One way or another, this codex has been hot for the entire hundred and sixty years."

"Exactly."

I picked up the photograph. "How do you come into this, Missy?"

"I knew you were going to ask that question."

"How in the hell do you know so much about it?"

"That question, too."

One answer dawned on me. "Did Kevin ever own the codex?"

"Almost," she said wistfully.

"Almost?"

"He was outbid."

"By whom?"

"The guy in Baghdad, I guess."

348

"So this was when? Ten or twelve years ago?"

She shrugged. "I was still married to Kevin."

"Fifteen or twenty?"

"Danny, please."

"This is not about your age," I said testily, "but it's almost as important."

"I'm glad that's understood. Once Kevin became known in any particular market, all kinds of things came his way. One thing always led to another."

"How much for the codex?"

She pursed her lips. "Kevin dropped out at seven and a half million."

"Francs?"

She smiled a faintly indulgent smile. "Dollars. The bidding was international. The currency was agreed on beforehand: American dollars, in cash."

"Cash? Jesus Christ."

"Seven and a half was over our budget. To tell you the truth, when it was stupid stuff like shoes and bathtubs, Kevin thought it was funny. He thought people deserved to be shorn of their money, if that's the way they wanted to spend it. It was like he owned a gambling joint or something. He was very knowledgeable about it, and just as cold-blooded. A good businessman in a weird business. The Syracuse Codex was different."

"Why?"

"Several reasons. One: the money was too big. Two: the people involved went from fun to unsavory, with no in-between. The aristocrats and eccentrics, the reclusive collectors and wildly successful software magnates who collect rock & roll memorabilia somehow turned into cocaine dealers, arms merchants, third-world politicians with blood on their hands, savings & loan crooks–shady, belligerent, vulgar people. They had tons of money and it was all cash. But the things we saw at their parties. . . ." She shivered. "Ugh. Neither of us liked it any more. On top of that, Kevin's research had made him nervous about–well, he called it the *karma* of the codex."

"Karma," I observed, "is Sanskrit for *deed* or *action.*"

"Yes?" Missy said. "Well, going right back to Theodosus, a number of people associated with the codex died in unseemly or untimely ways, or both. There's an entire apocryphal history. . . . But that wasn't the real reason. The real reason was that the Syracuse Codex was so goddamn illegal, such a thorough-going piece of roguery, as Kevin liked to say when the stakes weren't so high, such out-and-out international grand theft, along with smuggling and tax-evasion, that he didn't see why we should want any part of it."

"So why did you?"

She ignored this. "Finally, the fork in the road became un-mistakable. We had some really close friends, a husband and wife. She was born rich. He was a famous drug lawyer who made his reputation defending potheads in the sixties for free. After they married, they started a family, and, despite his wife's money, he felt he needed to make a living. Since drug law was his thing, he started taking on drug clients who could afford to pay him. At first this meant high-profile LSD dealers and chemists. Then it became cocaine dealers, first the mules, then the suppliers, and then came the syndicate heavies. Ultimately he found himself in court defending narcotics operators he *knew* had killed people, or had had them killed, or both. Really powerful, really dangerous people. They paid him hundreds of thousands of dollars to keep them out of jail, and he did it. He was very good at it. But he also came to despise them, and finally he hated himself most of all. His whole life came into question. You see what I mean?"

"I see what you mean about the lawyer, but I fail to see what this has to do with the codex."

"One day this lawyer decided he'd had enough. He tapered off his case load and retired. Just up and quit. Moved the wife and kids to Tahoe. Designed and built a house. Almost two years later one of his old clients looked him up. Big heroin dealer. A very bad man. The DEA had the guy dead to rights: possession, transportation, and sale of hundreds of kilos of heroin; money laundering, contract murder, tax evasion—the works. He needed expert help. Our lawyer friend turned him down. The guy said hey, I paid for your house. The lawyer said yes, that's true, and I earned it. Now I'm retired. I'm done. I can't help you. The guy said, you sure? The lawyer said he was sure. The guy said he understood. They shook hands. The guy got another lawyer. The other lawyer did what he could, but the bad guy got sentenced to twenty-five years without parole. About a year after he was sentenced, our friend and his wife disappeared forever."

"No trace?"

"None."

"Once he'd been locked up, the old client got to brooding."

"That was the general opinion."

"I guess making money's not the cherry festival it's cracked up to be."

"As to the codex, Kevin and I were torn. We discussed the possibilities endlessly. One minute we'd say, this is our last big score; let's do it and get out. On the other hand we had plenty of money and, by then, Kevin's father had died, so Kev had nothing left to prove and nobody to prove it to. He'd almost doubled the fortune his grandfather's trust had settled on him, and his father had witnessed about two-thirds of that increment before the Alzheimer's got him and he couldn't tell the difference anyway. Kevin hung in until he doubled his inheritance, just to achieve the round figure. It was a personal goal thing—even though by the time it was accomplished, the old man had died. Don't think about it. I tried not to. Anyway, okay, that was done. He'd proven his manhood. Why get in a tizzy about it?"

"Because it wasn't about the money," I answered.

She waved it off. "Finally we had one last day to think it over. And still we couldn't decide. Opportunities like this don't come along every day—hell, they don't come along in a lifetime. The Syracuse Codex is a prize beyond value. But in some kind of basic and karmic way, the codex was almost too weird to touch. It was a global object, a treasure that belonged to all humanity. No private individual should be able to assert domain over it. If that were true, then we had no business trying to corner it for profit."

"Admirable," I said. "So why not buy it and donate it back to the Bibliothèque Nationale and defend their stewardship against all comers?"

Missy looked at me. "That's a pretty cool sentiment," she pointed out, "for a guy who doesn't have a Lalique to make water in."

"Not being so delicately encumbered, I have plenty of time for the odd thought."

"We thought that thought," she said primly, "but the price was steep."

"So what determined you to get into the bidding anyway? Seven and a half million dollars? Jesus. I can hardly bring myself to say it."

"It's a lot of money," she agreed. "But what changed our minds was, we heard about the ring."

"The ring," I said stupidly.

She tapped a lacquered nail on the photograph. "You remember the story?"

"There were two rings. . . ."

352

"No, there were three rings. There was the pair that Manar had made–"

"Manar, Manar. . . ."

"The father? Theodosus' father?"

"Theodosus' father commissioned the original two rings. Right. From the guy in India."

"Very good. He had one made for Theodora, and one for himself."

"Manar's ring ultimately passed down to Theodosus."

"Right. And what did Theodosus do?"

"Ah, yes. He had an imitation ring made, the third ring, which he carried to Constantinople."

"Do you remember what it was made of?"

"Hell, I don't remember what the first two were made of. I was in bed with hypothermia when I heard the story, remember?"

"The stones in the first two were amethyst. The stone in the third ring was garnet. All three were convex-cut, or *cabochon*– little globes. The word derives from the Old French for head or cabbage. You can get with cabbage-head, can't you, Danny? You've always liked etymologies."

I smiled thinly.

"All three were made by the same jeweler, and the three settings were identical, the two of gold, the one of brass."

"Okay, we've got that straight. So what about them?"

"Just as we were considering the codex auction, the third ring came on the market, Danny. The one made of garnet."

I was completely taken aback. "Someone found the actual ring? Guaranteed?"

"Guaranteed. Records of the design were discovered in India, including, get this, the jeweler's original sketch, signed by him and countersigned by the purchaser, Manar himself. The signatures shared a Vedic lunar date, too."

"That damn drawing must be worth a fortune."

She shook her head. "You're catching on, Danny."

"I don't believe this."

"Neither did we. But. . . ." She tapped a fingernail on the manila envelope. "We received a photograph."

"Those damn photographs—was it this damn photograph?"

"No, of course not. A different one."

"So where—?"

"It came from a ten-percenter, a picker whom we knew only by his reputation. There was little doubt that the ring was genuine."

I shook my head. "So now what?"

"Kevin, and Kevin only, had a chance to buy the ring—get this—before it went onto the open market."

"You mean the *open* open market?"

"No. I mean the underground open market."

"How did you rate the preferential treatment?"

"Two reasons. First, there was Kevin's reputation for honesty and ready cash."

"Prime considerations, no doubt. And the second?"

"The ring was, shall we say, *fresh?*"

"Fresh?"

She nodded. "Extremely fresh."

"Like, the garnet ring came pickled in warm blood in a mayonnaise jar?"

She made a face. "Let's just say it was so fresh that the previous owner thought he still owned it."

I had to smile. "That's pretty fresh."

She nodded. "We were in Paris at the time. The codex, meanwhile, was ever-so-briefly in Marseilles. The timing was such that we had to bid on the codex before we could attempt to purchase the ring. The machinations behind the ring deal were complicated. There were middlemen in different countries. Two or three languages were involved."

"So you went for the codex."

"We decided to go for both."

"Both?"

She nodded.

"The Big Casino," I surmised.

"All this happened in two days. We didn't sleep at all. We decided to stall the ring deal while we went after the codex. If we didn't get the codex, we could still go for the ring. With the codex relatively out in the open, the ring would be worth millions. If we wound up with both... Well. Even now, the thought of owning both the garnet ring and the Syracuse Codex completely overwhelms my Prozac."

"I think I have a glimmer of comprehension of that sensation."

"I must take a moment to compose myself." She sipped her tea and made a face. "This is cold."

"Get on with it. We already know you lost the bid."

She nodded distantly. "We had a direct line from our hotel in Paris to the auction in Marseilles. The proceedings were very exclusive, of course."

"Exclusive to a menagerie of world-class villains."

"Without doubt. In any case, we had a budget. In order to secure both the ring and the codex, our price for the codex could not exceed seven and a half million. It was a day I'll never forget. We had a bottle of champagne on ice right next to the phone. Kevin wouldn't open it until after the bidding because he wanted a clear head. Right away, the numbers went beyond what we'd expected. You know," she added parenthetically, "it's simply amazing how much money there is in the world."

"Can it."

"You don't believe it," she sighed. "Most people don't. Anyway, by the time the auction was over, *we* didn't believe it either. The holding price was five million–five million! The bidding went up a half-million dollars at a time, with no more than thirty seconds between bids. Up up and up. Within three minutes we were out of the running. Three minutes!"

"You're breaking my heart. Who got it?"

"Oh, Danny, don't be so cruel. Can't you at least get into the spirit of the chase?"

"We're running out of time."

"We just sat there," she resumed despondently, "with the phone between us, watching that unopened bottle of champagne as the numbers ascended. Finally, the thing was knocked down."

"How much?"

"I told you. Ten million."

I shook my head in disbelief. "Ten million dollars for a slice of veal."

"Actually, it's parchment."

"Oh. Did you drink the champagne anyway?"

"What?" Missy blinked. "Funny you should mention that. Yes." She assumed an odd look. "We drank it the next day."

"You waited until you had bought the ring?"

She shook her head vaguely. "At first we thought that was exactly what we'd do. 'Oh, well,' Kev said after the codex was auctioned, 'we'll just buy the ring. We'll spend a hell of a lot less money and make a bigger profit.' I had to agree with that, of course. But we went to bed that night with a bad feeling."

"Why?"

"It's difficult to explain. There was a rational element, which simply had to do with the fact that the garnet ring was even more of an illegal antiquity than the Syracuse Codex, if only because it was more recently stolen. We knew the history of the codex, more or less. But about the ring we knew only that it was verifiably genuine and genuinely available.

"The irrational element was that we simply shared a bad feeling about this ring business. Losing the codex seemed like a clear sign that we should just forget Theodosus

356

altogether. But it was just a feeling. Kevin put it aside and made the call anyway, signaling our interest. Then we set about doing the hard part. We waited."

"In your first class hotel suite in the middle of Paris, you waited."

"In the heart of the Sixth, mind you," she clarified. "But waiting is waiting, you know. Finally it was the police who put an end to it, along with our delusions."

"The police?"

"The next afternoon five or six French cops appeared in our hotel suite. Boy, did they have news for us. Our jewelry 'associate' had been found murdered, and rather spectacularly so. 'Semaphorically fixed,' as that nasty French Inspector put it; in other words, the man's murder was meant as a warning. All the blood had been drained from his body. A thumbprint from his one remaining digit revealed his identity to the police. The only other meaningful clue found with the body was a bloodstained scrap of that square-ruled notepaper—the sort French school children use? The Inspector showed it to us." Missy shuddered. "On it were Kevin's name, the address of the hotel, and our suite number."

"This is beginning to sound a little bit like the circumstances surrounding that case in Sea Cliff," I pointed out thoughtfully.

Missy nodded. "Kevin was magnificent. He declared that this murdered man was obviously a hoodlum, and, but for his timely death, there, perhaps, had gone our own untimely ones. May God forgive him for speaking thus of the dead, Kevin added, though he stopped short of actually making the sign of the cross. He convinced the police that it was completely obvious that this nefarious dead man had targeted us for robbery or kidnapping or worse. He refused to construe it any other way. No other explanation could be possible. Indeed, much to our chagrin, it turned out the fellow had a considerable record for just such activities—burglary, auto theft, attempted murder, and whatnot–but none for, say, smuggling, or receiving stolen goods. So, getting an eyeful of the opulence of our hotel suite along with a glass of excellent cognac, and with a little help from the manager, a personal friend, who smoothed things over and endorsed our impeccable credentials, the French Inspector saw to it we were put on the London boat-train by midnight, with a police escort, yet. The conductor was kind enough to find us a bucket of ice, and yes, to answer your question, we finished the bottle of champagne just as we pulled into Calais. There was a glass for our escort as well. We overwhelmed him with gratitude. Kevin and I were a couple of dilettantes, and we considered ourselves well out of a nasty situation. So." Missy pushed her teacup aside. "Kevin never dealt antiquities or ephemera or anything else, ever again. And for sixteen or seventeen years I never gave the Syracuse Codex or the ring of Theodosus another thought."

She gave me an imploring look. "You must believe me."

"I've always loved your stories, Missy, whether they're true or not. Are you telling me that what we have here is *déjà vu* all over again?"

"Yes. No. I mean, not exactly."

"What's changed?"

Again she slipped a fingernail under the edge of the photograph and levered it up so I could see it. "Last year, Tommy Wong came to me with a proposition." She let the photograph fall back onto the table, face up. "He told me that Renée Knowles had located the Syracuse Codex."

"Renée had found the Syracuse Codex? Our Renée? Where? How?"

She shook her head. "Not important. What was important was that she had it."

"And?"

She held out her hand. "And then Tommy Wong placed the garnet ring of Theodosus on this very palm."

358

Thirty-four

"Missy, it's eleven-thirty."

Missy turned a twinkling diamond bracelet on her wrist and glanced at it. "So it is."

"You think you could wind this up?"

She smiled contentedly. "It's atomic."

I sighed. "Wong's gone."

"Don't worry. For what he thinks I'm showing up with, he'll wait."

"And what, exactly, does he think you are showing up with?"

She smiled sweetly. "You."

"Missy, how could you do this to me? Whatever it is, I hastily add, that you're doing?"

"Oh, come on, Danny. We know you have the ring."

This left me dumbfounded. "The ring," I laughed. "Of Theodosus? *I* have the ring?"

"Sure."

"You just finished telling me that Tommy Wong has it."

"Had it. Past tense."

"What happened?"

She shrugged. "It got away from him."

"It *got away* from him? What did it do? Call a cab?"

"Not important. But it didn't go far."

"Okay, we'll put that detail aside while you tutor me as to my strand in this braid of avarice. Tell me, now, from whom did I steal it?"

"Silly boy. You stole it from Renée." She patted my hand. "After you killed her."

"That isn't funny, Missy. I thought your intuition told you I didn't kill her."

"That was before I found out she was the last person to have the ring."

"And who told you that?"

"Tommy. He always knew where it was."

"Maybe he killed her."

"He says you killed her."

"That's brilliant. How about this: she gave me the ring for safe-keeping and then *you* killed her."

"Danny," she huffed, "don't be ridiculous."

"Don't *you* be ridiculous, Missy. I never even heard about this goddamn ring until Bowditch played us his tape, over a week after Renée was killed. You were there, remember? Even then, I had no way of knowing the ring had been spotted anywhere in the world in fifteen hundred years. Bowditch certainly didn't mention it. I only find out about stuff when people like him or you decide to tell me about it. And all this time I was thinking this whole to-do was over the Syracuse Codex. How stupid can I get?"

"Oh, Danny, don't be so hard on yourself."

I turned up my hands. "If it's my fate to look ridiculous—"

"After your looks go," she said distractedly, "it's about all you can expect."

"Then I definitely got started early."

"It's not so bad, darling. Maybe you could do the evening news. Your job is to scare them, not entertain them."

I touched one of her wedding rings. "Which husband gave you this?"

"My first."

"That was the orthopedic surgeon?"

"He could do anything with his hands," she sighed. "That's

360

how he seduced me. He did card tricks, played the saxophone—he even made his own shoes. Each shoe had individual toes," she wiggled the fingers of her free hand. "Like Bugatti's?"

"That's the creepiest thing you ever told me about one of your husbands."

"It wasn't until after I married him that I found out that he did *everything* with those hands." She shivered and looked away. "I don't want to talk about it."

"Enough! Listen to me. You still wear his ring."

She flattened her hand on the table, the better to admire the ring. "I can't bear to pawn."

"Missy, you've never set foot in a pawn shop in your life."

"Of course not. Are they as dreadful as people say?"

"The point is, does this ring still mean something to you?"

"It's a diamond. Of course it means something."

"He didn't want it back after the divorce?"

"He *begged* me to keep it."

"So you wouldn't forget him?"

She made a little face. "All I can remember are those busy hands." She brightened. "And the place in Ketchum. That was nice. And he had a friend who—"

"Missy, look at me."

She looked away. "Why?"

"I swear by your first wedding ring, which means so much to you, that I've never laid eyes on that garnet ring."

She looked back. "It's called the Ring of Theodosus."

"That makes sense. But I've never seen it or touched it or smelled it or felt it or even heard of it until Sergeant Maysle's lecture the other day. Perhaps more relevantly, I don't care about it. All I care about right now is getting my hands on whoever killed John Plenty. Then I'd like a good night's sleep. Do I make myself understood?"

She said, "If you had seen it, you'd feel differently.

361

I shook my head. "Most people aren't wired for acquisitive greed—not like you are, anyway. Can you understand that?"

"In a word? No."

"Let me try another tack. The garnet ring's a knock-off. What could it possibly be worth?"

"It's a beautiful ring. It's legendary. The associative value alone is incalculable. The ring's worth a fortune, and you're an idiot."

"This ring got Theodosus killed. Did it stop there?"

"Yes, it got him killed. In Anchialos, right between Sozopolis and Mesembria." She smiled sweetly and took back her hand. "Ali was very specific."

"You know the story well."

"Inside and out. Up one side and down the other. In the dark like my own husband's—" She stopped.

"Hands," I supplied.

She shuddered. "Just the first one."

"What makes the knock-off so fascinating?"

She told off her fingers. "It's associated with an immortal story. It mitigates the blame accrued to Theodora for her part in her son's murder."

"What are you talking about? She was going to kill the kid anyway."

"Danny," Missy explained patiently. "There are apologists for *everybody*." She held up a third finger. "Then there's the Syracuse Codex. The two items are complementary. Each corroborates the other. Each has disappeared and resurfaced time and again, all over the world, so you've got romance. Plus, like the codex," Missy was now counting her forefinger a second time, "the ring has profound historic value. Shall I go on?" She went on. "It turns out the Madras jeweler is known and collected. That's how documentation for the design turned up in the first place."

"Bowditch couldn't remember his name."

"Ramahandras," she said promptly.

I looked at her.

"Danny, people are looking for this stuff."

"How much is the ring worth?"

She shrugged, exasperated. "Kevin would have known how to get a good price."

"A million?"

"Don't act so stupid!" she shouted. More calmly she added, "Stupidity doesn't become you."

"Ten million?"

She eyed me shrewdly. "With or without the codex?"

I sighed. "My head hurts."

"Danny, you're exasperating. Remember the price at which, as I just told you, Kev and I quit the bidding for the Codex?"

"Seven and a half million."

"That's right. It sold for ten, and that was seventeen years ago. So now think. What's a fair price?"

"Whatever the market will bear," I parroted, bored.

"That's my Danny. If these items were in Texas, and Texas were in hell, they'd still be the hottest things around. Throw in August, too. Museums want them. Collectors—"

"Bowditch wants them," I reminded her. "People with guns want them. Call it off. Citizens have died. Borders have been crossed. Taxes have been evaded. Institutions have been pilfered. There must be cops and agents and hired thugs and bounty-hunters and depraved ten-percenters looking all over the world for both the ring and the codex. Let's say you and Tommy do get hold of them. What's to be done? The safest thing would be to keep them. The only out might be a finder's fee or a reward from an insurance company, which might protect you. But they've never been insured—right?" That stopped me. "That's the angle Renée saw," I hastily concluded. "That's what got her into it. Right? No insurance? Therefore no law?"

"Sure, Danny," Missy agreed sarcastically, "that and ten million dollars."

"Which one got Renée killed? The codex or the ring? Do you know? Do you care?"

"About Renée Knowles?" She pursed her lips, incredulous. "What else is there to care about?"

There came no answer to this. "Missy," I whispered. "Not you. . . ."

She drew herself up. "Danny Kestrel, how dare you suggest–?" She looked away; she looked back; she slapped me. "Certainly not!"

For as long as I'd known Missy, I'd rarely caught her being serious. She never seemed able to lock on to any real reason to become concerned or upset about anything, about, say, the destruction of Beirut. And somehow she always and easily pulled me into her persiflage. But now she displayed gravity I'd never seen before. Furious she said sternly, "Danny, you're missing something here, something *fundamental.*"

"I am?" I drew a finger over my cheek and looked at it. No blood. I showed it to her. "What am I missing?"

She pushed my hand away. "Only Renée Knowles was interested in the Syracuse Codex or the Ring of Theodosus or anything else solely because of money. The rest of us care about what they *mean.*"

"Oh," I said. "I thought we were going to talk about murder. But, okay, let's discuss culture. Or, as you put it, what they mean. And what the hell do they mean? Ten million? Twenty? To somebody somewhere, that's exactly what they *mean.*"

Missy denied this. "The money is secondary. Look at the people involved in this mess." She made with the fingers again. "There's Theodora herself. . . ."

"Theodora's been dead for sixteen hundred years!"

Missy insisted. "Longevity makes a big difference, Danny. Compare Theodora to, say, I don't know, Marilyn Monroe.

Think of the ring as a love letter to Marilyn from Jack Kennedy. Now do you get it?" She thought for a moment. "Did you listen to the radio this morning?"

'This morning' sent my mind to John Plenty's darkened loft. For a moment I smelled whiskey and gunpowder, and saw the gleam of light on broken glass and that damn shoe. "No," I said quietly. "I didn't listen to the radio this morning."

"Some guy announced he has the copy of the Beatles' *White Album* that John Lennon signed for John David Chapman, two minutes before Chapman assassinated him."

"Oh, no," I wailed. "I'll talk. I'll confess. I'll do anything. Just don't hit me with the pop culture anymore, along with the people who died for its sins, and the people who can't get enough of feeding off of it."

"One point five million, Danny."

"Missy, please. You're making me sick."

"I seek an analogy you can grasp. Try to factor in the things that may be unimportant to you but are as life's blood to others. Imagine: Marilyn Monroe and John Lennon and even John F. Kennedy, the 35th president of the United Sates, may well be forgotten a hundred years from today. Two or three hundred years from now, let alone fifteen hundred, it's more than possible that the United States itself will have been forgotten; if, indeed, there's anybody around to do the forgetting. And if they are around, what's the one thing they might remember about us?"

"The invention of television?" I immediately suggested.

She smiled compassionately. "The Syracuse Codex and the Ring of Theodosus represent more than mere *Zeitgeist* culture, Danny. They're history. They're artifacts of a timeless story. They've developed apocryphal histories of their own. Almost everything else is gone. It's true they're extremely valuable; you're perfectly right to think that, at this point, as a market reality, they're pretty much beyond price. I dare say that if you were to attempt to donate the ring to a museum, for example, you'd find that the museum's directors and insurance carriers—not to mention the modern-day government of Turkey—would find a way to ruin you over it. At the very least they'd whittle your commission down to practically nothing. You'd spend most of it on lawyers defending yourself against charges that eloquently detail how you stole the ring in the course of a ten-year rampage of pillage and rape you don't remember because of your multiple personality disorder but got away with because of your penchant for cross-dressing, and this museum and its insurance carrier have joined forces to get you off the streets in a spirit of civic cooperation unprecedented in the annals of corporate Byzantine bauble acquisition. *Et cetera ad nauseum.* Do you hear what I'm saying, or do you not?"

"What you're saying is, since even a legitimate repository would try to fuck me out of such a valuable antiquity as the Ring of Theodosus, I should just turn it over to you because you know what to do with it. Right?"

"How utterly percipient of you, Danny Kestrel."

"I'm flattered to be in the loop at all, I'm sure. But I don't have your goddamn ring, Missy. Today is the first time I've even heard of it surviving at all. Okay? Now what?"

Without hesitation she said, "Now you tell that story to Tommy Wong."

Tһırtʏ-fıvє

Despite her banter, which I was beginning to perceive as dangerous beyond mere treachery, Missy's drift contained an element that I'd missed before, which was that only some of the people involved in this matrix of thieves gave a damn about the money. This shook my thinking. If the cannibals come to the feast because they're hungry, what are the fanatics there for?

Renée was duplicitous and avaricious and vamping for her main chance; willing to sacrifice almost anything to get ahead; piling up fortune against misfortune, weapons against adversity, success against poverty, little misanthropic coups against the world's reluctance to acknowledge her existence. Ambitious to the point of sociopathy, she pursued a vision of success no one else understood, a vision she'd taken to her grave, if the term vision applies. She'd sacrificed everything, including her life, in pursuit of what may never have been anything less than unobtainable.

Theodora herself? She'd had everything, only to be brought down by a "cancer" at a relatively tender age, barely in her forties. Yes, look at Theodora. She'd had it all. . . .

Renée wasn't stupid. Like Missy, she probably knew the story of Theodora as well Sergeant Maysles did. Had she learned anything? Had Renée discovered in Theodora a model against which to measure the scope of her own aspirations? A milestone such as, for example, possession of the Syracuse Codex? Or the Ring of Theodosus? Or both?

367

Like a snake thought to be a hologram right up until the moment it strikes, a theory had formed, as if in the night, without my realizing it. Renée had come to identify with Theodora, the orphaned prostitute, who, by her fierce and tireless efforts, managed to aggrandize to herself an entire empire. She'd sold her body to whomever. She tortured and killed by the score. She perpetrated the death of her only son. And for what? It was true that she had instigated good works. It was true that, if she were perceived as a despot, she was perceived as a successful one, and that very success justified the extremity of the measures necessary to assure her reign—"no alternative between ruin and the throne." Several writers considered her a proto-feminist.

But for what? So that, despite the attendance of four thousand servants, despite scattering alms on all sides, despite endowing temples and schools and orphanages, a cancer might unstring her knees, as Homer put it, and fit her for the cobblestone shirt?

Not a bad idea, for one paranoid and alone. But it seemed too sentimental for Renée Knowles. Theodora, who had lived it, would no doubt have accepted her early death as the next roll of the dice, and would rather have endured it while couched in the honor and finery of an empire, than sweat out no dice at all in a shack next to the town dump. Renée would have felt the same way. She'd die alone, amid her self-referential collections in Pacific Heights, while her husband's hookers came and went, before she'd nod among tulips and grandchildren on the front porch of her cowboy's ranch.

So something else was afoot. Renée had found something that caused her to violate all the principles she'd come to understand, to throw out the unsentimental tools by which she'd levered herself up in a tricky world of vague liaisons, unwritten double-crosses, secret cash deals. In a world where she was only as good as her word, and her word was only as good as the last deal she'd made good on, Renée had double-crossed somebody, and that somebody was bent enough to kill her for it.

Renée had misjudged. She'd overreached.

What had clouded her judgment? The value of the codex was certainly sufficient to encourage any number of people to have killed her for it, if that were why she died, but if so, the killer came away from the murder empty-handed. So far, so obvious. But why had Renée reneged? On whom? And why had it subsequently gotten John Plenty killed? It was true they'd spoken the night she died. I saw the exchange. And I believed John when he explained to me that she knew she was in trouble, that she'd been tempted to get him to help her, and that she had changed her mind. He even flattered himself that it had been her one good deed in life. But John died anyway. Why? Was ten million dollars the price of why? Ten million bucks. . . .

Clearly, Renée had no such money available. The Codex was far too precious, far too hot, and far too expensive for Renée to control it by herself. So what was she doing in the mix? Working on commission? Why not? If Tommy Wong were to be believed, just about any commission on ten million dollars would amount to far more than Renée had been able to grift up to then. But who would have trusted her that far?

So how about this: she was a *mule.*

I liked that.

Renée Knowles never had a piece of the action. She couldn't have, because she had no economic clout. This would mean she was working for somebody else. So who? Gerald Renquist? Certainly he'd been in on it. But the amount of money required to play the game ruled him out, too. As it did his mother.

Which, once again, left only Tommy Wong. And now it turned out that Wong had actually been in possession of the

Ring of Theodosus—not in Baghdad or in Paris or at the South Pole, but in San Francisco, and very recently.

If Missy was to be believed, Wong had decided that I was now in possession of the ring. If so, it could only be because he thought I'd gotten it off Renée, just before she was killed. But I wound up with the Syracuse Codex instead.

Why didn't this add up? Had Dave and I missed the ring in the BMW? Was this extremity even conceivable? Had Renée Knowles become the first person in fifteen hundred years to be in simultaneous possession of both the Ring of Theodosus and the Syracuse Codex?

That possibility might have looked so momentous to Renée as to appear more like an historical imperative rather than an opportunity exposed by mere chance, of a gravity sufficient to screw up anybody's judgment. And therein might well lie the answer. This solution might explain why Renée had deviated from the sacred path of her ambition, betraying every contact, not to mention risking her life. The possession of these two priceless antiquities would have magnified her accomplishment beyond anything a little girl might ever have imagined, riding her wingless Pegasus reluctantly homeward in the chilly light of a fall afternoon. Theodora's rise to power, resonating with her own success, must have sweetened Renée's anticipation of victory.

Renée had not been able to resist a play that was, simply, suicidal. It had cost the lives of others, too.

It would have been interesting to hear what Tommy Wong had to say about these things.

But. . . .

The driveway was circular, the landscaping scrupulous, the mansion and its grounds tasteful and extensive. A glint of sunlight darted from the Pacific Ocean down a bowered path alongside the house, bringing with it the fresh taste of cool marine air. Gulls wheeled in the thermal draft rising from the cliff above China Beach, directly behind the house. A couple of finches chattered on the chimney cap. The front door stood open as if there were a garden party out back, as if we were expected.

Ecstasy lay across the threshold of this door, sprawled ungainly, bloody and dead, with brand new holes in his head, front and back.

Missy tripped over the body, stepped back to take stock of Ecstasy's fate, and fainted.

Ecstasy had taken his medicine while running away from it. His entry wound was posterior, at the top of his spine; the exit wound would be anterior. I turned him over. His little .25 automatic remained stuffed up the sleeve of his jacket, unfired. The sagittal crest above his right eye was blown away.

I stepped over him, into the silent house.

Across the marble tiles of the entry foyer, the Cajun lay at the foot of a sweeping teak staircase. One of his arms protruded between the newel post and a baluster, twisted unnaturally. Below the hand, his tomagotchi peeped feebly. The Cajun's corpse featured two extra holes of its own, close together, in his chest. A .32 automatic pistol lay at his feet. He'd gotten it out of his pocket, but he hadn't managed to fire it.

Except for the insidious waft of expended cordite, it was a beautiful house with a lot of wood paneling, paintings, gilded cornice moldings, sumptuous drapes, and oriental rugs. One flight up the mahogany staircase tendrils of smoke rose slowly in the light angling in through an immense, north-facing window. You could probably see Bolinas from up there.

A door in the western wall of the foyer opened into a handsome library. I found Tommy Wong there, and he wasn't reading. Tommy Wong would never read again. Somebody had drained all of his blood into a trash can.

371

They'd tied him to a chair and cut a wrist. When he didn't talk, they cut the other one. Or maybe they cut the other one after he talked.

It was hard to say. Clarence Ing would figure it out. But it wouldn't ever make any difference to Tommy.

Ostensibly a delicate narcissist, Missy could probably have found the fortitude to sit through a video of her own plastic surgery. But a hole in somebody else's head? Cue the swoon. I draped her, wilted in couture, across three chairs in the dining room, whose main door let onto the east side of the foyer, opposite the library. I closed the front door for propriety's sake and returned to study Tommy Wong.

The wound in one wrist had drained into a rubber wastebasket, the other into a crystal punch bowl. Because it was taller, the waste basket had allowed less of a mess, but as it contained the greater volume of blood, it seemed fair to speculate that it had been the first receptacle pressed into service. A bath towel over Wong's knees was soaked in blood. These details seemed grotesquely fastidious. They wanted to torture the guy without ruining the rug?

They'd seated Wong in a ladder-backed chair that looked a lot like a Renny Mackintosh, except for the armrests, to which Wong's forearms were lashed, wrists up. The incision in the right wrist was sufficient to sever the veins but no deeper. The second incision, in the left wrist, clove to the bone.

Each sleeve of his shirt and jacket had been slit to the elbows for access. One arm was tied with a necktie, the other with a belt, articles poached from Wong's immaculate ensemble—a freshly-pressed, pale yellow shirt and dark tan suit complimented by soft leather loafers. His arms and trunk were secured to the back of the chair by a long red sash embroidered with gold thread, borrowed from a venerable silk kimono displayed on the wall above the mantelpiece. Wong sat with his back to the hearth, and the whole scenario

372

had been arranged so that someone could sit comfortably on the facing sofa to watch him suffer, and to sip, the while, a glass of chilled Chardonnay.

As I surveyed the scene, it occurred to me, apropos of nothing, that the two finches I'd noticed outside must have been perched atop the chimney cap of this very fireplace.

The wine bottle stood close to a half-empty glass on an end table adjacent the couch. In between them was a corkscrew of the type that uses a threaded wooden barrel. The cork, still impaled on the screw of this device, remained damp. Only the single glass had been poured, and the portion not entirely consumed. Condensation lingered on both glass and bottle. It seemed incredible to think that the perpetrator may not have worn gloves.

The wide sash no doubt had been handy, not applying so tight a constraint on the man's arms as to deprive his wrists of their proper circulation, nor so obtrusive as to deprive the spectator of his spectacle.

Except insofar as they might have swayed Tommy Wong in his preference to die slowly or quickly, ordinary human emotions could not have found a part in this scenario. Somebody sipped wine while Wong's life drained away in thick gouts. The brilliant red in the glass bowl harmonized disconcertingly with the scarlet of the kimono and sash, set against the otherwise quiet tones in the room.

Ranged around this scene was a truly impressive library, and among its many volumes I soon descried a section thick with titles like *Theodora: Portrait in a Byzantine Landscape; Theodora, Empress of Byzantium; Justinian and Theodora; and Theodora and The Emperor.* George Frederick Handel, it appeared, had composed an oratorio, *Theodora,* of which there were a very old score, with some conductor's penciled notes, and various recordings. Unusual, if not unexpected, the library seemed to consist almost entirely of first editions. A selection of works on the post-Christian Roman Empire was tall and wide. There were a very old, multi-volume edition of Gibbon's *Decline and Fall of the Roman Empire,* bound in vellum, a deluxe edition of *A Bibliography of Edward Gibbon's Library,* a collection of his letters, his *History of Christianity,* and a first of his *Autobiography,* as well as a collection of his early works in French. Procopius had his own section, too. The multiple volumes of his *History* were there, as well as various editions and translations of his *Secret History* including a facsimile of the original, Ανεκδωτα, along with his servile inventory of Justinian's public works, *Buildings.* Perhaps it had been this atypical and by all accounts most boring latter work by Procopius that had inadvertently initiated Tommy Wong, architect, into the cult of Theodora?

The room had little else to offer, other than decades of reading, and there didn't seem to be any *cabochon* garnets lying around. Wong's desk was neat and uncluttered. There were a shaded Prairie lamp and a telephone; a golden pen set; a blank memo pad, each cream-colored page embossed with the crimson logo of the Pachinko Hotel Group; and a glazed sandstone sculpture of two intertwined carp, one swimming into its center and the other swimming out.

I considered this sculpture, which allegorized, no doubt, the Tai Chi of yin and yang. Masculine and feminine, active and passive, one force waxes as its complement wanes, one fish arrives as the other departs, life feeds death and *vice versa.* I looked toward Wong's body, trussed in a collectible chair and backed against his stone-veneered fireplace, hard by a two-hundred-year-old brass hamper stacked with fragrant mesquite. One fish waxed powerful, sipping a fine Chardonnay; drop by scarlet drop, another had ceased to exist.

There were cut-glass decanters of brandy and bourbon in the built-in bar, a sink with gold fixtures, various glasses, a

374

bottle of Old Overholt. Bottles of mineral water, Kirin beer, and one of horseradish stood in a refrigerator under the counter, along with another of Chardonnay. I found no golden saucer bearing a garnet ring.

Wong's complexion had been too fair for a serious drinker in his sixties, his frame too trim and slight. When I met him, he looked in excellent health. Whether his story about Renée's little fraud with the Chinese trunk had been true or not, he had declared it a mistake to do business while drinking. But now, of course, everything he'd said to me would have to be reevaluated or disregarded altogether. On one hand, since he did lots of business, one might assume he didn't have much time to drink. But he had mentioned his predilection for a rye Manhattan, and there was the fifth of Old Overholt, along with vermouth and bitters. At the least, one might conclude Wong had been a genial host.

Right up to the end.

Tһirty-six

I hadn't heard about a scene like this in thirty years. One cut wrist left Wong maybe half an hour to make serious talk, if he could stand the shock. Usually the mere sight of the knife or razor was enough to get the information, if there was any. Either way, it was the odd man who could stand such treatment.

The half-empty glass reminded me of something. I went to the bookcase and pulled out a modern paperback of Gibbon's master-work. Its table of contents referenced *Portrait of an Empress*, the passage on Theodora read to us by Bowditch.

But the reproach of cruelty, so repugnant even to her softer vices, has left an indelible stain on the memory of Theodora. Her numerous spies observed and zealously reported every action, or word, or look injurious to their royal mistress. Whomever they accused were cast into her peculiar prisons, inaccessible to the inquiries of justice; and it was rumoured that the torture of the rack or scourge had been inflicted in the presence of a female tyrant insensible to the voice of prayer or of pity. Some of these unhappy victims perished in deep unwholesome dungeons; while others were permitted, after the loss of their limbs, their reason, or their fortune, to appear in the world the living monuments of her vengeance. . . .

Droplets yet fell from the chair arms, ". . .insensible to the voice of prayer or of pity." I replaced the volume on its shelf. Perhaps Tommy had prayed. But had he bothered to beg for his life?

For, surely, he had known his assailant. A path of destruction led directly to him, but there was no sign of a struggle here. His inept soldiers had been felled, their wounds accurately inflicted. What if, moreover, Wong hadn't even heard the shots? Perhaps Ecstasy and the Cajun had shown up only after the fact of Wong's death, and not to interrupt the inquisition? This seemed very likely. Cowed by certainty of failure, Ecstasy had been unable to do anything other than flee his fate, while the Cajun, at least, had made an effort to ward it off. What if, indeed, Wong had been expecting the earlier party who, having punctually arrived for a meeting with him, had calmly ordered him tortured to death?

Wong himself could have been working for the person who killed him. What if, having also somehow failed, he'd paid the ultimate price, meticulously exacted?

Or had Wong found his sordid end by withholding some vital piece of information? If not saving his own life, at least, might he have thwarted someone else's plan?

Ecstasy and the Cajun had failed to deliver. Wong had failed to deliver. Wong and—who else? Renée, Gerald, John. . . .

And Missy. Missy had failed to deliver, too.

I hurried through the library door. Halfway across the foyer I could see into the dining room, where stood the three chairs, empty.

As I stooped to pick up the Cajun's weapon, I realized the front door was open.

I didn't even bother to pick up the gun. Instead I walked to the front door, stepped over Ecstasy's mortal remains, and had a look outside.

377

The Jaguar was gone. I cursed that car for its silent operation, and cursed myself for letting Missy slip away.

She must have realized the danger. No wonder she fainted. When she woke up, she ran. If the sight of a violent death upset her, the intimation of her own demise must have overwhelmed her Prozac entirely.

I stood over Ecstasy and tried to think. I hadn't done anybody much good lately, but it annoyed me considerably that Missy thought she had a better chance alone than she did with me.

My Missy. My high-society friend. Practically the only person I knew who had more than just a couple of nickels to rub together, and now it looked as if she were seriously courting the banal destiny of a common criminal.

Our friendship seemed to have resolved itself into a marketable quantity. She'd traded me in. She had suckered herself back into the codex/ring deal, which, given her Paris experience, seemed ill-advised to say the least.

Ecstasy's dead eyes offered their endorsement.

In view of the ways in which various players had cashed out lately, rapacious individuals like Wong and Renée Knowles and Gerald Renquist, where did that leave Missy? Who was left?

Renée's husband certainly didn't give a damn about antiquities. All he cared about was hookers and the local football team. But even if Knowles did care, even a motel-soap magnate such as himself would hardly have the bankroll to play in the Codex League—would he?

I couldn't accept Knowles as a player. There couldn't be so much demand for one-night-stand bars of soap that he could afford ten-million-dollar antiquities, let alone two of them. He was worth a few million, tops. Thousand-dollar prostitutes and single-malt Scotches and an afternoon football game with no clock to punch looked like high cotton to him. Even if he was worth ten million, even if he could get an angle on a legitimate, non-violent purchase price, he wouldn't be playing this game. One way or another, separately or together, the Syracuse Codex and Theodosus' ring were well beyond his reach. The guy wasn't wired for the ruthless cupidity being exhibited by the players of the Codex League. Wrist-cutting? Not Knowles. Not by a long shot.

I paced between the bodies of Ecstasy and the Cajun, talking to myself. A little voice in my head took occasion to remind me that, cupidinous or not, *I* was now the party holding the Syracuse Codex. And how easy it had been! All I had to do was get copulated, kidnapped, bludgeoned, shot, hypothermified, interrogated, and disillusioned. The hardest part of it was spending all my time with people who didn't care about anything but money. But since it was the only kind of people I was meeting lately, maybe I'd learned something from them by osmosis? After the codex, how difficult could it be to take down a ring? Why not go for broke? Maybe all I had to do was donate a little blood into a rubber wastebasket, and I'd find myself looking a fortune right in its pointy little teeth.

But I'd never been one to seek such achievement. All I'd ever dreamed of was endless wet jungle or vast blonde planes of uncarved maple. A fortune beyond my dreams? Why? My dreams were modest traumalogues. I didn't need money to play them. They were sponsored by my government.

Buy a nice set of scorps and rifflers, said the little voice, and devote the rest of your life to whittling shepherd's staves for the Pope, for the Greater Glory of God. Jesus Christ, I responded disgustedly, do I get to keep my shoes on? But the little voice insisted. All the birdseye maple you want—think of it. You could incise Latin mottoes in spirals along the shaft. Get it? The shaft? With that kind of money, I fretted, unamused, I could probably go down to Stanford and get

379

Latin incised directly onto my DNA. Or your nuts for that matter, rejoined the little voice. As Picasso said, art comes from the balls. Why not let it end there, too?

Finally came a coherent if chilling thought: whether I understood Missy's motives or not, whether she understood them or not, Missy couldn't say she didn't know what she was in for. Well, she could, but nobody would believe her. Certainly not the cops.

But what about Dave? Even now the old bastard was working at the boatyard with his back to the street, as ignorant as a flat tire. When they came to get him, he wouldn't stand a chance. Not too far away, I wasn't sure where, he'd stashed the Syracuse Codex; I wasn't even certain he'd taken the trouble to hide it well. Even now, however, the prize was glowing on the codex-detector of some internecine picker. Not just any picker, mind you, but the same picker who was going around town letting the blood out of people, as well as shooting and burning them, not to mention gutting some of them and cutting the wrists of others, and all for the sake of a thin stack of parchment. This picker didn't stop at anything, let alone propriety, let alone innocence, age, civilization, an honorable discharge, or diesel breath, in his quest for the parchment grail. I had gotten Dave caught up in it. Was I going to get him killed, too?

Yo, Danny boy, spoke the little voice, seeing its opening, which it ever abided, you got Dave into this. Just like you got John Plenty into it. Just like—

Hey, I interrupted. John Plenty got himself into this. He was in love with Renée Knowles long before I bumbled onto the scene. Remember?

Quit kidding yourself, said the voice. Renée let him off the hook. Remember? John said so. They followed *you* back to *him.* You're at least that paranoid, aren't you?

John had an affair with her. . . .

He had an affair? She was using him.

380

For what?

Who knows? Transshipment?

This stopped me.

I paced over to the Cajun's corpse. The tomagotchi seemed to have run out of gas. It lay peepless on the rug, no score on its blank screen. So much for Zou-Zou. Though on the move, the Cajun had seen his two bullets coming. Ecstasy may have seen him try to pull his own gun to buy himself a chance, only to be dropped by two well-placed rounds, squeezed off so quickly as to sound as one, and so accurately as to impact their target two inches apart. No obvious holes in the walls, no stray rounds seemed to have been wasted. Taking note of this deadly marksmanship, Ecstasy had sought the exit. On the run, he got it from behind. A third excellent shot.

Transshipment. . . .

It's in there, dummy, the little voice chided. Data retrieval. . . . You don't often do crates. Remember?

I remembered. When I framed the Renée Knowles nudes for John, he asked me to throw in a crate. Crating art is a specialty; I offered him the phone number of an outfit that did it. "Oh yeah," he said, "Girly uses them all the time." "So use them now." "Oh she's not in on—" John caught himself and said, "Just do me a favor, Danny, and build the crate. What's the big deal?"

I don't know, I said to myself, staring down at the Cajun's blood-soaked pineapple shirt. What's the big deal?

But at the time I said, Sure, John, I'll whip something up. But I only have this apple core plywood here, and it's expensive; it costs ten times the shop grade they use in crates. Hey, John said, bill me.

But then he added, Our usual deal is you provide a slot that allows for packing material. I'm familiar with crating protocol, I said, familiar enough to eschew it. John ignored this and suggested, in a strained tone which, in retrospect, must have been annoyance with his ineptitude at mendacity. How about you provide two slots for two pictures instead of one. Right, I said, same dimensions?

And John made a face. No, he said, as if thoughtfully. From the watch pocket of his jeans, he retrieved a folded piece of paper. Figuring backwards from the theoretical canvas, he began sheepishly. . . . I haven't framed it yet? I asked, confused. No, he said, with a grimace, you haven't. You have a new framer, I began. No, don't worry about that, he said quickly. Just make the slot so it'll accept nine by thirty inches. Including the packing material? I asked. Yes. The previous painting I'd framed for him measured four by thirty by fifty inches; plus foam padding, it would have required a crate slot some ten by thirty-six by fifty-six inches. I mentioned this. Oh, said John dismissively, maybe it'll just be a drawing. Can you have it by Friday? Friday was just a couple of days away. So the conversation had turned to that problem.

In the back of my mind I'd been thinking, lo these many months, that John had started using another frame boy. And beating myself up as to why. Was he dissatisfied with my work?

Well, John had stuck with the same old frame boy, all right. Right down the line.

Once you've identified a reliable sucker, why change?

So now I'd seen John's "painting" at last, in the back of Renée's BMW. He hadn't had to paint it himself because it had already existed for fifteen hundred years. Its Lexan case measured about three by fourteen by twenty-four inches. Throw in the usual packing material—three-inch Sonex around bubble-wrap around a heat-sealed plastic wrapper—you get snug with John's specification. John would have needed only a simple tool or two to notch the crate for the vacuum valve.

Renée's teeth would have done fine.

So John Plenty, too, had been sucked into the voracious

382

gyre of the Syracuse Codex. I'd never considered him a close friend, but what possible reason could John have found to deceive me? Kind of like Missy, the little voice quipped, except she wasn't a marine. Given our military service, John and I had been colleagues after a fashion. Brothers in experience. But within that he'd always kept his artistic self walled up in a special fortress, to the which I, a mere artisan, would never have access, It was a piece of his puzzle that could never be explained.

He played you for a chump, the little voice flatly declared. Re-evaluate everything he ever told you.

For love of Renée, I decided, John had at some time smuggled the Syracuse Codex somewhere and somehow to somebody.

The somehow part we now know. Danny Kestrel built the crate. Good boy. Arf. It took two years to figure that one out.

The little voice pestered me. "She," John had said. "She didn't need–" what? John had been talking about Renée, right? Renée didn't "need" to get Girly involved in this transaction, let alone her art-crating service. Was that it? John had come directly to me. It was only the one crate. I had a framed painting sitting right there in my shop. Why not kick out the crate, too? Give the money to old Danny. So what if the ply-wood's more expensive? The difference amounts to a pittance. Not to mention that the usual fabricators would almost certainly refuse to crate it by Friday. . . .

You're straying, Danny, said the little voice. Want to get paranoid?

I looked around me. From astride the library threshold, I could see all three bodies.

Who me? Paranoid?

Strictly for argument's sake, the little voice persisted, what if that pronoun *she* hadn't referred to Renée? Or to Missy? Or to any other *she* you've met lately?

CROOKS, BRINE, & DRINKER

Thirty-seven

The warm, omnividient sun provided a stark contrast to the cool occlusive library I'd left behind, as I trudged the twenty blocks from Tommy Wong's mansion to the pickup truck. Its rays abraded the sclerotic fissures of my eyeballs like filaments of windblown sand. They forced their way through the slits of my eyelids as they would cracks in the siding of an old house, to lie up in the musty corners formed by dry-rotting plates and studs; little windrows of meaningless spindrift, adding and subtracting to themselves, minute harmless transactions by which very little accrued to the good or to the bad. . . .

Everything used to be so simple.

A sense of doom urged me over those pedestrian blocks. The human day hung suspended while the surface of the planet rotated beneath it. Lunchtime had come and gone, the mail would arrive, your soap operas would manifest and deliquesce, along with the odd telemarketer and ball game, maybe even a paycheck before dark, and, finally, a couple-three murders.

There were only so many players left. If I were to call Bowditch's attention to them, he might fit the collar with no more trouble to myself. But now I had a thing to straighten out, and there was no time for Bowditch. I felt sure that Missy was heading straight for the abyss. Though she had played me off against forces I had only recently begun to fathom, let alone admit as formidable, and for, in any case, her own reasons, which, outside of greed, I didn't fully comprehend, Missy was still my friend. She'd made a mistake running off, but I had little doubt she was about to make a bigger one. Even as I walked, Missy was driving toward the heart of the matter. Everyone had abandoned precaution. The pretense of civilized behavior, ever precariously established, had dissolved. People had been getting killed over the Syracuse Codex and the Ring of Theodosus for quite some time, but for the moment matters had accelerated. Somebody figured they had enough cover to make the score and get out of town, out of the country, likely out of the hemisphere, before the authorities could catch up with them, so a few lives no longer mattered. The only reason they ever did matter was that there were laws governing interactions between customers and suppliers. If you wrote contracts and honored them, if you wrote checks and they didn't bounce, if you promised to deliver goods and did so, the law protected you. If you didn't, the law protected your customer. But if customers and suppliers go around killing each other, what's a law-abiding body to do?

Just lie there, if it's dead.

The sun lit up the Avenues like a realtor's dream, clean and bright and fogless. You could see the deco capital of the south tower of the Golden Gate Bridge from Clement Street; it looked like it was just beyond the rooftops in the next block, just within reach, though it was at least two miles away. Parents were pushing strollers with attached umbrellas to protect their replicant's fair integument from the brutality of a sun brought so near by the emissions of its parents' sports utility vehicle. A scent of garlic chicken wafted on the afternoon westerly. A

dry cleaner's wall vent blasted passersby with the claustrophobic reeks of carbon tetrachloride and fried polyester, a toxic
jet of compressed air from the inverting fun-house floor. . . .

It was past one by the time I got to 35th at Anza. The truck
started. John Plenty's .25 was still under the seat. I had the
idea that a random discharge out the truck window had an
excellent chance of striking someone with an interest in the
Syracuse Codex—but that would be too easy. Instead, like the
guy who's been thrown from the horse, I drove right back up
25th Avenue. At El Camino del Mar I took a right onto
Lincoln Boulevard and barreled for the Marina.

I had only the one guess. Then Bowditch would be welcome
to take his chance. But first, I owed Missy the guess.

I know it sounds stupid. You might think that, Missy being
the kind of person to whom nothing really bad had ever
happened, she would be precisely someone I couldn't get
along with. It's not that I'm exclusively sympathetic to tragic
fuckups. It's just that people like Missy take very few things
at all seriously, and those few things are, to my mind, strange.
Renée had viewed people of Missy's ilk as targets, as fodder
for her ambition, not worth additional consideration
whatsoever—certainly not as people. But then, Renée had no
use for people at all. She'd alienate or betray anybody,
anywhere between a stranger and an intimate, the former
Mrs. Knowles and the cowboy who merely loved her: she'd
done it without a thought. The sole exception in a long line
of consistencies, so far as I had been able to discern, had
been John Plenty. She might have loved him. But within the
context of her interaction with him, the exception had proved
but a momentary aberration. She had used him until he wasn't
useful anymore, then dropped him. Only at the last moment,
at the Renquist Gallery, in the face of a helpless situation,
had she made the exception. The only reason to have dragged

John Plenty into it at that point would have been that she didn't want to die alone.

Renée knew she was being watched that night at the Renquist Gallery. Whoever was watching her would have known, as I had only recently discovered, that John Plenty had, at one time at least, been marginally involved in Renée's designs on the codex and the ring. In the nick of time, so far as John was concerned, Renée had realized that, if she were to ask his help, it would only seal his fate as well as her own. Whoever was watching her that night would have no compunction over taking out the two of them. And, for all I knew, they both had it coming. If so, leaving the art opening together may only have made the package that much neater. And there you had it. John Plenty went to his grave, the poor sap, thinking Renée had done him a good turn at last.

A total stranger got Renée out of her fix—temporarily, at least. My unexpected presence bought her a little time. Was it enough? Obviously not.

As far as Renée was concerned, I was just a handy stranger. Willing, pawnlike, male. The rest of that night—physical impressions on the musculature, dents on the neural fuselage, sighs in memory—lingered like fingerprints on aluminum. Time and weather would efface them.

Missy. Well, it's hard to explain. Sure, she'd thrown me over for a chance at what she perceived as the big time. But she hadn't shown herself willing to get me killed—not yet anyway.

Like I said, it's hard to explain. . . .

No it isn't. It looked to me like Missy was about to get herself killed. So, before I called Bowditch and showed him John Plenty's studio, which nobody had likely discovered yet, and explained my way out if it, and then showed him Tommy Wong's place and explained my way out of that, I thought I'd make a stab at pulling Missy's fat out of the fire.

387

Later she would think of it as karmic liposuction, and thank me.

Much later, when things had cooled off, Missy and I could sell the codex for seven or eight million dollars and split the profit.

See? I think they call it enlightened self-interest.

I parked next to the Harbor Master's office in the Marina Green, on the last block of Scott Street. There are three phone booths there. A quick call to Information gave me the address I needed. Another call to Bowditch would give him something to do. As usual, I got his voice mail. I left the two addresses, Wong's and Plenty's, and hung up.

The green Jaguar was parked on a hydrant at Jackson and Steiner on the northeast corner of Alta Plaza, a four-square-block park in the heart of Pacific Heights. The car couldn't have been there for more than an hour, but it already had a ticket tucked under the driver's-side wiper. That's a $250 fine in San Francisco. One of the costs of doing business.

The house across Jackson was damn big. Whoever designed it had forgone the Victorian. This place went right up to the height allowance and spread from there, expanding to every nook and cranny that hotly contested variances could make available to it. It had a three-door garage, a service entrance, a deck with trees growing on it, bougainvillea overflowing the south-facing portico, gables, a turret, lightning rods, trellises, topiary hedges, cypresses trained into pointy twists like auger bits, a satellite dish—and still it seemed to be a single-family dwelling.

The front door would be reserved for formal occasions, and those in the know would use a side door. But which side? And which door on which side? Pinnacled by this cusp of etiquette, I marched right up to the front door and rang the bell. When a guy opened it, I fitted the business end of John Plenty's target .25 to one of his nostrils and backed him up

388

the way he'd come. Since nobody else had been standing on ceremony, why should I?

I kicked the door closed behind me. We were alone in a big vestibule, the kind in which you could store a couple of prams and eight or nine overcoats and several pairs of gum boots and still have room for the grandfather clock and an umbrella stand. The doorman was a piece of work, however. The gun didn't bother him at all. He kept his hands in plain view and moved slowly, cool as a cucumber with no fear of pickling. He wore an embroidered cashmere vest that might have been from Afghanistan or Guatemala; its buttons were black shark's teeth. Outside the vest a leather shoulder harness kept the butt of an automatic about the size of a paving stone from falling out of his armpit. He wore wool pants and Birkenstocks sandals, I'm not kidding, and had a moustache on him that made him look like Meher Baba, except his complexion had a hundred thousand miles on it and the mous-tache didn't begin to hide a knife scar that traversed his cheek from the hair above his left ear to his Adam's apple. If this was a butler, then I was Junipero Serra.

Still, it made me feel good to make his acquaintance. Here was the butler to mix it up with John Plenty, to set cars on fire, to let the blood out of people. Here was the butler, I felt sure, capable of swatting the two barflies sticking to the rug at Tommy Wong's house.

"Say, fella," I said, backing him into the room. "Have I not been seeing a lot of your expertise around the ville of late?"

Moustache wouldn't say. Some guys are modest like that. I looked past him. Nobody else was in sight.

I tried again. "What caliber's the cannon?"

He just watched me. I was confronting a professional at last.

"Been fired today? Three or four times?"

His black eyes only showed me my own reflection.

389

"Where's the woman with the Jaguar?"

Moustache's livid scar twitched back and forth as if of its own accord, like a hair on a projector lens. The rest of him kept still.

"What are you waiting for?" I rotated the pistol until its butt was parallel to the floor, so its sight scoured the inside of his nostril. "A weather forecast?"

He let me rap him once between the eyes with the butt of the gun, just to show me he could handle it. Then, as I drew back to hit him again, he took the gun away from me.

I know how it happened. The guy was fast and had fifteen years on me—okay?

We scuffled over the terms, strictly *pro forma,* and I hurt him less than he hurt me. Much in the way that even a domestic dog, let alone a wolf or a coyote, will find the blind pony in a herd, this guy seemed to know instinctively that my legs were hurt. He delivered a backwards kick with his heel to the bullet wound in my calf, a real eye-opener. He gave the rest of me a good working over, too, and when he was finished, I was bleeding anew from both knees down. He himself wound up with a nicked nostril and, I'm not happy to report, both guns.

Moustache was well-trained. He hurt me in order to wrest control of the situation, but he didn't kill me. I didn't even lose consciousness. After this tender preamble, he made little ado about showing me the basement.

As the house was on the north-facing slope of Pacific Heights, its basement was not like your basement; it had a splendid view of the Golden Gate Bridge, Sausalito, Belvedere, Angel Island, Alcatraz, part of the Richmond Bridge, and a long stretch of sunny Berkeley, all the way north to El Cerrito, about fifteen miles away. I had just begun to admire this vista when Moustache sat me down in a chair facing away from it. The chair was entirely of polished teak, very heavy, with broad arms and a straight back. Moustache drew thick drapes over the windows, plunging the room into darkness. Candle-flames appeared here and there in the gloom, and the room began to fill with the damp peat odors of incense and lamp oil. A bolt racked. A door creaked on its hinges. There were whispering, a rustle of fabric, foot-steps. It sounded and smelled like a sacristy just before communion and seemed equally remote from salvation.

Except for the curtains, the walls were lined from floor to ceiling with tchotchke-laden shelves. Over-stuffed chairs and book-heaped tables were scattered about, but the remarkable article of furniture stood on a carpeted dais directly before me, draped in textiles shot with gold and silver threads. A carved and painted eagle clutched one of two gilded globes atop the tall stiles of its back.

Well, well, I thought. A throne in a democracy.

Moustache abruptly adjusted the angle of my chair, squaring it with the throne. With a rustle of fabric and an odor of mildewed cork, moving as if choreographed by rheumatoid arthritis, Mrs. Renquist appeared before us.

No surprise there; it was her house. Still, if I hadn't known as much, I might not have recognized her.

Girly Renquist was draped in purple textiles so ponderous and stiff they hung like sculpted stone. Her feet were shod in golden slippers. A multi-tiered, bejeweled necklace draped her ample bosom. Matching pendants descended from her earlobes nearly to her shoulders. Her eyes didn't look right, and after a moment I realized that their pupils were 'pinned,' that is to say, miotic: diminished in her impassive face, they shone like two lights in a distant stereo cabinet.

Because my lower lip had begun to fatten around the split Moustache had administered to it, my *Renquist* sounded more like *Mwrenqwiss*. She ignored the greeting and took her seat.

After a while I said, "I suppose you're waiting for me to blurt something?"

Slowly she deigned to notice me.

"How about Moustache drives you over to Coit Tower," I suggested. "Exactly halfway between the top of the Filbert steps and the No Parking sign, there's a pile of dog shit. Kneel there, and eat your fi—"

The butler clipped me over the ear with his pistol butt— much heavier than John's .25, much heavier than Ecstasy's, for that matter. As bell-ringers go, it rang well.

Mrs. Renquist tented her fingers under her chins and considered me. Maybe 'consideration' is the wrong word. She looked like she'd just flooded an anthill with gasoline and struck a match to it; now she was settling in to watch it burn.

Before my ears stopped ringing, she said, in a world-weary tone, "What is it with you, Danny?"

I shook my head as if flies were besieging it.

"What could you possibly offer that we'd be so interested in? Where does your certainty come from?" She examined the back of one hand and scratched it, rattling copious bracelets. "Do you really think you know something we don't know?"

My modest laugh allowed the fat lip to shudder against its teeth. "On the contrary. I'm quite certain you know a great deal more than I do, Mrs. Renquist. I'm the one guy around town you can always count on to know next to nothing. A veritable empty vessel. Has nobody ever pointed out that your first person plurals make you sound as pretentious as Richard Nixon?"

She beamed. "Flattery, Danny, will get you even less far than your artless protestations of ignorance."

"I can see that," I agreed woozily, still trying to shake the ringing from my ears, "But where is it, exactly, we are trying to get?"

"Come, come, Daniel. It's not where but *what* we're trying to get." She sighed laboriously. "May we dispense with these tedious preliminaries? Can't we agree that you know what it is we seek, and where to find it?"

I shook my head. "Why not? But it's not going to do you any good. Because, as I keep attempting to explain to anybody who might listen, which is nobody, I have no idea what's going on, and never have."

Her smile vanished and she flicked her left hand. Moustache whacked the other side of my head.

He hadn't moved his hand more than a foot, but I saw stars and the ringing redoubled. "Jesus," I mumbled, drool running over my chin. "This guy's good. Where'd you get him?"

She made no response.

I said, "Baghdad, by any chance?"

She frowned thoughtfully. "Danny, how perceptive of you to have guessed so nearly. As a matter of fact, he's Kurdish. Of course, Kurdistan is a world apart from Baghdad; but still, you were so very near the mark. Perhaps you've traveled there and know its peoples?"

Despite the interrogative tone, it didn't sound like a question; it sounded like cocktail chatter. I ignored it.

Silly me. She moved the hand. I got hit.

"That was a question," she pointed out.

"No," I said. "I've never been any closer to Kurdistan than a bowl of goat yogurt."

She smiled. "It's a good thing Attik can't understand you. If he could, he might undertake to hit you . . . autonomously." She chuckled. "The Kurds are very interested in autonomy."

"Why?"

"You're insulting him."

"Me? Insult Attik? How? Since when does a fly insult the jackass?"

Attik struck again.

It wasn't transmission fluid leaking out of the ear closer to Attik, but I tried to laugh anyway. "Oh, dear, Mrs. Renquist, you're going to have to curb Attik's English lessons before he hurts somebody."

Perhaps not pleased with this very slight betrayal of information, Mrs. Renquist drew back into the cushions of her throne and looked a little grim.

"This was the guy, wasn't it?"

"Really, Mr. Kestrel," she began. "If you insist on—"

". . .This Attik clown here—"

"Wait!" she ordered, forestalling an additional blow.

". . .Who you used to sucker that TV news guy?" I shook my head, like a dog shedding water. "I can't remember his goddamn name. But it wasn't Gerald. Or was Gerald there, too?"

She watched me.

Bile thickened my diction. "It was Attik, at your orders, who made the fake sale to Haypeak during the Gulf war. Not your son."

Girly said nothing.

"Am I wrong?"

Out of the gloom to one side of the throne she fished a little brass bell.

I wasn't finished. "Did Attik kill Gerald too, Mrs. Renquist, because he bungled the exchange with Renée?"

She clutched the bell in both hands, a finger in its mouth, and watched me.

"Did he have to kill the weather girl? I won't remember her name. . . ."

"Carrington," she said quietly. "Who said he killed her?"

"I did. An unexpected witness? Was he told to kill her, or was it an *autonomous* decision?"

She loosed the body of the bell, letting it dangle limply from one hand by its intricately carved wooden handle, considering me the while. Then she turned her wrist, ever so delicately, until the bell emitted its faintest tinkle, as if she were trying to see how quietly it could be rung.

At once a door to the left of the throne opened to reveal a hooded figure. Mrs. Renquist swept a couple of languid fingers in my direction. Head down, the figure approached me. With it came a cloud of patchouli.

The creature knelt beside the chair to gently align my forearm along the top of the armrest, palm up. I resisted. As the heel of Attik's hand landed just above my ear, the figure looked up, and I saw that the hooded face had been hideously scarred.

Coagulation had barely begun. Circular and recent, the wound suppurated plasma and gleamed with unguent. Certainly the cheek and sagittal crest had been gouged to the bone. The face looked like a reef exposed by a low tide.

"This is Teddy," Mrs. Renquist said. "Recently, Teddy was viciously attacked."

"A broken bottle, by the look of it."

"Yes," Mrs. Renquist said thoughtfully. "Wielded by a friend of yours. Do you hear, Teddy?" she added, as if speaking to a child. "The man with the bottle loved this man in the chair. They were like brothers."

Attending his work, Teddy again cast the caldera of his eye socket in my direction. A hideous grin turned up one side of his mouth, but the other side drooped.

"There is damage to the nerves," Mrs. Renquist explained. "The symptoms are . . . unfortunate."

"Yeah." I smiled hugely at Teddy. "Looks like John landed one, all right."

Teddy's grin faded, his face twitched, and he viciously cinched the strap.

"John Plenty most ungratefully stole from us," Mrs. Renquist said. "When he was nobody, we plucked him out of that horrid warren of communal art studios in the shipyards at Hunter's Point. He'd been studying the figure in secret while slathering big, meaningless abstractions for the public—except he had no public. One look at his figure studies and we called him a fool. He was wasting his talent on Surrealism and Expressionism, so-called intellectual painting. Rubbish. We offered him a ten thousand dollar portrait on a dare, more money than he'd ever seen in his life. He painted the picture in a month. A masterpiece. Immediately he had his own studio, money in the bank, all the women he could . . . paint. Eventually he commanded seventy-five thousand dollars a picture." She snorted with disgust. "By now, if it hadn't been for us, John Plenty would be painting with his fingers in some veteran's ward."

"He'd probably be alive, too," I pointed out.

"That's good money," she roared. "Only six or eight thousand of which," she added with a sneer, "John paid for one of your miserable frames."

"Well then," I said, "John must have been doubling my price back to you."

Mrs. Renquist hissed and fell silent.

Having secured my right forearm to the arm of the chair by means of a couple of stout velcro straps, Teddy moved to attend the left one. Despite being careful not to occlude Mrs. Renquist's view of me, and despite his wound, Teddy worked smoothly. Do a thing enough times, you're bound to get good at it.

Mrs. Renquist said with contempt, "John Plenty had the most reputable gallery in town—the Renquist Gallery—money in the bank and not a care in the world. But then he had to get mixed up with that . . . that. . . ."

"Tramp," I suggested. "Guttersnipe."

"Guttersnipe," she repeated, as if trying it out. "We find the slur insufficient, but it fairly unveils a tip of the iceberg. Like a fool John fell in love with her, which only made him easier to deceive. Renée led him into *attempting* to deceive us." She suddenly clutched the bell in both hands, so that it clinked as if strangled. "To deceive us, his mentor," she muttered.

Both my arms secured, Teddy scuttled over the carpet and faded into the gloom beyond the throne. He moved with no more apparent gravity than an empty plastic bag, afflated along a sidewalk by a breeze.

"His Queen?" I asked softly.

She nodded assent, imperiously.

"John Plenty, Renée Knowles, Tommy Wong—they defied their Empress?" I whispered, so quietly I wasn't sure she'd heard it.

Teddy reappeared bearing two crystal punch bowls and three burgundy towels. He placed a towel on the floor beneath each arm rest, and on each towel he positioned one of the bowls. He lay the third towel over my lap, taking care to tuck its ends under my thighs.

Mrs. Renquist's eyes had come only part of the way back from wherever she had sent them.

"They defied us," she said simply.

Thirty-Eight

The tool was a dog-legged piece of functional wickedness. Removing a single screw split its handle lengthwise to accommodate a replaceable blue blade that was little more than an elongated double-edged razor. Teddy played with it as if warming up for a game of mumblety-peg. Holding his right hand flat and palm down, he placed the knife across the back of it. Then he whipped the hand out from under the exposed blade and caught it by the handle as it fell, the hand still facing downward. Without pause he smoothly flipped it behind his back, up and over his left shoulder, and caught it by the handle with his left hand. A slip certainly would have resulted in a nasty slice. Not as bad as the wound already inflicted to his face, but nasty nonetheless.

"Smooth," I said. "It's like you can see right through the crust."

Teddy's rotted, smoke-stained teeth turned his disfigured grimace into an X-ray plate of a piranha's head.

His prowess displayed, however, my own was yet to come. Teddy produced a stubby screwdriver and set about changing the razor-blade. Out with the old blade, bloodstained and nicked, in with a new one, which gleamed like an alloy cooked down from a thousand African violets. Teddy dropped the used blade into a punch bowl; it skittered down the glass slope and up the opposite side, only to slide back down to the bottom, like a trapped spider.

"A carpet-layer's knife," Mrs. Renquist observed, opening a cigarette tin. "Teddy brought it to our attention. It's the tool we've found superior to all others." She selected a cigarette and passed its length under her nose. "Teddy used to stretch a little rug."

Teddy looked up at me. It would be a while before his sad eyes resigned themselves to his new deformity. "You've sunk a long way from the trades, boy," I noted sternly. Teddy stuck out his lower jaw and glowered.

Mrs. Renquist smiled over her cigarette. "It slits the toughest carpet in a single pass, but carpet-layers frequently slit a palm or thigh by mistake, too. That's why they refer affectionately to this treacherous but useful companion as their *Bloody Mary*." She touched one end of the cigarette to a candle flame. "Not without a little awe, we note; in much the same tone by which one might refer to a pet rattlesnake."

"You'd think this exotic crowd would come up with something a little more fetishistic."

"Oh, we've tried all manner of claptrap. Attik, for example, has a lovely knife. Did he show it to you?"

"That's this one's name? No. He only showed me his *yubi-waza*."

Mrs. Renquist smiled. "It's traditionally employed to castrate the sheep." She pursed her lips and vacuumed excess smoke from the air around her face. "The problem is," she held her breath, "most blades lose an edge all too quickly, in paring flesh."

Paring. I heard it.

She exhaled loudly. "Human flesh is surprisingly tough. Ask any surgeon. Paper, too. You wouldn't think that cutting flesh or paper would dull an edge, but it does."

Despite the obfuscating odors of patchouli and incense, those of her cigarette reached me, and I recognized the distinctively commingled reeks of tobacco and so-called tarball heroin. Much as a proper Chinese diner quickly chopsticks food three or four times to his mouth before pausing to chew it, Mrs. Renquist inhaled sharply three or four times from her cigarette, taking the smoke deeply into her lungs, before holding her breath for a long time. When she exhaled, very little smoke reappeared.

Teddy tightened the screw in the handle of the Bloody Mary. "The problem was," Mrs. Renquist abruptly continued, "we kept having to sharpen the knife. Every time there was a call for its services, we'd have to sit through the honing. It was Attik who insisted the knife be prepared *in situ*. This slowed things way down. On the positive side, you can imagine the negative effect on the hecatomb."

Hecatomb. I heard it.

"If he or she hadn't already fainted, that is. There is no question, however, of sharpening the knife beforehand. Attik thinks mere repose, even in a sheath, dulls a blade. Sharpening, moreover, is tedious. He begins with a rough stone, using not oil but his own spit, and continues to a fine stone only when good and ready."

I thought to perceive deep analogies between what Attik and I did for our livings, brothers in *hwettan*, but held my tongue.

"Insofar as our modest hecatombs would have to watch this process, there was some inherent psychological value. But on the whole we found it time-consuming and, frankly," she smiled thinly, "inconvenient. So." Her smile twitched and collapsed as she shifted heavily on her throne. "We compromised on Bloody Mary. The changing of the blade is sufficiently cognate to ancestral etiquette to satisfy Attik's sense of tradition, and sufficiently quick to satisfy our need for efficiency. Teddy likes to do the changing; something about the screw gives him satisfaction. Bloody Mary's customers, so far, have lodged no complaints." The royal humour begat

400

an idiotic smile in the ruined visage of her sycophant. "You will let us know, Mr. Kestrel, if you are, in some fine point, discommoded?"

Teddy presented the knife, handle first over the back of his wrist, for Attik's inspection. Attik took it and turned the new blade against the dim light, tested its edge with his thumb, and shaved a few hairs off the back of his hand.

"Mrs. Renquist," I chirped. "May I speak?"

As if I'd interrupted a reverie, she allowed a moment to pass before she answered, showing just a trace of annoyance. "Yes, Mr. Kestrel?"

"Before we . . . begin . . . wouldn't you like to know about the ring?"

"Ring, Mr. Kestrel?" She cocked her head. "What ring?"

"Why, the Ring of Theodosus, of course." I looked from her to Teddy to Attik. Attik was using the blade to plane a little curl of cuticle off his thumbnail. "The garnet one." I looked back at her. "Isn't the ring what this is all about?"

She stroked her chins with the back of a forefinger. "Is it, Mr. Kestrel?"

"Well what the hell else—I mean, a lot of people have been getting killed lately. I just assumed that—"

"Ah ah ah," she said, wagging the finger my way.

"What. . . ?"

"People get killed when they disobey their Queen," she said, as if lecturing a child.

"Are . . . you my Queen?"

For the first time since my arrival, a look of true discontent overran Mrs. Renquist's features. She wasn't looking at me when it happened. But it appeared that a sudden spasm of heart-burn had stabbed up from her intestines, disrupting an important social occasion. An inconvenience that would —must—pass. "Mr. Kestrel. . . ." She paused as if to master her impatience. "You don't have the ring, Mr. Kestrel. You've never been in possession of the ring."

They must have killed Wong for it. So much for that card. For all I knew they'd disposed of Missy, too. That her car was out front explained nothing, really. Maybe she had parked on a hydrant in front of Girly Renquist's house so she could grab a cab downtown. Maybe she was shopping even as I was preparing to die. Maybe the location of her car was just a coincidence. But if they weren't going to bring Missy up, I wasn't either. What did that leave me? I couldn't see a way out. The codex seemed especially unplayable. The moment I offered it, Dave was a dead man. Getting him killed would be a pretty lame way to repay him for saving my life. Whether I gave up the codex or not, I was about to be dead anyway, merely the latest victim in a long concatenation of destroyed lives.

Oh well, I thought. Maybe Dave will figure out how to turn the thing into enough diesel to motor *Rummy Nation* to Mexico.

"You know," said a voice, "just because Danny won't take you seriously? It doesn't mean he wants to die."

Now she shows up. "Yee-hah," I roared, so suddenly that Teddy jumped. "If humor was good enough for the Tet Offensive, it's good enough for *Byzantium*. Ancient mother-fuckers, newly minted, laugh or cry, we're all gonna die–!"

Attik cut me short with a crashing blow to the top of my head, the most severe yet. Acting crazy may have confused the Cajun, but it was just a dandelion to the weedeater of this operation.

"You see?" Missy persisted. "And besides, as you pointed out yourself, Danny doesn't have the slightest idea where the ring is."

"I was bluffing," Mrs. Renquist said quietly, "until you interrupted."

Standing within the same shadows that had engendered the loathsome Teddy, Missy quietly but stubbornly reiterated, "With all due respect, your Grace, Danny's never even seen the ring."

Her Grace didn't seem particularly disturbed by Missy's insistence. On the contrary it appeared that, not only did they know each other, they knew each other well.

"And," Missy added, "since he's useless to you, may I beg from you the favor of his life?"

My jaw dropped. Even Attik grunted. Teddy pouted, disappointed.

"Explain yourself." Mrs. Renquist commanded; but she was watching me.

I'd never thought Missy remotely capable of servility. Yet now she stepped out of the shadows manifesting every sign of it. While apparently far from unfamiliar with the ersatz throne-room, she also seemed tremulous; as if, dialectically speaking, she was making propositions on thin ice. Tenuous, Byzantine ice. Ice that cracked not only as she skated, but ice that consisted entirely of perilous fissures in the first place.

"Tommy Wong has the ring," Missy said.

Mrs. Renquist didn't smile at this. But she seemed to take some satisfaction in being able to say, "No, my child. He doesn't."

Missy, I almost said, what are you doing? *She* has it.

"Have you spoken with Tommy since yesterday?"

Teddy wouldn't deny himself a little snicker.

"Silence!" his Empress bellowed, startling all of us. Teddy did not hesitate to sink to his knees, lowering his head all the way to the carpet at the foot of the dais. The hem of his djellaba visibly trembled.

"Indeed I have spoken with Tommy since yesterday," Mrs. Renquist replied evenly. "Just this morning, in fact. He didn't– doesn't–" She corrected herself. "He no longer has it."

403

Missy looked around the room, then back at Mrs. Renquist. "What's happened to Tommy?"

Nobody spoke. For some reason, Mrs. Renquist continued to watch me.

I did not know Missy's game. I didn't even know what planet she was playing it on. And while I was more than willing to grant Girly Renquist the benefit of her insanity, I was wary of the insidious cunning that often accompanies madness. Before Girly might draw some dangerous conclusion, therefore, I ventured an abrupt revelation.

"Tommy's dead, Missy."

Missy started, as if visibly shocked by the news. Before I could add that I'd seen Wong's body not two hours before, Attik delivered a thundering blow to the side of my head, his best shot yet, with so thorough a transferal of inertia that a vertebra clicked in my neck and sparks filled my eyes. I nearly lost consciousness, and choked bile onto the towel in my lap.

"How disgusting," said Mrs. Renquist. "Teddy!"

Teddy sprang up from the floor and set about dabbing a fresh towel about my lap with leering familiarity. My head was filled with the screeches of air brakes and mating peacocks. For all I understood, Teddy intended to emasculate me, but he should have known better than to make sudden moves around a disoriented veteran. I lifted a shin up into his crotch and toppled him. Teddy hit the floor clutching his testicles. He flailed his head against a corner of the dais, raking afresh the wound in his face, and screamed in agony.

I cleared my throat and hawked a little bile his way. "That one's for John Plenty, you mutilated asshole."

Before Attik could break my head, which I had no doubt he intended to do, Teddy rallied. He rose to his knees and, with a yowl like a scalded cat's, smashed one of the crystal bowls across my knees.

Now both Missy and Mrs. Renquist screamed, and I must

404

have emitted some sort of roar as well. I hooked the toe of one boot behind Teddy's head, planted and rotated the heel of the other squarely on the wound in his face, as if his eye socket were a smoldering cigar-end. Teddy didn't take this quietly. But Mrs. Renquist must have screamed louder because Attik, his ear attuned to the wavelength of her orders, now delivered an efficient whack, not to the back of my head, but to the back of Teddy's, with the butt of his heavy pistol, and it was good night, Teddy. Like a flick of the wrist will lift up and lay down twenty feet of rope foot by foot, Attik's gun butt sent a standing wave through Teddy's entire torso. He stretched along the rug for a nap, blowing bubbles through the blood in his broken nose like an overheated dog.

Teddy's dissonant hash settled, we all took a break.

Except Missy. No fool, she got her oar in right away.

"If Tommy Wong is dead," she said through tears and clenched teeth, "then I know where that goddamned ring is."

Mrs. Renquist, who had redirected her glare of distaste from Teddy to me, now settled it onto Missy with thoughtful interest. "Go on, dear," she encouraged, almost pleasantly indulgent. "We're waiting."

"Do you know where his body is?" Missy asked tremulously.

Mrs. Renquist glanced toward Attik, who nodded perceptibly. "Yes, we do." She had a second thought and looked at me. "Or did."

Very nice, Missy, I thought; and I said, "You still do, although," I added, as ominously as I thought prudent, "Inspector Bowditch won't be long in discovering it." I looked at Missy. "Any time now, the identity of the dead guy at Pier 70 will have led Bowditch to Tommy's construction foreman."

Mrs. Renquist looked at Missy. "Pier 70?"

Missy, who appeared to have been taken unaware by this

information, turned to her and said, "We have no time to waste." She drew a breath. "I have a request, your Grace."

Her Grace straightened her posture.

"It's not much," Missy hastily added. "A matter of justice, really."

Everybody knew what this request was. Or we thought we did. But Mrs. Renquist wanted Missy to say it out loud.

Missy plunged ahead. "I'm going to tell you where the ring is in any case. You know that. But Danny. . . ." She glanced under her eyelashes in my direction, like a schoolgirl admitting to a crush in front the assembled student body, and, I had to admit, she looked convincing. "Danny is . . . a special friend. In the past, as you know, he's done good work for both of us. I've been in very close touch with him lately. We've talked at length about the present situation. I can assure you that he knows next to nothing. He's in his present position purely by happenstance. If Gerald hadn't panicked Renée into—"

"We do not speak the name of that treacherous interloping opportunist," Mrs. Renquist said sharply.

Instead of remarking that it sounded just like a chip off the old porphyry, Missy curtly nodded her assent, and quickly pressed her case. "Yes, of course. But even now, I assure you, he still knows nothing. Our own stupidity—please, let me finish—enabled him to make one mistake after another until, finally, he blundered his way here. He only came, as he imagined, to save me. Why should he have to pay for the errors we ourselves made? If Tommy hadn't sent those three idiots after him—"

"Yes. . . ." said Mrs. Renquist thoughtfully. "They were pesky. Utterly incompetent."

"I agree," said Missy meekly. "But it was very difficult to understand what to do, what with Tommy interfering every step of the—"

"Yes, yes," Mrs. Renquist interrupted impatiently. She noticed that her cigarette had gone out, and held its burnt end to the candle flame.

"Your Grace," Missy said, as if screwing up her pluck, "if you could see your way clear to free my friend, I will give you the usual assurances that he will . . . behave."

Usual assurances? I might have discounted a little framing, too. But for once I kept my mouth shut.

The room lapsed into silence while Mrs. Renquist smoked. Then, in the voice of curdled maternity, she said, "Daniel, do you understand that Melissa is guaranteeing your life with her own? Do you understand that you are in the reciprocal position of guaranteeing hers with yours? Do you understand that these mutual sureties amount to nothing less than *blood betrothal?*"

I must have hesitated. Certainly there remained in my throat the taste of blood. In the end, however, I couldn't have responded more reverently than if I'd been addressing Hera herself. What else could I do? Turn the poor woman down?

"I do," I said, in my most solemn voice.

The Renquist took three quick tokes off her cigarette and settled back on her throne. "Granted," she said tightly, without exhaling so much as a wisp of smoke. After another pause, during which she seemed to be in appreciative equilibrium with the mere fact of being conscious at all, she daintily stubbed the half-smoked cigarette into the mouth of a golden ashtray shaped, I noticed at last, like a silently roaring Chimera. "Now my child." She replaced the half-smoked cigarette into the metal tin. "Where is our ring?"

Missy spoke in the most neutral tone I'd ever heard her use, as if reciting a rote lesson. "Gerald's pact was not with Renée; it was with Tommy. If either of them was ever caught or severely compromised, if either of them was unable to safely dispose of the ring, each was. . . ." Missy hesitated, her

407

neutrality faltered. "Each was . . . you know . . . to swallow it."

Silence, absolute and complete, filled the room.

"Tommy used to practice."

Silence.

"Swallow, retrieve. Swallow, retrieve. Swallow. . . ."

Silence.

Missy added, in a very small voice, "Now you know where. . . ." She could hardly bring herself to finish, ". . .to . . . look."

Mrs. Renquist glanced at Attik. Twin portals onto an obsidian wasteland, Attik's eyes revealed nothing.

Nobody looked at me. Why should they? As usual, I had no idea what they were talking about.

"It's true," Mrs. Renquist said thoughtfully, "that Tommy had rather a strange look on his face as Attik . . . interrogated him. But, my pet, we thought her agreement was with that *creature.*"

"Gerald—"

Mrs. Renquist shot Missy a fierce glance, but Missy stuck out her chin and continued.

"Gerald was in the covenant, but he never once had the ring. So Renée never had it either. Tommy only wants the codex, as you know. But he's never let the ring out of his sight."

For all the attention the murder of Gerald Renquist was getting from his own mother, Missy might just as well have been discussing flux density in Humbucker pickups. The woman just wasn't affected. Gerald Renquist's mother only wanted to think about Tommy Wong's ring.

"He watched Bloody Mary with rather a fascination," she said thoughtfully. "We remarked it at the time, but thought little of it. He was having a glass of wine as we made rather a spectacular entrance. It was early for wine. Even white wine. We don't wonder. . . ."

408

What's to wonder, I was thinking, as I looked at one of my own wrists. It was a pale, freckled thing, traversed laterally by three folds where the skin hinged between palm and forearm, subtended by one main vein and a couple of minor ones running parallel to it. Think of flying into Burbank on a hot fall night. Just beyond the lights of the runway, past the twinkling suburbs ramping up to the silhouetted coast range, everything is on fire; it's glowing like the pit of hell beneath its own smoke. Who wouldn't watch? It's the end of the world, and it's fascinating.

On the other mandible, Tommy might have been concentrating, closely watching as his wrists were slit, so as to metabolically forbid as it were the possibility of puking the Ring of Theodosus into the very hands of his enemies. If so, such fortitude would rank Tommy Wong among the great warriors of avarice.

As if reading my mind Mrs. Renquist observed thoughtfully, "That's a pretty cool customer, isn't it." After another moment she declared, "We'll have to go see for ourselves."

"Oh," Missy said faintly, "can't we stay here and watch television?"

Mrs. Renquist ignored her. "Get the car."

Without not a word but two flicks of his Bloody Mary, Attik set me free and solicitously helped me step over the snoggering mess that was Teddy. Bits and shards of shattered punch bowl crunched underfoot.

I have few standards by which to judge such things, but "the car," an immaculate Bentley, looked brand new. Don't those things cost a quarter of a million dollars? Attik took a respectable-looking tweed jacket off a hook next to the garage door. With a belt in the back, leather buttons, and elbow patches, the jacket made him look like one of those courtly gentlemen you see hanging around a hotel ballroom, assessing

409

the shy widows. The coat was tailored to accommodate a twelve-shot Israeli pistol in the armpit.

Missy sat in back with Mrs. Renquist. I sat up front with Attik. We used Steiner to drop down off the north slope of Pacific Heights to Lombard. We drove right past the gallery, but Mrs. Renquist didn't even look at it. Attik took Doyle Drive and exited onto Park Presidio. The car was utterly silent. The day was lovely. Thick afternoon sunlight filtered gracefully though the eucalyptuses of the Presidio, mottling the Bentley's hood like an epileptic's daydream. After the patchouli of the curtained death chamber, the fresh air was very pleasant. I had to suppress the urge to jump out of the car only when Attik let the speed drop below forty. "I would have done this differently," I chided him, as he turned west on California Street. "You can get off Doyle into the Presidio—right before the toll plaza? From there you can either turn north, past the statue of Strauss and under the plaza itself; or you can turn south out of the parking lot and go back under Doyle. Either way you skim along the top of Baker Beach on Lincoln and come right out at 25th Avenue and El Camino del Mar, with not three stop signs on the whole trip. See?"

Attik ignored me of course and maintained his silence as well as his route, and we arrived at Tommy Wong's place soon enough. The villa looked much as it had just a few hours before. The circular drive was empty. The landscaping showed not a leaf out of place. We found, upon mounting the steps, the front door still ajar.

So Bowditch hadn't picked up his messages.

Loosening the button of his jacket, Attik went inside while we waited on the porch. The two finches had removed their conversation from the chimney cap to a power line that bordered the property. For another minute, the day remained beautiful.

Attik reappeared to invite us into the house.

410

He had moved Ecstasy to the wall next to the dining room door. Ecstasy looked a little stiff, unable to relax fully into his new position. Since he wasn't in the right of way, the Cajun remained at the foot of the staircase. The foyer was quiet enough to hear flies buzzing.

Missy balked at the library door. "Could I please be excused? I–"

This sounded like something Missy might better have left unsaid, and my heart skipped a beat. But in her zeal Mrs. Renquist completely overlooked the fact that Missy wasn't supposed to know what horror awaited us beyond the door, and she took Missy firmly by the arm. "Courage, my child."

Tommy Wong was still tied to his chair, and he was still dead. His lips had begun to recede a little, so his smile was showing a little gum. His drained complexion was the damp gray of curing cement. His eyes, half-opened slits, still gleamed, life-like. His hair was immaculate, every strand in place.

Attik didn't hesitate. He produced his Bloody Mary, freed the dead man's wrists, cut away the red sash, and rolled the corpse onto the floor. It was only by brute force, accompanied by some unusual noises, of the sort you hear at a suspenseful moment in a hushed movie theater, that Attik succeeded in straightening the cadaver sufficiently to lay it on its back.

"Your Grace," murmured Missy, and she smacked her lips weakly. "I don't think I. . . ."

"Hush, Dear," Mrs. Renquist said. "All shall be known in a trice."

That Attik's Bloody Mary was sharp, anyone would agree. It slit open Tommy Wong in two passes, from abdomen to sternum and from appendix to pituitary gland, gliding as facilely through the walls of his stomach as if they were of no more substance than the linen of his shirt; as if Tommy Wong's

411

corpse itself were no more than a bill from the electric company.

There was very little blood by now. Even so, Missy began to inhale in sharp little gasps.

Attik rooted in Tommy Wong's stomach with one hand, staring the while, as if thoughtfully, at the kimono over the mantelpiece.

Missy groaned.

Attik grunted and withdrew his hand, now festooned with the glistening wheaten toroids of a popular breakfast cereal.

Missy pulled aside the plastic waste basket that already contained half of Tommy Wong's blood supply, fell to her knees, and vomited noisily.

Attik wiped the prize on Wong's shirt and showed it to his mistress. Mrs. Renquist donned a pair of oblong reading glasses in order to inspect it closely. "My goodness gracious," she said approvingly. "The Ring of Theodosus at last."

Thirty-Nine

The nice thing about jewelry is, a woman can wear it through any customs shed in the world with near impunity." Missy smiled and contentedly touched her hair. "Especially if she's beautiful."

We were trudging along 25th Avenue toward Geary Street, where we would stand a chance of getting a cab.

"A third trip up this damn street," I grumbled, "I'll have to get me some Spandex shorts and a mid-calf pedometer."

All around us, normal people attended their evening chores. Couples pushed strollers to the grocery; dogs dragged their masters to the park. A guy with a necktie draped over one arm hurried past us with a briefcase in one hand and a bouquet in the other.

"So long as it's not the Star of India," Missy added.

"Yeah," I responded listlessly. "The Star of India." I wasn't really interested in this conversation. A good hour's sleep had last come my way while I was marooned under Pier 70. Blood seeped through my jeans below both knees, one ear was bleeding, both of them were ringing, and I had a headache fit for Raskolnikov. Somewhere along the way I'd chipped a tooth. I was still alive, though, and that seemed like an accomplishment. The evening was lovely. The last rays of sunlight skimmed over the coastal fogbank at their flattest angle, thick and tangible, coating the world with an autonomous purity.

413

Autonomous. . . .

I idly brushed my hand over a boxwood hedge. "How does the Ring of Theodosus stack up with the really big stones?"

"Modestly. On the other hand nobody's ever seen it, so it's legendary."

We walked in thoughtful silence. When next Missy spoke, I looked up to find us in the middle of an intersection I did not recall entering. A car was stopped inches from the crosswalk. When the driver caught my eye, he shook his head.

"Girly's been after it for a long time," Missy was saying.

"Maybe she deserves it."

"God help those who think otherwise."

"I don't think there are too many of those left by now."

"Oh," Missy corrected, "there's always somebody."

"It only takes one megalomaniac and a couple of gorillas to make a war, it's true."

"What's a megalomaniac? Tell me again."

"A psychopath locomoted by delusions of wealth, power, dominion. If she somehow manages to impose these delusions on other people, she's upgraded to Empress. Altogether, a sociopath."

"You've been doing research," Missy surmised.

"Also, she can obsess on the grandiose. Is the Ring of Theodosus grandiose?"

"Once word gets out about what's been happening in San Francisco, the Ring of Theodosus is going to scan as grandiose."

"I'd say it's a matter of sooner than later."

She looked at me. "Who's to tell?"

I stopped walking. "Bowditch, Missy. Remember Inspector Bowditch? He works for the Homicide Division of the Police Department, and he's not about to go away. Very likely he's the next person you and I are going to meet. When the press asks about the rash of murders sullying San Francisco high

414

society lately, he'll have something to tell them. Then we'll see grandiose."

"I'd forgotten about him."

"Likely story. In any case, Bowditch hasn't forgotten you."

A taxi appeared and Missy hailed it. The driver slowed, had a good look at us, and sped away.

"I'll have that guy's medallion," Missy declared.

"He's probably late for his poetry workshop."

"If only I had my cell phone."

"Good idea. You could send out for pizza while we wait for a cab."

She snapped her fingers. "When the pizza arrives, we'll hijack the delivery vehicle."

"Four out of five scientists refuse to use them, you know."

"Pizzas?"

"Cellphones."

"How could they be so recalcitrant?"

"Phone here." I tapped my head. "Satellite there." I pointed skyward. "If microwaves bubble cheese on pizza, think what they do your brain."

"The cell phone's the greatest invention since the underwire bra," Missy insisted stubbornly. "They wouldn't let it hurt us."

My finger came away from my temple with blood on it. "I'll see that yours is buried with you."

"That's not funny."

"In the plague years they tied a little bell to the pinky of the hastily buried. Think of it as progress."

"That's way less than not funny."

I wiped the blood on my jeans. "Missy, what's bugging you? Death used to make you laugh."

She professed amazement. "I lose out on a million-dollar deal, and you wonder what's *bugging* me?"

"Missy," I said quietly, "you don't need a million dollars."

415

"Little do you know."

"A lot do I know. You've got money coming in from the eight directions, always have, always will. What's with a lousy million dollars?"

She chewed her lip. "I've never done anything, you know. Anything substantial, I mean."

This was absolutely true, but I didn't say so.

"I've traveled, sure. I sit on museum committees. I've eaten oysters with statesmen and pasta with opera divas. I've slept with all the really interesting billionaires on both coasts. . . ."

"And married three or four of them. It's your life. Get used to it. Give the rest of us a break."

"I will not get used to it," she said petulantly. "I won't. I've spent eighteen years chasing this deal, and I'm not going to lose it now."

"Missy, are you insane? We were lucky to get away with our lives back there. In fact, when you're done feeling sorry for yourself, you might want to explain how you managed to leverage us out of Girly's clutches in one piece. That guy with the carpet knife is no joke. And another thing. I don't want to hear about how life is passing you by like it's some kind of taxi. It's death that just passed me by, not life."

Missy said pensively, "Wasn't it John Lennon, who said that death is nothing more than getting out of one taxi and into another?"

"Go quote that to his left shoe."

"Don't be stupid."

"Speak for yourself."

"That's exactly for whom I speak."

"Look," I said, with some heat, "I, for one, am very pleased to find myself back on the bricks, taxi or no taxi, and I intend to stay on them. Whatever you're thinking, count me out. Done. Fired. Terminated. Kaput. Let's get over to Clement or Geary or wherever, find a cab or a bus or a rickshaw, you go your way, and I'll go home. I'm going to apply a bath to my dirt, aloe vera to my wounds, ibuprofen to my back, ice to my head, and whiskey to my soul. Then I'm going down to Original Joe's and eat the thickest New York steak in the building, very rare, with my bare hands. After that–which reminds me." I patted my pockets tentatively. "Do you have any money?"

"Not like I'm going to have," she said, watching me.

"That's good. Because I– What's that mean?"

"I'm glad to hear you've had it with this business, Danny."

"And you haven't? You want more of this horseshit? You want to watch another guy get gutted while you puke into a wastebasket full of blood? Go ahead. Take the first taxi you see to the next crime you can find. I'll walk home."

"It's not going to be that easy, Danny."

"Watch me do it hard, then. I'll crawl to Folsom Street if I have to."

Still she watched me.

"What? What's not going to be so easy?" I said uneasily.

"You owe me one," she said quietly.

"I *owe* you one? One what?"

"One favor."

"I owe you a favor?"

By now we had reached another intersection. The sunlight slanted down the cross street, west to east, and bathed Missy's surgically tweaked complexion like an irradiant emulsion. She was tired and it showed her age. Her normal makeup– too much, too thoroughly applied, in a child-like attempt to thwart the caustic hunger of time, as the shadow of the taxi she feared most drew across her lovely face, so feared as to enable her to delude herself into thinking her money might help her avoid it–this makeup was missing. Her pricey cosmetic surgery vividly declared itself in the all-seeing sunlight. But Missy didn't talk tired.

417

"Daniel Kestrel, how quickly you forget. Were not you strapped to a chair less than two hours ago, your life-force poised to get drained into a punch bowl like so much cheap brandy?"

"Cheap brandy?" I blinked. "Missy, I haven't heard you use so colorful and original a simile since your first husband got caught in that orgy with—"

"Don't change the subject," she snapped. "Did I or did I not intervene on your behalf?"

"Just why in the hell do you think I got myself into that predicament in the first place? I went to Renquist's house to save your ass." I jabbed a finger into her shoulder. "Yours, yours, yours."

"Thanks, I'm sure. Once tied to that chair, however, your chivalrous motives were rendered quite moot, weren't they."

"*Moot?*" I sputtered. "My chivalrous motives, as you put it, stemmed from nothing more than my deep, personal regard for your miserable, white, upperclass *ass—*"

From out of nowhere an elderly woman appeared and shook an umbrella in my face. "When are you homeless people going to learn that you can't be arguing among yourselves like this? You've got to stick together. Besides, you're a very cute couple."

Missy summoned a withering *hauteur* and said, "Homeless? Madame, I'll have you know that I own five homes on three continents."

The woman looked at Missy, then at me. "Oh, my," she said.

"I'll take care of her," I assured the woman, taking Missy's arm. "As winter comes on, she gets irrational. She's afraid of the cold. Could you spare some change?"

"Remember," the woman said, handing me a twenty, "you've got to stick together."

418

"San Francisco," I said proudly, as the lady walked briskly away. "If we don't take care of each other, who the fuck will?"

"Exactly." Missy plucked at the twenty, but I was faster and pocketed it. She shook free of my arm. "I saved your life—yes or no?"

I capitulated. "Absolutely, Missy. Yes, you saved my life. I'm forever grateful. Forever in your debt. Without your intervention, I'd be Hecatomb 57. You want me to carry your books to school?"

"No," she replied immediately, "I want you to hand over the Syracuse Codex."

I stared at her, dumbfounded.

"Then we'll call it square," she added sweetly. "And your benefactress is right. We mustn't fight like this. And we shan't, Because once you've given me the codex, we'll never see each other again."

"Square," I repeated, "and finished."

"Done. Fired. Terminated. Kaput."

"But. . . . Will we still be friends?"

She gave me a big smile. "You bet."

419

FORTY

Half a block later I asked how she knew.
"Simple," Missy said. "You haven't mentioned it since the day you first heard about it."

"Since Bowditch played Maysle's lecture for us?"

"Correct."

"You, of course, knew about it all along."

"And I, of course, never stopped talking about it."

"But you know much more. You know for example that Renée Knowles and Her Grace the Renquist were in cahoots to corral both the Ring of Theodosus and the Syracuse Codex."

She shook her head. "Renée worked for Tommy. I worked for Girly."

"Worked?"

She nodded. "Past tense."

"Oh," I said skeptically, "you're dead too?"

"Girly only wanted the ring, Danny. She went too far, but now she's got it. Many have died, including her own son. Girly sees that as some kind of historical inevitability, by the way, and once you buy into that past-life stuff, the sky's the limit. The way it stands now, Girly will fare happily with her long-lost ring and skip town before your friend Bowditch catches up with her."

"Long lost ring. . . ."

"You want to figure it out, Danny? Don't cleave to reason. Think back on the story of Theodora. You don't have to have

420

read all the books—although I know you boned up on the subject while you were thawing."

"Yes," I smiled, "the warm bath of history."

"Well, Gibbon's digest will do nicely. Everything Girly Renquist does can be found in it—by Girly's lights anyway. Whoever got in Theodora's way, whoever was disloyal, whoever made a mistake, Theodora dealt with summarily. Girly behaves likewise. That's all the logic you need. You also need to adjust the scope of the prize downward, from the Roman Empire to a single antiquity. When Theodora's son showed up, she killed him outright. So what if the boy managed to string it out for a couple of days? As for Gerald, he got to go to Stanford in the fabulous seventies, and live a full life afterwards. *Then* Girly killed him. But to her, it adds up to the same thing."

"But why? What empire was he threatening?"

"Make a little allowance for the wheel of meat and the mutations of history, why don't you? He was threatening the heritage of Girly's past life. The codex was ancillary. Girly didn't care about it. To her the codex was merely a means to the ring, which is the true synecdoche of her soul—or something like that. The codex was merely another apocryphal byproduct of her career, no more or less germane to its actual progress than a first edition of Gibbon. Or of Procopius, for that matter. Her clippings, as it were. Gerald was welcome to the codex. But the moment he made a move on the ring, he betrayed his mother. She found out right away, of course. In fact, she claims that history and her astrologer told her in advance."

"But Gerald never had the ring."

Missy shook her head. "That was hardly Girly's fault, and it was hardly from want of trying. In essence, Girly nailed the right guy for the wrong reason. The real wrinkle was that

Gerald was even further into the double-cross than she knew. Not only that, he wasn't the *only* double-crosser."

"Sounds to me like Girly was the only one who wasn't double-crossing."

"You know what? That's exactly right. Take Renée, for exam-ple. Once she got the codex away from Girly, she had no intention of letting go of it—as you know," she added sweetly.

"Wait a minute: Girly was trading the codex . . . via Renée . . . to Tommy . . . for the ring . . . via . . . Gerald?"

"Very good, Danny. She was indeed. The idea was for two more or less innocent minions to meet under innocuous circumstances—John Plenty's opening. . . ."

"Innocuous?" I said incredulously.

"Innocent?" she said incredulously, and laughed. "Make the exchange and that was to be that. But Tommy didn't trust Girly at all, and he was right."

"Did he know she had killed before?"

She brushed that aside. "She had the codex and that got the better of Tommy's judgment."

"Did Tommy get the ring legitimately?"

More brushing. "He paid for it, if that's what you mean."

"That's not what I meant."

Missy shrugged impatiently.

"So what the hell happened? What went wrong?"

"Tommy shouldn't have attempted to do business with Girly in the first place. He had the experience of that couple in Mill Valley to go by. When it comes to dealing with Girly and Attik, everybody is in over their head."

"That seems obvious. So why did he attempt to deal any-way?"

"Girly knew he had the ring and threatened to leak the in-formation. If the rest of the world found out Tommy had the ring, the rest of the world could force him to give it up."

"But he had similar leverage—no?"

"He wasn't ruthless enough to use it. Besides, Tommy was in his right mind. He knew that once everybody started down that road, everybody would lose."

"A Mexican standoff."

"Not quite. Girly told Tommy that if he screwed her out of the ring, no matter what else happened, Attik would kill him. Word for word, that's what she said, in the most pleasant tone you ever heard, over a very expensive lunch."

I withdrew my eyes from an approaching intersection and slid them over the automobile roofs along the opposite sidewalk, until I could see the side of Missy's face. "You were there. You dined with them."

She didn't meet my gaze. "I was there."

One of the mysterious bonds that moored Missy to me gently parted. "Then what happened?"

"Tommy panicked and re-hired those three jerks from wherever, in a pathetic attempt to protect himself from Girly. Later, that turned into a pathetic attempt to intimidate you into giving up the codex."

"Which I didn't even have," I pointed out.

"Not yet, anyway," she pointed out.

I frowned. "Re-hired?" She shook off the question. "So what happened at the gallery?"

"It's hard to say. The best guess is, Renée saw Attik as she was coming in. At any rate, she smelled a rat." Missy smiled. "She wasn't very drunk, you know."

"She just wanted to live," I said quietly.

Missy corrected me sharply, "She just wanted to live with the Syracuse Codex."

"Then it didn't work out at all, did it."

"No. Anyway, Gerald had his own ideas about what was going on. But, you see, we think—"

"We?"

423

"We *thought*," she corrected herself, "that Gerald and Renée fully intended to make away with both ring and codex on their own bike, as it were. But things went awry."

I nodded grimly. "Things went awry."

"Gerald went to Tommy that night to get the ring. Tommy balked. He didn't trust Girly, and Gerald couldn't talk him into trusting her for just that one evening."

"Renée, meanwhile, was over on Jackson Street getting the codex."

Missy nodded. "Gerald was forced to show up at the opening empty-handed, with every intention of telling Renée to turn around and take the codex back to Girly. But something spooked her before she managed to speak with Gerald."

"You said she saw Attik."

"Okay, maybe she saw Attik. You knew he was working in the kitchen that night?" My jaw must have dropped. Missy smiled. "White jacket and trousers. Anyway, Renée had a couple of drinks to pass the time."

"Maybe she had a couple of drinks to calm her nerves, because she had already thrown a wrench into the works by hiding her car."

"It was merely a precaution, I suppose, that turned into a pivotal disaster. In any case, the already shaky bond between her and Gerald dissolved completely the moment she realized he didn't have the ring. Panicked, Gerald pressed her for the keys anyway. His line was, Tommy would give up the ring only after he actually had possession of the codex, and that he could be trusted."

"Which left Renée in a tight spot."

"Untenable. She couldn't give up the codex and go back to Girly empty-handed. She probably couldn't even go back to Girly with the codex and without the ring. And what she and Gerald really wanted to do was blow town with both of them."

"What a pretty picture. So she got herself an escort and dropped the mess directly into Gerald's lap."

"Yes," Missy nodded. "So everybody thought. But there was a problem."

"No," I said. "A problem? Like, for example, she had the codex in the car but Gerald had the keys?"

Missy dismissed this. "You don't think she had a spare at home?"

"Uhhh," I said, "I don't have a spare at home."

"You'll recall," Missy said sweetly, "in the kitchen, how Renée very suddenly downed a glass of champagne?"

I frowned.

"Or was it Chardonnay?"

I nodded slowly. Perhaps my mouth was open. Slow or fast, it must have appeared a very stupid nod.

Missy said carefully, "The glass of wine downed whole was duly reported. Upon hearing this report, Girly assumed–"

"She assumed that Renée had swallowed the ring," I concluded.

"You could not have convinced her otherwise. From that moment, Renée's fate was sealed."

"Son of a bitch. She never even had the ring."

Missy shrugged. "Right girl, wrong reason."

"But," I protested, "it was Tommy who–"

"Oh," Missy agreed perfunctorily, "Tommy agonized over the unfortunate turn of events."

"Yes, I'm sure," I surmised bitterly. "But he still had no codex."

"He still had no codex. Gerald nervously went ahead with the charade over the car keys. Coming as it did on top of Tommy's reneging, your presence very likely unnerved Gerald completely. He was supposed to drop the ring into Renée's purse as he retrieved the keys. Had he not gone through the motions, Gerald might well have saved his own life, and Renée's, too. Instead, he took the keys anyway. So Girly *thought* the exchange had been made, and that Renée was up to no good."

"Did Gerald ever know where Renée's car was parked?"

"It didn't make any difference."

"Attik followed Renée as instructed."

Missy nodded.

"And when she couldn't come up with the ring...."

Missy said nothing.

I shook my head. "Why didn't he kill me, too?"

"He was being discreet."

I laughed in her face. "Shortly thereafter, he caught up with Gerald. Discreetly, of course."

Missy made an impatient circling motion with her hand. You're playing catch up, this gesture said. "Inspector Bowditch picked you up before Girly could sic Attik on you, Danny. It was a near thing. By the time you got home from the police station, Girly had figured out most of what was happening, and made you for the charming *naif* you've always been."

"Gerald was empty-handed too," I persisted. "Or, should I say, he was working on an empty stomach?"

"*Voilà.*"

I shook my head. "What a fucking mess."

Only few blocks remained until we reached Clement Street, where there would be some chance of transportation.

"What about Djector? He looks to be a guy capable of lying, cheating, stealing, and maybe even killing, for something he wants."

She glanced at me, then away. "That's what we wanted you to think."

"That's what you. . . ?"

"I was trying to protect you, Danny. You understand, Girly wanted to clip you right away."

"Clip me?"

"But I said no, Girly, Danny's a bright boy. Let's throw him off the track just a little, just insofar as we ourselves are concerned. Maybe he'll come up with something. And look what happened." She smiled. "I'm so proud of you, Danny."

"Djector never fit in at all?"

"Actually he did, but only until last year. When he saw the violent turn things were taking, he quit. Like Kevin Carnes quit. They got smart. Or," she added, "cowardly. At any rate, Manny got out."

"I suppose 'cowardly' depends on your point of view," I observed acidly.

Missy grimaced. "It didn't discourage Tommy Wong."

"Wong's case seems self-explanatory," I bitterly observed. "All things being equal, and less than transcendent, would you rather die from a slit wrist or disembowelment?"

Missy said frankly, "I don't plan on dying at all."

FORTY-ONE

U p ahead we could see California Street, which, unaccountably, seemed deserted. That was fine with me. I still had plenty of questions.

"Was all this a rerun of the Mill Valley fiasco?"

"To the extent that Tommy wanted the codex badly enough to trade the ring for it, yes. To that purpose, he visited Moira Carrington in Mill Valley. You recall her interest in gems?"

I nodded, then abruptly said, "Wait a minute. *Moira Carrington* had the ring of Theodosus?"

"I'm explaining this backwards. Don't rush me." She smiled a little smile. "Her interest in gems was rapacious, it's true. But it wasn't blind."

"Tommy had somebody with him? For, uh, driving and whatnot?"

"Tommy had Gerald with him. For driving and whatnot."

"God almighty. And they seemed like such nice people."

"They *were* nice people. When Tommy and Gerald visited Ms. Carrington in Mill Valley, Haypeak had yet to return from Iraq. This is not to say that Moira didn't want to keep the ring. And she intended to keep it. But Tommy and Gerald reasoned with her. When she resisted, they whistled up that Cajun guy with his two idiot friends."

"That was the first time he hired them" I realized.

"But Moira Carrington was no Danny Kestrel." Missy gave my forearm an affectionate squeeze. "She was no Renée Knowles, either. All those small-time gorillas had to do. . . ."

428

"Small-time gorillas?" I said aloud. And with that thought came the abrupt realization that, if I'd always considered Missy's cop-show argot an affectation, I'd always been wrong.

"All they had to do was walk into her living room, and the deal was as good as done. Tommy made her a very reasonable offer—her money back and that much again, twenty thousand in all. Moira was so scared he had to explain it twice. Once she understood how graceful an exit Tommy was offering her, she went for it. Gratefully, she went for it. And you know what?"

"Uh. . . . What?"

"Haypeak never knew a thing about it."

"You're kidding."

"She never told him. It was too bad, too. From her experience he might have learned a thing or two about proper behavior. Her flirtation with the black market easily could have ruined her career, not to mention gotten her killed. The moment she saw the last of those five weirdos, Moira Carrington swore off gem smuggling, and she never breathed a word to anybody about her brush with adventure. I bet she still couldn't sleep." Missy stopped walking. "Haypeak, on the other hand. . . . Danny?" she asked thoughtfully. "Can I change a pronoun?"

I stopped walking, too. "I beg your pardon?"

"Yes," she determined, "I owe it to you." She started walking again.

She took my arm and talked without meeting my eye. I tasted dread in my mouth. It tasted like blood.

"We used Carrington like we used Haypeak," Missy said.

"We," I repeated softly. It wasn't dread I was tasting. It was the inevitable.

"She was in London in a swank hotel, waiting for Haypeak to get out of Baghdad. Moira Carrington fell for the ruined-heiress grift like a barometer falls for a hurricane."

429

Grift? "Missy—"

"Don't interrupt. I was good, you know."

I stopped and assessed her. "As the ruined heiress?"

"Flawless."

"I'll bet you were."

"Come on," she said, pulling my arm. "I got out of that London hotel room with $10,000—all the cash Moira had on her—and a handshake. I promised to pay her back fifteen thousand—that's fifty percent interest—within a year. As collateral, Moira Carrington got the Ring of Theodosus."

"Where the hell did *you* get it?" I sputtered. "Did she know what it was?"

"She pretended not to." Missy smiled hugely. "She was going to rip me off, of course."

"Are you telling me that you ran the same scam on both of them?"

Missy nodded enthusiastically. She was almost laughing.

"Didn't you think it just the least bit strange, not to say coincidental, to find two such buzzards—Carrington and Haypeak, I mean—so alike in the same nest? Didn't you think they might be cops or stool pigeons or too stupid to use—something?"

"Quite the contrary, darling. I thought that two buzzards in the same nest, as you so quaintly phrase it, was the most natural thing in the world. Look at Kevin and me. Look at Girly and Gerald. As for stupid. . . ." Her gesture encompassed the whole word. "Avarice eclipses everything," now she laughed aloud, "even greed."

"All right," I nodded, amazed, "all right. But why all the subterfuge?"

"Simply? Tommy and Djector were so hot they were glowing in the dark. They'd been chasing all over Europe for years, trying to put some kind of deal together. Renée's entire antiquities operation, for example, was a cover for Tommy's pursuit of the codex. Don't get me wrong. Kevin's memorabilia, Djector's art-repping, Renée's picking, Tommy's book-dealing–it was all legitimate. The codex/ring endeavor, however, was fraught with false leads, mendacious connections, and great expense. Our alliances came together and fell apart. We squabbled, we made up, we quit, we took vacations, we came back. We went broke and quit for a year, two, three. A lead dwindled into thin air. Another came to our attention. Altogether, we were entirely too flamboyant, credulous, naive–honest, even–not to mention self-defeating, devious, unprofessional, and erratically financed. A lot of the wrong people knew who we were, and I'm not talking about the authorities, here.

"But then, Tommy and Djector managed to score the ring somewhere in Europe. This was years after the guy who had contacted Kevin and me in Paris got himself killed. I happened to be in London. I was more than willing to help; but I wasn't about to get arrested for something as idiotic as not declaring a stolen antiquity to an airport customs officer. That bit I laid on you this morning, about Tommy putting the ring in my hand? It's true, but I didn't say where he did it. It happened in London." Missy's eyes glowed with the memory. "We knew we would be relatively safe if we could get it into the United States. Once on our own turf we would sort out sticky little details like possession," she smirked. "We had some wacky idea for a time-share deal, like the Ring of Theodosus was a condo on Maui." She laughed sardonically. "Tommy would wear it for a month, I'd have a turn, then Manny. . . ."

"Just around the house," I said. "In the bath and whatnot."

"Danny, you are such a pill. We had gained control of both ring and codex," she stated flatly. "But the ring was in England, a country which is pretty serious about its customs, and the codex was in Iraq, where all of a sudden there was a war on."

"How did you possibly manage?" I asked, trying not to overdo my fascination.

"We managed very well, thank you. But in the end. . . . It was somewhat like political geography," she added thoughtfully. "Because Girly and Gerald happened to corner the codex in Iraq, and Tommy and Djector and I happened to corner the ring in England, we suddenly had two coalitions where there had been only one. It was like this mountain range had arisen between us. . . ."

"You were redefined by your experience, your possessions, your weather—your crops, as it were."

"Yes," she smiled, "we were defined by our crops. Meanwhile, the Carrington woman may have been truly frantic about her boyfriend, but she didn't forget to have her publicist meet the plane at Heathrow with a couple of reporters in tow, so she could fret live on CNN."

"Journalists have publicists?"

Missy shook her head. "Djector happened to be right across the channel, in Deauville, buying a horse. At the time, he and Tommy were seriously thinking about smuggling the ring into the states stuffed up the behind of some million-dollar foal—"

"Missy," I interrupted, "your mythomania heaps my credulity."

She didn't lose a beat. "There is, however, the well-known propensity of the DEA to X-ray imported animals to the point of giving them cancer. Even so, Tommy and I were ready to take the chance of moving the ring from Harwich to Deauville. But at some time or other, Djector had been involved in a deal with somebody who had mentioned Ms. Carrington's predilection for gems. Manny was in a racetrack bar and saw her on television, getting off a plane in London, and knew he'd found a way. Think about it, Danny."

"Oh, I'm thinking about it."

432

Missy obviously took pleasure in the memory. "I made the connection at her hotel and the rest was easy. As a result, we had a global media network tracking both our pigeons for us. Can you imagine? It was very amusing. If we wanted to know where either of them was at any given moment, all we had to do was turn on a TV!" She laughed a laugh like I'd never heard from her before; it was hearty and . . . piratical. "Of course," she added, "when it came down to cases out there in Mill Valley, one of our two fifteen-minuters failed to comprehend the inexorable logic of the endgame."

"Endgame. Yes. So you . . . adjusted his picture."

She said, "Some finesse was involved."

"Robbery, arson, murder. . . ."

"Haypeak brought it on himself."

"That's a lot of finesse, all right."

"If Tommy had been involved, the outcome might have been different. It would certainly have been different. He simply couldn't have brought himself to pull a trigger."

"Or have someone do it for him."

"Absolutely."

"Whereas, just having somebody tuned up a little bit. . . ."

She shrugged.

"All in a day's work," I bitterly surmised.

Missy turned not a hair. "Carrington drew Tommy as her nemesis, and it worked out. Haypeak drew Girly, unfortunately. But still, he brought it on himself. As for the Carrington girl, it's was unfortunate that she happened to be there when her boyfriend's partner showed up to do business. It's almost as if fate. . . . On the other hand, while it was a very long time before anybody caught onto what had really been stolen, why they'd been killed, or who had done it, the ring has never been mentioned. How much finesse do you want?"

"You're right. I must be losing my perspective. Are you

433

sure they failed to see the light? Did things really have to go so far?"

Missy cleared her throat. "Girly considers such explanations beneath her. At any rate, Djector heard about it–everybody heard about it; and that's when he bailed out. But you know what?"

"What?"

"That's when Gerald decided his mother had gone over the top."

We waited for a light. One of those scooters that sounds exactly like a reciprocating saw rounded the corner and made its way up the block, west on California, absolutely the only vehicle on the street.

"Let's think about this, Missy. You, personally, have been after the Syracuse Codex and/or the Ring of Theodosus since– when? Since you were married to Kevin Carnes?"

She nodded.

A thought struck me. "Did Kevin leave you because–?"

"I left Kevin," she corrected firmly.

"Sure. Okay. So how many people have died since you got interested?"

"Nine," she promptly answered, "since I got interested."

"Does that included the unknown contact in France?"

"Okay." She shrugged. "Ten."

"Now, when you do get your cold little hands on the codex, what are you going to do with it? Where are you going to go? Who or what is going to stop you from getting killed, too?"

"It's simple, Danny. I have no intention of keeping it. I'm going to sell it for a bundle. Once it's passed through my hands, I'll be safe."

"You're not worried about Her Grace, the Renquist, and Attik, Her Hammer?"

"Quite the contrary. Even as we speak, police and other entities are forcing them to flee to Argentina or some other place equally far afield. Meanwhile, six months in a faceless suburb of Albuquerque or Tucson couldn't be safer for little old me."

"Little old you? So plain. So unremarkable. So inconspicuous. So undistinguished. You going to trade the Jaguar for a Buick?"

"Of course not. A new paint job will do nicely. You always speak in such extremes, Danny."

"Bowditch isn't stupid, Missy. He's going to get wind of this."

For the first time in five blocks, Missy's gaze met mine. "How is Bowditch going to get wind of this?"

I shrugged. "DNA from the puke in Tommy Wong's wastebasket?"

She smiled thinly. "The only way he's going to find out, Danny, is if you tell him. And if you tell him anything at all, he'll quickly grasp that the codex was once in your possession, too. How do you think he's going to like that? How do you think you're going to like it?"

I pursed my lips.

"For gosh sakes," said Missy. "Taxi!" And she stepped off the curb, directly into the path of a cab.

To avoid killing her, the driver locked his brakes and the taxi screeched to a halt, acrid smoke swirling from its wheel wells. The cabby leaned out the window and said, "I don't normally pick up crazy people, god fucking damn it."

"It's true that my friend is mentally ill," Missy said, opening the back door. "But he only takes it out on himself by reading poetry and such. Get in," she said gently.

"Yeah?" The cabby dropped the flag. "I write poetry."

"Clay and Scott," Missy said. I might well have invoked the names of a few poets to test the waters; but Missy placed a peremptory hand on my forearm, and the ride proceeded in silence.

435

The cabby U-turned and drove east on California to Divisadero, where he turned north. Along the way the darkening twilight encouraged him to switch on his headlights. He turned east on Clay and stopped at Scott a block later.

"Give him the twenty," Missy said, adding, "Change, please," as I handed it over the seat.

I got out and stretched my legs, an unpleasant exercise, as they felt and sounded incompletely caramelized. They looked it, too.

We began to walk over the hill of Alta Plaza Park, diagonally toward its northeast corner, where Missy's Jaguar waited on the hydrant at Steiner.

"May I ask you a question?"

"Sure."

"It seems we are about to switch to your incredibly conspicuous getaway vehicle. Why?"

"There are money and a credit card hidden under the make-up mirror on the passenger-side sunshade. In the trunk are a computer with fax and email capability, not to mention my A-list society database, a cell phone, and a thoughtfully packed portmanteau."

"Oh."

The southern half of Alta Plaza rose steeply before us. Two tennis courts and a playground occupy a terrace just below the top of the hill. From the crest above them you can see a great deal of the San Francisco Bay. Far out to sea the sun had set. A subtly-graded twilight above a few tangerine-tinted clouds elided from cornflower blue to an ultramarine violet, straight over our heads. A new moon appeared at the lighter edge of this blue, accompanied by Venus. From the center of the bay winked the revolving light atop Alcatraz, five times a minute.

It was a beautiful place from which to be contemplating crimes. We paused by a bench next to a telephone box to catch our breath. The air had cooled considerably. It was the dinner hour, and only a little traffic obtained in this residential neighborhood. A private school across Scott was dark and deserted. Below us sat Girly Renquist's immense home, in total darkness.

"Not a light," I observed.

"She's long gone," Missy said.

"So why the precautions?"

She looked at me in the darkness. "I got us this far, didn't I?"

I had to agree with that.

"Danny?"

"What."

"Are you going to keep our bargain?"

"If you say so." I gestured toward the phone box. "Wouldn't you rather call Bowditch?"

She ignored this. "You promised."

"I promised."

She laid her hand on my cheek, tenderly, it seemed, though two or three days of whiskers grated her palm. "Square?"

I nodded.

"You won't see me again," she said quietly.

I didn't know what to say to this. Missy had been growing on me from the moment I'd met her, I'd forgotten how long ago. Maybe I was just realizing that I'd always assumed she would always be around, that her antics would provide amusement in my senility even if I never actually saw her, even if I only read about her in the society columns. Whatever my feelings, I stood still for the kiss she gave me, which wasn't quite sisterly, and not quite unchaste, either. It was a kiss from Missy, a woman I had never figured out. Perhaps that's where her charm lay.

Missy didn't even bother to remove the three $250 tickets that fluttered beneath a windshield wiper. The Jaguar's engine

437

was so quiet it was hard to know whether or not it was firing. The car moved as Missy bade it, and we were carried back across town, one last time.

The boatyard was deserted. The Jaguar's headlights picked out masts athwart sawhorses, the keels of hauled-out boats, piles of rigging and odd timbers, a rusted 55-gallon drum overflowing with empty oil cans and spent beer bottles. Missy parked under the sign, headed out. Afoot we threaded our way through the shadows until, rounding a big cleated tire of the haul-out crane, we found Dave right where I'd left him. A couple of tin-shaded floodlights glared down on the iron workbench, where a paint-spattered boom-box quietly muttered jazz among the tools. A can of Olympia beer waited on a cleat next to a pack of Camels and a butane lighter.

He didn't hear us approach. Years in engine rooms had ruined his hearing and, as he almost had the injector pump back together, his concentration was up. The housing hung at an odd angle in the bench vise, freshly painted bright red and sprouting new fittings.

Dave turned to select a T-handled Allen wrench from a box full of them, and spotted us over the half-lenses of his reading glasses. Certainly he noticed the shape I was in, and the company I was keeping, too. But he retrieved the wrench and fitted it to a bolthead.

"Evening," he said. "Out for a stroll?"

Across the inlet, under the lights of the distant shipyard, a plume from a high pressure steam hose scoured the hull of the dry-docked hospital ship. The electric whir of a gantry motor drifted over the water. A moth oscillated one of the lamps over the bench.

"Dave," I said. "It's time to retrieve the Syracuse Codex."

438

fORTY-TWO

We dinghied out to *Rummy Nation* and fired her up. At 250 rpms the asthmatic diesel sounded like a pile driver on an ant farm. But she chugged us determinedly away from her mooring, giving the buoys surrounding her sunken sister ship a wide berth. Missy had no sooner settled into a lawn chair in the cramped wheel house than she began to sneeze helplessly, the fit incited by spoors of mold rising from the companionway. Dave solicitously handed her his bottle. Missy took a swig of rum, only to have the sneezing redouble.

Dave laughed and produced a pink oil rag. "Oh, my god," Missy said, but daintily blew her nose with it.

Dave's eyes gleamed. Putting to sea, if only to journey a mile or two over the bay, had him contentedly gruff. In a wide turn around the easternmost pontoon wall of the shipyard, *Rummy Nation* was but a chip at the foot of the industrial gigantism of steel scaffolding, gantries, halide work lights, cables, chains, and leaking steam pipes. "Swell's up," Dave said, squinting into the darkness. "Might have a taste of winter in a day or three." He spun the wheel so as to angle over a gleaming ripple in the deceptively tranquil sheet of the bay's surface. The stem met the swell with a little smack and dropped into the trough behind it. A can of aerosol ether bounced down the three companionway steps, there to conjoin with other objects as they rearranged themselves below. A little brine sluiced along the foredeck, divided around the wheelhouse, and coursed astern with surprising energy. Missy squealed and picked up her feet. We rocked over the swell and beyond, scuppers leaking.

Twenty minutes later, maybe a mile east and south of the dry dock, Dave threw *Rummy Nation* into neutral and drifted up alongside a bobbing channel marker. The buoy had once displayed a number, but corrosion had effaced the paint long since.

Dave retrieved the six-foot gaff from the trailing dinghy and hooked the buoy's mooring chain with it, to adjust the boat's position. Then he fished the pole beneath the buoy until he hooked a loop of yellow nylon line and brought it aboard, over the davit block. He bent three turns of line over the drum of the pot windlass and engaged the solenoid with the toe of his sneaker. The electric motor whirred and line streamed up and over the davit down to the winch and into a galvanized tub at the foot of the davit. The line spewed a little rooster tail of brine tangent to the rim of the block as it came aboard.

Dave happily muttered to himself, taking satisfaction from the proper workings of the mechanical chaos that filled his life. The efficient disarming of the BMW's alarm system, the methodical restoration of an antique injector pump, the etherless firing of his diesel and its metrical wheeze, the smooth take-up of the pot winch–these eased the few hours of restless sleep allowed the alcoholic, and cheered his mornings.

Missy shivered and hugged herself against the cool marine air. I plucked a quilted flannel jacket off the back of the lawn chair and draped it over her shoulders, and she absently thanked me. Her eyes shone in the dark, wholly absorbed in watching the surface of the water, where the quivering yellow line disappeared into the center of dark concentric ripples. Dave slowed the winch, tailing the inboard line into its tub with one hand, steadying the outboard line with the other, until the line tautened with the weight of something no longer sitting on the bottom. Water began to well to the surface, pushed by the rising crab pot.

"I was wondering, Missy, whether you'd ever actually seen the thing?"

She answered, without thinking, "Yes. I saw it when—"

She stopped.

"You saw it in Mill Valley," I said quietly.

She did not take her eyes off the pot line. "We have a deal, Danny."

Once I might have chided her mildly. But I didn't feel mild. I felt sick. We were aboard a small boat; the rolling and the stinks of mold and diesel and rotting fish might make anyone queasy. But had we expected to drag up some sharp-toothed mucilaginous creature with luminescent antennae and fins like scimitars, I could not have conjured more trepidation. I knew I would never see Missy again, after tonight; but now I wondered why I'd ever bothered to see her at all.

The pot breached the surface, and the winch ceased. Dave hesitated long enough to allow the crab pot to sieve most of its seawater back into the bay, then handily swiveled the davit until he could unspool line sufficient to ease the payload to the deck.

The pot landed with a clank. Missy abruptly stood up, a thin plume of her breath visible against the dark interior of the wheelhouse. "What's that?"

"Chain," Dave said. "Otherwise she'd float." He kneeled over the pot to unravel two or three inscrutable knots at its mouth, which in the course of its sojourn at the bottom of the bay had never been open to its usual prey. Likewise, to forestall some human predator poaching its contents, it hadn't been marked by its own buoy.

The mesh of the trap opened to reveal the outer of four or

441

five black heavy-duty polyethylene garbage bags, sealed with fiberglass tape. Dave retrieved his boning knife from his belt sheath and carefully filleted the bags, layer by layer. This was an odd moment. Watching the blade, I could only recall the last filet I'd witnessed.

"We took a page from the codex itself," I said, "in concealing it."

"Do tell," Missy muttered, indifferent to everything outside Dave's progress.

"I do tell. Dave deep-sixed your treasure after I last saw him. I've never known its whereabouts. It's similar to the way Ali acted as a blind for Theodosus, don't you think? Ali kept the ring while the boy visited his mother, you'll recall—"

"I do recall," Missy replied, with distinct disinterest. Dave cut the last bag. A shard of light glinted off its contents.

I shrugged. "One plays what cards one is dealt."

Dave stabbed the knife into the wooden deck and left it quivering there. "Argh," he laughed softly, and lifted the box. The stem of the vacuum valve momentarily tangled in the mesh of the crab pot, and he held the box off the deck while I disentangled it. When I stood up again, Dave handed the box to me. I righted it so that, handed to Missy, it was face up. "There you go, darling."

The flannel jacket fell to the deck as she took it. For a moment Missy peered as if myopically at the box, at the top page more or less visible through the translucent lid despite the bad light. Then she sat back into the lawn chair as if faint, as if bewildered, clasping the box to her breast as if it were a child.

"The Syracuse Codex," she whispered.

Rummy Nation banged against the channel marker. Dave took up the gaff to fend us off. "Now what?"

"That's up to Missy."

442

She caressed the plastic box. Her lips moved as if she were reciting a text. Per-haps she knew the codex by heart. The diesel coughed thirty times per minute. It was one of Dave's studies to see how few rpms the Hicks would make and still turn over.

"Where to, Missy? How about Jack London Square?" I pointed across the bay. "You could take a cab to the Oakland Airport."

She looked up abruptly, as if surprised to see us, but said nothing. She looked cornered, as if all she wanted in the world was another minute in which to savor her triumph.

"I never thought I'd see Missy James at a loss for words," I said. "You want to go to your car?"

She nodded distantly. "Yes," she said softly. "Please take me to my car."

Dave lay the gaff on the deck alongside the wheelhouse, kicked the transmission into gear, and spun the wheel. The modest vessel clanked and shuddered and began to make way. He gave her a little throttle. The dinghy fell in astern of us, like a foal following its mare. The channel marker began to diminish as if it were the thing moving, and soon disappeared into the gloom.

Despite all the sounds of a small vessel under power, the silence among its passengers was palpable. Missy cast abrupt glances toward the shoreline of San Francisco, toward the south bay, toward the lights of Oakland. Dave and I watched ahead, each wrapped within his own thoughts.

By and by we rounded the end of the dry dock, steering a middle course between its outer pontoons and the sunken *Stripéd-Ass Bass*. Dave pointed up at the looming hospital ship. Though a good hundred yards aport, it looked like her stern was directly above us. "Don't want no Burmese mangrove to fall outta the hawsehole when they clear the chain locker, argh hargh hrg. Crush a crabber like a friggin tick."

Hawseholes and other hazards safely astern, we drew abreast of the boatyard. "Run right up to the dock," I suggested.

Dave nodded. He could anchor out and dinghy back in while I saw Missy safely on her way, or he could wait. Either way, he and I could then proceed to drink everything we could get our hands on, the curse of this damned plastic box and its attendant fanatics lifted from our lives for good.

"Don't forget to stop at your local friendly vacuum station every five thousand miles," I said to Missy, as Dave put the transmission in neutral. "Got to keep the atoms in pure stasis, entirely separate from the weevils of putrefaction."

She neither smiled nor spoke. She didn't even turn her head. She was watching the dock as if it were a tectonic plate, taking a geologic age to drift out to meet us.

The bow drifted alongside the outermost piling. Dave stepped outside the wheelhouse and smartly dropped the plaited loop of a thick line over a cleat bolted to the corner of the dock. The other end of the line was already fast to a starboard cleat in *Rummy Nation's* stern. The little vessel continued its inland drift. The line lost its slack and began to tighten audibly.

"Already gone, are you?" I said quietly. Had I been a stranger trying to pick her up at a bus stop, Missy might not have ignored me any more pointedly. I was no longer needed. But as she tentatively put a foot atop the pier-side gunwale, ready to step ashore, she said, "Goodbye, Danny."

They had been waiting among the shadows and now appeared, almost on cue. The stern was moored. The bow had drifted nearly to a halt. Walking forward, Dave stopped beside the house and bent to pick up the gaff, which was underfoot. A voice said, "A pretty landing, governor. Now the bow line, if you please."

It was almost on cue. If Dave had been in the bow, if the bow were moored, if Missy had been on the dock, then the timing would have been perfect. Life is all about timing, son, the drill instructor used to say, as he buried one end of his pugil baton in your gut.

I'd never heard Teddy speak; he had some kind of London accent. Not hesitating for a moment, not doing badly for an old drunk, Dave launched the gaff straight at him.

Teddy, one foot poised on the bow gunwale and ready to step aboard, almost a mirror image of Missy, had to fall backwards onto the dock to avoid getting impaled.

The gaff did this work and more. Tracking right past Teddy's nose like an aluminum snake, fully extended in its strike, the gaff disturbed the aim of Attik. Ten or twelve yards inland of Teddy, in the shadow of a stack of rental dinghies lashed upside down to the pier, Attik only had time to throw a single shot toward Dave before batting the gaff off course with the barrel of his pistol.

The big Israeli automatic sounded loud over the water, as if some one had bashed the side of a dumpster with a three-pound maul. A hollow-point round exploded an entire forward corner off the top of the wheelhouse, well above Dave who, in launching the gaff, had lost his balance and fallen backwards into the narrow slip of deck between the house and the starboard gunwale.

"Take care where you shoot!" bellowed a massive female voice, a contralto worthy of a diva who sees her entire *raison d'être* momentarily within her grasp. And in a move incommensurate with the order of an Empress, Mrs. Renquist clutched at Attik's gun arm. The assassin's second round passed no more than a couple of inches over the prostrate Teddy's hapless head, gouging a groove along the boards of the pier beyond him before its fragments lifted up to spatter the creosoted piling that anchored the end of the floating dock, just outboard of me.

Since shooting had started, and knowing only what I'd

observed in the past hour about motor-sailing, I kicked the gearbox lever into what I assumed was reverse, then threw myself headlong and backwards, toward the aft dockline. The little engine bogged down but kept chugging, and gradually, discernibly, her screw began to take hold.

Recoiling, Missy had already fallen backwards into the boat, behind the wheelhouse, and landed, unfortunately, over the washtub full of crab-pot line. She received a severe shock to her spine and momentarily lost control of her precious plastic box, which clattered to the deck. Lefthanded I retrieved the sheath knife, breaking off its tip, which remained embedded in the deck, as I rolled over and beyond the Lexan box, to saw at the dock-line. This seemed to take a long time, with all of us exposed to whatever ordnance might come our way.

Dave, feeling his boat lurch out of control, instinctively stood straight up beside the wheelhouse. This shielded me and Missy, too, but gave Attik his target at last. The big pistol boomed a third time and the thimble-sized round knocked Dave six feet straight backwards over Missy and right on top of me.

The impact of Dave caused the knife blade to stray through the webbing between the thumb and forefinger of my right hand. The dock line parted, but had remained whole long enough to cause the unsecured bow to initiate a turn counter-clockwise around the moored stern, and the entire vessel slid past the end of the dock, wallowing sternward and increasingly sideways toward the bay. This slow careen would soon have us broadside to Attik's line of fire, and probably entangle the dinghy painter in the prop. The dinghy was effectively winding clockwise to port, around the stern, as if it hadn't moved at all, though still tethered to *Rummy Nation.*

"Icthyphallic," Dave gurgled, "motherfucker. . . ."

I put my mouth close to his ear and said, "Is there a gun in the house?"

446

"Fishdicked fomenter of incest," he choked, barely audible. "Needlefishdickedsistermonger. . . ."

"A gun," I insisted, only to hear a faint argh hargh hrgh of puzzled introspection, which bode no good for Dave. I gave the throttle a kick and rolled the other way, to cut the dinghy painter. The severed line drifted out of the port supper on the stern of the boat, the side opposite the dock.

Now there was more shooting. It was probably only a moment before I recognized the sound of a weapon entirely different than the Israeli pistol, but it seemed like a very long time. No lead seemed to be coming aboard, however. Then Teddy screamed like I'd heard men scream before, and died.

"You goddamn sons of bitches!" a man shouted and the new gun boomed again, a roar far heavier than the Israeli pistol's. "You killed my wife!"

A woman screamed.

The Israeli automatic barked.

"Yogurt-eatin bastard!" The bigger gun discharged four times. Lead pellets clattered among the wooden rowboats and galvanized fittings and aluminum masts, and rolled along the pier like so many ball bearings. But none of this seemed aimed at *Rummy Nation.*

Abruptly, the guns fell silent.

Blood trickled out of one corner of Dave's mouth. It looked black in the darkness. "Argh," he breathed, ever so faintly.

"Keep laughing," I hissed as I peered over the gunwale.

Gunsmoke drifted over the dock. The two lamps over Dave's workbench shone as the epicenters of a chorded web of light. From where Teddy lay on the dock, one of his arms twisted up into my sightline. Teddy was no longer a factor. Behind the stack of dinghies an indecipherable discussion was under way. The voices sounded incongruously reasonable, if terse. And then three blasts of buckshot raked the pile of inverted rowboats. Wood splinters twirled up and fell

447

back, ticking onto the dock and into the water. The rounds were fired from Dave's workbench, where now I saw a man sight along a pump shotgun, its barrel propped atop the tools and gear there. A box of shotshells, its flap open, tilted atop the red pump housing.

"Kramer!" Mrs. Renquist shouted from the shadows. "Let's talk!"

Kramer Knowles?

Double-nought pellets blasted six-inch splinters out of the rowboats. Knowles pumped the spent shell expertly, without compromising his aim. "You're through talking, you treacherous bitch!" He rained pellets onto the dock and its rowboats until his gun was empty.

Mrs. Renquist screamed the while, an hysterical ululation nearly lost to the roar of the shooting. But it was loud and eloquent enough to suggest that a prolonged barrage might drive her mad—or madder, one should say.

"What's the matter, you fucking whore?" Knowles yelled, calmly fitting shells into the smoking breech. "You never been shot at before?" Rounds chambered, he loosed three without aiming. Those rowboats would never float again.

I slid out from under Dave and crawled toward the helm, taking the knife with me. At that moment the Israeli pistol began banging away from above and inland of the rowboats. Attik was shooting for effect, around the front of the haul-out crane, and his fire was inaccurate. Sparks ricocheted all around the tools and metal parts heaped on Dave's work-bench. Pieces of rubber chunked off the crane tire, right into Knowles' face. Knowles rolled off the workbench with shotgun tucked against his chest, like a trained Marine should. His next two shots, straight up, blasted the two worklights into darkness.

The helm was full to starboard. I spun it all the way to port and goosed the throttle. Though by now well clear of the dock, *Rummy Nation* had been trying to show her stern to it.

Left alone, she might have backed right around the end of the dock and up the other side. My idea was to straighten the wheel enough to continue backing east and away from the dock, possibly until we got to Sacramento, keeping as much boat between us and the shooting as possible. And I was well into this maneuver, having put forty or fifty yards between the bow and the end of the dock, before I realized that my move had betrayed Missy's position entirely.

Despite being badly injured, Missy had managed to crawl around the front of the wheelhouse and fall over the port side of *Rummy Nation*, into the dinghy, and she had taken the codex with her. In all the shooting, half under Dave and behind the house, I hadn't noticed.

Slipping into shock, soon to be unable to feel anything or even to walk, Missy crouched helplessly in the dinghy. Disoriented and dazed, she yet clung to her Syracuse Codex. Until I corrected the helm, she'd managed to cling one-handed to the port side of *Rummy Nation,* keeping the larger boat between herself and the gunfire.

My move inadvertently and completely exposed her. She lost her grip and got left behind, not twenty yards from the end of the dock – a perfect target. Light from the boatyard bathed her incredulous face. She looked our way, then back towards the dock, and finally placed the invaluable prize of her long quest between herself and the guns ashore, just like a shield. It must have been one of the most difficult decisions of her life. Reaching over it, in obvious pain, she dipped an oar into the water beside the dinghy. She could not have wielded this oar any less effectively if she'd only had one arm, and its blade only knifed the water ineffectively.

Despite being besieged herself, Mrs. Renquist noticed. She began to scream like a dog being slowly run over by a car. Attik, rattled no doubt, fearless more likely, foolhardy in fact, loyal no matter what, abandoned his position and caution

449

forthwith. He sprang from the embankment, down onto the stack of rowboats, and thence to the floating dock. He crouched and ran, throwing shots over his shoulder toward Knowles. Knowles stood up and returned fire, screaming oaths as if they would make him bulletproof. Sparks ricocheted on all sides, but he was oblivious. His buckshot tore splinters from the dock timbers in front of and behind Attik, and rang on metal fittings. Flowers of dark blood began to bloom on the handsome tweed jacket. Knowles fired steadily. He made every shot count; the shotgun held seven rounds, times nine pellets per shot. As Attik approached Teddy's corpse, he turned his pistol slowly away from Knowles, even as pellets visibly minced his tweed.

Then Knowles ran out of shells. In the sudden silence, though by now sixty or seventy yards away, I thought I distinctly heard the metallic clink of a firing pin as it fell on the empty chamber. This was impossible, of course. The diesel stack was thumping just a few feet above my head. But I saw Knowles look around, momentarily disoriented. Then his eye fell on the box of shotshells, just a foot or two behind him.

But now Attik glowered down on Missy like a deity, molten with rage. Mortally wounded, his body now twisted through and beyond the turn he'd judged, its rotational skew augmented by a dozen ballistic swats. Blood welled from the corners of his mouth.

"Danny!" Missy screamed. "Danny!"

Even as he fell, Attik raised his killer's pistol and emptied it, shot after shot, directly at Missy James, who ineffectually flailed her oar a mere forty feet away. Before Attik crashed face first to the dock, both of them, Attik and Missy, were lifeless.

I could only watch.

Fully half the rounds hit her. Upon impact hollow-point bullets mushroom, broadening into a path as thick as the

450

butt of a pool cue. They did terrible, fatal damage to Missy. And they did equally fatal damage to the Syracuse Codex. A number of bullets hit the box before they hit Missy, and so her expensively nurtured complexion sustained not only the impacts of hot fragments of lead, but also a foray of plastic splinters as well; as well as the subtler abrasion of papyrus atoms.

The little dinghy took hits, too. Only one at the waterline might have sufficed, but there were several. Dead and clutching no more than shards of her aspiration, Missy James sank with the dinghy and the Syracuse Codex, into the bay. Only miscellaneous smithereens remained afloat, trailing ink and blood, the dissipating filaments of a dream that had proven, at last, less than immortal.

FORTY-THREE

Rummy Nation backed through the perimeter of buoys and squarely into the topmast of the sunken *Stripéd-Ass Bass*. The prop flailed at the gear down there; its blades tangled with a submerged stay, just above the spreader, and stopped. With a sick clank from the transmission and a wheeze from its cylinder, the little diesel died.

Deep within his flickering consciousness, Dave realized something had gone wrong. His lips moved feebly. Otherwise he lay perfectly still.

There we bobbed. About sixty yards of water separated us from the pier. Only the sounds of water were audible. Because of the mercury vapor lamps high in the air high above the hospital ship, target visibility wasn't too bad. It was so quiet that I thought work must have stopped in the vast drydocks. Maybe we had an audience? Maybe they would call for help? Maybe they thought we were shooting a movie instead of bullets?

Leaning over the stern to assure myself of the hopelessness of our situation, I heard voices. Turning, I saw Knowles in front of the battered rowboats. I couldn't make out what was said, but I clearly heard two pops. They sounded like penny firecrackers. Knowles roared and fired the shotgun from his hip. Silence. Knowles chambered a round. He lowered the barrel. He fired again. Then he slowly sank to his knees.

I glanced east to the towering shipyard, two hundred yards

452

away. Steam rose into the spotlights atop one of the gantries, two hundred feel above the bay. The machine's winches whirred and stopped and whirred again. A load of I-beams settled onto an iron deck; a second later I heard the crash. The dry dock appeared to be carrying on with its work. Was it possible that nobody over there had noticed all this shooting over here?

I peered over the wainscot of the wheelhouse, through the windshield glass.

Knowles staggered down the dock, his steps uncertain on the water-borne boards. He leaned as if facing a high wind. Hinges grated as he stepped, as if with a lubber's uncertainty, from one floating section to another. The snubbed lines belaying the entire rickety structure creaked as they stretched taut over a swell, and he almost fell. A halyard began its rhythmic strum against an aluminum mast, then ceased.

Knowles side-stepped the body of Teddy and came to that of Attik, who lay across the dock with one leg in the water. He prodded one of Attik's eyes with the barrel of the shotgun. But the corpse, being a corpse, didn't mind at all.

Knowles looked toward what was left of Missy.

The holed dinghy had swamped and settled out from under her, leaving behind an appalling detritus. The swell had begun to dissipate the pieces, large and small, of Missy James and the Syracuse Codex, among a jerry can, a styrofoam cooler, several beer bottles, and an upended rubber boot.

Knowles certainly must have expected the treachery of a feeding frenzy; but, bent solely on dispensing revenge, he was not distracted by the collateral glows of fame and wealth. His survey of the devastation was proprietary. He stood swaying, the shotgun couched in the crook of his arm, with the nonchalance of an inebriated duck hunter, with not a care for the sodden and irretrievable scraps of the shattered codex. Some of these remained on the water's surface and

453

shimmered dimly in the uncertain light. Others lay obscurely sandwiched, in delicate equilibrium between the tension of the surface and the unambiguous pressure of the depths. And others, having yielded to the inevitable, wallowed feet and even yards below, eddying side to side but ineluctably downward. All would eventually find their way to the bottom, retreated forever beyond legibility or value.

Knowles didn't give a goddamn about the Syracuse Codex. Not then, not ever.

Again, he fell to his knees. The change of posture half took him by surprise. The stock of the shotgun whacked the dock as he extended it to steady himself.

Knowles looked toward the stack of dinghies. The visible surfaces of these, the hapless recipients of so much gunfire, showed great numbers of freshly torn splinters and gaping holes. If there were a seaworthy vessel left in there, it would be far down in the belayed stack. Knowles was badly wounded. The fire-cracker pops I'd heard had come from the muzzle of John Plenty's target pistol, which Attik had left with Mrs. Renquist. As Knowles stood over her, she'd squeezed off two rounds. Both pierced his abdomen. That's when he killed her. But it wasn't why he killed her.

Knowles braced the stock of the shotgun on the dock and angled the barrel some thirty degrees above it. He launched a round in *Rummy Nation's* direction with a laugh. A moment later, pellets descended harmlessly onto the roof of the wheelhouse, and into the water around the boat.

It wasn't exactly like being shot at. We floated fairly out of the range of any shotgun, even a long-barreled one. Knowles knew it. I knew it. Nevertheless, I dragged Dave into the shade of the wheelhouse. Dave had a sucking wound, but that meant he was still breathing.

"They killed my wife!" Knowles yelled weakly. It gave him

some trouble to pump the action, but when he had, he loosed another round in our direction.

Nothing save a direct hit in an eye could do us harm at this range. A pellet cracked one of the two panes of glass in the windshield, but didn't penetrate it. Lead balls skipped off the roof, dinged the stack, ticked against the decking forward and the galvanized tub aft, and sprouted little eruptions as they hit the water.

"They killed my Renée!" His anguish echoed over the water between us.

Knowles awkwardly pumped the action, casting an exasperated, almost jack-lit glance to his right as he did so, to where Missy's body floated amid shreds of codex. Perhaps, having lost his wife, not to mention his health, Knowles intended to blow away the world in recompense?

It seemed fair enough.

He raised the shotgun to his shoulder, toward *Rummy Nation,* wavered, then crumbled onto his left side.

Preceded by a shriek of feedback, a bullhorn fired up.

"This is your basic San Francisco Police Department Tactical Squad," a voice said calmly. "Throw down your weapon and put your hands on top of your head."

Bowditch's amplified voice sounded as measured and bland as an intercom echoing over a used car lot, asking for a salesman to pick up line four.

Spotlights began to play over the boat yard.

"Throw down your weapon, Knowles," the electronic voice barked, annoyed, tired, and ineluctable. "They're all dead. You won. Hands on top of your head, and face the spotlights."

Knowles did not respond. I could see his hand moving ineffectually about the trigger of the shotgun. But he did lift it.

A single rifle shot rang out. A little geyser of splinters erupted from the boards of the dock not a foot from Knowles' shoulder.

455

"That's across your bow, mister," the bullhorn said.

The boat was turning. Strange noises were coming from the stern, where the tangle of rudder and prop and topmast rigging resisted the change. Dave lay on deck between the helm and the forward wall of the wheelhouse, curled into a fetal position. His breathing had bubbles in it, and a dark froth was staining his beard. I shouted over the gunwale. "Knowles! They're all dead. Call it off! Bowditch! He's hit! Hold your fire!"

Knowles made no response. An eerie, echoing silence descended, and gradually the night air became rein-habited by the stretching of dock lines, the creaking of hinges, halyards tapping their masts, water lapping hulls and pilings.

Three uniformed police officers took turns covering each other, crouching and scampering as they approached the three crumpled forms strung out along the length of the boat dock. One stopped by the first corpse. A second stooped by the second. The third officer stopped at Knowles. The officer kicked the butt of the gun, and it came away from Knowles' hand and fell into the water. The officer knelt to feel Knowles' throat for a pulse. Then she cautiously looked up, toward *Rummy Nation,* and I recognized Sergeant Maysle. She stood away from Knowles slowly, still covering him with her service pistol, and spoke into a microphone clipped to her shoulder. A reply squawked back.

Knowles was dead or dying. Sargent Maysle continued to cover him, now holding her service pistol with both hands. But she wasn't looking at him. Or me.

Sergeant Maysle was watching the floating remnants of the Syracuse Codex, as they rose and gently fell on a passing swell.

BYZANTINE LEGACY

FORTY-FOUR

Bowditch was as pissed as Moby Dick by the time he got his hands on me.

There was a lot to explain. Renée's missing BMW, for a minor example. But all anybody could do was talk about it because nobody officially found the thing. Abandoned on China Basin it was soon stripped of its fenders and doors, the hood and trunk lids, engine, transmission, differential . . . . Despite the missing parts and a fried electrical system, it was still a brand-new BMW, so somebody soon hauled off the chassis, too. None of it was ever found.

Clarence Ing found the Ring of Theodosus. Down at the morgue. It was on Girly Renquist's wedding finger.

Bowditch had me all framed and ready to hang on a wall, nonetheless. There was insufficient evidence to charge me with car theft; and I was able to make a coherent argument for having seen the ring only once, at Tommy Wong's. But Bowditch thought he had a pretty good fit on me for receiving stolen property—the Syracuse Codex. I of course took every opportunity to remind him that, in light of twelve or fourteen murders, this was a relatively mild offense. And then, once more, Clarence Ing got his oar in. He found a single gold bead embedded in two grams of dogshit caught in one of the peculiar suckers lining the soles of Teddy's hightop sneakers.

This tiny bead was a perfect match for the remaining examples to be found in Renée Knowles' missing earring, the one found crushed into the entry hall carpet of her home. This piece of material evidence pretty much wrapped up her murder.

Undeterred, Bowditch went me one better and charged Dave with complicity. It was in reading the warrant, by the way, that I found out that Dave's real name was Absalom D. Peptol.

Dave didn't give any more of a damn for Bowditch than he did the warrant. He was just glad to be alive. He lay in the hospital for four months with a large bullet hole in him, cheerfully suffering its various complications. The surgeons removed the better part of a lung along with his gall bladder, and strictly enjoined him against the further depredations of cigarettes and alcohol. Rummaging about his insides, however, these same doctors had assessed his liver as a miracle unknown to science. They sewed him up and regularly displayed him to specialists and students, as a medical curiosity.

Meanwhile, I finished carving that maple-and-blood wood frame for Michelle Canton, putting myself in the way of some much-needed cash. Other work came in, and time passed.

But Bowditch remained really browned about the codex. I refused to tell him anything and, soon enough, obstruction of justice got added to receiving stolen property. Even in light of my tipping him to the murders of John Plenty and Tommy Wong, not to mention those of Ecstasy and the Cajun, a grand total of two murder scenes and four stiffs to get himself on the news about, Bowditch continued to hound me. So when I finished the hand-carved frame, I had to use the money to hire a lawyer. A guy with a shingle across the street from the city jail took the money, told me not to worry, and stopped returning my calls.

In the midst of this, which took months, I had the inspiration to invite Sergeant Maysle to dinner. Bowditch was soft on her. My idea was to see if she wouldn't put in a word on my behalf, try to get him to lighten up. Not to mention, Sergeant Maysle was a smart, beautiful woman, and we could discuss it over two dinners, if she liked.

Fat chance. By that time, Sergeant Maysle's translation and commentary—entitled, appropriately enough, *The Syracuse Codex*—had been published. Complemented by the spectacular events in San Francisco, the ensuing publicity enabled the Sergeant to take an extended unpaid leave from the police department. She traveled all over the U.S. and Europe on the strength of the book, and, of course, the story made a sensation in Turkey. She never worked as a cop again. The Smithsonian commissioned her to write a catalogue to accompany a major exhibition of Byzantine antiquities, prominently featuring the Ring of Theodosus, of which the museum had become custodian pending resolution of the thoroughly arcane question of provenance. This story, too, Maysle turned into a series of articles and eventually a book. The museum show made such a splash it may still be traveling. A year after Dave got out of the hospital I opened up the *Examiner* one afternoon to read that the good Sergeant Maysle had won a $350,000 "genius grant" from a widely-respected philanthropic organization. The article was so hastily slugged it was accompanied by her graduation photo from the police academy. The next picture of her that I saw appeared in *National Geographic*. She'd changed her hair and was not dressed as a cop. She was lecturing on the Byzantine mosaics still to be seen in the churches of S. Vitale and S. Apollinare Nuove, in Ravenna, which depict, among others, Justinian, Theodora, and, it is believed, Procopius' boss, Belisarius. The article detailed how book sales and her "genius" award had enabled Dr. Maysle to establish the Cabochon Research Foundation, headquartered in Paris, for which she was "profoundly grateful." Only the old-timers in the San Francisco Police Department would call her Sergeant, anymore. But it had been a very long time since Dr. Maysle had visited San Francisco.

Earlier, about three months after the phantasmagory in Mike's Boatyard, certain lab tests came back to Clarence Ing. Nobody's fool, he'd ordered them on a hunch and, once again, Clarence got results. His tests determined, beyond a doubt, that the Syracuse Codex was a forgery.

Three days later, at a meeting in the D.A.'s office, Bowditch had a stroke.

He wound up in the same hospital that Dave had been in. Different wing, different building, same institution. I went by to say hello, only to find a different man than the fading but pugnacious bulldog I had known. In a month he'd lost thirty pounds and aged ten years. His complexion had gone from rubicund to ashen. Five machines were keeping him alive. I was so shocked by the change I could hardly speak. Mrs. Bowditch, a kindly, attentive, worried woman, herself in bad health, sat beside Bowditch's bed the whole time I was there. She refused to let us discuss work-related subjects, let alone Clarence Ing's lab results. This left only the subject of Bowditch's Chronic Obstructive Pulmonary Disease, which nobody wanted to talk about either, and the visit which started out as awkward quickly became pointless. I hardly knew the guy, after all. My presence clearly upset him, but, in fact, he seemed confused about why it upset him, which in turn disconcerted me. I'd gotten used to his badgering. In the hallway outside his room Mrs. Bowditch explained that her husband had to let go of all that stuff in order to get better, and one way for me to help him do that would be not to visit him again. I didn't blame her.

Without Bowditch's persistence the investigation fell apart. Nobody cared about a fake codex, so I was off the hook for

460

receiving stolen property. Experts stated that the penmanship was crude, what they could read of it. The main clue was the forgery's hand-laid paper, which was traced to Fabriano, the venerable Italian manufacturer, whose experts were able to assign it an age of twenty-five years or less. Since this material is easily purchased anywhere in the world, little or nothing could be established beyond its age and marque. With the ink Clarence had worse luck, as too little of it survived salt water immersion to analyze. That only the top sheet inside the plastic box had any writing on it at all didn't help. The box wasn't even made of Lexan but common plexiglass, manufactured in warehouse-sized lots and distributed globally, and that was the end of that trail. As a small consolation, this particular detail explained why the box hadn't stopped or at least deflected Attik's bullet fragments. Even the vacuum gauge had been faked. Fished off the bottom of the bay by a scuba diver, it turned out to have been robbed off an ordinary bicycle pump.

Every trail went cold. No evidence could prove one way or the other whether the codex everybody had been chasing had ever been genuine at all. This doubt extended all the way back to the clandestine deal in Iraq. If never genuine, of course, then a lot of people had died for nothing. The newspapers had a field day with it.

"'At least ten people dead,'" Dave quoted one day, from the subhead of a Sunday feature. The article was accompanied by quotes from Dr. Maysle's book and her author's photo. "'And for what?'" Dave was back in the hospital by then, due to ongoing vexatious symptoms, and had gotten quite adroit at vexing the hospital staff. Even now, laying aside the *Chronicle,* he retrieved a pint of rum from beneath his pillow. "Besides, it's fourteen, ain't it? If Bowditch croaked, we could make it fifteen."

"If you croaked, we could make it sixteen."

461

His laugh disintegrated into a deep, protracted cough. "Christ, " he said, when he could talk again. "I want a cigarette."

I declined a swallow of rum. "They released him yesterday."

"Is he going back to work?"

I shook my head. "He's in a wheelchair. A year of therapy, his wife told me, and maybe he'll be able to walk with a cane."

"That sucks," Dave said warmly. He was taking a second pull on the pint when a male nurse appeared.

"Goddamn it, *Mister* Peptol," he scolded. "We're trying to get you vertical out the front door, not horizontal out the back one. Give me that bottle at once." He held out his hand. "Gimme gimmme."

Dave cheerfully relinquished it, asking, in his most reasonable tone, "How do you expect me to get any better without my medicine?"

The nurse upended the bottle over the sink. Hardly anything came out. "The idea is to get *off* medication." He dropped the empty into a trash can. "Especially *self*-medication." He set about thumping Dave's pillow, tidying up, and taking readings from a pistol-like device, whose tip he inserted into Dave's ear.

"It shakes a man up," Dave said, tranquilly submitting to the examination, "to hear about a guy like Bowditch getting wheeled over the threshold of his retirement."

"His wife told me they have a little ranch on the southeast shoulder of Mount Lassen. It backs right up to the national park. A few horses, a hundred fruit trees, a hammock slung on a sleeping porch, satellite TV. . . ." Dave winced. I shrugged. "They're looking forward to it. Bowditch figured out a long time ago that the only way he could afford to retire was with some kind of disability to round out his pension

462

and social security. He didn't know how to go about it without getting shot."

"A million-dollar stroke," Dave said. "On the job."

"Worth every nickel, more or less. He didn't have to stop a bullet."

"So what if he can't walk?" Dave asked rhetorically.

I was sitting with my back to the door. "That guy gone?"

Dave nodded.

I slipped him a fresh pint.

• • •

We motored in with the tide yesterday morning.

It's been nearly a year since we were last in Puerto Angel. They've rebuilt the jetport since the hurricane, upgrading the service while they were at it, so there are quite a few more gringos here than the last time we visited, plus it's cruising season and the harbor is choked with boats. But a guy at the chandlery remembered Dave and secured us the loan of a private mooring for a couple of weeks.

Dave of course says I should have seen it thirty, forty years ago. He says the same thing about all of Central and South America. But it's true that, thirty-five years ago, he used to pick up a hundred bales of marijuana at a time in a little village just north of here, right off their turtle dock, right in the middle of town. A bale meant fifty kilograms, some eighty-seven pounds, of dope. A turtle dock meant live sea turtles upside down on their carapaces, dying in the sun. That part hasn't changed. The Mexicans still make a soup and a highly regarded suntan lotion out of sea turtles.

Dave never stopped sailing till he got those hundred bales to Juneau, where a guy selling to pipeline crew bought every kilo aboard for cash. Pot was legal in Alaska, see, and blah blah blah. So where's the money now, Dave, somebody always asks. And Dave always laughs right with them, hearty as can be.

These days you can get a thousand gallons of dry diesel in Puerto Angel. You can buy something to drink besides *pulque* or tequila, too. They have all the shipboard provender you need, fresh, canned, or freeze-dried. They've got spar varnish, winch handles, hoses, belts, filters, fasteners, fish-finders, water-makers—that chandlery Dave prefers is first-rate. There's a bookstore with a large English-language section, though by now we both read Spanish almost as well as we speak it. You can find fabric softener, batteries, French newspapers—there's even a cyber-café; not to mention a shaded poolside barstool, from which Dave can order a proper Bombay and tonic, with ice made from distilled water.

Consuelo's gone ashore with Dave, today, leaving me to my bench under the awning on the afterdeck. I still take a lot of pleasure in wood carving, and don't really care much for drinking in the waterfront bars or shopping at the *mercado*. Tomorrow I may step ashore to visit a coffin-maker I met two or three trips ago. It's a family operation, four or five generations old, and they do real nice woodwork.

Southern Mexico, Central and South America, even the open sea provide me with all the wood I could ever find the time to carve. Little hand-planed boards, rough-sawn logs, pieces of ancient furniture, everything in between, in any species you care to name, there's plenty to work with. I've got several years' worth of boards stickered and drying— insofar as the sea air will allow them to dry; they're stacked below the fore and aft companionways, and a few other places, too.

Byzantine Legacy is a two-masted Baltic schooner, 107 feet at the water line, with a big house amidships and another one aft. Nordic fir construction throughout, with not so much teak and brass brightwork, she has lots of interesting fittings and gear collected up from a century of continuous seafaring. We're only the fifth owner, and there's a shelf of salt-stained logs in the saloon dating all the way back to the day she slid down the ways in Öberstaad, Denmark, in 1893.

She's been refitted twice. Once in 1943, in Chile, and two years ago, at our behest, on the Caribbean coast of Nicaragua. Every time we ship the Canal or make port, people take her picture. A proud vessel, she is. More than willing to sail, she accepted with equanimity the four-banger Cummins diesel that Dave found in Key West. That damn engine stayed on the foredeck for nearly a year, tarped and thick with naval jelly, until Dave had gathered up several crates of parts necessary to the refit, and then we hauled her in Copañahual.

A couple of years without a major project had been enough for Dave. In Cancún he'd taken up with Gwen, a Florida housewife on the lam from her doctor husband, or so she claimed, and Dave forgot about the new diesel for a while. She was a hellion. Once she coldcocked Dave with an oar, not that he didn't deserve it, but overboard he went, with us doing six knots. Somehow we got him back, and he loved every minute of it. But Gwen met a delivery skipper in Zihuatanejo, whose current charge featured a heli-pad and a swimming pool, not to mention electricity, a washer and dryer, and hot running water, and she disappeared in the blink of an eye. After he'd gone on a good drunk for about a month, long enough to say good riddance but not so long for him to quit sulking, Dave threw himself into the modernization.

Of fair size, we're anchored at the very end of a long dock. A few folks come out for a look, but they pretty much leave us alone. I'm working on a frame for a large photograph of the boat to send to Consuelo's family. It's the first frame I've made since I left San Francisco. The Mexican taste runs to elaboration, so I've been taking my time and having some

465

fun with it. The motif is manta rays. You've never seen manta rays like the ones off the west coast of Mexico. They're as big as Volkswagens and that's impressive, but I've never looked at them in quite the same way since I noticed that *manta* is Spanish for blanket. The frame has an octopus, too. Its tentacles embrace the top and one side and fondly entangle a mermaid with Consuelo's face.

Just now, a little puff of wind took a few wood chips over the side. As I idly watched them dissipate on the swell, I was reminded of the bits of plastic and paper floating on the bay, that night in San Francisco. It seems like many years ago now, though it's only six. Or maybe it's seven.

•••

Missy's second husband, Kevin Carnes, attended her funeral. Afterwards I approached him. He seemed to be everything Missy had said he was, decent, modest, and smart. About Kevin, and maybe only about him, she hadn't been lying. She should have stuck with him. I took his phone number.

Kevin had followed the story in the papers, of course. When I finally called him, more than two years after Missy's funeral, he remembered me, and was very interested in what I had to sell.

Kevin Carnes paid five million dollars for the genuine Syracuse Codex. On the off chance that he might turn out to be cut from the same cloth as Missy or Girly or ten or twelve other dead people, I refused to let Dave witness the trans-action, and never mentioned his involvement to Kevin. Without Dave, certainly, there would have been no deal to make. But Dave had been shot up pretty badly as it was. He could hardly work at all. The doctors had told him that, between his drinking and the gunshot damage, he should

466

expect a foreshortened life. I wasn't going to let him walk into a trap with me, and that's the way it went down, but you should have seen Dave the night I left the boatyard with the genuine codex under my arm. He looked like a dog watching over the fence as the guy he knows as The Can Opener climbs into an airport jitney, bags in hand.

On the other hand, Dave should have seen me sweat as, all alone, I took the dedicated elevator up to the penthouse of the Hotel Argent. That's the name. I'm not kidding. It's on Third between Market and Mission.

Just me and the Syracuse Codex. The elevator opened directly into the penthouse living room, and no sooner had I stepped out of its doors than two gorillas patted me down. Right away they found the little pistol and confiscated it. That could have been the end, but it wasn't. Quite the contrary, they showed no disrespect. They didn't even relieve me of the codex, which I had wrapped like a big Christmas present, in red and green paper with sleighs and reindeer all over it, a fourteen-loop scarlet bow, and a hand-calligraphed envelope with a computer-chip greeting card inside that featured the Andrews Sisters singing *Frosty the Snowman.* It was that time of year. Quite the contrary, they relieved me of themselves: they simply disappeared. And the next thing I knew I was sitting on a silk-upholstered sofa with a globe of Armagnac in one hand and a Cuban cigar in the other, looking south over one of the damndest views of San Francisco I'd ever beheld. Kevin took the Syracuse Codex into another room, where he had somebody set up to authenticate it. This took a while but the time passed pleasantly enough. At length the two gorillas reappeared with two pieces of matched luggage, a valise and a suitcase of tanned pigskin the color of oiled teak. When they'd put down the bags and gone away again, Kevin suggested I have a look inside.

Have you ever seen fifty thousand one-hundred-dollar bills?

467

Darling, as Missy herself might have said, of course you haven't.

Five million in hundreds is twenty-five feet tall. The notes stack up like J. Edgar Hoover's files on the Mafia, or the Mafia's files on J. Edgar, or maybe both. They stack up thick and voluminous, comprehensive and ineluctable, and formidable and undeniable. It's impressive.

When I was satisfied, I closed the suitcases and left them parked where they were, between me and the view, with my feet up on the taller one. Kevin asked whether I cared for a second Armagnac. I cared. He offered the label on a brand new bottle for my inspection. I waved it away, saying I wouldn't know what I was looking at. He opened it and poured a modest amount into a fresh glass, stemmed and small like he mentioned it was supposed to be, and he checked the bouquet before handing it to me.

I raised the little glass in his direction. "Chins up,"

Kevin Carnes gave me a puzzled look. Then he said, "Just a moment." He went to the sideboard and retrieved a second glass, a mate to the one I held, and poured a little Armagnac for himself.

"Chins up," he repeated, and gently touched the rim of his glass to mine.

We sipped. It tasted very fine. We sat on the sofa and watched the view. We were way downtown, a ten-minute walk from the Ferry Building. But you could see beyond San Bruno Mountain from that penthouse, clear past the south end of the city.

I indicated the suitcases on the floor in front of us. "I should have brought a handtruck."

Kevin smiled graciously. "You'll think of something."

We watched the view some more. You could almost count the lighted windows on the passenger jets queued for final approach, some twenty miles down the bay.

I expressed a minor curiosity. "Kevin," I asked him, "did you know Renée Knowles?"

"Pardon?" Kevin replied, interrupting his own thoughts. But before I could repeat the question, he answered it.

"No," he said. "I never met her."

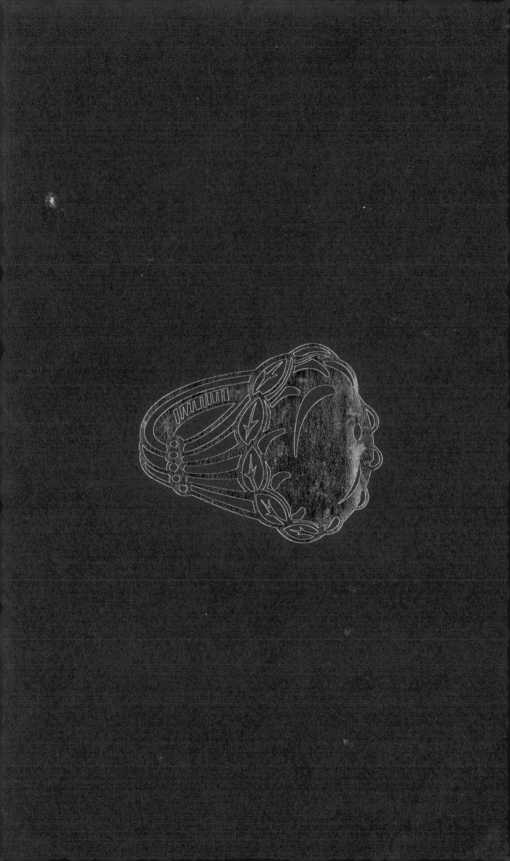